Diana Appleyard is a writer, broadcaster and freelance journalist. She worked as a BBC Education Correspondent before deciding to give up her full-time job to work from home, a decision which formed the basis for her first novel, *Homing Instinct*. She lives with her husband Ross and their two daughters in Scotland.

Also by Diana Appleyard

HOMING INSTINCT
A CLASS APART
OUT OF LOVE
EVERY GOOD WOMAN DESERVES A LOVER
PLAYING WITH FIRE

and published by Black Swan

TOO BEAUTIFUL TO DANCE

Diana Appleyard

BLACK SWAN

TRANSWORLD PUBLISHERS
61–63 Uxbridge Road, London W5 5SA
A Random House Group Company
www.rbooks.co.uk

TOO BEAUTIFUL TO DANCE
A BLACK SWAN BOOK: 9780552773058

First publication in Great Britain
Black Swan edition published 2007

Addresses for Random House Group Ltd companies outside the UK
can be found at: www.randomhouse.co.uk
The Random House Group Ltd Reg. No. 954009

The Random House Group Limited makes every effort to
ensure that the papers used in our books are made from trees that
have been legally sourced from well-managed and credibly
certified forests. Our paper procurement policy can be found on
www.randomhouse.co.uk

Typeset in 11/13pt Melior by
Falcon Oast Graphic Art Ltd.

Printed and bound in Great Britain by
Cox & Wyman Ltd, Reading, Berkshire.

2 4 6 8 10 9 7 5 3 1

Mixed Sources
Product group from well-managed
forests and other controlled sources
www.fsc.org Cert no. TT-COC-2139
© 1996 Forest Stewardship Council
FSC

To Beth and Charlotte, despite their constant
reminders of my losing battle with age

Acknowledgements

I would like to thank my publisher, Linda Evans, and agent, Sheila Crowley, for their constancy and support with a book which has taken a while to deliver! Thanks also to Tess and Harold for the loan of their beautiful house near Fowey where I could absorb the landscape and enjoy many windy walks in the mind of Sara. My family, for putting up with me being away with reasonable grace, and my mother and sisters for being at the end of the telephone line. The publicity team at Transworld are always terrific, and I would also like to send thanks to the newspapers and magazines who support my writing and short stories, with particular regard to the Femail team at the Daily Mail, especially Rachael.

Chapter One

'Perhaps you should have left him years ago.'

Sara hesitated, secateurs poised to snip off the withered, paper-thin petals clinging to what had been a most beautiful pale pink rose. In death, its colour had faded to the sepia of parchment, and even as the words circled lazily around her head, she thought how odd that something so lustrously beautiful could turn, with such apparent rapidity, into such decay. She snipped, decisively, and the dying rose fell to the earth.

'Oh, I don't know. There was the money, after all.'

Catherine, a large hat like a raffia wheel keeping the sun off a face which had recently undergone a chemical peel and was still therefore at the rather delicate stage, chewed the end of her sunglasses. 'A fatuous comment. And one I know you do not mean. Don't even attempt to fib to me, Sara Louise Atkinson. I know you inside out.'

She leant back into the rickety deckchair, tapping in mid air a critical foot encased in the latest wedge-heeled sandals, observing her oldest friend through narrowed eyes.

Sara straightened, her right hand pressing against the stiffness in the small of her back, rolling her neck as she did so and feeling a satisfying click. The gate definitely needed painting. Pale blue, she thought. Pale blue, to reflect the sky on a good day.

'I'm not ready . . .' Not ready to what, she thought? Not ready to discuss the fact that she, too, had been effectively deadheaded? She smiled to herself. She liked the analogy. There was no room for sentimentality or self-pity. Not here.

She took a long breath. 'I'm not ready,' she said, slowly, 'to come up with any form of judgement. I'm sorry. I know you want me to feel angry and betrayed but I don't honestly know what I feel, and I cannot look upon anything at the moment as a certainty. It's as if . . .'

'As if what?'

'As if I'm not really here.'

She looked up into the clear blue sky, as, high above her, a rook wheeled towards the tall fir trees beyond the gate, cawing loudly to its mate, heading for home at the end of another busy twig-gathering day. For a startling moment, she thought she might cry. Cry now, why? When she'd driven all the way here and unpacked most of the boxes and looked out over the sea from the tiny window of her bedroom without a trace of self-pity or even sadness, simply a steely determination to *live*, not to go under, not to be anything that anyone might expect her to be at this particular moment in time?

'Oh, darling.' Catherine leant forward, as if to get up, but found she could not rise with any form of swiftness or elegance from the unwieldy chair.

'Don't you have anything more sodding comfortable?'

Sara laughed. 'I paid two pounds fifty for that at the local shop. Don't mock.'

'You were robbed.' Catherine floundered for a

moment, her knees, in smart white cropped trousers, waving perilously. For a glorious moment Sara thought she might go over backwards. But Catherine had not survived two marriages and numerous abrupt changes in fortune to have her dignity compromised by cheap garden furniture. With a graceful leap, she landed on her feet. Behind her, the deckchair sighed into a collapsed heap of stripy material and awkward wooden elbows. Sara's Labrador, Hector, asleep in the grass, awoke and regarded it with mild surprise. Did it need investigating? Mostly harmless, he decided, and sank his head back upon his blonde front paws. His chocolate brown eyes watched Sara closely, awaiting a movement which might herald the dinner his internal clock informed him was long overdue.

'I need a drink.' Catherine set off towards the open front door. Hector followed her path with mortified eyes. Right direction, wrong person.

'There's white wine in the fridge,' Sara called, to her retreating back. Stretching, she pressed the back of her soil-stained hand to her mouth, feeling the warmth of the sun deep within her skin. After just a week at the cottage, her skin was beginning to freckle. Freckles, or the first signs of age spots? Who was there to care? She closed her eyes, briefly, the setting sun luminous behind her eyelids.

'You'll go quite loony here,' Catherine said, minutes later, pressing an ice-cold glass of wine into her hand.

'Why?'

'Because there's nothing to do. What will you do all day? I'm so worried you're going to be lonely.'

'There's *everything* to do. That's what I like about . . . all this.' Sara gestured around the garden. It wasn't sufficiently organized to be called a garden yet, simply a patch of ragged grass with the odd ancient rose poking its gnarled head above the tallest weeds by the

11

low stone wall at the front of the cottage, the sad, shrivelled remains of last year's blooms hanging forlornly from spindly stems. It had been a proper garden, though, once, she thought. When the cottage was loved.

It had lain practically derelict and forgotten for almost two years, the estate agent had told her. Before that, it had been owned by a rather batty old man who had kept himself busy, apparently, collecting old newspapers and empty tins of baked beans which he stored in piles in the narrow corridors and behind closed doors. He had died here, alone, and the cottage had stood empty ever since. Before his death, during his tenure, both the garden and cottage had fallen into severe disrepair. The cottage dated back to the early seventeenth century, and Sara guessed it must have been at least fifty years since anyone had done anything to repair or even paint it. It had simply crouched into the hillside, prey to the vagaries of storms, sea mists and the high winds buffeting the south Cornish coast, waiting patiently for rescue.

When she had pushed open the door, just under three months ago at the beginning of January, the air within musty and stale, there was a palpable sense of loneliness and death which quite appealed to her. They were two injured souls, the cottage and she. She would be needed, here.

Once contracts had been exchanged, the estate agent, a friendly young man called David, said he knew of someone in the village, a mile down the road, who could help to tidy up the garden for her, but she said no – she wanted to do it herself. She had always enjoyed the feeling of being tired out from hard work in the fresh air, and relished the challenge of rolling up her sleeves and getting on with something she could *do*. The doing was all.

In London, their 'garden' had consisted of a long, narrow roof terrace with smart teak decking, decorated with ornamental steel grey metallic pots containing exotic and dangerously spiky species of cacti – they required nothing more strenuous than the odd tweak here and there. Matt at the time was going through a minimalist de-clutter phase, and Emily remarked it was a bit like trying to sunbathe within a surreal pinball machine.

They had once had a big garden – well, big for London – when the children were small and they were in funds, living in an end-of-terrace Edwardian house, facing the common, in Wandsworth. Enclosed by a lovely high crumbling red brick wall, it was overgrown and wild, a secret garden. But with two young children and working part-time for Matt as his PA, Sara hadn't had the time or energy to bring it under control, and the wild brambles tapped on the kitchen window, a living, growing reproach to her neglect. Buddleia, which she hated – she knew this was irrational, but she always thought of it as a very common plant – ran riot, and the briars choked the roses. Then, once both children were at school all day and she had a little more time to try to bring the garden to heel, they had yet another financial crisis and Matt moved them on. What equity they had streamed into the business to keep it afloat, and they decamped to a rented, run-down three-storey town house, which had previously been lived in by students, in a far less fashionable area of London, with only a small paved courtyard as an apology for a garden. She did not reproach Matt for the abrupt downturn in fortune as she knew well by now that running your own business was almost inevitably a rollercoaster. He was doing his best, working himself into the ground, and success, he promised her, was just around the corner.

When the girls were nineteen and sixteen, he finally hit the jackpot. After years of highs, lows and near bankruptcy, he had pulled in a number of big contracts and was in a position to be able to float the company to bring in new investment. A year after the flotation, he had had an offer from a much bigger media conglomerate. After long and painful negotiations, during which time Sara was seriously concerned for his health, such was the stress as they picked over every tiny detail, they agreed he would stay on as managing director, while they became the majority share holder. The initial cash windfall – a third of the overall sale price of the company – meant they could move out of the narrow town house, wave goodbye to the crack dealers at the end of the road, and usher in a new life in a smart penthouse apartment by the river. Matt felt the move was more than justified by such Herculean effort and stress. It should have meant a time of celebration for Sara, and would have been so, undoubtedly, if only she had not hated the apartment on sight. It had simply never felt like home. She felt uncomfortable, inappropriate, set against its sleek contemporary lines with its immaculate gleaming stainless steel kitchen. She would have far preferred a house in the country, something like an old rectory with a big garden, but Matt said he would hate the commute and he needed to stay in town, for now. So Sara put her dreams for a peaceful, rural life on hold. When he retired from the company, she told herself, in five or so years' time. Then they could have the life Matt so richly deserved. Travelling, gardening, theatre trips, reading in the sun – growing comfortably older together. In time, there would be grandchildren, an extended family. A new life, the next phase.

* * *

'Thanks.' She took the glass of wine from Catherine, and ran her finger over the icy, beaded exterior.

'That fridge is bloody awful. You must let me help you . . . we can have a lovely day tomorrow buying things for the home.'

Sara smiled at her, shaking her head. 'The fridge came with the house. There weren't any relatives, so everything was just left. And I can't afford to replace it at the moment.'

'Why didn't you just chuck it out? You really should have. Honestly, Sara, I can't believe you can't afford . . .'

'It works.' She shrugged. 'You should have seen it before I set to work with the cream cleaner. I quite enjoyed it, actually. It was nice to make a difference.' She sat down carefully, facing Catherine, on the low stone wall in front of the cottage. Her eyes half-closed against the setting sun, she squinted over her friend's shoulder at the faded white façade of the little house, the exterior paint cracked and chipped to reveal bare patches of old stone, like the missing pieces of a jigsaw. The white-painted window frames were visibly rotting, with jagged splinters and gaping holes, which was presumably why the wind had howled through the house when she first came to view, back in January. She would need to replace them, no doubt, and added them to her mental list of tasks. So much to do. The thought pleased her.

'What are you smiling about?'

'I'm just thinking how far I have to go.'

'I think you've gone quite far enough. It took me *seven hours* to drive here. There's not even a railway station for forty miles. There's an understandable need to escape, darling, and there's being deliberately perverse at the expense of the poor souls who don't want to lose you *completely*. This is practically a different time zone.'

15

'You sound like my mother. I know it's remote. It's perfect.'

'How will you see the girls? I can't see either of them here,' Catherine added beadily. 'It's not exactly spacious, is it? Hardly what they're used to.'

'Lottie's coming down at the beginning of next week. She's been staying with Mum while I – get things organized. I don't know about Emily. She's so busy with her new job . . . and she's not really—'

'Talking to you?' Catherine jumped in. That wasn't what Sara had been about to say, but she let it pass.

'That won't last, you know that,' Catherine continued with some satisfaction. 'It's just petulance. She expected you to do the "normal" thing and hang onto the apartment while Matt had to move out into a flat or something. You were the injured party, after all – why shouldn't you keep that lovely place? Then you could have indulged in intense retail therapy with her in tow, and wallow in all the material benefits of guilt alimony. Christ, darling, it's no more than you deserved. She could hardly have expected you to bury yourself in this –' she searched for the least offensive adjective she could find – 'eccentric cottage without even a mobile signal for comfort. This,' she said, looking about the tiny garden with thinly veiled distaste, 'is the domestic equivalent of a hair shirt. I wouldn't have dreamt of buying somewhere poky like this. He'll think he's won, you know. You've made it far too easy for him.'

'You've been divorced too often.' Sara smiled, unoffended. She had known Catherine too long to be upset by her astonishing lack of tact. 'And is that really the "normal" thing to do for a wife who is no longer required? To seek vengeance by effectively squatting in the former family home?'

Catherine ignored the question and continued crossly, 'At least I know how to make the best of a bad job. There's always some consolation, there has to be. I'm sure he gave you, didn't he, a really decent whack . . .'

'Stop fishing, Catherine. It's none of your business. Anyway, nothing's sorted out as yet. There's no formal agreement, the apartment isn't even sold yet.'

'Doesn't stop me asking. I just need to know you're all right, I do worry . . .'

'No, you bloody well don't. You want to know exactly how much money I squeezed out of him and all the gory details. Don't forget how long I've known you, too.'

Catherine grinned, unperturbed. 'Well, you should have every penny, really, considering. You don't want to think of her . . .'

Sara opened her eyes wide, and looked at Catherine sharply. 'No, I don't want to think of her.'

'Aren't you the tiniest bit curious? To know how long, that kind of thing? Why when we all thought you had the ideal . . . it was *such* a shock . . .'

'For someone who claims to be on my side, you sometimes trample upon my sensibilities with less than fairy footsteps.'

'Sorry.' She made a little moue with her red lip-sticked mouth, her eyes still beady with the desire to root out more information. 'Shift up.' Catherine moved towards her and parked her elegantly clad bottom on the wall next to Sara, regarding the cottage with narrowed eyes. 'It's so—'

'Small? Run-down?'

'All of the above. It's as if you are deliberately putting yourself into *exile*. You don't know anyone here, what on earth is the attraction? A holiday cottage, I could understand, but to *live* here? All the

17

time? Surely, with Matt's money, you could have bought something much more . . . oh, I don't know, pretty. Welcoming. I miss you. We all miss you. No-one can understand why you took off like that. Why not a cottage in Dorset? Or Kent? I mean, they count as the country, and at least they're within shouting distance of London and you could pop up to see us whenever you wanted. What on earth are you going to do for *pleasure*? Anyway, don't you want to live some-where which is much more in keeping? Just because Matt's gone doesn't mean . . .'

'In keeping with what?'

'In keeping with your former standard of life.'

'It wasn't *my* life,' Sara said, patiently.

'Yes, it was.'

'No, it wasn't. It was Matt's life. The apartment never felt like my home. But Matt was so enthusiastic, I just went along with him – after all, it was his money, he deserved it after so much bloody hard work and you know how good he is at persuading people to do what he wants. It was always pointless to disagree once he'd got the bit between his teeth.' She shook her head, ruefully. 'I don't know why I didn't dig my heels in more after we first looked round – this sounds rather mad, but the apartment didn't want me, either. It had awful vibes.' She laughed. 'I've only just fully admitted that to myself. I found it cold, unwelcoming. I tried to convince myself that it was far more practical, much easier to lock up and leave if we ever got the time to travel or take longer holidays, much more convenient after our decrepit old houses.' She smiled bitterly into her wine glass, her mouth turning down at the corners. 'Buying the apartment was supposed to be our fresh start. Put all the troubled years behind us.'

'After life in Brixton among the crack dealers.'

'Exactly. And with the girls practically off to university, Matt promised he was going to start stepping back from the business, make a gradual exit, so we could travel, maybe even buy a house in France.'

'Do you think he was having a breakdown?'

'Why?' Shocked, Sara looked across at Catherine, who shrugged, taking a sip of wine. The deep red of her lipstick left the trace of a smile upon the glass. 'It must have been something like that, surely. It's so out of character. He was the last person I would ever have expected to— It must have been a moment of madness. *Why* would he?' She paused, regarding Sara intently, her eyes narrowed.

Sara knew exactly what she was thinking. Trapped within that pause, like the beating wings of a moth, was an accusation Catherine would never actually acknowledge, even to herself. That it was somehow – although this was, surely, irrational – Sara's fault. Her fault. That she had 'let herself go', taken her marriage for granted, not smartened herself up to keep pace with Matt's rising star, a man who was fighting and winning the ageing process and seemed to become better-looking as the years passed. Had she committed – in Catherine's eyes – the cardinal sin of ageing, without frantic resistance? Did a lifetime together count for nothing compared to smooth, elastic skin and eyes uncreased by age?

Whatever Catherine said, however vociferously she denounced what Matt had done, the moth's wings of this accusation beat behind her eyes. You are amusing, you are entertaining, intelligent company, you look well for your age, you have supported him through all the dramatic ups and downs of his career, you are the mother of the two children he adores – but you have let yourself become comfortably old. And that is not

19

what men want, however intelligent they may be. It is your fault, your fault.

Catherine, of course, pleaded not guilty to any such folly, although she currently had no man to please. She was in the process, at almost fifty, of being nipped, tucked, peeled like a banana and stretched into a facsimile of youth. At occasional unkind moments in a harsh light, Sara thought she was beginning to look a little drag-queen with her unnaturally unlined eyes and perfectly smooth forehead. Like a sheet of blank paper, Sara thought, devoid of expression.

I'm not sure I want you here, she thought suddenly. This is my new place, my new life. You want to pick over the past, and place it in context, and make truths of something I cannot begin to understand or rationalize. For the moment, I just want to be. I want to pull on a pair of old jeans and cultivate my garden. I don't want to carry over my past life to this place or care about what you deem important. Here is new, and innocent. I'm not 'Poor Sara' here. Why can't you see that? That's why I wanted it so badly. Because it was untouched, there were no fingerprints of the past. And now you are raising ghosts.

'Let's go inside.' She drained her glass, and, standing up, she took a step towards the front door. Catherine remained seated.

'You can't hide from what's happened,' she said, frustration making her cruel. 'You'll have to face it one day.'

Will I? Sara thought. Actually, she decided in that moment, I don't think I will. I think I am going to wilfully bury my head in the sand and do exactly what I want to do, and refuse to allow myself any attempt to make sense of what has happened and just see what happens.

'Hector.' At her voice, he raised his head, his ears

lifting in what he hoped was a fetching, come-hither manner. It worked. 'Dinnertime,' she said. At the familiar words, he bounded to his feet and shimmied sideways up to her, thrusting his head against her thigh. His besotted eyes fixed on hers, smiling his ridiculous lopsided Labrador grin, the soft dark skin of his mouth curling up over his sharp white teeth.

'Dingbat,' she said fondly, her hand resting on his broad, warm head. 'Noodle.' He trotted on ahead of her, thick tail wagging, through the front door, and down the narrow passageway which led to the tiny kitchen at the back of the house, where his bowl lived next to his wicker basket. He had swiftly learnt the geography of the house, and the moment he'd flopped down at her feet on his blanket the very first night, the cottage had become home. His, at the moment, was the only company she craved. Within his calm deep brown eyes lay her sanity.

It was, she had to admit, a dreadful kitchen, long and thin, and more like a lean-to than an actual room, with a corrugated-iron roof. Rain sounded like an aerial bombardment. Catherine had reserved her greatest disapprobation for the kitchen, as Sara had shown her round. 'You can't cook in here,' she said, horrified.

'Why not? There's a cooker –' Sara gestured at the truly ancient Baby Belling stove resting on a rickety white cupboard with a cracked glass door '– and I brought the microwave from home.' It stood on the work surface at the side of the sink, its sleek steel lines gleaming incongruously against the 1960s beige Formica cupboards.

'Ha ha. It's insanitary. That's not an oven, it's a –' she peered at its small metal label closely '– Good God, I haven't seen one of those in years.'

'Oh, for goodness sake,' Sara said, rattled. 'I'm not

going to have to live with all this for long. I'm going to apply for planning permission to extend . . . next time you come down you won't recognize the place.' In her mind's eye she could see the kitchen she wanted, three times as big, with part of the roof glass, like an atrium, and French windows leading out onto the small wilderness garden at the back, facing the lane.

Over the lane, behind the tumbledown stone wall, spring shades of purple and moss green moorland, deep in bracken and brambles, rose steeply, before merging into lush pasture. This pastureland, dotted with impossibly white fluffy sheep, rolled over the crest of the hill and then fell away like the undulating folds of a blanket into a neat patchwork of stone-walled fields in the valley beyond. A timeless landscape, unchanged for centuries.

The front two rooms of the cottage presented a major challenge, two tiny parlours with ugly mean little hearths. She'd have to find an architect, someone to help her work out a way of opening up the front of the house, knocking down the walls to create one big room. The small windows would have to be enlarged without ruining the façade of the cottage to maximize the incredible views over the cliffs with the water stretching away to the mist of the horizon, where the sea met the sky and became one.

At first she had thought she might be frightened, overawed, by such a vast expanse of nature without fellow habitation around her, but when she stood in the front garden, one hand on the gate, as the estate agent put his key into the lock of the front door before her, she looked out across the sea and felt as if something deep inside her had connected and found a home. This was the right place.

* * *

'Why should I have left him years ago?' They were sitting, with their feet up on one of the remaining unopened boxes, deep into the second bottle of wine. Outside, the sky was midnight blue, edged with indigo.

'Because you look more peaceful than I have seen you look for years. Not that I think this is a good idea,' Catherine added hastily. 'Why don't you keep this place, as you are obviously determined to, as a holiday cottage, and then once you get the settlement you can buy a flat in London? I hate the thought of you pottering around down here, alone. You must let us help. Stop being so fucking *brave*,' she said, leaning forward and touching Sara's knee in a tipsy gesture of affection.

Sara smiled. In her way Catherine meant well, she really did want her to be happy and it was understandable that she had been alarmed by her abrupt flight. It was also understandable that she wanted to pick over the drama of the situation, and store away for future use the nuggets of riveting information due a best friend, such as whether Matt had begged her to take him back, and how he had reacted to her decision to leave so suddenly. One of the reasons why she was such entertaining company was because she always knew everything about everyone. You could always trust Catherine to come out with the question normal people would think too indelicate to ask, but desperately wanted to know. As a young girl, she'd revelled in drama and liked to place herself at the very centre of whatever action was going on. It was no surprise, Sara reflected, that she had led such a turbulent life.

'I'm not brave,' she said. 'I'm surviving.'

I wonder, Sara pondered, turning over in bed an hour later, beneath her heavy quilt, if this peacefulness comes from the fact that, now, I have to live my life by my rules alone. I always thought that having no one else to consider or put first would be the most terrifying prospect. Instead, I am beginning to think it might be a life of quite infinite possibility.

Chapter Two

Richard was very obviously drunk. He slumped, half leaning against the wall in the hall, one hand resting on the dimmer switch as if he might suddenly plunge the entrance hallway into pitch darkness. In the other hand swung a glass of red wine, tipped at such an angle it was perilously close to spilling out on to the pale blond floorboards they had had bleached and varnished when they moved into the apartment, at great expense.

You are not a happy man, Sara thought, as she walked past him, avoiding his eyes, pushing open one of the arched oak double doors to the main living area with a practised foot, holding in both hands a wide tray of artfully arranged canapés. Asparagus rolled in Parma ham, king prawns in filo pastry, tiny croutons topped with beluga caviar and smoked salmon blinis. None of which she had had to make herself, thank goodness, canapés, were such twiddly, time-consuming little things to create. They had been prepared by the catering firm she had booked months before, in preparation for Matt's fiftieth birthday.

Not that he looked fifty. Sara glanced over at him, leaning elegantly, an elbow resting at shoulder height, against one of the marble pillars in the open-plan living room which stretched almost the entire length of the apartment, as she moved through their guests. She smiled as they took canapés off the tray with difficulty, between their fingers and thumbs, trying not to drop bits of food into their glasses. She saw Matt glance over at her, and knew he would be annoyed that she was handing out the canapés herself, when there was a team of waitresses standing idle in the kitchen. Although he was now sufficiently wealthy never to have to work again, he loathed the thought of being ripped off and was obsessional about getting value for money. He could never resist a deal. Sara teased him, saying it was part of his northern up-bringing, that he always had to be the one who came out on top. Buying his new Range Rover (his fiftieth birthday present to himself, with all the bells and whistles such as satellite navigation and in-car DVD screens), he had spent hours on the Internet finding the lowest price. He had to feel he was in control. The winning, to Matt, was all. Many of the people he came up against in business found him abrasive and Sara was the only person who knew best how to deflect his temper. His staff lived in fear of his black moods and sudden rages, but then within moments the storm would have passed and he would be expansively charming once more. Sara alone knew his mercurial nature stemmed from the misery of his childhood, and forgave him.

From the moment he had exploded into her life, plucking her out of her safe middle-class existence, she had sold her soul to this attractive, frustrating, complex man. As her mother said on her wedding day, life with Matt would be anything but boring.

She did not want to drink any more this evening and handing out the food gave her an excuse. Never a particularly successful drinker, her head began to reel after two or three glasses of wine. The easiest way was to keep busy, to have something for your hands to do. Matt liked to drink, and over the years she had found it far easier to remain relatively sober to smooth down any ruffled edges. Drink brought out his chippiness, the belligerence simmering beneath the urbane exterior.

As she glanced over at Matt, he took a long drag of his cigarette, blowing the smoke out over the head of the slim woman standing in front of him. Rachael was one of Sara's friends, made when their daughters were together at primary school. Sara knew Matt found her dull. She was married to a banker in the City, a man Matt would refer to as a tosser ex-public schoolboy, a chortling buffer with a receding hairline and expanding waist, tonight in his 'off work' uniform of striped shirt, moss-green corduroy trousers and suede brogues.

Matt caught her eye as he looked up, and grimaced, turning his mouth down at the corners, which meant in their language, help, I'm trapped. Sara raised her eyes to the ceiling, and he smiled.

He was wearing a beautiful tailored black Armani jacket, a white collarless shirt and dark designer jeans. His dark hair, once jet black, was now flecked with charcoal. He kept it cut very short and standing up slightly from his forehead. It suited him, as most things suited him. With his unlined olive skin and tall slim build, he could easily pass for a man ten years younger.

New clients introduced to Sara would look from one to the other in surprise. How did a sleek, expensively groomed man like Matt fit with a wife like Sara? A comfortable-looking woman, attractive, but thickening around the middle, whose blonde hair, escaping from a careless bun, had been allowed to fade to a mix of pale grey and lemon grass, who tended to wear clothes for comfort, rather than style. Her eyes were beautiful, hazel with a rim around the iris of deep chocolate brown, but they were surrounded by the fine laughter lines of age, the skin beneath beginning to puff and bag. Both she and Matt now needed glasses for reading, but whereas Matt opted for a slim pair of oval rimless designer frames, she chose half-moon tortoise-shells, which hung, generally forgotten, on a chain around her neck.

While many of Sara's friends swore by Botox or even, like Catherine, had gone the whole hog and had a facelift, she had no desire to meddle with nature. She could *see*, of course she could, that they now looked remarkably unlined for their age, but she thought they no longer looked like *themselves*. They looked like beautiful dolls, permanently wide-eyed as if they had just sat on a pin. Was that to appear youthful, to have an expression of permanent surprise?

It was not, however, entirely correct of her friends to say that Sara did not care *at all* about the ageing process. She didn't like becoming plump, or lined, or having knees which emitted gunshot noises if she stood up too suddenly – she just had better things to do than try to hold back time by joining a gym or having endless, expensive beauty treatments. Besides, Matt never complained, or seemed to notice her rolls of flab. Their love-making was constant, reassuring and highly pleasurable. They also seemed to be alone amongst their married friends in that they actually talked to each other and enjoyed each other's company. At no point could she remember ever having been bored when she was with him, or feeling that they had run out of things to say. Given a choice, she would rather be with Matt than anyone else.

* * *

For the party tonight the girls had insisted she at least make an effort to look glamorous. They had swept her off to a fashionable department store in the West End, a place Sara would normally avoid like the plague, where the price tags made her blanch – how could anyone justify spending so much on a dress? The rake-thin assistant, who existed presumably entirely upon pine kernels, looked her up and down with barely concealed disdain, swallowed bravely, and ushered her into a luxurious changing room, saying that she would bring her a selection of suitable dresses, although they didn't have so much *choice* in her size. She then produced a series of insubstantial dresses in floating chiffon, designed for an anorexic sixteen-year-old, not a chubby middle-aged woman nearing fifty who did not feel it was fair to inflict the sight of her upper arms on the wider public.

She could feel herself getting hotter and hotter as she tried on the dresses, and at one point became trapped trying to get a dress with a tight bustier-style top off, wedging her arms above her head as if about to dive into a swimming pool, and had to call the girls in for help. Emily looked at her in horror and said, 'God, Mother, have you *seen* the size of your thighs? How can you bear it?' Meanwhile Sara emitted muffled protests and implored them to tug, praying that the assistant didn't pull the curtain aside at that precise moment to reveal her big pants and dimpled thighs to the entire floor.

Eventually the girls pronounced one bearable. It was made of black silk, with a reasonably high neckline – Sara decided cleavage was a no-no with the crêpey skin dividing her breasts. The bodice was reasonably tight fitting without being too uncomfortably grippy, and it definitely made her look slimmer. The skirt flared out into a flattering, mid calf-length, and with heels she thought she would feel almost elegant.

'Are you sure this isn't a bit young for me?' she asked, for reassurance, turning this way and that to see herself from all angles in the full-length mirror. Standing on tiptoe to simulate high heels, she twirled around and the silky skirt flared outwards.

'Do *not* do that,' Emily said, her head critically on one side. 'Sumo-wrestler knees, Mother. Bad sight of the week. Keep them covered at *all* times. But, overall, it's OK. I don't think anyone will actually be *frightened*.'

Lottie, much kinder, was sitting on the ornate changing-room chair trying not to laugh, composing her features into an expression of encouraging approval, thin legs crossed in skinny jeans.

'It makes you look really nice,' she said, nodding. 'Honestly. You hardly look fat at all.'

'Thanks,' Sara said.

Of the two girls, Emily was most like Matt, in looks and personality. She'd recently finished a degree in journalism and was about to start work on a commercial radio station which was owned by a friend of Matt's – although she flared up with rage if the word 'nepotism' was as much as breathed in her hearing.

Lottie, three years younger, was currently on a gap year. She hadn't done as well as she had hoped in her exams, and had been forced to take up a place at her second choice of university. It was a rather soulless, campus university in the Midlands and she'd been miserable there from day one. A friend suggested she come travelling with her to Thailand, and against their parental wishes she had chucked in the course after just three weeks and disappeared. Matt said she was a fool, but Sara said she was, after all, on the cusp of becoming an adult and she had to start making her own decisions, even if they were the wrong ones.

Before the party, Lottie had been home from Thailand for just a week, and they were doing battle with university forms yet again, something which Sara had hoped had gone for ever. She was nagging her to get on with it, but you couldn't push Lottie too far as she simply retreated and curled up within herself. She bruised, emotionally, far too easily – as a child she'd been constantly saving fledgling birds, baby mice and stunned hedgehogs from the side of the road, only to see most of them, inevitably, die, whereupon she cried heartbroken tears and buried them in shoeboxes packed with cotton wool. The garden in the house by the common was dotted with little crosses made from lolly sticks.

'Tell me truthfully. Is this me?' Sara asked, opening the door as Catherine arrived, half an hour earlier than the other guests. The dress had felt much tighter when she put it on tonight.

'Heavens. A little – well,' Catherine put her head on one side, composing her features, 'It's a little – funereal – but it suits you.'

'Explain exactly how that is a compliment?'

'It's just not your normal kind of thing. But no. Honestly. It's lovely. Very . . . slimming.'

'Gee, thanks. You look amazing.' She looked Catherine up and down. Catherine was wearing a skin-tight dark green satin sheath dress, and impossibly pointy black court shoes, more weapons than footwear.

'I know,' she grinned. 'I might even pull tonight. I am on the lookout, between you and me, for a nice young man. Don't care what he does – I just want to feel firm young flesh beside me.' She shivered with pleasure. 'You should hear what Alice says. You know she's met a twenty-four-year-old guy at the gym? A musician – of course he's after her money but apparently . . .'

Sara shuddered, and held up a manicured hand. For the first time in years she had had a manicure yesterday, and kept glancing down, surprised, at her painted red nails. They did make her hands look more elegant. Perhaps she should look after herself a little more; the manicure and pedicure had been fun, although she'd been very embarrassed at how much dead skin had been rubbed off her feet. It was like descaling a kettle.

'Spare me,' she said. 'I am too old for scurrilous tales.'

'*All night*,' Catherine replied, ignoring her. 'At least FOUR times.'

'I'd be so *bored*,' Sara laughed, despite herself. 'Wouldn't you? And my back locks if I stay in one position for more than ten minutes, and I get dreadful pins and needles. I drive Matt mad tossing and turning all night. Anyway, who's to say that we old married couples don't have amazing all-night sex?'

'Do you?' Catherine asked, fascinated, following Sara into the hall and unwrapping her cashmere pashmina, while looking at herself appreciatively in the mirror.

'You know perfectly well I wouldn't tell you even if we did. I'll hang that up for you. You don't want to keep it on, do you?'

'Nah. It's like being wrapped in a horse blanket. Bloody things. At least you still *have* sex. Most of the long-term married people I know – and God knows, there aren't all that many left – haven't slept together for years. Chrissie says the nearest thing she gets to an orgasm these days is the new Boden catalogue hitting the doormat. She and Clive haven't shagged in four years. She thinks it may well have dropped off.'

'No Milo?' Sara asked, diverting the subject. Catherine often told her far more than she needed to know about the sex lives of their friends, whom Sara then bumped into in Waitrose and thought, 'Blimey'. Milo was Catherine's only child, who had been invited because the girls thought he was so cute. He was currently doing nothing after his A levels, which he'd taken at an expensive boarding school, paid for by Catherine's second ex-husband. He had done spectacularly badly and had recently announced he was starting a band rather than going to university. Catherine said so far this consisted of sleeping all day, strumming a few exhausted chords on his guitar, sitting on his bed wearing boxer shorts before pulling on the same clothes he had been wearing for a week and disappearing into the night, failing to return until the early hours. She only knew he was in the house, she claimed, by the empty Marmite jar on the kitchen table and the trail of toast crumbs leading to his bedroom. Emily had promised that if he did start a band, she'd try to get him some airplay on her radio station, maybe even an interview. Matt said it was highly unlikely, because he was usually too stoned to start a sentence, let along a band.

Catherine doted on him, and Sara thought privately that she had spoilt him, allowing him to run wild and treating him less like a son than a petted confidante. He was hilarious on the subject of his mother's complicated and eyebrow-raising love life.

'No, sorry. He had a better offer, some kind of heavy jamming and smoking session at a mate's house.'

'Don't you mind?' Sara said.

Catherine smiled at her, pityingly. Sara had always been so naïve about these things.

'My disapproval isn't going to stop him, is it? They all smoke weed. He'll grow out of it. Anyway, I'm hardly in a position to complain, am I?'

'True.' Sara disapproved deeply of her friend's occasional cocaine habit, although Catherine claimed she now had it firmly under control.

Catherine grinned at her. 'You're such a prude. Everyone does it. One day I just know you're going to break out and do something outrageously wild. No one can be so perfectly behaved all the time.' She glanced down with satisfaction at her flat stomach, encased in tight green satin. 'This cost Maurice's credit card over a thousand, I'm pleased to say,' she said. 'Roland Mouret,' she added, inserting a cigarette into ruby red lips. 'Thank God for my dear ex-husband and his flexible friend. Ha! That makes two little flexible friends he possesses. The only trouble is I cannot breathe. Don't let me eat *anything*. Not even the teeniest weeniest nut. I sense that tonight I am going to meet a stunning new man.'

'You know most people coming already,' Sara pointed out. 'I didn't invite many of Matt's work colleagues, because the list would have been endless. Most of our parties seem to end up business meetings with drink, and I wanted this to be a proper birthday party, just for friends. So sorry, no toy boys I can think of. I should have got the girls to invite some of their friends, but then I'm not sure that would have gone down very well, the thought of you preying upon them . . .'

'Like an elderly mantis? Thank you, dear friend. Talking about being disapproved of – is your mother coming?'

'She couldn't leave the dogs, and Matt won't have them here.'

'Thank Christ for that. Sorry. But you know she

always looks at me as if my life has gone so tragically awry. Richard's not coming either, is he? Such a groper.' She shuddered at the thought. 'As if I'd go anywhere near him. I'm not that desperate.'

'I could hardly *not* invite him. He's Matt's oldest friend, and he's been through a bad time.'

'*He's* been through a bad time! Are you in touch with Jo?'

'I spoke to her last week. He's not paying her anything at all, you know. She's beside herself. I think his business is going under, yet again. Matt hates me taking sides but it's so . . .'

'No wonder he'll be here, then. He'll be trying to tap Matt for a loan.'

'Matt's not that stupid.'

'Let's hope not. Why on earth does he put up with him, though? He's bound to get hideously pissed.'

'*Please* don't give me something else to worry about, there's enough as there is. The caterers only got here half an hour ago, they're still putting out the glasses. At least Richard's not my problem, thank goodness,' Sara said. 'Can you grab a drink, while I make sure everything's in place?'

Catherine picked up a glass of champagne from the kitchen table and wandered into the living room. Even knowing the style of the room as well as she did, she paused in the doorway, her eyes wide. Sara had arranged hundreds of candles on every available surface, and their flickering, cathedral light mingled with the tiny white spotlights suspended on steel wire cords which ran the length of the room just below the high ceiling. With the huge arched warehouse windows reaching from floor to ceiling, the view over London was breathtaking. Tonight, the panoply of lights within the room seemed to stream out into those of the city, stretching away like glittering gemstones on a sea of black velvet.

Having put the canapé tray down on a coffee table, Sara paused for a moment to look out of the window at the far end of the room, the chatter of their guests rising and falling behind her. Moments later, she sensed Matt standing close by.

'Make them all go home now,' he breathed softly, dropping his mouth to kiss her black silk shoulder. 'I'm bored of talking rubbish to people who are not you. Whose idea was this?'

'Yours. And after all this cost and fuss?' she asked, as his arms folded around her, a feeling of warmth spreading from his touch.

'I'm sure it was yours, actually. Why didn't we just take the girls out to dinner somewhere horribly expensive?'

'Because you like parties,' she smiled, leaning back against his familiar contours. Their bodies fitted perfectly together, like the pieces of a jigsaw. 'Stop pretending.'

'How well you know me.' His hands slid upwards to the underside of her breasts, smoothly gliding over the layered silk. Automatically she breathed in, feeling her stomach turn over. Even after twenty-six years of marriage, he could still do this to her.

'Let's go to bed,' he whispered. 'Sod the party.'

She laughed. 'Grown-ups don't do that sort of thing,' she whispered back. 'We're not teenagers, remember?'

'Who cares? Go on. I dare you. We can lock the bedroom door. No one will know.'

'No,' she said, pulling away from him. 'You shocking man. How can you think such a thing? Come on. Once more unto the breach,' she ordered, smiling at his reflection. His arms tightened around her, pulling her back, close to him.

Catherine, looking over at them, silhouetted against the dark window, grimaced in envy. They were the only couple she knew who touched each other in that intimate way. As if they still loved each other. If only. No. She mentally shook herself. She was not going to wallow in any form of self-pity, that was the trouble with drinking too much champagne. It made her maudlin.

'Not going to go,' Matt said in a childish voice, and Sara could feel his mouth smiling against her ear. He smelt strongly of aftershave and cigarette smoke.

'You have to. You're the host. Go sparkle,' she said, her breath misting the window.

'Twenty-six years of me,' he murmured. 'Twenty-seven, actually, with the year we spent dating. How on earth have we got this far? You are the most tolerant woman, you know. Do I have to make a speech?'

'You love making speeches.'

'What if I break down in tears when I thank my lovely family for all these years of blissful happiness?'

'The girls will be physically sick?'

He laughed. 'I will say it, though. Not exactly in those words,' he added hastily. 'But I do believe it, you know.' He pressed his mouth against her neck in the briefest of kisses, his voice low and insistent. 'You're everything to me. I couldn't have achieved any of this without you. You are infinitely precious – *essential* – to me.' Sara closed her eyes, her heart filled with a rising sense of joy. They were so very lucky.

'I love you,' she murmured. Then she swivelled in his arms to face him. 'Now go and do your social thing. Go chat someone up,' she added briskly.

He smiled, his mouth curving at the corners, dark eyes glinting. 'You look beautiful, tonight.'

'Do I?' she said, surprised.

37

'Yes.' He nodded, looking down at her, his eyes fixed intently on her face. 'Never leave me,' he added suddenly. She stared up at him, astonished – it was not the kind of thing that Matt would ever normally say. As their eyes met, she felt a sudden jolt. What had she seen, just then? A flicker, a shadow of uncertainty, even fear, flashing behind his eyes? She shook herself. I'm imagining things, she thought. Her eyes searched his face, but abruptly he had turned away and walked back towards their guests, reaching out to take a glass of champagne from a passing waitress. He drained it in one swallow.

'Just hang on a minute.'

Richard reached out to grip Sara's elbow as she walked towards the kitchen carrying two over-flowing ashtrays and four empty wine glasses.

'What have you been saying to my wife? Or rather my *ex*-wife?' Drunk, his northern accent was far more pronounced. Sara looked around, hastily, to see if anyone else could have heard, but the rest of the guests were too far away in the living room. He must have been waiting here, by the door, to catch her.

'This isn't the time,' she said, quietly and firmly, pulling away to try to make him release his grip, but her hands were too full and there was nowhere she could put the ashtrays or the glasses down, so she was forced to stand close to him, trapped.

'Would you like me to call you a taxi? You seem rather tired,' she said, trying to keep her voice light.

He leant towards her, his face red and sweating. She drew back as she smelt his stale breath, his mouth close to her face. 'Come on, I know you've been talking to her, encouraging her. She's been threatening me with her solicitors. Bloody Legal Aid, just because it doesn't cost *her* anything. It's costing me a fortune to fight this, she knows I can't afford . . .' She could see how blotchy his skin had become, his eyes red-veined, the skin beneath puffy. He used to be so good-looking – he and Matt were lethal womanizers when they shared a flat, when she and Matt had met.

Richard's first marriage had lasted just five years and then he'd married again. Sara liked Jo, his second wife, and she'd been sympathetic when Jo rang her a month or so ago, in tears. It was an awful mess, and Matt had told her not to take sides, even though Richard was patently in the wrong and, to her mind, spiralling out of control, drinking far too much. She and Jo hadn't been particularly close friends, and Sara had been, initially, surprised by the call. When she put the phone down, she realized that what Jo wanted was for Matt to intervene, because he was about the only person that Richard still listened to.

Sara had talked to Matt, as she'd promised Jo she would. He'd said it wasn't their problem, but, knowing Matt as she did, she knew he would have tried to reason with Richard. This had clearly not gone down well. So why had he come, tonight, if things were so tricky between them?

'Richard, *please* will you let go of me. Pop round tomorrow, if you want to talk to Matt. It's none of my business, and I'm not having this conversation with you now. It really isn't the time or the place. If you don't want me to call you a taxi, drink some water and go and join the others. We'll pretend this conversation never happened.'

Under her steady gaze, he dropped his hand – but as he did so he half turned, and the glass in his hand tipped, spilling the dregs of red wine over her skirt. They both looked down at the small spreading stain, edging out like dark blood over the black silk.

'Sorry,' he said sarcastically, without a hint of apology in his voice.

She looked at him, appalled. 'That's all right. I am sure it will wash out.' She glared at him, and he stepped backwards, away from her. His eyes were full of knowing.

Just go *home*, you bloody man, she thought, walking swiftly away from him towards the kitchen. She felt deeply disturbed, not just by his drunkenness but by the way he had looked at her – almost as if he pitied her. If only she hadn't had to invite him. She must tell Matt that he was horribly drunk – he must have been drinking long before he arrived. Sara normally tried to see the good in everyone, but right now Richard was testing that ability to its limits.

However, she kept getting waylaid, and didn't have a chance to talk to Matt before the speeches started. Collected in their living room were almost all the friends they had made during their twenty-six years of marriage, former neighbours from their three homes before the apartment, friends Sara had made from the girls' primary and then secondary schools, clients of Matt's who had become friends. Richard was the only friend he had kept since childhood. Sara had wanted to invite his mother, but Matt said there was no point as she wouldn't come. She hated leaving her bungalow in Manchester, and she drove Sara mad by constantly asking how much everything in the apartment had cost.

Half an hour later, Matt tapped on a low coffee table with his champagne glass. When that failed to achieve quiet, he paused, and then said loudly, 'Will you all shut up for *one* minute?'

The good-humoured babble within the room faded to a series of whispers and then there was silence. Everyone turned, smiling, towards Matt.

'I thank you. I am very glad to see you all here, given how far some of you have come. Now, since you have all spent the evening drinking my very expensive drink and eating my delicious food, you can pay me the honour of listening to my considered thoughts on the subject of my attaining the extraordinary age of fifty.' He gesticulated around the room with his champagne glass. 'Goodness, that is old. At least I don't look it,' he said, smiling self-deprecatingly. 'I certainly don't feel fifty. The picture in the attic –' he leant forward, conspiratorially '– looks even younger than I do.' He raised his eyebrows, and everyone laughed.

Emily, who'd worked her way across the room to stand next to him, raised her eyes to heaven. 'Boasting again,' she said, loudly enough for everyone to hear. Laughter rippled across the room.

'If I can't show off tonight, when can I?' Matt argued. 'I was told never to count my chickens, but I think that, tonight, they are well and truly hatched . . .'

Out of the corner of her eye, Sara saw Richard stumble into the room, the people nearest to him glancing over, alarmed and embarrassed at the fact he was so unsteady on his feet. She must try to get him home, she thought, right after the speeches. She had thought about asking him to make a speech – thank goodness she hadn't.

'Just get on with it,' heckled one of the guests.

Matt held his glass up in front of him, a smile on his lips. 'This is my party, and I can do what I want to. Little did I think that I would be standing here today, twenty-six years on from my wedding, surrounded by so many people who claim to be my friends, and, of course, my family. I am a fortunate man,' he added. 'I've been lucky in business – well, actually, it's mostly genius, but I'll pretend it is luck so the rest of you

41

don't feel too inferior – but most of all I have been extremely lucky in my family. I promised my wife I would not embarrass her tonight, but I can't help myself.' He reached out to take Sara's hand and she took a step towards him, her face pink. 'I have not always been the most demonstrative of husbands and I haven't always been there when I was most needed, but I have a beautiful wife who has stuck by me for an inordinate length of time, and given me two stunning daughters, for which I am truly thankful as we used to say before our school dinner . . .'

'*And* a beautiful girlfriend.'

The murmur of laughter stopped as if someone had clicked their fingers. One by one, like dominoes tumbling, everyone turned towards the doorway. Richard stood, swaying, a look of triumph on his face.

'Don't forget your beautiful girlfriend, Matt. Shouldn't you thank her, too? Oh, has she not been invited?' He looked owlishly around him. 'How peculiar. But I suppose you did your celebrating earlier, didn't you? Somewhere a little more *private*.'

Matt's fingers tightened in a spasm around Sara's hand. He was staring at Richard, his face taut with fury. He wore an expression Sara had never seen before – rage, blind rage, distorting his features into a man she did not recognize. A pulse beat beneath one eye and the corner of his mouth twitched convulsively. She looked slowly down at his white-knuckled hand, gripping hers – time seemed to have moved into a surreal dimension, as if she was underwater, unable to reach the surface. Then she caught his eye and the shadow became the man. A stranger. In that moment, she knew that it was true. Matt seemed completely lost for words. There was no denial, no defence, nothing to save the appalling moment.

'That's right,' Richard said loudly, trying to stand upright, putting out a hand to balance himself against the door frame. 'No mention of her, is there, in your little résumé of your perfect life?'

He turned to leave, and, as he did so, his hip caught a cut-glass rose bowl on a table just inside the door, filled with exquisite pale pink roses. For a moment it spun, and then seemed to hang in the air, before crashing to the ground. As it shattered, the shards of glass, like perfect daggers of ice, flew out across the pale floorboards. How beautiful they are, Sara thought, as, one by one, the roses dropped to earth and lay among the broken glass and rivulets of clear water.

'I'll clean it up,' she said, clearly, into the silence. 'Don't worry.' Before her the guests parted as she walked, with dignity, towards the kitchen to fetch a dustpan and brush.

Chapter Three

The caterers had finally left. Sara couldn't find the chequebook, and had had to turn out several of the kitchen drawers to try to locate it, when all the time it was sitting in its folder in her leather handbag in their bedroom, the handbag Matt had bought for her when they were on holiday in France last year. Sara didn't normally like designer labels, but this was just the right size for popping over her shoulder when she walked to the shops.

Her signature was little more than a squiggle, and the words on the cheque jumped about as she wrote them, as if they had a life of their own. She had thought Matt had paid the caterers in advance, but apparently not. As she handed it over, she glanced at the printed names on the cheque. Mr M. S. de Lall and Mrs S. L. de Lall. They had had a joint account for twenty-six years, ever since they married.

In the appalled silence, Richard had stood aside to let her pass, and then moments later, she heard the front door slam. He had gone, his mission accomplished.

'He's an idiot, a fool, you can't believe him, this is *madness*.' Catherine was the first to reach Sara, her

44

hand reaching out to grasp her shoulder, to make her turn. Her fingers dug into Sara's skin, but Sara pulled away from her. She could not bear to be touched, she did not trust herself to speak. She put a hand out to steady herself against the cupboard door.

Catherine's voice rose. 'It can't be true. How can it be? Sara, *listen* to me. Turn round. Please, darling. Matt would never . . .'

'Not now,' Sara said, calmly, without looking at her, taking out the dustpan and brush and shutting the door. 'Not now.' She paused and took a deep breath. She couldn't seem to make her eyes focus, and for a moment she felt so dizzy she thought she might faint. 'Could you . . .' she whispered, resting her forehead on the hand placed against the closed cupboard door.

'Yes? Anything.'

'Could you see everyone out? I think we'd better, I'm not, I really need to, just for now . . .'

'Of course. And put that away, please, darling. You must sit down.'

Sara, still holding the dustpan and brush, said nothing and walked away from Catherine, through the kitchen, past the waitresses, who stared at her, stunned. She could not go back into the living room, could not face any of the familiar faces, could not bear to register their shock. What could she say? How could she face any of them again, the people who had witnessed such an extraordinarily public humiliation of Matt, and her family?

Breathing hard, she slid open the glass doors leading out on to the roof terrace.

Outside, the cold wind hit her, and she wrapped her bare arms around her body. Before Sara, the lights of London stretched away. It was a perfect, clear night, the stars overhead iridescent in the black velvet sky.

She took a step forward and placed one hand on the

wrought-iron railing. The metal was icy under her hand, but she gripped it without feeling the cold, rocking backwards and forwards without knowing that she did so. Richard's words ran through her mind, over and over, as if on a loop of tape. 'Your beautiful girlfriend, your beautiful girlfriend, your beautiful girlfriend . . .'

She did not care about the humiliation. What mattered most was the fact that Matt had been shamed in front of his own children.

Richard was not lying. She knew that. He had looked at Matt with a bizarre kind of triumph, as if challenging him to deny the accusation in front of all those people, the people who knew him best in the world, knowing that he could not do so. And he had not. The smiling assassin had hit his target, and he knew that there was nothing Matt could either say or do.

If it was revenge, it could not have been better executed. Whatever. The words were said, and could not be unsaid. They had dropped, like perfect pools of poison, on to the shining floorboards and they could never be retrieved, and now the stain was spreading inexorably outwards over every part of their life.

She dropped the dustpan and brush on to the decking, and brought both hands up to her face. Gently, she touched her skin, feeling the ridge where the soft flesh under her eyes met her cheek. How guileless and naïve have I been? she wondered. Her fingers came to rest in the defined creases at the very corners of her eyes, and she closed them, feeling her pupils flickering and darting from side to side. In that one moment, the familiarity of her life had become an alien landscape.

She stood looking out over the city with no notion of time, until through the glass she heard her name. She half turned just as Emily wrenched the doors open.

'He's gone!' she shouted, her eyes wild.

Sara started. 'Who? Richard?'

'*Dad.*' Emily was sobbing, her beautiful face twisted with grief. '*Dad*'s gone. I tried to stop him but he pushed me away! Like he didn't care! What's happening? It's completely insane . . .' Emily's words seemed to catch in her throat, and she fell forward, through the open doors. 'Why didn't he just say straight out it was rubbish, how could he just *leave*? Didn't he think about us at all?'

Sara held out her arms, and Emily folded into them, trying to make herself as small as possible, and through the thin chiffon dress Sara could feel her daughter shaking. 'Why?' she repeated, over and over again, her voice rising hysterically.

'Shush,' Sara said, holding her tight. 'Shush, I don't know. I don't know anything, at the moment. Come on. You're cold.' Silently, she led Emily back into the kitchen. All the guests had left, and the apartment was eerily quiet. The waitresses were standing in a huddle around the kitchen table, and, as Sara put a hand on Emily's shaking shoulders, one coughed and then asked if they could, possibly, have payment and then they could leave. They had cleared up the glass, the woman said, her voice low with embarrassment, emptied the ashtrays, collected the glasses and all of Sara's cutlery and plates were stacked in the dishwasher. The trays which had held the canapés were piled up neatly on the central island in the kitchen, its black marble surface wiped and gleaming. They had done an impeccable job.

'What do you want to do with the cheese?' the waitress asked.

Sara looked at her, stunned. She realized they had not reached the cheese. 'Just take it away with you,' she said, trying to smile.

'Do you want me to deduct it from the overall cost?'

'No, no, please, just take it away.' Just go! Sara screamed, inwardly. Where was Lottie? Leaving Emily sitting at the table, she walked quickly through the hall into the living room. Someone had left a coat on the chair in the hall, she thought, as she passed, a rather lovely black velvet one. Part of her brain began to work out whose it might be, while another part thought, 'How can you be thinking this, now? How can you think anything is important? Your life has exploded, and you are worrying who has left a *coat*?'

In the living room Lottie stood with her back to her, her outstretched palms resting on the window, as she looked out into the night.

'Dad's gone,' she said, into the window.

'I know. Emily told me.'

'I think he hurt her. She went to stop him, and he pushed her away. Like he had to get away from us and he couldn't bear to stay.' She spoke mechanically, as if too shocked to register emotion.

'I'm sure he didn't mean to . . .'

'Stop defending him!' Lottie shouted. She turned, and Sara could see her heart-shaped face was streaked with lines of mascara, her beautiful hair falling down from the chignon she'd had put in, today, at the hairdressers, as a treat.

'Darling . . .'

'I can't think.' Lottie put her hands to her face, her hands shaking. 'Don't say anything. Don't even try to defend him. You can't make this OK, Mum.'

'I know. Not tonight. We all need to sleep.'

'Where do you think he has gone?' Her voice became low, child-like, afraid.

'I don't know.'

'You could call him.' There was a pleading note to her voice. 'Just ask him if it is true. I have to know. I can't sleep, not knowing.'

'No.'

'I'll call him.'

'He won't answer his mobile. What would you say to him, anyway? We're all going to have to calm down. Tonight isn't . . .'

Lottie's face crumpled. 'I know.'

'Hush.' Sara moved forward, to embrace her.

'Some party!' Lottie said, into her mother's neck, a trace of her normal voice. Sara laughed.

'Memorable, certainly.' Her voice was low, and bitter.

'You can say that again. Do you think it could be *true*?' Lottie said the word slowly, with appalled fascination, as if examining it from every angle. 'We would have known, surely. Dad's not that much of an idiot. He loves you – us. He *does*. What do you think, Mum? You know him best. Surely you would have known – you *must* have known?'

'Darling, I have absolutely no answers. I promise you this is as much of a shock to me as it is to you. We need to sleep and then tomorrow we can try to . . . I don't know, see what is to be done.'

'How can you be so calm? How could Dad do something like that? It's *repulsive*, gross. You've always been . . . how could Uncle Richard say that? And in *front* of everyone?'

'I don't know. I really don't.'

'If it isn't true, why did he walk out? This was his party. He's a coward to just leave like that, it's pathetic, like a *child*, running away.'

'I have no idea.'

'It must be true. Otherwise why would he run away like this?' She clenched a hand against Sara's shoulder. 'I hate him. How could he be so stupid? Such a bloody coward?'

'You don't hate him.'

'If it is true, he isn't who I thought he was. And I need him to be the same. He's my *Dad*. This doesn't happen to us, it's like being in some kind of film.'

'This isn't about you,' Sara said. 'Please don't think it is.'

'But it is, isn't it? It's about all of us, our family, and nothing can ever be the same again.' She began to cry, the tears sliding down her face.

Sara said nothing, because there was nothing she could say.

Lottie reached up and angrily wiped away her tears, smearing mascara across her cheek. 'I haven't even given him his present, yet. I bought it in Thailand, and I was saving it right to the end, when everyone had gone and it was just us, just family. I thought it was really special, and now it's all – it's all fucking *ruined*.' She wrenched herself away from Sara and ran out of the arched living-room doors, her footsteps echoing through the silent apartment. Her bedroom door slammed.

Sara walked out of the living room, having blown out all the candles which had not burnt themselves out. As she reached forward to pull the double doors closed, she saw Matt's Blackberry lying on the table next to where the glass bowl had stood, just inside the doorway. He never normally went anywhere without it. She stepped back into the room and picked it up. Almost without knowing what she was doing, she pressed the arrows until she reached his message inbox. The latest message read 'private number'. As if in a dream, she pressed the 'enter' button.

'I love you,' the screen said. 'This will be *our* year.'

Chapter Four

The cottage huddled against the hillside on the far peninsula, as if trying to shelter from the driving wind and rain.

'Are you absolutely sure you want to bother seeing this one?' asked the estate agent, battling to hold on to the flapping property brochure, as he tried to close the door of the car. Sara turned up the collar of her raincoat, and stared through the mist at the distant little house.

'Quite sure,' she said.

'OK. It's your call.'

They'd stopped at a junction to check the map, because the last sign to Lanteglos had fallen down, pointing, rather hopelessly, into a field of miserable-looking sheep, who stared defiantly back at them as if to say, do we *look* like a village? It was a quite dreadful day, and Sara wished she'd put on a warmer coat. On the train, the heating had been turned up like a furnace, and the wind cut her like a knife as she stepped on to the platform to change trains at Plymouth, to take the smaller branch line to Liskeard. From the station she had walked up the hill to the estate agents, noting the preponderance of electrical appliance and pet shops, for some bizarre reason, on

51

the High Street. Peering into the shop windows while trying to mentally establish the geography of the town – this might, after all, be her nearest place to shop – she thought how very little there was she actually wanted to buy, unless, of course, she suddenly felt the need for rabbit nail clippers or a flat screen TV.

The agents had lined up three suitable properties for her to view that afternoon.

'Why on earth Cornwall?' Emily had said, as they sat around the kitchen table in the tiny service flat Sara was renting, just off Kensington High Street. It was a shabby, depressing two-bedroom apartment, with paint peeling off the walls, decorated in an inoffensive but soulless hospital cream. It reeked of temporary habitation, which suited Sara just fine – you could neither care nor attach any emotions to such a place. It was, she realized, a place of limbo, which suited her mood exactly: living, and yet not actually *alive* in any recognizable sense of the word. She woke, she washed herself, she dressed, she made coffee, she walked Hector, she cooked rudimentary meals like poached egg on toast, tasting nothing, all with little or no conscious thought or emotion. Catherine said that she was still in shock, but it wasn't quite that – she felt rather as if she was waiting. Waiting for someone to pull back the curtain and reveal it had all been a grotesque joke, and that normal life was about to resume. Matt too appeared to be waiting – waiting for her to come to her senses and return home, according to Emily, who had appointed herself their go-between. Lottie wanted no contact with Matt, but Emily had been to see him the day after the party, at his office.

Most of her waking day was spent two steps away from reality, watching but not participating, as if there was a time delay between herself and the rest of the world. She'd never taken pills for anything, and shrugged off Catherine's suggestion that she should see her GP and perhaps ask for tranquillizers or anti-depressants. Sara did not want her senses muffled further – she already felt a little like the living dead. Her calm thoroughly unnerved Emily, who appeared to want drama and rows, although Lottie seemed to understand why she had absolutely no desire to talk about anything but the most boring mundanities. She felt that if she simply trod water for a while, the world might tip back on to an even keel and her path forward might come clear. Yet every morning she woke, looked at the blank walls and realized afresh that what had been done could not be undone, and her future lay entirely in her own hands. This was a quite over-whelming prospect for a person who had played the supporting role to her husband and then family for twenty-six years. Taking the initiative was a highly daunting prospect.

When Matt failed to reappear the morning after the party, she had packed a small overnight bag and asked the girls if they would come and stay in a hotel with her for a day or so. She could not bear to stay at home, surrounded by his things, the very walls bearing the imprint of those words. Hector could sleep in the car. She knew that it was perhaps not the most rational thing to do, but she refused to sit in the apartment, waiting for Matt to come home and try to explain.

Her days of passivity – that was one thing she *had* decided – were over. She was not going to sail, swan-like, over this, and forgive Matt, and smooth life back to normal. If the children had been younger, possibly, yes. But not now. Not now she and Matt were about to face a future on their own, a chance to rediscover their lives together before they had had children. Even knowing nothing of the circumstances of his –

whatever it was – she recognized the need to take action on her own terms, as a way of regaining at least a little of her shredded dignity.

For how long, she wondered, had she been passive, unknowing Sara, welcoming Matt home when he was late, cooking for him, running his bath, when all the time he was late home because he had been having *sex* with someone else? Had he rejoiced in his duplicity, congratulated himself on running two such disparate lives? Had he needed the thrill of deceit? *Did* she bore him, when all the time she had congratulated herself on the strength of their relationship, the longevity of their marriage, their tender love-making? The thought made her feel physically sick. Did he think she was overweight, sexually unattractive? Had he made love to her out of pity, all the time thinking of her, whoever she was? No, she would not wait for him to *choose* to come home. When he came back, she would be gone, and not contactable, at least for a while, until she could think clearly and decide what action to take. Above all, she did not want to hear him say he was sorry. The truth was far too complicated for that one, small, inadequate word.

Matt had apparently returned home towards the end of the second day – Sara had no idea where he had been, and had no desire to know. Shocked to the core at finding the apartment empty, he rang her mobile and begged her to come home. Sara listened, said nothing, and then switched off her phone. Lottie was refusing to talk to or see him, and only Emily had seen him. She now flitted between the two of them, and Sara resolutely refused to ask her any questions about how he was, and whether they had discussed the future.

After a week of staying in a hotel, she made the

decision to rent a flat for a month, at first. Catherine and several other girlfriends tried to persuade her to come and stay with them, but she did not want to stay with anyone. Above all, she did not want to *talk*. She could not bear the inquisition that staying with a friend would bring. But she could not hang around in limbo for ever. There were practicalities. Life went on. Emily was starting her job after Christmas, Lottie needed to submit her entry to university for the following year and she, Sara, needed to— That was where the logic broke down. What *did* she need to do? The only phrase that came to mind when she challenged herself with this salient point, was 'get away'. It was neither a sophisticated nor a thought-out response – simply a compelling need to be somewhere where no one knew what had happened and she could breathe and think clearly. And try, desperately, to make some sense of what had happened and decide if she and Matt had any kind of future together.

Christmas was a grisly affair – her mother had invited them up to Yorkshire but Sara could not bear the thought of being clucked over by her mother and her friends, some of whom, according to her mother, were now saying they had always thought that Matt was rather '*fast*' and not to be trusted. Emily spent the day with Matt at home, and she and Lottie had gone to Catherine's. For the first time in many years, Sara had got drunk. It hadn't helped.

Emily had found a flat to rent with two girlfriends, near to her new job, and was in the process of moving some of her things there from the apartment. Lottie didn't have to be anywhere until next October, and as for Sara, there was no pressing need for her to be anywhere, or do anything. Her road map had vanished overnight. If she was not to be Matt's wife, who exactly was she to be?

The decision to move to Cornwall had come in the midst of a sleepless night as she tossed and turned, wondering if the stance she had taken made her more, or less, ridiculous, and whether she really had the courage to leave him for good. Even now, no concrete details had emerged, but it was clear from the snippets that Emily let fall that Matt, infuriated by Sara's decision not to see or speak to him, was spending a lot of time with this woman, although Emily said there was no sign of her at home. Catherine had set herself on to a mission to uncover the truth – she said if anyone was going to find out every minute detail from whatever source, it was she, and Sara realized, without bitterness, that under all the concern her friend was having the time of her life. She had told Catherine not to embark on her detective work – there was no point. She would far rather be told by Matt, eventually, once the dust had settled, than be fed gossip and rumour. Catherine grimaced at this and asked, 'But how do you know he *will* be telling you the truth? It's much better to be armed with the facts,' and Sara realized, with a jolt, that Matt *might* lie to her – after all, he had been lying to her for who knows how long. The truth she had felt was the bedrock of their relationship had crumbled into ashes.

They had holidayed in Cornwall as a family when the girls were in their teens – Matt hated it, with all the queuing on single-track roads and forcibly cheerful days on a chilly beach – but something in the landscape and the coastline had touched her. I could live here, she had thought at the time of the holiday, and then forgotten all about it. But the mind has a way of storing such connections. It was, anyway, no madder than any other ideas she had had, and she had to go *somewhere*. Staying in London was not an option. She was terrified of bumping into Matt, and Emily had told her that on several occasions he had waited in his car for hours outside her rented flat, to try to ambush her into communication.

Emily announced that taking sides was pathetic, and it was causing a rift between the two sisters. Lottie said she could not understand how Emily could bear to even talk to Matt. Sara told them she did not want either of them to be forced into the position of having to choose between two parents, and encouraged Lottie to call Matt, but at the same time she could not help being hurt by Emily's decision to spend the majority of her time with her father. Emily said, point blank, she thought it was ridiculously childish of Sara to refuse to at least *talk* to him, to which Sara replied, keeping her voice carefully controlled, that it was not Emily's decision and she would not be bullied one way or the other. Matt had *chosen* to leave them that night – a decision Sara regarded as unforgivable. To leave them with the turmoil that Richard's words had created, and not even try to give an explanation? How could she sit down calmly and discuss the situation with him?

The Formica table in the kitchen of the service flat was littered with details of properties, which Emily had been flicking through with increasing dismay. Lottie sat huddled on the sofa, her hands wrapped around a polystyrene cup of coffee, the sleeves of her jumper pulled down over her fingers. Hector lay sprawled across her lap, his fat paws twitching against his pink stomach in a puppy dream.

'I don't quite know *why* Cornwall,' Sara said, in response to Emily's question. She ran her hand through her lank hair. She must wash it, but looking after herself seemed quite irrelevant. 'I just feel a need to be by the sea – we had a holiday there once, do you remember, when you were about fourteen?' Emily nodded. She remembered it: a holiday of struggling to a stony beach down a long, damp path, with towels, buckets and spades, a cool box and a bag which held books on the way down, plus Lottie's carefully collected stones and shells on the way back. Emily had moaned constantly, saying it was the least enjoyable holiday she'd ever been on, and she was way too old for beaches. Lottie, meanwhile, was in seventh heaven, pottering about with a fishing net, dropping shells and little shiny stones into a bucket while Emily sulkily read novels and shivered under a towel. Matt had only been able to join them for three days, because he was negotiating an important deal, and he had made it clear, as only Matt could, that he was not enjoying himself. He said it reminded him too much of the holidays in his youth, sitting miserably on a beach in Blackpool while his father drank in the pub. Besides, he liked the sun, and was growing used to the five-star luxury of business trips.

That morning Emily had marched into the apartment, dumped her bag on the kitchen table and told Sara that Matt was threatening to sell the apartment if Sara did not come home. She was, Emily added, sick of their inability to communicate, and it was 'doing her head in'. She then followed up this bombshell by announcing that Matt could not believe Sara was considering leaving London before they had even had a chance to talk and allow him to explain what had happened. The clear insinuation – from Matt, via Emily – was that Sara was being a very silly and irrational woman indeed.

Over the past three weeks she hadn't taken any money out of their joint account – she was paying for what she needed, such as food and the rent and deposit for the flat, from a building society account in which she'd stored a small legacy inherited from an aunt who had died several years before.

There was enough in the account for a deposit on a very cheap house, but Sara was very worried about how she would pay the mortgage with no income, and still have enough money to live on. Unless she took money from Matt, she would have to get a job. Catherine thought she was insane not to take him for every penny she could, if she was determined to leave her home – which, she implied, was impetuous and risky in the extreme. Catherine's theory was that she should have stayed put, to get the best chance of having the apartment awarded to her, if it did eventually come to divorce.

Sara, however, was determined to manage without handouts from Matt. The thought was repulsive. How could she leave him with her head held high, and then run back to him for cash? If she had any chance of a new independent life, she must not be beholden to him. She was very clear on that point. The girls, yes, of course, but not her. Her mother could bail her out if she got desperate, although this was an admittedly unattractive option. Even if in the distant future – well, at present there was no suggestion of an 'even if' – she returned to Matt, she would still have the house she was planning to buy. A bolt hole, something quite of her own. Independence, she could now see, was vital for survival. She had been too trusting and dependent, and she did not ever want to be so vulnerable again. What a position he had put her in, she thought. To have her loyalty and love rewarded in this way. She was trying not to be bitter and angry, but it was so very hard to be noble, especially when there was the risk of bumping into him at any moment. In Cornwall, it would be so much easier to be noble from a distance.

Her friends desperately wanted to do something to help, but Sara refused to either stay with them or have long gossipy lunches picking over the details. Her friends, especially Catherine, wanted to know how she *felt* – and the honest answer, that she had no idea, puzzled and irritated them. How could they help, if she would not let them understand? Of course it was the very *public* nature of the revelation which riveted the imagination: so dreadful. Their separation was, naturally enough, the hot topic of the moment at many dinner parties among their friends. The general consensus of opinion was that Matt had been an idiot, and that Sara ought to take him to the cleaners – not only could she get half the money from the sale of the company, she was also due half his pension, and with one daughter still in full-time education, she had every chance of getting their home. For a man who had riled many in business, there was more than a hint of delighted come-uppance.

Sara understood her friends' vicarious interest and their need for regular bulletins on her mental and emotional wellbeing (or not) and any decisions she was planning to make, but fuelling the fascination was more than she could bear. She could take no pleasure in being in the eye of the storm. The only solution, she felt, was to flee and leave all this mess behind.

So now she was sitting in the cramped front seat of a small Ford, driving along single-track country roads bounded by high, grassy banks, in the pouring rain. Periodically they had to stop in a lay-by to let a tractor or car pass, and each mile seemed to last an eternity. The last cottage they'd seen had been far more suitable than the one they were heading for, the estate agent claimed. That cottage was neat, and recently renovated, with new double glazing and a gas fire with 'real' living flames in the small, immaculate living room. A mile from the sea, it had an easily managed garden, spaces all ready for bedding plants. Ideal for a retired person. But I'm not retired, Sara thought. I'm just beginning.

'Nearly there,' the estate agent said, with a nervous smile. He found Sara a difficult woman to fathom; she didn't volunteer any information about herself and her circumstances, and although she was well dressed, well spoken and clearly middle class, she hadn't shown any interest in the big expensive properties they currently had on their books. In the office, he'd tried to steer her towards a spacious Georgian rectory, which had wonderful views, an acre of garden and a price to match, but instead she'd tapped the glass in front of the cheapest house they were selling, a little, falling-down cottage they thought would take years to shift, because it was in such a decrepit state. Most people didn't even want to look at it, when they realized how remote it was, and how much work needed doing simply to make it habitable. It didn't even have central heating.

Eventually he stopped the car in front of a five-barred gate. Leading to the little cottage was a grassy track, about twenty yards long, not firm enough to risk parking the car.

'It's a bit muddy,' he remarked, reaching down to unfasten his seat belt.

'That's fine,' Sara replied cheerfully, and opened the car door, hanging on as the wind threatened to wrench it from her grasp. Stepping out and stretching, the view made her catch her breath. There was almost nothing between the cottage and the sea, just a small front garden, a low stone wall and then, fifty or so yards beyond some tall fir trees to the right of the garden, the edge of the cliff. Beyond that the sea, steely grey, stretched away to the distant horizon, the tips of the waves flecked by crescents of white foam. It was like standing on the edge of the world. The nearest house she could see stood on the next peninsula, at least five miles away. Above her a seagull wheeled, catching the rising currents of the air and then hanging, as if suspended in space, before dropping like a stone towards the sea. Away in the distance a ship's bell rang – an eerie sound, with no sight of the ship through an impenetrable grey mist. The agent glanced sideways at her. 'Are you sure you want to live *quite* so far away from civilization?' He smiled.

'Quite sure,' she replied, her voice rising above the wind. 'Can we go in?'

He led her around the front of the cottage, and opened the gate, with difficulty, as it was hanging off on one hinge. He walked towards the front door, and, as he struggled with the key, she paused, one hand on the gate. This could be my home, she thought. The idea had come out of nowhere.

Inside, the air was musty and stale. The cottage felt as if there had been no life within the walls for a long time. Piled up in the corner of the corridor, in front of the kitchen, were stacks of old newspapers, and, on the floor in the kitchen, lay discarded, rusty tin cans. Sara looked at them in surprise. Had no one thought to tidy up? The two front rooms were still furnished, but with the kind of very old cheap furniture you might find at a car boot or jumble sale, varnish peeling, threadbare armchairs with dusty antimacassars over the backs. It looked as if someone had simply walked out of the door one morning, and never come back.

'The old man died,' the estate agent said, noting her expression, his face apologetic. 'I'm sorry it's such a mess. He had no family, so I'm afraid it's just been left as it was. He didn't even make a will, so the profits from the sale will go to the state.'

'How sad. He must have had some interests, surely? A charity he'd rather the money went to? People around here must have known him.'

'Not really. It's that old cliché, he kept himself to himself. Just pottered around here, didn't even have a car, walking into the village a couple of times a week for newspapers and essential food. The locals say he didn't talk to anyone. Bit of a mystery, really. The villagers say he had a daughter, but she disappeared, apparently. I don't know about his wife – she must have died young, too, or he was divorced.'

'Poor man,' Sara said, picking up one of the newspapers. The date was 1987. 'How long had he lived here?'

'Oh, fifty or so years. Almost a lifetime. Odd to make no mark, in such a long time, isn't it?'

'Perhaps he didn't want to be found,' Sara said.

'Or was hiding from someone.'

'How romantic,' Sara smiled.

'Not much romance about this place, though, is there? It's a bit of a dump. Sorry, I'm not selling it very well, am I? But I can't see you in a place like this.'

'I can,' Sara said.

Chapter Five

She woke to feel Hector's breath warm against her face. Reaching out, she stroked the soft hair on the top of his head as he arched up against her hand like a cat. His eyes, from the edge of the bed, peered enquiringly into hers, clearly informing her that she had overslept, and breakfast time was long overdue. He then laid his head dramatically on the bed next to her arm, and she heard the sound of his tail thumping on the bedroom floor. She must get up to let him out, he'd need to pee.

The duvet and bedspread lay heavy on her legs, the weight pinning her down. She had been glad of them in the night, as the air in the room was chilly. Turning her head, she saw the inside of the window was covered with condensation, and the top of her head felt painfully cold. It was early spring, and by the time the sun reached its full height at lunchtime it was so warm you could walk outside in just a T-shirt, but the nights remained cold. By contrast with the top of her head, her body was drenched in sweat, not just from the heat of the bedclothes, but from the hours she had lain awake, tossing and turning, trying to find escape in sleep from the thoughts chasing themselves endlessly around her mind without resolution.

During that night there had been moments in time when a great void seemed to open up and she felt a terrifying loss of self, as if she was falling into a sea of nothingness, her identity gone, and she had to grasp at thoughts, names, places, as she fell. Help me, she thought, giving up on sleep and staring out at the black night through the thin curtains. Help me. I don't quite know *who* I am, here. Will I be able to stick at this, and be alone, or will the loneliness drive me to a kind of madness? She had always thought of herself as a calm, practical person, who did not flap and had little sympathy with neuroses. But so much of her security had disappeared – she was beginning to realize just how much she relied on Matt, how much she needed his physical presence. It wasn't simply that nebulous concept, 'love', it was his companionship, his friendship. The warmth of his body beside her at night, the reassuring unspectacular routine of their lives together, the unthinking confidence with which she had planned ahead, holidays, social events, visits to the theatre, Christmases. All taken for granted, all, now, gone. Without any of this certainty, there was an endless void. Thank God for the girls. And dear, beloved Hector who gave, at least, a basic structure to her day with his simple needs of food and exercise. She must sleep, she had told herself. Close your eyes. What can harm you? Fear is a purely negative emotion, it leads nowhere. There was so much to do in the morning, and she'd be exhausted. But it was only as the sky began to lighten outside the window that she fell asleep, just an hour before Hector's face appeared inches from her own.

As she opened her eyes, he whined, and she smiled at him, feeling the nagging fears beginning to slide away. 'I would go mad without you,' she said, out loud. Excited and encouraged by her voice, a fat blonde paw slid up on to the bedspread, followed by another, and then, as subtly as he could, he levered his bulk on to the bed and flopped down next to her, squirming his body against hers and thrusting the back of his head against her neck, front paws bicycling as she reached out from under the duvet to rub his tummy. Then he rolled over, sighed, and heartily licked the side of her face.

'You just live, don't you?' she said, looking into his eyes, just inches from her own, filled with the purest of love and anticipation of the pleasures of the day ahead. He wagged his tail, his mouth curving into his Labrador grin.

'Enough,' she said, laughing. 'I'm getting up.' Through the window the sun cast a languorous trail of light upon the bedroom floor, full of the promise of the day.

'Fifty years I've been walking these cliffs.'

'Really,' Sara said. 'Every day?'

'Aye, rain or shine. See this?' He plucked at an incongruously bright yellow fleece, the kind of modern windproof garment she'd only ever seen previously being sported by the bike riders in the Tour de France. 'I've put this on today and I'm glad of it. You're not wearing enough clothing. That wind today, on the tops, it's like ice, spring or no spring. It'll go right through you, in a thin little jumper like that.' He looked at her appreciatively.

'I'm quite warm enough,' she said, folding her arms across her chest.

'You see,' he said, not really listening to her, happy simply to have an audience, leaning on his long walking stick, breathing heavily, 'If I wear too many layers but no fleece, I get a sweat on, and then when I'm on the top of the hill that sweat freezes. Then I get a chill.'

He looked at her triumphantly. 'I can't afford a chill, not at my age. I'm eighty, you know,' he added proudly. Sara shook her head in amazement, which was clearly the reaction he sought. She tried not to smile.

'It's all right for a young person like you. Muddy today, isn't it? Not as good as yesterday, I went further then, the path was dry. Made good time. But then I had my walking boots on.' He looked down, approvingly, at Sara's new walking boots. 'I've these on today, for the wet.' He lifted up a foot, all the better to demonstrate a curious pair of cheap green wellington boots, which he had cut off, just above the ankle. 'They're a bit more slippery, but they keep my feet dry.'

'How marvellous. They look just the thing.' Sara cast about for another topic of conversation. 'How much further are you going?'

'Another mile and a half, all the way to Polruan,' he added. 'Went to Polperro and back, yesterday. That's quite a walk.' Sara nodded in admiration, although she had no idea how far that was.

'You here on holiday?'

'I live there,' she said, gesturing at the cottage, half a mile down from the headland, upon which they were standing. It looked tiny, from the distance, like a doll's house. 'I've just moved in.'

His face lit up. 'No!' he said. 'Not old Mick's cottage?' She nodded, smiling at his obvious pleasure. This was clearly going to be big news in the area. 'It's falling down, that is. He never did nothing to it. Stuck there, day after day, hardly ever came out, never even said as much as a "how d'you do". But then, with his daughter . . .' He shook his head.

'What happened to her?'

'You don't know?'

'No, no idea.'

67

'Not for me to tell you, not with you living there. Where've you come from, then?'

'London.'

'Lunnun!' He said the name with a mixture of relish and disdain, as if she'd said, 'Timbuctoo.' 'Never been there, never wanted to. What brings you here?'

Sara was very tempted to reply, 'My husband has been having an affair with a woman who is apparently much younger than me and I felt it was prudent to leave for the sake of my sanity,' but chose instead to say – perhaps lamely, by comparison – 'I felt like a change.'

'Big change. Must be a bit lonely, if you're all on your own,' he said. There was something definitely leering in his expression, and Sara decided this prospective friendship needed either nipping in the bud or the establishment of clear boundaries, despite the fact he was eighty.

'No, I'm fine,' she said firmly. 'My daughters are coming to stay and I aim to come and go, quite a bit.'

'Ah. Been into Liskeard yet?'

'Yes, I went shopping there, yesterday.'

'Bit of a dump, isn't it?' He laughed, his breath wheezing. He wiped a dewdrop off the end of his nose. 'You'll like Fowey better, everyone does. Awful in the summer, though, can't move. All the tourists, still they spend the money. I'm a widower,' he added.

'Are you? I'm sorry. I'm . . .'

'Oh, I'm all right,' he said. 'I walk every day, fit as a flea. Can't let life get you down, can you? As long as I've got my health.' He looked down at his skinny legs, encased in strange loose black leggings, which ended several inches above the cut-off wellingtons.

'You certainly look very fit,' Sara said.

He smiled, delighted, straightening himself up on his stick. 'That your dog? Bit timid, isn't he?'

'Er, yes,' Sara said, as Hector hovered behind her legs. 'He's not normally like this,' she added, as she tried to shove him out from behind her.

'He looks a bit puffed. Not like me.' He slapped his thigh. 'Right, I must be off now,' he said, as if Sara had been holding him up with unnecessary conversation. 'I'll see you again, then. Now you're local.' He headed off swiftly, his bony knees moving at sharp right angles away down the narrow muddy track.

'I'm sure,' Sara called, to his yellow back. 'Goodbye.' Without turning, he waved his stick high in the air, as farewell.

'Come on, you useless dog,' she said. 'If I can climb this hill, so can you.'

Hector trailed along behind her as she climbed the last few yards towards the summit of the headland. Just below the top she stopped, her lungs bursting, her thighs on fire. She had thought she was reasonably fit, but walking in this high, thin air was exhausting. She would get fit and lose weight, if she walked the coastal paths every day.

Hector's head hung down as he tried to keep up with Sara, his whole body aching. If he had to climb another hill he might well sit down and refuse to move at all. It was all very well looking forward to walks, but walks in the past had their parameters; he knew how far he was going to go, in a nice flat park, but here he was being made to march well out of his comfort zone. And then there was the sea. On the day after they had moved in, Sara had taken him to the beach. He had thought he liked water, but this did not taste or act like normal water. It moved, often quite vigorously, and when Sara had thrown a stick into the sea he'd bounded in after it, expecting it to float, but it had been caught by a wave and disappeared, which meant

69

he had to swim around in circles looking for it. Instead of the water staying the same it swirled about and got deeper, and when he attempted to swim back to shore it seemed to be physically trying to stop him. He was paddling away like crazy, but nothing was happening, in fact – and, correct him if he was mistaken – he appeared to be going *backwards*. Sara then had a very unkind fit of laughing when he tried to drink the water, because he was naturally rather tired and thirsty after so much exertion. Instead of tasting as normal, it tasted most peculiar, and Sara had to sit down she was laughing so much as he snapped his jaws open and closed, wrinkling his nose in disgust, sneezing at the saltiness.

Today Sara thought she would try to walk to the second headland beyond the cottage, but, after reaching the summit of the first, she could see how very far that might be. Beneath her was a steep path, then a stile, a long meadow full of sheep – she wasn't quite sure how much she trusted Hector with sheep – and then the path ascended via what looked like hundreds of stone steps, cut into the hillside. She decided enough was enough. Instead, she turned round and took the path back to her cottage. But then, as a compromise for not having walked as far as she'd planned, she carried on and took the stony path down the side of the cottage, which led to the little grey-pebbled cove she had begun to think of as her own.

As she reached the tiny beach, the path became a series of stone steps, worn into grooves not simply by human footsteps, but by the ebb and flow of the tide. The sea was about twenty or thirty yards out, and before her lay a tideline of muddy brown seaweed, mixed with detritus, old ropes, plastic bottles, driftwood. To her right ran a wide stream of clear river water, the rivulets cutting swathes of different depths through the sand and tiny grey stones as it flowed home to the sea. She splashed through the stream, deciding to investigate as she hadn't been this far yesterday, glad she was wearing her new boots. As she walked further towards the waterfall which poured down over a small rocky cliff from the headland, something caught her eye, in a narrow inlet by the mouth of the stream.

It was a dead baby dolphin. Hector saw it too, at the same moment, and ran barking towards it. Sara, her heart sinking, moved closer. The dolphin must have lain there for days, its sleek, formerly grey skin a discoloured dark brown, and, as she came nearer she could see its belly was grotesquely distended, yellowing. She wanted to touch it, but drew back in horror when she saw the dolphin's eyes had been pecked out by seabirds.

'How did you die?' she said, aloud. The dolphin's mouth was open, agape, as if in surprise, and Sara could see the line of tiny jagged white teeth. Even in death and decay it was quite, quite beautiful, the smooth, curving symmetry of its body incongruously perfect amongst the flotsam and jetsam of the beach. Leaning forward, she saw a tag around its tail. 'Do not touch,' the label read. 'South West Wildlife Trust Aware.'

She had bent the tag over, so she could read it, and, as she did so, she realized how the little thing had died. Twisted around the dolphin's tail was an ugly tangle of green nylon fishing line, attached to a short length of rope. More knotted fishing line lay around its body, and on its dried-out skin lay deep gashes, presumably caused by the dolphin thrashing about trying to rid itself of its deadly encumbrance.

Sara put her hand to her mouth. 'You poor, poor

71

thing,' she breathed. Hector looked down at the dolphin, and then back at her. 'Just a smelly dead fish,' his expression seemed to be saying. 'Can we go home? I'm hungry.'

For reasons she could not quite fathom, Sara could not bear to walk away. The contrast between the graceful, natural curve of the dolphin's body and the grotesquely ugly man-made tangle of nylon line made her suddenly, unaccountably, furious. How stupid, how thoughtless, we are, she thought. How little we understand or care about this extraordinary world around us.

She walked slowly, thoughtfully, back to the cottage. Obviously fishing line was a danger to many creatures, not just dolphins, but how could you stop the fishermen trawling the coast? It was their livelihood, after all. Perhaps not many dolphins died in that way. Perhaps the death of this little dolphin was just a freak accident. She had no idea such a thing as the South West Wildlife Trust existed. It must be relatively efficient to have found and tagged the dolphin so quickly. She presumed that people must report deaths like this to the organization, when they were walking along the beach.

At the cottage, the red light of the new answerphone she had only just installed that morning was flashing with a message. She used to like finding messages when she came home, but now she found herself frowning, and mentally shook herself. She must stop dreading contact with the outside world. She pressed the 'play' button, and then turned to hang Hector's lead over the back of a chair.

'It's me,' Lottie's voice was subdued. 'Can you call me? Soon?'

Chapter Six

'She needs to be with you. I know you wanted time to settle in, but I think she should come down sooner than Monday. She's just *sad*, darling, and I don't think it is helping, being up here with me, so far away from you and . . .'

The name was left unspoken.

The phone had rung just as Sara was picking up the receiver herself to ring Lottie back.

Lottie had taken Sara by surprise by saying she would rather stay with her grandmother in Yorkshire, than move with her into the cottage. Emily, meanwhile, had said she was far too busy with her new job to 'possibly think of schlepping halfway across the country to the arse end of nowhere', to quote her precise words. It was, Sara realized, perhaps just a little too much reality for either of them to witness her moving the few items of furniture she had taken from their home to Cornwall. Besides, they both had strong reservations as to the potential of the cottage as their new home. Emily, having looked at the details with disdain, said it looked little more than a hovel, and was her mother trying to make some kind of point in being such a martyr? Sara said, simply, that it was all that she could afford.

And Sara knew that Granny's farmhouse had always been a place of safety for Lottie, even if she was made to play endless games of whist and help with the church flowers. Sara suspected she craved that kind of mundane normality, with everything else in her life in such turmoil.

'Lottie's out with the dogs at the moment,' her mother said loudly – she firmly believed your voice needed to *carry* on the phone – and Sara held the receiver away from her ear, wincing. 'She's not eating. I made her steak and kidney pie for lunch, you know it's her favourite, but she wouldn't even touch it, just pecked away. She's far too thin. I can't stay on long, I've to make the sandwiches for bridge tonight and I must wash Badger. He rolled in fox poo this morning, I hope he'll go in the river with Lottie. Dreadful smell, right through the house. For all we know she's become dyslexic with all this bother.'

'Anorexic. No, she isn't, she's always been very slim.' Sara had some sympathy with Lottie, her mother's pastry was like eating carpet underlay.

Sara's father had died ten years previously, and since his death her mother had filled her life with what she termed 'good works', such as the church and various voluntary organizations. She was, she said, busier than she had ever been. Not happier, but busier.

'Darling? Did you hear me?'

'Sorry, Mum, I was miles away. She's bound to be sad. Can I talk to her now?'

Her mother sighed. 'I told you, darling, she's out with the dogs. I can't hang on too long, I'll get her to ring you back.'

'Of course,' Sara said, smiling. 'I won't keep you . . .' There was no point in reminding her mother that she had actually rung her, as she would have forgotten.

'I don't mind Lottie stopping with me, but we've got

to think what is best. I'm only her grandmother, it's you she needs. I really have to rush, darling, it's my only chance to pick up the, for the concert, oh, you know, the things—' Her voice rose, impatiently.

'Tickets?' Sara hazarded.

'That's it. Tickets, for the choir recital on Thursday. Are you eating properly?'

'I am.'

'I bet there's nowhere to shop. Is there a local shop? You're going to spend a fortune on petrol.'

'There is, in the village about two miles away. Pelynt.'

'Wherever. I bet you don't have half the things we get these days in the village shop. *Baguettes.*' She paused, to let Sara take in the sheer exoticism. 'Oh, blow the tickets.'

Sara knew this was her mother's shorthand for saying she had decided she had the time to talk, and wanted to say something specific. 'I know you'll explain it all to me in time but I really cannot understand why you felt *compelled* to rush off halfway across the country. Why didn't you come up here if you wanted to get away? Your home is always here for you, you know that, darling.'

Because, Sara thought, then I really might have felt as if my life was over. I'd be clucked over and pitied by all your friends and before I knew what was happening to me I'd be in a tweed skirt and flat shoes handing out slices of cake at the church coffee morning, not to mention being paired off with Mary's fiftysomething son who played the organ, still lived at home and was clearly gay.

Sara had now admitted to herself that a great deal of her decision to leave London and all their friends had a great deal to do with the aura of failure, of the dreaded, 'Poor Sara, it must be so *awful* for her.' In

Cornwall, she could not feel like a specimen on a microscope slide. She knew no one, and no one knew what had happened.

'I like it here,' she said, defiantly. 'It's very beautiful, honestly, Mum, you'll love it. Lots of windy walks and pretty villages.'

'I can't help thinking you've been rather rash. It's not like you, you always thought things through. If you don't object to me speaking my mind, I don't think moving all that way away is the best thing for the girls. One minute they had a family and a home and the next you're all scattered to the four winds. And you've left Matt rather in the lurch, not that I could ever condone an – oh, what do you call it? An affair. Nasty French word. Your father couldn't even boil a kettle, and I bet Matt's just the same. I know what he did was dreadful – I don't know the details, and I don't want to – but there must have been a chance to patch things up. Twenty-six years of marriage, it's an awful lot to throw away, darling, especially these days when people seem to get divorced over a little tiff. It must be so confusing for the girls – where are they supposed to call home? With you, or Matt? It's just been all so *sudden*.'

Sara closed her eyes. Not now, she thought. Not when I am feeling so fragile from lack of sleep and I am surrounded by boxes and indecision. I need my mother to be on my side.

She took a deep breath. 'Please understand, Mum, that I *have* thought this through. I can't go back, at least not yet. And don't tell the girls that you think I should. That isn't fair. They have enough to cope with as it is.'

'Oh, don't worry, you know me, I'm the soul of – what is it?'

'Discretion.'

'Exactly. Have you spoken to Matt?'

'Once.'

'And what does he say?'

'It has nothing to do with him.' Sara said, quietly. 'This isn't his decision. I don't need to ask his permission. It's my life now, Mum.'

'You're still his wife, darling.'

'He should have thought about that before he climbed into bed with someone else.'

Her mother snorted disapprovingly. 'I told you I don't want to know all the gory details. But, you know, darling, men will be men. I can't help thinking you are being a touch melodramatic by leaving him like this. Why couldn't you have stayed and worked things out? It's hardly the first time a man's gone off. He hasn't *murdered* anyone.'

'How would you have felt if I'd been the one to have had an affair? Would you think Matt was justified in leaving me?'

'You're not that stupid. Besides, you're rather past the age for all that palaver, aren't you?'

Sara quietly seethed. 'That's not the point. I might. Why is it so very different for Matt?'

'Men never think they're too old. Your father . . .'

Please, Sara thought. Please don't tell me that my father had an affair. I need to be able to cling on, at least, to the fact that I had a blissfully carefree childhood and my parents were faithful and adored each other and there are no skeletons to come tumbling out of the cupboard.

'Your father didn't have an affair as far as I know, but how *do* I know? I know that he was a good husband and a good father, and I'm very grateful for that. I've had a very nice life, and so have you, until all this happened. Was Matt ever a bad husband to you, before?'

'Not really. We've had our ups and downs . . .'

'Oh, who doesn't? I've no idea why the modern generation seems to think that marriage should be all sweetness and light, it's about bloody hard work and sticking at things. And Matt has been a wonderful father to the girls. He didn't have an easy start, and he's done so well with the company and everything. *Does* an affair really matter so much, darling? It probably meant nothing at all to him.'

Sara had to prevent herself from shouting. She took a deep breath. 'Yes it does. It does to me. It means he lied to me. I can't take him back. How would I ever trust him again? Besides, you always used to tell me I should do more with my life. Well, now I'm going to. I am going to get a job.'

Her mother snorted. 'A job, now? At your age? Doing what? Besides, it's all very well for you starting again, but what about the girls? They may be nearly grown-up but they need stability. They still need their home and their parents. I don't hold with all this giving up and rushing off. It's pride, isn't it? You think he's let you down.'

'One of the main reasons I left,' Sara said, willing her voice to stay calm, 'was because of the girls. Should they really have a doormat for a mother, who would accept anything just to keep the peace and a nice comfortable home around her? Matt took away, in one fell swoop, everything I thought our marriage stood for. I could not live a lie, especially not for them. I think Lottie agrees with me. She wouldn't talk to Matt for weeks after – after he walked out on us.'

'I bet Emily doesn't. She's a right monkey, that one, she'll know which side her bread is buttered. I don't see her high-tailing it down to Cornwall.'

'She has her new job,' Sara said, remembering that Emily so far had not given her any idea when she planned to visit. Catherine had promised to come soon, but there were no such promises from Emily. Despite her determination not to think of either girl taking sides, she felt a flash of jealousy. Then she had a disturbing thought. Had Emily actually met this woman yet? What if she had, and hadn't told her? What if this woman – girl – had moved into their home? Her heart beat faster, and for a moment she felt faint.

'What? I'm sorry, Mum, I wasn't listening.'

'I said, you shouldn't have left so quickly. Perhaps you should have given him more of a chance.'

'Why?' Sara asked, indignantly.

'You could have nipped it in the bud. Anyway, why couldn't *Matt* have moved out, if anyone had to? Then there wouldn't have been all this disruption. I know it must have been awful, hearing like that – Lottie told me that much, I wouldn't let her tell me more – but I don't understand why you couldn't have sat down with Matt and talked it all through. I don't think you've really given him a chance to explain, darling.'

'I don't really want to have this conversation right now, Mum. You have no idea how difficult . . .'

'See this through Matt's eyes, darling,' her mother cut in. 'To him it was probably just a fling, you know, a midlife thingy, sex.' Sara stared at the phone. Her mother never failed to surprise her. 'And have you even given him a chance to explain, yet? It's been nearly three months, darling, that's an awful long time not to talk at all.'

'Once. I talked to him once.'

'What did he say?'

Sara hesitated. She hadn't told anyone about their conversation, not even Catherine, who was panting to know.

'You don't have to tell me, darling. I know I sound like I'm criticizing, but I'm always going to support you, you know that. I'm just so worried about you, all alone in that funny little house, so far from everyone. I'd love you to come here, or shall I come down?'

'No!' Sara said, quickly. She wound the cord of the phone around her finger, looking out at the little wilderness garden through the smudged glass of the window. It would be a relief to talk about it. She took a deep breath, and told her mother what happened.

She was loading the dishwasher in the service flat when her mobile, which was lying on the kitchen table under a newspaper, rang. She'd taken it off 'divert' as the girls and Catherine said they were fed up with not being able to get hold of her, and it had been at least a week since Matt had tried to call her. She did not think for a moment it would be him.

'It's me.'

'Hello, you,' she said automatically, as she always did, and for a split second, nothing had changed. A thrill ran through her, the sheer pleasure of hearing his deep, confident voice. In that split second, she felt safe. Then she shook herself. No. Nothing was the same.

'Don't hang up. Please. Thank God you've finally answered. I've been trying to get you for days. Well, two weeks and one day, to be precise.'

'Mmm.'

'How are you?'

'Fine. You?'

'Oh, brilliant,' he said. 'On top of the world. Never been better.' He laughed, bitterly. 'What do you think?'

'Don't be facetious.'

'Don't refuse to speak to me. How do you expect me to feel? This is completely insane. You *left* me, Sara, and I—'

She stared at the phone, then closed her eyes. 'Stop this, Matt. I'm not ready . . .'

'How's Lottie? Is she with you?'

'She's not so great. Yes, she's here.'

'Why won't she see me?'

'I don't know. It isn't my decision, it's up to her.'

'I suppose I should feel lucky that at least one of my daughters can bear to be in the same room as me.'

'I don't want to talk to you about this. You know how sensitive Lottie is. She's devastated, Matt.'

There was a long pause.

'Can I see you? Please? I can't talk to you about any of this over the phone, it seems crazy. I need to hold you, Sara, oh, God, I need to see you . . .'

'Please. Don't.' Tears were pouring down her face. 'Don't do this to me,' she said, her voice little more than a whisper.

'I love you,' he said. 'I love you, love you. Can't you imagine what it's been like for me? The flat is so empty, it's like someone has died. I hate going home. Thank God Emily's been here, she's kept me sane. I . . . I just can't . . .' He was crying. Sara stared at the phone. Matt never cried.

'Hush,' she said, without thinking. 'It's OK.'

'No it isn't fucking OK!' he shouted.

'Don't shout. Stop it. Look, for God's sake, Matt, *I'm* the one, I'm the one who had to stand there, listening to your best friend tell me that you had a *girlfriend* – what a ludicrous term – in front of everyone who knows us best. I stood there, in my lovely new dress and my painted nails, as everything that I thought was my life, everything I had always trusted to be real, was shattered. I've been to hell and back, Matt. Please. Don't tell me how hard it's been for you. Don't tell me how hard it is to come home to an empty flat. Imagine coming back here, to this shitty little place which feels like a prison, not knowing which way to turn . . .'

'Come home. Come home, then.'

'I can't,' she sobbed, leaning back so suddenly her back collided with the hard cold white porcelain of the sink.

'Why? Why not?'

'Because I don't know you!'

'That's absurd, Sara. How can you say that?'

'Because the Matt I love could never, *never*, have done anything like that to me. You've taken away everything I thought was mine, you've made my life seem little, my love, unimportant, next to whatever you have . . . whatever you have with her! It's the lies, Matt, it's the lies, for how long, how long . . . ?'

'Don't.' His voice was very quiet.

'I can't help it. Can't you see? I can't be with you. I can't make sense of any of this. I must have been so wrong . . .'

'When? When are you going to change your mind?'

'I don't know.'

'How can it be better? Being apart?'

'I can think. Plan what to do.'

'That's not what Emily says.'

Sara took a long, shuddering breath. 'Really? And what does Emily say?'

'She says you're in pieces.'

'Oh, does she? That's very supportive of her.'

'They shouldn't be taking sides.'

'Well, maybe you should have thought of that, shouldn't you, when you were slipping off to sleep with someone else, Matt, lying to me, to all of us. Who is she? Tell me! TELL ME!'

The line went dead.

Chapter Seven

She had barely given it a tap, when the entire wall came crashing down. One moment she was holding a hammer, the next it had become a toothbrush. Before her horrified eyes, the wall began to crumble, she was enveloped in clouds of dust and then, corner, by corner, the entire cottage began to sag and fall in on itself, like a pack of cards.

At this precise moment she woke up, and looked about her, her heart beating wildly. The cottage walls were still there. Crumbling and patchy, but still there. Her bedroom was just the same – the same too-short curtains barely covering the window, same floorboards with a gap just in front of the tiny cracked corner sink, with the mildewed mirror above. Same rickety chair, where she'd placed her jeans and T-shirt the night before, neatly folded, with her deck shoes lined up at the base of the chair. The book she'd been reading as she fell asleep, a romance set in Provence, lay open on top of the heavy quilt.

Exhausted, she fell back against the pillows, feeling her pulse rate gradually returning to normal. When she'd first opened her eyes, everything had seemed blurred, not quite real, as if somehow caught between a dream life and the solid, defined realities of consciousness. It took a moment for her vision to settle, and in that twilight moment, there was a twinge of the fear.

She was working on the fear — it kept creeping, uninvited, into moments of her daily life. When she drove the car home from the shop, with a bag of food on the passenger seat — bread, milk, eggs, dog food — in that one, crystalline instant when she switched off her engine and girded herself to pick up the shopping and get out of the car, there it was. She didn't think this was depression — it did not settle upon her like a dark, heavy cloud, rather it lurked, with shadowy grey fingers, at the very edge of her consciousness, reaching out to touch her when she least expected it, taunting her — you think you're surviving, in control, but you're not, are you? You're scared. Is this better than swallowing your pride and accepting Matt back? Believing him if he said it would never happen again, closing your mind to suspicion?

The trouble was, she realized, that being on her own, she had far too much time to think about herself and ask herself how she felt. Life, before, had been far too busy and structured, and the question, 'Am I happy?' was quite irrelevant. Now she found she was constantly testing herself as to whether she felt happy, miserable or simply numb, poking her feelings, trying to establish what they were, how she could capture happiness and recreate the sensation. Does walking the cliff paths make me happy, or simply tired? As I lie in a hot bath after a long, cold walk, am I pleasantly happy, or just warm? Does eating make me happy, or does it simply satisfy a physical need? It was, she had decided, quite exhausting to analyse how you felt all the time — not to mention pointless and counter-productive, but she could not prevent herself from doing so. Introspection, she had found, was a thankless, exhausting task, which led nowhere apart from into more confusion and unhappiness. Look outwards, she told herself. Not inwards. Be busy. Get on with things. Let contentment come to you, rather than seeking it out and attempting to manufacture the feeling.

Occasionally, she would find herself singing along to a song on the radio as she drove through the narrow lanes towards the cottage and she'd think, 'Aha. Caught you. Happy.' And then the moment was gone, and the fear settled back upon her. What I need, she told herself, sternly, is just to get on with things and stop analysing. The trouble was, there *was* something missing. It had occurred to her more than once that it would have been much easier if Matt had died. Cruel, admittedly, but then at least she would not have this constant nagging sense of being incomplete, of having failed. Her life, she could not help but think, was always going to have that bitter gap. And I'm not like that, she thought, sadly. I'm not bitter. I don't want to be a victim. Matt's selfish and thoughtless actions have turned me into someone I have no desire to be. And here, in the cottage, she was no one. Not Emily and Lottie's mother, not Matt's wife, not even her mother's daughter. She was the beginning of a new person, who didn't quite know who she was, let alone whether or not she was happy. At the moment, days were for surviving and nights a relentless quest for the bliss of sleep.

The evening of Catherine's visit during Sara's second week at the cottage, she had decided this could be a life of infinite possibility. This was true, but it was quite hard to be so brave and optimistic when you were lying in bed, quite alone, with the wind making the wisteria tap on your window like something out of *Wuthering Heights*, knowing that yards from your little house lay the sea, not a solid, comforting thing, but a vast, moving, mysterious entity with endless unknown depths, and that the future was equally without form or structure and was entirely up to you.

During the day, she loved the sea, especially when the sun was bright and the sky overhead a kingfisher blue. Then she could feel, for the most part, brave, and confident. But at night everything seemed to close in on her, and the fear came and she felt lost, such a tiny thing, amidst so much space. Then she would hunch the bedclothes and quilt around herself, like a cocoon, and think, 'you brought yourself here. You *chose* this. This was a conscious decision, and at the time you thought it was a brave thing, a healing thing. You needed it. Now you are being a coward, a useless creature, a scaredy cat, frightened of your own shadow. Be rational. There is nothing to fear.' Forcing herself to breathe slowly, she would start to count out, one by one, the certainties in her life – her love for Lottie, for Emily, her mother, her friends. Hector. Matt.

I am still in love with him. I'm furious with him, I despise him, I am so very disappointed in him, but I love him. He is the man I married, and I can never change that.

Catherine's visit had not helped. It had been too soon, she realized. She needed to establish the anchoring points of her life here before she brought in the past. With Catherine the chaos had returned, the need to discuss and try to make sense of what had happened.

Be sensible, she told herself, firmly. She was just as much Lottie's mother and Emily's mother, no one had deserted her, so many of her friends had sent letters and flowers. She had not been forgotten. She had a large, if now distant, network of friends who were desperate to see her and make sure she was OK. Work would start soon on the cottage, once she had found some builders – and there was so very much to do, so many decisions to make – but she did not have Matt to share the burden. When they had renovated their home on the common, she had never bothered him during the day at work with small queries, but she knew that at the end of the day he would be home, and all the myriad questions which had built up could be discussed jointly, and settled. Whenever anything important needed to be settled, she automatically thought, 'I'll see what Matt thinks'. It wasn't as if she couldn't take a decision for herself – it was rather that she always had his second opinion, and she trusted his judgement.

Nothing seemed to faze Matt – he said that having lived with his father, anything that life could now throw at him was a breeze. Maybe that was why he was so successful in business – what could be more frightening than his childhood memories of a violent, drunken father who regularly woke Matt by throwing his mother down the stairs? It had made him a risk-taker, an adventurer, but one who seemed to need to be able to come home to the safe haven of the family they had created together, so very different from his own. Or so she had thought. Well, she mused, he might have needed the safe haven of his family, but he apparently needed something else as well – another kind of risk. Perhaps she had given him too *much* security, un-wittingly provided the firm ground from which he could launch his sexual adventures.

What *had* made him do it, to take such a risk? He must have known that, eventually, he would be found out. If he didn't love her, Sara, anymore – was that a possibility, despite his protestations? – why hadn't he told her? Were there other parts of his life she knew nothing about? She lay in bed, thinking hard. Little things drifted into her mind, little things she hadn't thought particularly significant at the time. For the last year or so, his hands had trembled in the mornings. She noticed it when he was holding his coffee cup, and she remarked on it. He dismissed it, saying he was just stressed from work, he'd take a few days off soon. And he had a tic which seemed to beat constantly, he'd developed a habit of pressing his finger against the corner of his eye, to hide it.

He was clearly under stress, but was that stress caused by the guilt of deception? He must have felt *something*, she thought. He couldn't have divided his life so very easily. He must, she thought, have been, secretly, in turmoil. She tried, briefly, to imagine how she would feel if she had fallen in love and was sleeping with someone else, without Matt knowing. She shook her head. It was impossible to contemplate. Bizarrely, she felt a pang of pity for him. It must have been eating away at him, the guilt – no wonder his hands were shaking.

Why? 'Why' was the word which ran round and round her mind, as she lay in bed telling herself, 'I must sleep.' She went over so many situations, analysing entire conversations, the way he had looked and acted, searching for clues, for unexplained late nights, any loss of affection or distance from her. There was nothing. Until that moment at the party when the darkness had moved across the back of his eyes, she had not known. Not even suspected, not one tiny inkling. How had he hidden it from her? She knew that Catherine thought she must have at least suspected something was going on. Had other people known, their friends, his staff? His PA Sheila knew him nearly as well as she did – had she known? Sara didn't think so – the shock on all their faces when

Richard had dropped his bombshell had been so very genuine. There hadn't been any horrified murmuring, no, 'Oh *no*, that this should come out now,' – it had taken them all by complete surprise. No one could pretend to such an extent. This had been a secret. A secret life, from which she and the girls and everyone else they knew had been excluded. He often spent evenings socializing after work with clients, travelled to meetings abroad in Europe and the States. Thinking about it now, he had endless opportunities for infidelity, but she had never felt insecure because she thought that was not the way they lived their lives. He called her constantly when he was away, there were no mysterious absences or times when she could not get hold of him. Or so she had thought.

So why had he done it? Was it *because* it was secret, the thrill of no one knowing? Was there a distant side to him she had never known existed? Or was he unhappy and bored with her, and she had never realized? Had there been others? That thought made her turn, restlessly. Maybe she had been skipping about like bloody Doris Day while all the time he had been sneaking off into dark corners, booking hotel rooms, meeting women in bars. Behind the face she knew so well, was there an entire person she did not know? Could he be such a convincing actor?

And then there was the question of love. Sex, yes, she could just about understand. Catherine had once said that any woman could make a man sleep with her if she tried hard enough. Sex, she said, was so integral to male self-esteem that if a woman absolutely threw herself at him, he would be forced to act upon it, because otherwise he was not fully a man. Sara had thought Matt was that rare thing, a genuinely honourable man who realized there was too much to lose for the cheap thrill of casual sex. She had thought that their marriage was based on friendship, as well as love, and that he respected her too much to betray her so cheaply.

Sara wasn't a fool, she wasn't so naïve that she didn't realize how men talked when they were together, even – especially – civilized, sophisticated men. So had Matt been unable to stop himself, had he fallen *in love* with this woman, and did he love her *more* than his family? Was it an emotion he could not control? Had he been planning to leave her?

The trouble was, she thought, as she lay there, increasingly hot and unsettled, miles away from sleep, I do not know. And I do not know if I will ever know. And that means that everything I have based my life upon for the past twenty-seven years does not appear to have any validity.

She put her hand on her stomach, feeling the soft, pliant skin. Was it so very simple – she was too fat? Sexually unattractive? It seemed so superficial, she could not believe that this was the reason. Matt had never complained about the way she looked, he had always been so tactile. Their love-making never faltered. That was largely why she'd never bothered to diet much, or go to the gym, persist with jogging or contemplate cosmetic surgery – friends did, because they thought they had to, to 'keep' their men from straying. Sara had been pitying, she loathed that attitude. But had she been naïve? Maybe she had been far too complacent and not made enough of an effort to stay young-looking and slim. She shook her head. That was so hard to believe. Matt had said he loved her because she was secure, she didn't torture herself with worry, or follow the latest diets and chase an image she was never going to attain because getting old was getting old, no matter how you tried to cover it up or exercised away the lumps and bumps, which invariably came back the moment you stopped.

'Can you hear me? This bloody line keeps breaking up.'

'You're not driving, are you, darling?'

'No, don't worry, I've pulled over in one of those lay-by things.'

'They're not lay-bys. They're passing places. Be careful. Can you see a sign?'

'I haven't seen one for miles. There was one, but it was leaning over too far and appeared to be directing me into a field of sheep.'

'That's the one. Turn left there.'

'I turned right.' Lottie sounded as if she was about to cry, and Sara's heart turned over. My child. Did you ever grow out of that tug, even when they were in their forties and bank managers or whatever? Did you ever grow out of the urge to rush to them, put your arms around them and try to shield them from the harsh realities of life?

'Well, turn round,' Sara said practically.

'Easier said than done.'

'Did you bring a map?'

'No.'

Sara felt a wave of familiar impatience. Hopeless Lottie, who had always relied on everyone around her to sort out her life. She seemed cast adrift in the business of trying to be an adult, clearly not helped by the current situation. Maybe Matt had been right. Maybe she had sheltered her too much, and not equipped her with the tools of independence and responsibility. Emily never had any problems getting from A to B, in fact she positively relished any kind of practical challenge requiring ingenuity. Lottie, however, seemed to approach life with a kind of hopeless optimism, and when things did not go well, due to a complete lack of planning, she looked about for some-one to blame. It was never her fault.

'You took it out of my car before I went to Granny's.'

Sara sat on her impatience. 'No, I didn't. Anyway. Just turn round and go back to that signpost. Then go the opposite way, and just keep on coming. Don't turn off at all. When you get to the fork in the road, after about a mile, with a small grassy bit in the middle, take the right fork. That leads to Lanteglos – and go right through the village, with the Spar shop on your left-hand side. About a mile on there's a yellow house – there will probably be some hens in the road. Don't hit them, for goodness sake – and two miles on from there you'll see the Volvo parked in a lay-by. I know it's a passing place, but the road doesn't go anywhere from here, it just becomes a track to the farm. The cottage – it's mostly painted white – is opposite the car. Have you got that?'

'I think so,' said Lottie dubiously.

'Attagirl. You should be here in about fifteen minutes. I'll put the kettle on.'

'Thanks. I'll need a cup of . . .' Her voice, which had been quite audible, changed and became a Dalek noise, and then disappeared altogether. The signal had been lost. Sara put down the phone and looked around her.

What would Lottie think? She'd risen early, and, in her nightie and dressing gown, set to work. She had decided to have a bath once she'd finished cleaning, because she knew she would be dusty and sweaty. That was one of the beauties of the cottage – you could wander around stark naked if you wanted to, as long as you looked out for the postman. He was the only person you were likely to see all day, unless the farmer or his son came past on their tractor, to feed the sheep, or a group of walkers passed on their way to the cliff-top paths leading to Polperro and Polruan.

The rituals of the morning helped to banish the ghosts of the night – clean teeth, splash face, brush hair, let Hector out. Simply opening the front door on to the garden was a gift, now that summer was coming. This morning the sun was just beginning to climb in the sky, and the garden was bathed in a soft, pale golden light. By noon, the sun would be directly overhead, scorching, iridescent yellow in an aquamarine sky. At this time, however, the light was muted, a gentle awakening as the rooks stretched their wings in the fir trees beyond the gate, making exploratory cawing noises ending in spluttering coughs, to test their voices ready for the full throttle of homecoming at about five in the evening, when the entire garden became a cacophony of greetings and territorial bickering.

Catherine had asked how she could bear such a din, but Sara shrugged and said you got used to it very quickly, and anyway, the rooks were here first. It was their home far more than hers. That did not stop her, however, from bellowing at them from time to time, 'Just bloody shut up, will you?' as they flapped, squawking, from tree to tree, swooping down over the garden, or disappearing towards the horizon on mysterious missions while their mates shouted hysterical reminders. A rookery was not, she acknowledged, a soothing or peaceful thing to have at the end of your garden.

She stepped out on to the lawn, the grass under her bare feet covered with dew.

Within minutes her feet were soaked, and covered with the tiny white petals of the daisies – she must mow the lawn. Only she didn't have a mower – there was hardly a need for one at the apartment, and Matt had long ago sold their old one.

Her hands curved around a comforting cup of coffee

as she looked out over the moss-covered wall, towards the sea. Not once, not one morning, did it ever look the same. This morning it was in a sexy, lolling-about Mediterranean mood, almost turquoise, fading to navy blue towards the horizon. She padded over to the wall. The roses she had deadheaded when Catherine was here were beginning to grow, and from the blunt-ended stems pale green leaves were unfurling, tinged with a deep red. Earlier, as she'd been brushing her teeth, she was delighted to see a pale pink bud on the wisteria outside her bedroom window, like a small plump pineapple. Now, looking up at the wisteria from the garden, she could see the entire climber was dotted with buds. It was too straggling, but she'd soon get that under control. Gradually, the grey fingers of the night were beginning to curl up and retreat, as the sun warmed her face and she planned the day.

Walking back inside, she looked around, trying to see the cottage through Lottie's eyes. Of course she would think it was very small and, at the moment, shabby. What she hoped, most of all, was that Lottie would be able to see the potential, not to mention share the sensation of peace which had wrapped itself around Sara from the moment she had walked in through the front door. Nothing could keep the night thoughts at bay, but once she was awake, the cottage did its best to soothe her. This healing power had nothing to do with her physical surroundings – the air of peace lay in the atmosphere, the way the old walls had absorbed the centuries of life within. You could try to create an impression of calm using sofas, carpets, curtains, ornaments, paintings, flowers – but what you could not create was an atmosphere. That was what had connected with Sara, the sense that the soul of the cottage wanted her to stay.

But, practically, it was a mess. There was nothing

she could do about the kitchen, but she'd made the two little living rooms as comfortable as possible, sweeping the boards, putting down two of her favourite Moroccan rugs, which were too wide for the floor space and curled up at the edges where they met the wall. Her furniture looked far too big – she had taken the cream sofa and two armchairs from their apartment, their proportions designed to fill the space of the former loft. Here, the three-seater sofa was so long it filled an entire wall, and with the armchairs, there was barely room to tiptoe around the edges. Lottie would say it looked like a furniture showroom. But there was nothing she could do until she started knocking down walls, if that was possible without the entire house falling down. There was her dream – her subconscious had picked up this fear.

Yesterday she'd wandered along the lane and picked some greenery and flowers, to brighten the rooms. As yet there were no curtains up at either of the windows in the front rooms – what was the point, when she planned to alter the windows? At night, not having any curtains gave them a blank, austere feel, and she hated to look out into the blackness, terrified by the irrational fear of seeing a face peering back in. But during the day both rooms were flooded with light.

She made another cup of coffee and decided to wait for Lottie outside. Having washed herself as best she could in the old bath – you had to sit almost bolt upright, it seemed to have been designed for an exceptionally small person – she'd dressed in cropped beige cargo trousers and a white T-shirt, noting with pleasure how tanned her arms had become. There was a deep tan mark around her forearms – builder's tan, Matt used to call it. Stop it, she thought to herself. I must stop making Matt a point of reference, as if I can only see the world through his eyes. But I *have* looked at the world through his eyes, she realized. I tried to see everything from his point of view so I could filter out the things he did not like, or would annoy him, so his life would be less hassled. How many women, she wondered, experienced this? As if everything around you had to be scanned to prevent potential arguments and create harmony, dirty plates picked up, car keys put back in the appropriate place, television-programme details studied to select ones he might like. It was, she thought with a smile, as if she had viewed the world through Matt-glasses. And now she had to use her own eyes, and rediscover what *she* liked. From the food she wanted to eat, to the way she set out the furniture, the music she listened to, what she wanted to watch on television, even how long she stayed in the bath – all these decisions were hers, and hers alone. It was a kind of freedom, she thought. A compensation for failure?

Sitting on the wall, gazing at the cottage, she realized how excited she was about showing it to Lottie. This was the first time she had had anything that was so completely her own.

She heard the little Polo car before the red bonnet appeared around the last bend. They had bought Lottie the car last year – Matt had insisted on giving her a brand-new one because he said it would hold its value much better, and added he held out little hope of Lottie ever earning enough money to buy herself a new one. He had bought Emily a new Golf two years previously, a top-of-the-range model in black. He said Lottie was better with something less powerful, while Emily smirked as she knew her car had been more expensive.

'I'm so glad you're here.' For a moment, Sara just held her. With her arms tight around her younger daughter, time stood still. It felt just the same,

the instant connection and complete sense of un-
adulterated love and protectiveness.

'Come in. Don't expect much,' she warned. 'It's still
quite a jumble.'

Lottie's eyes had been wide as she tried to shut the
gate – 'It won't, the hinges are broken,' Sara interjected
– and as she walked towards the front door she turned,
to take in the view. 'Wow,' Lottie exclaimed, looking
out over the sea, her eyes moving over the water, to the
peninsula, around the high cliffs, the sea breaking on
the rocks beneath and then up, at the cloudless
sky, the gulls and the rooks wheeling and calling high
overhead. 'It's beautiful,' she said, simply.

Sara reached out to take her hand, pleased beyond
belief. 'I know,' she said.

Inside, Lottie pottered about while Sara boiled the
kettle, picking up familiar objects, wandering in and
out of the front rooms, smoothing her hand over the
back of the sofa which dwarfed the right-hand sitting
room, remembering.

'You haven't put any photographs or paintings up
yet,' she called, and Sara called back that there was no
point because there were so many changes to make.
Hector had nearly turned himself inside out with joy
at seeing Lottie, prancing about, rubbing against her
legs, thrusting his wet nose into her hand. As soon as
she'd walked in through the front door she had sunk
down, her arms tight around his neck, pressing her
face into his fur, breathing in his familiar smell. Sara,
who knew she was crying, walked on ahead into the
kitchen, leaving them together. Hector and Lottie had
always been a team, ever since he was a puppy. She
had let him sleep on her bed, which had no doubt con-
tributed to the fact that he had become so soppy. To
Emily he was quite useful as a reason to get out of the
apartment for some fresh air and exercise – she liked

the *idea* of having of a dog, but she hated the muddy paws and hairs on her lovely clothes. And sometimes he was just too much in her face, and she pushed him away. Lottie, however, loved him as an essential part of the geography of her life.

Sara handed Lottie a mug of tea. 'Let's sit outside. I'm afraid we'll have to sit on the wall – I must buy some garden chairs and a table.'

'I'll help you,' Lottie said. Sara smiled, as they walked out into the sunlit garden.

'Thanks. How was the journey?' She pushed a patch of moss aside to sit down.

'*So* long.' Lottie put down her mug on top of the wall and picked at her bitten nails, before putting her thumbnail in her mouth, tearing off a tiny splinter. Her hair, blonde like Sara's, was caught up, loosely, in a bun at the back of her head, secured with a glittery bulldog clip. It suited her, drawing the fine, slightly wispy hair away from her face, pale-skinned and delicately chiselled. Matt used to say she looked like the illustrations in Charles Kingsley's novel, *The Water Babies*. She was more classically beautiful than Emily, but she lacked her animation – Emily's face was so mobile, her dark eyes flashing, so that even though her features were less perfect than Lottie's, she made you feel she was beautiful because she was so vital.

Lottie's eyes looked haunted, especially in repose, the skin beneath shaded a delicate blue, like a bruise. When she was very young, Sara had had awful dreams about losing her, that she was too small, she disappeared into the crowd of a busy shop, or fell from her hands down gaping holes in the floor. Silly dreams, but the fear was there – that somehow Lottie might be taken away from her. As a child she had been much smaller than her peers, and was teased about it at school, sometimes cruelly – she ate almost nothing, no matter how Sara tried to tempt her, and she was so thin, like a little twig. Lifting her was like lifting a feather, she floated above the ground. We must toughen Lottie up, Matt would say impatiently, if she told him Lottie had trailed home from school, yet again, in tears, and how well Sara knew the look which passed over Lottie's face whenever her father criticized her lack of confidence – the sadness that she was not the kind of daughter he wanted, not tough and confident enough, like Emily. She was, she felt, second best.

When Sara had asked her mother how Lottie was, she had said, simply, 'sad'. And that was it. Too often Lottie was sad, even when there was no concrete reason to be so. Sara's heart would go out to her whenever she saw her pale, tear-stained face looking up at her as they walked together away from school as she murmured, 'They were mean to me again,' and Sara would sink to her knees to wrap her arms around Lottie and say, 'They are wrong, not you.' But then Matt would say, in response to Sara's concerns that perhaps they should move her from that school, that she had to learn to take it on the chin, she had to get used to people being unpleasant, that life was not fair, but a battle to be won. Sara wondered if they had been right in making her stay. The bullying hadn't ceased, and it was only at secondary school that Lottie seemed to gather a close group of friends around her and begin to find the little self-confidence she had. She'd always been a wonderful artist – as a child, her bedroom floor was littered with drawings – but she hadn't shone academically. Matt had been so in-expertly parented Sara made exceptions for him as a father, but now she could see that he had not been sufficiently understanding of Lottie, nor praised her talents. And now, perhaps, this attitude was coming home to roost.

'How was Gran's?'

Lottie smiled, pulling the sleeves of an old grey V-necked cashmere jumper of Matt's down over her hands, the cuffs, as usual, in holes. 'You know, Gran's. Lots of stodgy food I couldn't eat, long, cold walks with the dogs, ancient women popping round for incomprehensible chats about bobbins and cake tins and *very urgent* trips to take library books back. Is Granny the only person in the world who still uses the library?'

'Quite possibly.' Sara smiled. 'Sadly.'

'What I didn't like –' the thumbnail was back in her mouth '– was the way that all Granny's friends looked at me, as if I was ill. Even Granny seemed to be a bit careful with me, as if she mustn't upset me. It was pretty awful, really – I felt like an exhibit in a zoo. Will it go on being like this for ages? I'm bored of the weirdness.'

Sara looked at her thoughtfully. 'I don't know,' she said slowly. 'I'm not sure I'm far enough down the line to know when things will feel like normal. I feel a bit like that, too. A bit like I'm recuperating from a long illness.'

'I didn't use to think I liked routine,' Lottie said. 'I used to think that fantasy was much better than real life. But now I'm not so sure I do. This is all a bit too much change. It's awfully tiring,' she added, sighing, scuffing her feet in frayed turquoise silk ballet pumps backwards and forwards against the crumbling base of the wall. 'I have to think what I'm going to say before I say it, to everyone.'

'Do you feel,' Sara said, carefully, 'that life doesn't seem quite real?'

'God, yes!' Lottie looked about her. 'It's all completely bonkers. You've left Dad and we're selling our

100

home, and you've moved down to this mad place and Dad's looking at other smaller flats and it's like our lives has just gone *flump*. I don't know where I am, anymore.' She hit the top of the wall with the palm of her hand and then took a sip of tea from the mug held in her other hand. 'Does that sound normal to you?'

'Obviously not.' Sara laughed. 'It's a pretty good assessment, really. Are you cross with me?'

'Why?' Lottie regarded her mother, cautiously.

'For leaving Dad.'

'Oh.'

'Are you?'

'I don't honestly know. Yeah, a bit. There are moments, I have times, when I'm like really, really angry with both of you. Dad for having the affair – I mean, what was the point, he's so *old* for God's sake? – and then you for refusing to talk to him and then deciding to leave us and come down here when you don't know anyone and there's no earthly reason to actually be here, apart from trying to make some kind of insane statement, I suppose.'

'I never planned to leave you, Lottie. This will be your home too, I hope. And Emily's, when she wants to come.'

'She doesn't. I don't know anyone here, Mum, all my friends are in London. Why should I move here? I mean, that's not to say I won't, but it's very hard just to give everything up at home, all my schoolfriends, my social life. Kind of a weird prospect, you have to accept.'

'Oh? Does Emily definitely not want to come? Not even for a holiday?'

'No, she doesn't. Not yet. She's got work, anyway, and she says it's a really stupid thing to have done and Dad's gone mental. She sees his side. You know. She's still living with him most of the time, even though she's got her flat. I think she should move out, but she says Dad "needs me so much".' She put on a falsely intense voice, and grinned. 'You know, Emily, the drama queen.'

'He probably does need her.'

'Yeah. But he should have thought of that first, shouldn't he? Before he started shagging some bimbo. He can't have everything.' She glanced apologetically at her mother. 'Sorry.'

'Do you think I should have stayed? In London? That this won't work?'

Lottie looked out over the sea. 'I can see why you wanted to leave, but I do think this is maybe a bit too far. You've made us feel as if everything, absolutely everything has changed. It's a lot to deal with. You, here. Dad, in the apartment but kind of camping there and about to move out. Bits of furniture missing at home. It doesn't feel the same at all, like there are all these gaps. He's different, too.'

'Is he?'

'Yup.' Lottie finished her tea, and stared into the bottom of the mug. 'Kind of muted. Careful. Quieter. He doesn't shout way so much. I mean, I only saw him twice before I went off to Gran's, but he seemed to have changed quite a bit.'

'Really? In what way?'

'It was as if he had to handle me with kid gloves and be mega nice to me, and that was so freaky. He kept asking me if I was OK for money and could he buy me anything, like clothes or a new phone? Of course I took him up on it.' Sara flashed a smile at her daughter, who shrugged. 'Hey, I reckoned he owed me. I got the new Razorlight phone, really cool. And he took me shopping in Fenwick's and I bought a Ghost dress. Ghost! Emily was like, really green, because she was at work. But I bet she's got a lot of stuff out of him as well.'

'Sadly I have no money for clothes, so I can't offer you any bribes. The most you'll get here is lots of fresh air and healthy walks. You know I don't want you to feel you have to take sides, it shouldn't be like that. He'll always be your dad, I want you to see him.'

Lottie smiled at her. 'I know. But I want to be with you. Even if it means, like *no* social life. There's a lot to sort out, here, isn't there? I can help. You know me, I'm good at buying stuff. I have an impeccable eye. Cornwall has great light for painting, too. Can I have my own studio?'

'There is a *huge* amount to do,' Sara agreed. 'I suppose you could, if you want. There's not much room, though, it would have to be a very small one. Maybe in the attic?'

'Do you miss Dad?' Lottie examined her mother's face carefully.

Sara's smile flickered. 'Yes,' she said. 'Of course I do. I loved him.'

'Loved him?'

'Love him. I suppose. It's hard to say.'

'What a pair of idiots you both are.' She put the mug on the grass, and wrapped her arms around Sara, as if she were the mother.

'What about in the future? Will you see him? He really wants to see you – he told me to tell you.' Lottie screwed up her face apologetically. 'Sorry, but I promised I'd relay the message.'

'I'm sure he does. But I need to get settled here, first, before I can even think of that. Now, are you feeling strong? I want you to help me unpack the last of the boxes before we go shopping. Let's do that, then have lunch out and go to the garden centre in Liskeard and splash out on some chairs and a table for the garden.'

'Neat plan. I'm starving. I've been driving since seven this morning.'

'I'm so happy to have you here.' Sara stared into Lottie's eyes, their faces only inches apart, overwhelmed with relief.

'I know. Don't go all morbid on me, old woman. Where did you think I would go? Stay with Dad? I don't think so – he's always out at work and there's nothing in the fridge. And I can't afford anywhere of my own. So here I am.'

'I love you.'

Lottie made a small retching noise. She looked at Sara and then replied, as she always did.

'I love you more.'

Chapter Eight

'Is that your newspaper?'

Sara lifted it from the counter by the till, and put it back into her wire basket. 'Yes, sorry.'

'Damn and blast. I must have left mine at the end of the shop. Buggeration.'

Sara, looking at the speaker more closely, realized it was the woman who lived in the yellow house two miles from the cottage, with the hens, the hens she'd nearly run over numerous times as they pecked about the road.

She was about Sara's age, possibly a little older, with light brown hair, cut short. She had a handsome, weather-beaten face, and a mannish, capable air, enhanced by the thick grey fisherman's sweater she was wearing over navy blue trousers, tucked into wellingtons.

'I always get this one. Not very intellectual, is it? But I can't be arsed with the broadsheets and all those supplements – I just end up chucking the whole lot in the bin. Who's got time to read all that stuff? Terribly unenvironmentally friendly, I'm sure.' She smiled at Sara. 'I'm Helen, by the way. I've seen you driving about – you have a white Volvo, don't you?'

'That's right. I'm sorry, I nearly caught one of your hens the other day.'

'Don't worry. They've no road sense and an apparent death wish, but I can't bear to see them shut up in a hutch all day. I keep filling in the holes in the fence, but I suppose the grass is always greener.' She spoke in a clear, Home Counties accent.

'Look at all that money!' The teenage boy behind the till, his face an unfortunate panoply of acne, interrupted them by pointing at a large picture on the front page of the tabloid newspaper Sara was buying. 'You'd never think they'd hand over the money like that when you win the lottery. I thought you'd get just, like, a cheque. Fancy that,' he said in his Cornish accent, thick as clotted cream, shaking his head. Sara looked at him disbelievingly.

'I think that's just a publicity stunt,' Sara said, carefully. 'To show how big the jackpot will be this week. They don't give the winners the money in actual cash. It would be quite a lot to carry, wouldn't it, if you think about it?'

'I never! A publicity stunt?'

Helen caught Sara's eye and they both stifled a smile.

'You've bought Tremain Cottage?' Helen said.

'I have.'

'You're brave. It must need a hell of a lot of work.'

'It certainly does. I don't really know where to start,' Sara admitted. 'I'm still in a mess, haven't even unpacked everything yet. I'm camping, really, cooking on an ancient Baby Belling stove and a microwave. It's rather hard to think straight when you know everything's going to be replastered and whatnot. I really need to find a good builder.'

'You could start with me,' Helen said. Sara looked at her in surprise.

'I'm not a builder,' she said. 'But I am an architect and I know most of the builders round here. I used to have my own practice in Surrey, and I work from home now. It's amazing how much work there is around here, although most of it's on second homes, admittedly. People round here don't want to pay my rates.'

'How do you know I do?' Sara said, smiling.

'Big car?' Helen said.

'Oh, that's getting on now, and anyway it was given—' Sara had been about to say, 'It was given to me by my husband,' but stopped herself. 'I am on a budget,' she said. 'Honestly, I don't have lots of money. I wouldn't want to take you on, on false pretences. I'm hoping to do a lot of the redecorating myself.'

'I'd like to help,' Helen said. 'I tend to have two rates, anyway, one for jobs I don't particularly want to do but have to, to pay the bills, and one for work that really interests me. How old is the cottage?'

'I'm not exactly sure. About three hundred years?'

'Maybe even four. I'd love to come and have a root about. Is it in a dreadful state?'

'Pretty bad. I've tidied up, but there's no point painting anything, until I decide what I'm going to do. I didn't want to rush at it, and to be honest I've never actually renovated an entire house before, just bits and pieces, you know, rooms.'

'I'll come this afternoon, if you like. I haven't got anything on, apart from clearing out the henhouse, and I'd be thrilled to put that off.'

'That would be great. Thanks.' Sara smiled. 'About two?'

'Ideal. I'll see you then.'

From the interior of Helen's beaten-up Land Rover Defender came the sound of loud, hysterical barking. 'I won't let him out,' she said, fending off a large hairy Airedale dog as she climbed out. 'He's dreadful at jumping up and he gets thoroughly over-excited at meeting new people. His name's Nigel. Grim, isn't it? The kids called him that for a joke and I'm afraid it stuck.'

'Hector – my Labrador – is a bit timid. Maybe we need to introduce them slowly?'

'Nigel's all right once he gets to know you, but it is a bit like being attacked by a carpet.'

Sara laughed. 'We could always walk them together, later – if you've time, that is?' I mustn't rush this, she thought. I can't seem desperate to make a friend. Let's take it one step at a time. But thank God, oh, thank God, there seems to be at least one normal, intelligent person living nearby. Most of the women she'd bumped into so far in the Spar shop had been perfectly friendly, but either elderly or young mums coping with crying babies and hyperactive toddlers.

'He was my husband's dog and neither of the children will have him, understandably. So I got stuck with him, the silly old fool.'

'How long ago . . . ?'

'Three years. A heart attack. One of those things. He was older than me, but it was a shock all the same.'

'Come in.' Sara walked ahead of Helen and held the front door open for her, before following her inside. Helen peered into the two small front rooms. 'Hideously poky,' she said. Sara smiled. Helen was clearly not one to mince her words.

'I know, aren't they dreadful?' she agreed. Helen tapped the wall from inside one room, and then went back outside into the corridor. 'You may be all right,' she said. 'This is a stud wall, and the other one is probably the same. Not stone,' she added, catching Sara's baffled expression.

'I had thought I'd like to knock them both through into one big room and get rid of the passageway, but that would mean you'd step straight into a living room, which isn't ideal, is it?'

'Hmm. Unless you made a feature of the front door with a little porch, but never actually used it, and put the main entrance around the back. Most people don't use their front door, anyway, not when you park at the back.'

Sara smiled. 'That's a good idea. I want lots of light, but I doubt I'd get planning permission to make the windows bigger, would I?' She walked over and looked out of one of them, towards the sea.

'Is the cottage listed?'

'No. It probably should be, but it isn't.'

'That's good news. It's a bugger trying to get any kind of change, especially to windows, on a listed property. Now, show me the rest.'

She laughed out loud as Sara led her into the kitchen. Sara had swept the grey slate floor, polished the round oak table until it shone, and the fridge and stove were spotlessly clean, but even the vase of pink roses on the table could not hide the fact that this was a prefabricated excuse for a kitchen. 'Demolition,' Helen said, succinctly, looking up at the tin roof. 'What kind of kitchen do you want?'

Sara looked at her hesitantly. 'I'd really like to stretch out the whole of the back of the cottage, towards the road – I think there's room – and add another bedroom upstairs. I know it would have to be small, but I'd like a bedroom with a little en suite, so I'd have two bathrooms. And I've got this idea for the kitchen – I hope you don't think it's silly – but I'd really like part of the roof to be made of glass, like an atrium, so it would be a kind of conservatory.'

'Yes,' said Helen, slowly. 'But you'd look out on to

109

the road, wouldn't you, if you keep the kitchen at the back? How about building an extension at the side, stepped back from the main façade, obviously? So then you'd make the cottage longer rather than wider, which would look much better. You could keep the existing kitchen as a boot room, very useful when you have a muddy dog. Part of the roof would have to be flat, obviously, if you wanted to have another bedroom and shower room above, but then the end part of the roof could be a glass atrium. It would look great.' She smiled. 'Then you'd be able to look out over the sea – the view really is fantastic from here.'

'I would never have thought of that,' Sara said, gratefully. 'Thank you. I really need another bathroom, and with the children, one spare bedroom . . .'

'How many children do you have?'

'Two girls. They're not children, they're in their twenties now. Lottie's on a gap year – she's living here with me, she's just out shopping – and Emily, the older one, works for a radio station. She lives in London with her . . . with some friends, renting a flat.'

'So you came from London?'

'Yes.'

Helen looked at her, seemed about to say something, and then stopped.

'Let's drink our coffee outside,' Sara suggested. 'It's so lovely today. The smell of damp gets to me after a while. I'll show you upstairs later.'

They sat down on the wall, facing the cottage. 'I'm sorry I haven't got anywhere proper to sit. I've just ordered some garden chairs, and a table, Lottie and I chose them last week. Very exciting, my first big purchase.'

'Didn't you bring any from London?'

'No. They wouldn't have suited here, anyway. Can you see stainless steel in this garden?'

Helen laughed. 'Hardly. You didn't have an old house, then?'

'No. We, I, lived in a loft apartment. Part of a converted warehouse, in the docks area, with a roof terrace. Great view of the river, but not what you might call a garden.'

Helen looked at her, consideringly. 'I can't see you in that kind of environment,' she said.

Sara tucked a stray lock of hair behind one ear. 'No. I can't really see me there now either. Do you want another coffee?' She looked at Helen's empty cup.

'That would be lovely. I keep trying to give it up but I can't get started in the morning without it.'

'I'm the same.' They smiled at each other.

As Sara rinsed the two mugs out under the hot tap in the stained old sink, she thought, 'I must stop being so mysterious. Helen told me straight out that her husband was dead and she's obviously waiting for me to volunteer more information, but I'm really not ready to tell her yet that I have left my husband – it's so easy for word to get round and then – no. I don't want any labels. I don't want anyone I meet here to know. Not yet, anyway. Here, I am Sara Atkinson. That's all.' Only, she knew, she wasn't. She was still legally Sara de Lall, and this morning a thick A4-sized envelope had arrived. Turning it over, she saw the name of Matt's solicitors printed on the back. It was sitting on the hall table, under the mirror, and one of the reasons she had gone to the shop in the first place when she didn't really need to buy anything was as a kind of displacement activity, so she didn't have to open it just yet. Quite why she feared it, she didn't know. It was probably something to do with the sale of the apartment, it was unlikely to be anything too vile. Like divorce. Quite why she feared this, she wasn't sure. 'I just don't think I'm ready to consider that yet,' she thought. Too much was still unresolved.

With Lottie here, life was settling into a pleasing routine. Yesterday they'd climbed Raphael Cliff, and later today, if Lottie wasn't too late back from Liskeard, she had promised herself they would walk over Chapel Cliff before dropping down into Polperro and exploring the town, maybe have dinner there and get a taxi back. Living here was fun, Lottie had announced this morning, at breakfast. Like being permanently on holiday.

Helen was sitting with her eyes closed and her face turned towards the sun, as Sara walked towards her, carrying the mugs. 'Here you are,' Sara said.

Her eyes flew open. 'I'm just enjoying the warmth. This must be the hottest day, so far. You wait until the height of the summer, last year we had temperatures in the nineties, day after day.'

'How long have you lived here?'

'Three years. I waited a few months in Surrey after Jack died, and then I did what I'd promised myself I would – I sold everything up and moved down here permanently. We've had the house for years, as a holiday home. My kids thought I was mad, and that I'd die of boredom. But I adapted really quickly. Now I can't imagine living anywhere else, and when I go back to Surrey, or into London, I feel no connection at all.'

Sara smiled in recognition. 'You don't get bored?'

'God, no. I've got my work and I can pick and choose what I do. I'm lucky. It's all rather *Good Life*, really – I've got a flock of sheep, too, on the hill. Not to mention a couple of very dopey pet ones in the small paddock at the side of the house. Are you sure you haven't met them on the road as well? Very occasionally they make an arthritic bid for freedom and are spotted tottering down the road towards the bright lights of Liskeard. Everyone around here – especially

112

Tom the farmer – thinks I'm mad because I won't eat any of them. Have you met Tom yet?'

'A couple of times. I've seen his son, too, on the tractor.'

'Jim. Poor boy. He longs for city life, you know, but Tom won't let him go. Cheap labour, you know what farmers are like. He must be worth millions, but tight as a duck's arse, never spends anything on the farmhouse and it's a beautiful old place. He's a widower.'

'Do your children visit much?'

'Daniel pops down from the Midlands with his wife, usually in the summer – they've two young children – and Meg's away travelling in Australia for a year. On a gap year *after* university, if you please. Putting off real life, I suppose. I can't blame her.'

'They do seem rather slow to get down to work,' Sara smiled. 'Although Emily, my daughter, she got a job straight out of university, or at least, Matt –'

'Matt?' Helen raised an eyebrow.

'My husband. My ex-husband,' she said. 'Well – sorry, I don't know how to describe him. We're not legally separated, or anything like that. We're just living apart. That's why . . .'

'You're here.' Helen stood up decisively. 'Do you want to show me upstairs?' Sara realized she was not going to pry, and was relieved.

'This has real possibilities,' Helen said, minutes later, ducking her head to avoid the beams in the bedroom. 'These are really sweet rooms, and the bathroom's not *too* tiny, is it?'

'I know. Very Anne of Green Gables, don't you think, with the sloping roofs and little windows?'

'How big is the attic?'

'I honestly don't know,' Sara said. 'I haven't been up there yet.'

'No time like the present,' Helen said. 'Have you got a ladder? Here's the trapdoor . . .' She reached up, with both hands, and pushed the hatch away from her head. A shower of dust fell on both of them, and they peered up into the darkness, the rafters of the roof just visible through the gloom.

Sara went off to fetch a small wooden stepladder she'd uncovered earlier in the week in the shed at the far side of the cottage. It was grey with age, extremely rickety and covered in paint. She manhandled it, with difficulty, through the front door and up the stairs.

Helen climbed up first. 'Wow,' came her muffled voice as she peered up through the hatch. 'There's a lot of space up here. God, it's full of stuff, too.' She climbed up and stepped off the top of the ladder, making it wobble alarmingly, and Sara looked anxiously up after her. She didn't much relish the idea of having to balance on something so wobbly, but there was no other way up. Helen leant down to hold her hand as she reached the top, and heaved her up through the trapdoor.

In the dim light she could make out the outline of cardboard boxes, covered in twigs and straw, coated with a thick layer of bird dirt, and something much darker and more sticky. 'Bats,' Helen said, looking upwards. Sure enough, arranged in neat rows from the overhead rafters, were about twenty small bats hanging upside down, their wings carefully folded. They were barely bigger than plums. 'Pipistrelles,' Helen said. 'It's a wonder we haven't disturbed them.'

Sara was surprised to find she could stand almost upright, and moved quickly to one side, as she was directly under the bats. Charming they might be, but she did not like the thought of them flapping in her face. 'You could get at least one other room up here if we didn't tell anyone about the bats,' Helen said.

'Hang on, I think there's a light.' She reached out her right hand, and flicked the switch. The attic was abruptly illuminated by a bare bulb, hanging from a dangerous-looking, twisted brown wire in the centre of the roof. One of the bats opened an eye and regarded them solemnly.

'This must be such a fire risk,' Helen said, looking at all the straw. 'There's too much here for the birds to have brought in. The old man must have used this straw as insulation. Goodness.' She laughed.

Some of the boxes had split open, and Sara could see they were full of papers – not newspapers, but documents of some kind. In the far corner stood what looked like an old toy box. She picked her way over, making sure to stand on the wooden struts, terrified of putting her foot through the floor into one of the bedrooms below. As she reached it, she saw that on top of the wooden box was painted, in curly faded red letters, a name. Charlotte. What an extraordinary coincidence.

'Look at this,' Sara said. Helen, taking cautious small steps around the cardboard boxes, came over to stand beside her. Sara, crouching down, carefully lifted the lid. Inside was a pile of very old painted wooden toys. A clown, a puppet and a doll, with an astonishingly life-like face, and wide, unblinking eyes, lay staring up at them.

At that moment, unearthly music filled the attic – a haunting, sad tune, like the music from a carousel. They looked at each other in horror. 'What the hell . . .' Helen exclaimed. Then Sara started to laugh. 'It's a music box, as well as a toy box,' she said, pointing at the tiny figure of a ballerina on the back ledge, pirouetting amidst the swirling dust particles caught in the light from the naked bulb. 'Goodness, I thought we'd stirred up musical ghosts,' Helen said, sitting back on her heels, laughing.

'What an amazing antique, and I bet these toys are worth a fortune. There's something really spooky about dolls, isn't there?' She lifted the porcelain doll out of the toy box, and turned her slowly and carefully over in her hands, brushing the dust from her stiff white dress.

'I know. They scare me rigid, I didn't even like them as a child. You know . . .' An idea dawned on Sara. 'I met a funny old chap a while ago, walking the cliff path – you might know who he is. He wore a very strange pair of cut-off wellingtons, rather lecherous, lots of wild grey hair.'

'Harold,' Helen confirmed. 'Be careful with him, he thinks he's a real ladies' man. Anyone female is fair game. Never be enticed into his house to play Scrabble.'

Sara nodded. 'He said the old man who used to live here – Mick, I think his name was – had a daughter. He didn't tell me her name, but she might be this Charlotte. And he said something odd – he wouldn't tell me what happened to her, saying I'd find out soon enough. Most mysterious.'

'This is like something out of Daphne du Maurier,' Helen smiled. 'Our very own conundrum.'

'Have you ever heard anything about him, or his daughter? You've been here quite a long time, counting holidays . . .'

'Yes, but no one ever really talked to us. I'm only just being accepted as a local, and it's been three years since I moved. They don't confide in second-home people, we're just inblowers. God, I have to stand up. My knees have locked.' Creakily, she straightened up.

'Let's take the toy box down,' Sara said. 'I want to show it to Lottie. She should be home soon.'

Just then, they heard the front door slam.

Sara carried the box in both hands as she walked down the stairs. It was surprisingly heavy – she'd had to pass it to Helen very carefully down through the narrow hatch. Every time she bumped down a step, the lid opened fractionally and a squeak of music escaped.

They found Lottie in the kitchen, unpacking a white carrier bag. 'You'll never guess what I've found,' she said, triumphantly lifting out a bottle. 'Cloudy Bay!' As she lifted her head she saw Helen. 'Oh!' she said, surprised.

'Darling, this is Helen. I met her at the shop this morning, she lives down the road in the yellow house . . .'

'With the hens?' Lottie asked. 'The house with all those hens?'

'I am beginning to think that I am being unfairly labelled. There are other things in my life apart from being the owner of escapee hens.' Helen smiled, stepping towards Lottie. Lottie held out her hand to shake Helen's, but Helen ignored it, leaning forward to kiss her on the cheek. A look of disbelief crossed Lottie's face. Sara knew exactly what she was thinking. Mother's found another eccentric to be friendly with. 'Hi,' she said, shyly. 'What on earth are you carrying, Mum?'

'Look at this.' Sara set the dusty toy box down on the kitchen table, carefully moving aside the carrier bag and the bottle of white wine. She opened the lid. Nothing happened. She pressed down the little catch. Still nothing. Holding the lid shut, she lifted the box up, with difficulty, and found a stiff little key underneath, which she wound. Then she slowly opened the lid and the haunting music began.

'Ew!' exclaimed Lottie. 'Spooky. Where on earth did you find it?'

'In the attic.'

'We have an attic?'

'We certainly do. It's full of rubbish, but then we found this box. Oh – and we have bats.'

'Which you shouldn't really do anything about,' Helen said. 'They're protected, so we're not sure if we're going to be able to extend into the attic. I'm an architect – I said I'd help your mum.'

'Bats,' said Lottie, eyeing her mother thoughtfully. 'Not only have you bought a cottage which is barely in Britain, you have also bought a cottage which is top-heavy with bats. Anything else? No snakes in the grass? No scorpions lurking within the beams?'

'There are snakes,' Helen said. 'On the cliffs.'

'Actually, I like snakes,' Lottie said. 'Snakes are cool. What kind?'

'Mostly grass snakes, but we see the odd adder. They're really harmless – they just slither away when they see you.'

'Hector will never go for a walk again,' Sara said, looking at him.

'Wimp dog,' Lottie said, sinking to her knees and burying her face in his golden fur. He lifted up a paw and put it gently over her arm.

'I see what you mean about the timid,' Helen said. 'I can't see him and Nigel hitting it off.'

Lottie looked at them uncomprehendingly, and then put her hands over Hector's ears.

'Don't you listen,' she said, forgetting she'd called him a wimp. 'You're not bashful! You're the bravest, manliest dog I've ever seen.' Hector thumped his tail against the slate floor, puffing out his chest.

'Do you have a dog?' Lottie asked Helen, looking up at her.

'Kind of,' she said. 'He's in the car. Bit more like a curly mountain, though, than an actual dog.'

'Oh yes, I thought I could hear something barking. Can't you let him in? They could play together. It would be sweet. A little friend for Hector.'

Sara looked at Helen. 'I don't think "play" would be the operative word,' she said.

'He's kind of boisterous,' Helen said, screwing up her face. 'And he gets a bit confused between girl and boy dogs. He isn't terribly discerning, if you know what I mean.'

'How embarrassing.' Lottie was looking at Sara as if to say, 'Who is this person?'

'Helen said she'd take the cottage on as a project,' Sara said.

'Oh, cool. You've been looking round?' Helen nodded. 'Is it quite hopeless? Should we just get the bulldozers in?'

Helen laughed. 'Not at all,' she said. 'It's got great possibilities. The only thing I would change is this room – I said demolition, but actually if you put a proper roof on it, it could be a boot room, or a laundry.'

'Hear, hear to that. Mum, there's a letter for you on the hall table.'

'I know.'

'I think it's something to do with Dad. Looks official,' she said casually, lifting a squashy bag out of the white carrier, grey fish skin visible through the thin plastic. 'I bought halibut, as a treat. I was kind of overwhelmed by finding the Cloudy Bay and thought we deserved a good dinner. Parsley, too,' she added, waving the herb, before putting it carefully alongside the fish in the fridge. 'I am a genius. I thought of everything.'

'What an angel,' Sara said. She realized Helen was looking at her questioningly.

When Sara caught her eye, Helen looked away. 'I must be off,' she said. She leant forward and kissed

Sara on the cheek. She smelled of fresh air and wool. 'Great to meet you. What shall we do? Why don't I sketch out some ideas, roughly, and then we could get together later in the week? I know a couple of people in the planning department in St Austell, and some good, reliable builders too. I'll give you their numbers.'

'That would be the most fantastic help.'

Helen smiled at Lottie. 'Good to meet you.'

'And you.' Lottie waved a hand, casually. 'See you.'

Lottie waited until the front door had closed before she said, firmly, 'Lesbian.'

'Oh, for goodness sake, darling. Her husband died three years ago. She's not a lesbian.'

'She looks like one.'

'That may be true, I grant you. But she isn't. I'd know. Anyway, why should it matter?'

'How many lesbians do you know, Mother?'

'None.'

'Well, I know lots, and she's one.'

'I don't think you're right. Anyway, I am not a lesbian, so it's irrelevant, isn't it? It's just nice to meet someone local I think I am going to be able to get on with. Who might become a friend.'

'Be careful,' said Lottie darkly. 'You'll end up one of the "girls" and stop shaving your legs. Dad will come down to see you and find you entirely covered in fur.'

'Lottie, that's ridiculous.'

'I don't want my mother turning gay,' Lottie said, mock-dramatically. 'Isn't it enough that you have made me the victim of a broken home?'

'I am starting to get cross,' Sara said, laughing despite herself. 'Just because I have left Dad does not mean I am going to become a lesbian. Convenient as it might be for him to think so,' she added.

'Middle-Class Mother Dumped by Husband Turns

120

Gay,' said Lottie, in newspaper headlines. 'Shock,' she added, as an afterthought.

'Enough. You're being extremely silly. Right, this afternoon . . .' Sara looked at her watch. 'God, it's nearly one already. I propose we walk over the cliffs to Polperro. Hector hasn't had a decent walk today.' At two mentions of the word 'walk', Hector disappeared under the table. Not another walk, he seemed to say. I'm exhausted. I'm going to end up with legs like a dachshund.

'What about the letter?' Lottie said.

'Oh, yes.' Sara began to tidy away the coffee cups. 'Later.'

'Go and open it,' Lottie ordered. 'Stop prevaricating.' She took hold of Sara's shoulder, and firmly pushed her into the corridor.

Sara found she was actually closing her eyes as she ripped it open, Lottie standing behind her. This was silly. How could he hurt her? What could he change, or take away? Her eyes scanned swiftly down the printed page, until she came to a sentence which made her draw a sharp breath.

It said, 'My client requests that you visit our offices to discuss your financial requirements and to discuss placing the current separation on a more permanent legal footing.' She let the page fall on to the hall table. That sounded as if Matt did want to divorce. She closed her eyes, and put out a hand to steady herself against the wall. Why couldn't they just drift on like this? Why did they have to make a decision, so soon? But inside she knew the answer. Because Matt hated unfinished business. He hated not being in control. He was trying to frighten her into making some kind of decision, and forcing her to meet him, or, at least, his solicitor. He hadn't tried to make contact with her for over two months now – not since the call which had ended so abruptly. Emily had said, during one of their rare phone chats, that he had decided there was no point because 'she would not see sense'.

'What does it say?' Lottie picked up the letter.

Sara opened her eyes. 'Dad's solicitor says we have to meet to talk about money.'

'But that's good, isn't it?' Lottie said. 'He's going to have to look after you, isn't he? Dad wouldn't leave you in the lurch.'

'Why does Dad have to look after me? I'm not a child. I can look after myself.'

Lottie looked at her pityingly. 'Since when did you earn money, Mum? Of course Dad's going to have to cough up. You're his wife,' she added, as if to a dim child.

'He also says, through his solicitor, that he wants to put our relationship on a "legal footing", whatever that means.'

'Divorce?' Lottie said, lifting her eyes to Sara, her smile disappearing.

'I'm afraid it sounds very like it.'

Lottie's shoulders seemed to fold in on themselves. Wrapping her arms around herself, she leant back against the wall. 'Oh. I don't think I want you to be divorced. It's so final. I might end up with a wicked stepmother. Emily and I will have to stand next to her at the wedding in gruesome Laura Ashley dresses with glued-on smiles pretending to be grown-up about it and happy that our father has a second chance of happiness, whereas actually we'd rather eat our own hair than see him re-marry. God. Dad might even have more *babies*. Arg! Imagine! Tiny step-siblings! He wouldn't, would he?'

'Darling.' Sara tried to put her arms around her, but Lottie shrank back. 'I don't see why we have to make that decision just yet,' she said, as gently as she could.

'I think Dad's just trying to shock me into coming back. It won't work, though. I'm not going to be bullied into making the wrong decision.'

Lottie's head snapped up, her face suddenly furious. Sara looked at her, surprised at the anger in her eyes. 'Stop burying your head in the sand, Mum!' she shouted. 'Honestly, I take your side nearly all the time, but sometimes you go too far. You can't just leave Dad and think that he'll sit around, waiting for you to decide *if* you're going to come home. Can't you see Dad's point of view? He can't wait for ever. You've left the way clear for her, haven't you? You didn't stay to fight. God, now, Mum, can't you see? You've lost him! He's given up! That's what this letter means. He can't think that you love him anymore, so why shouldn't he be with her? Why shouldn't he divorce you?'

'What is her name?' Sara said cautiously, over-whelmed by curiosity. Lottie must know, as she talked to Emily nearly every night. Lottie had told her they'd decided to forget the initial rift – Emily said they needed each other too much at the moment for that. Sara hesitated. 'You don't have to tell me. I don't want you to feel you are being disloyal to Dad.'

Lottie looked over Sara's shoulder, her eyes filling with tears. 'Her name is . . . Karina,' she said slowly, as if the words were being dragged out of her. She reached up and angrily brushed away the tears from her cheeks. She took a deep breath, her thin shoulders rising. 'She's half-Russian. She's only two years older than Emily. I've met her, a few times, at Dad's office. She works for him. You must know her too . . .' she moved towards Sara, and put her arm around her neck. 'I'm so sorry, Mum,' she said, quietly. 'Maybe I shouldn't have told you, but it seems so silly when it's . . . when you're . . . when you know, you're talking about divorce. It's only fair that you do know. And he is with her, Mum. Emily says she's mad about him.'

A bell which had been ringing very distantly in Sara's mind sounded louder, and louder, until she was so deafened she stepped away from Lottie and put her hands over her ears. Of course. Of course it was likely to be someone she knew. Why would Matt have an affair with a complete stranger? Karina — what was her surname? — Nemcova.

Catherine had told her after the party that she had heard that the woman he was having an affair with was very young, in her twenties. At the time Sara hadn't given this information much credence, but it appeared Catherine and her mysterious source were spot on.

Sara knew Matt had poached Karina from a rival PR firm about two years before, and then she hadn't been long out of university. She was the daughter of a Russian millionaire and English mother. Matt had said she was a real piece of work, able to charm the birds out of the trees, and very bright — she had an Oxford degree — but rather spoilt. Some of the other staff hadn't taken to her at all, but he said she was bringing in contracts thick and fast. Last time Sara had met her, at the office Christmas drinks party, she had noticed the way her eyes followed Matt, and thought, oh dear, another of his staff with a crush. But, as usual, she'd dismissed it from her mind. If she'd worried about every woman who fancied Matt, she'd have been in a permanent spin. She thought hard. Had he talked about her much? In autumn last year he'd said he was putting Karina on to the account of one of his biggest clients, a mobile-phone company about to go global, and he'd joked she already had the chief executive eating out of her hand. There was something else, too. Last time he'd flown to Paris, the previous summer, she had been with him — he'd mentioned it, casually, and said she would be a real asset. He was taking a whole team to make the presentation, so it did not seem unusual. Why would she suspect?

'Karina,' she said slowly. 'I see.' And she could see her, clearly, in her mind's eye – tall, very slim, with a curtain of sleek brunette shoulder-length hair and huge chocolate-brown eyes. Beautiful, tailored clothes, with none of the grunge effect of Emily and Lottie. She looked poised, arrogant and old beyond her years. Yes, she had thought at the time, she did look a piece of work.

'Yup. Karina,' Lottie said, carefully, watching her mother's face. 'Don't look like that. You look as if you're going to faint. Are you OK?'

Sara nodded, and then, to her own utter amazement, she started to laugh. Lottie looked at her in horror. 'I'm sorry,' Sara said, wiping her eyes, her whole body shaking. 'You fool. Oh, you stupid old fool.' Of course, being Matt, it wouldn't just be anybody. It would be a stunningly beautiful young girl with a degree from Oxford and legs which went on for ever. Even in infidelity, he had impeccable taste. If you took two women who looked less alike, it would be her and Karina. The girl belonged to another world. Thank God she hadn't stayed to fight. Her shoulders shook.

'Have you gone quite insane?' Lottie said, staring at her mother in wonder.

'Probably. How am I supposed to react? Your father has been sleeping with a girl two years older than Emily for what could be more than a year, and all the time I've been pottering about thinking, hey ho, I must get the windows cleaned, and shall I book a weekend away in France because Dad looks tired and Hector needs his claws clipping, and all the time I was going about my daily life your father was falling head over heels in love with *Karina*. How very, very extraordinary.'

'Don't. I'm not sure I want to hear any of this,' Lottie said. 'Anyway, we don't know that he was in love with her. It might have been just, you know . . .' Her face wrinkled with disgust at the thought. 'And what would she see in him? He's so *old*.' Sara gently touched her daughter's face. 'Your father is a very attractive man,' she said. 'Lots of women find him good-looking, you know. Not to mention the fact that he's also, now, rather rich. It's a lethal combination.'

'Ew. Did they? Why didn't you mind? It never occurred to me. But then I suppose I took the fact that you loved each other for granted,' she said sadly. 'I never thought – it never entered my head – that Dad might go off with anyone else. He seemed to love you so much. You were always talking and laughing. I mean, I had friends' parents who never seemed to speak to each other. I thought we were so lucky . . .' her voice tailed off.

'I thought we were lucky too,' Sara said. 'I trusted him, you see.'

'Too much,' Lottie said sadly.

'Yes. But that's only with the benefit of hindsight.'

'Can we not talk about this any more? It's making me feel weird.'

'Yes.' Sara straightened up. 'This is not doing either of us any good at all. Let's go for a great long walk, and then we'll have the halibut and Cloudy Bay to look forward to when we come home.'

'I bought two bottles,' Lottie said.

'Good,' said Sara.

Chapter Nine

'Bristol first choice it is, then. Do you think they'll offer you a place?'

'Bloody well should do, with my brilliant CV and gap-year experience, which is only ever so slightly made up.'

'*My* brilliantly devised CV,' Sara corrected, looking at her over the top of her tortoiseshell half-moon glasses. They were sitting squashed together in front of Lottie's laptop, which was plugged into an old-fashioned dark brown socket beneath the desk. The socket had come away slightly from the wall, and Sara had had to jiggle the plug around to get the light on the laptop to come on. At any moment she expected there to be a blinding flash and a thousand volts would shoot up her arm. But then, as her mother always said, an electric shock is as good a tonic as a holiday. Quite how she'd worked that out, Sara could not fathom, but as with most of her mother's sayings, it was best not to consider too hard for fear of your mind boggling.

Used to broadband, neither of them could believe how long it took to log onto the Internet using direct dial, to send off Lottie's application.

'Do you think there's an old woman in Plymouth holding two wires together?' Lottie asked, as they watched the dark blue block at the bottom right-hand corner of the screen edging forward, agonizingly slowly. 'I haven't seen this for years,' she said. 'Come *on*!' Trying to get on to the university websites had been even more frustrating, because the screen kept hanging, and then for no particular reason a message would flash up. 'Your time limit is about to expire' one message read. 'Time limit?' Lottie cried. 'What's going on? Do we have to feed a meter, or something?'

Lottie had decided, after much deliberation, that she was going to apply for a fine art course and had given up on English Literature, which seemed far too popular, and she hadn't achieved the grades for anywhere she actually wanted to go. She had just enough points from her exams to apply for the degree course in art at Bristol University. Her application was very late, but when she'd rung the department they said they would consider her if she'd send in a portfolio of her work.

'You know,' Lottie said, sitting back in her chair. 'There are advantages to Dad not being here. He'd never agree to this – he wouldn't want me to take an art degree. He'd say it wasn't *academic* enough. It's rather nice to be able to follow my heart without being scared of what he says all the time.'

'He's going to need to pay your tuition and accommodation fees,' Sara pointed out.

'Oh. Bugger. Do you think he will?'

'Oh yes,' Sara said, smiling. 'I think he'll fall over himself to pay. You might even be able to squeeze a flat out of him.'

'Mother! What a dreadful thing to say! And for all your high words about not taking a penny from him.'

'That's me. Not you.'

'OK. I'm cool with that.'

Sara had let Lottie type out her CV first, for the 'facts

relevant to this application' section, and then laughed out loud as she read back Lottie's comments under 'additional qualifications'.

'I'm not sure Life Saving Grade Two is all that relevant,' Sara pointed out.

'But it said "qualifications",' Lottie argued. 'And I haven't got many.'

'You must be able to think of something more relevant than being able to float on your back using a pair of blown-up pyjamas.'

'It's a jolly useful skill,' Lottie said, giggling. 'Shall I put BAGA gymnastics Grade Three?'

'No.'

'Filling a blue egg with coins for the NSPCC and getting a badge?'

'No.'

'Grade One piano?'

'Is that all you got to?'

'Yes. You never made me practise enough.'

'Of course it would be my fault, darling. Come on. You must have something else you can put down. Move over.' Obligingly, Lottie shifted up so Sara was directly in front of the laptop, and then got up to pour them both another glass of the Cloudy Bay. Sara wondered briefly if they should have typed out the application before they started drinking, but it was too late now. She did seem to have become much fonder of wine, and she wondered if this was a good thing. She decided, on balance, it was – but she must be careful not to start drinking alone.

After five minutes, as Sara typed, Lottie became bored and wandered away. When she came back, she read the information over her mother's shoulder. 'Wow. I sound really cool. I'd give me a place.'

'Well, let's hope they will. Now, where else have you put down on this application?'

'Warwick. Then two other duff places, I hope they don't send me an offer.'

'Beggars can't be choosers,' Sara said, and then regretted it.

'Beggar, am I?' Lottie said crossly, holding her cool wine glass against her cheek.

'You know I didn't mean that. If you get an offer from any of these I'll be thrilled.'

'You only went to Manchester,' Lottie pointed out snippily. 'Not Oxford.'

'I met your father there, though, didn't I?'

'Imagine what your life would have been like if you hadn't met him. You might have had an amazing career. You might have been like a novelist, or something.'

'Unlikely. I don't think I ever really had the talent. I'm good at organizing, but I'm not very creative. You know, sometimes I do regret not having a real career. I was only twenty-four when I got married – I'd only been out of university for two years, and I was earning peanuts. It made sense to start working for Matt, and then when I had you two – I just couldn't imagine handing you over to a nanny. Matt didn't want that, either. So my brilliant career just never happened.' She smiled. 'I don't really regret it, you know. I wouldn't have given up those years when you were young for the world. It's the greatest joy, to see your children grow. I'm really lucky that I could be at home – I mean, there were times when your dad's business looked like it was going to go bump and I thought I'd have to go back to work full time, but Matt was never keen. Anyway, how can I regret the fact that I met Matt? You wouldn't be here, for a start, if I hadn't,' Sara pointed out practically. 'So we can hardly say it's a bad thing, can we?'

Lottie reached forward, her eyes scanning the application, and then she hit the 'send' key.

'That's me done,' she said. 'Now, what about you?'

'What do you mean, what about me?'

'What are you going to do?' Lottie sounded out each word, as if talking to a very small child.

'Oh.'

'You need a job. You said you did. You can't just potter about here.'

'I know. It's just with the cottage, and all the renovations . . .'

'You are prevaricating,' Lottie said, firmly. 'You can't just drift about, Mother. You're only forty-nine. You're not old enough to retire. Besides, if you're not prepared to accept handouts from Dad, you have to face the fact that you need to earn money. Get out in the real world, like the rest of us. Do an honest day's toil. You are no longer a kept woman.'

'Lottie,' Sara said patiently. 'Since when have you lived in the real world? The only job you've ever done was being a waitress and then you only lasted a week. Anyway, I'm not forty-nine. I'm fifty.'

'No!'

'I was fifty when you were at Gran's. She rang me. She assumed you had remembered and sent me a card or at least rung, and I didn't want to disillusion her.'

'God, no!' Lottie put her hand to her mouth, in shock. 'What evil children we are! We forgot your fiftieth birthday! Em too?' Sara nodded. Emily's lack of acknowledgement had been far more deliberate, she thought – it was much more like Lottie to simply forget. Lottie had been known to forget her *own* birthday. Strangely, what had hurt most of all was the lack of contact from Matt. He loved birthdays. She had once accused him of acting as if every day was his birthday, in that he relished finding excuses, any excuse, to splash out on a gorgeous present, open a bottle of champagne and take her out for a delicious meal.

On her fortieth birthday he'd flown her to Paris in a private plane and taken her to lunch at one of the city's most exclusive restaurants, in a five-star Relais Château hotel. There he had presented her with a small black velvet box. Inside was an exquisite eternity ring, made from white gold, inset with diamonds.

'Bit bling,' he admitted, cheerfully. 'But it's not every day you get to be so ancient. You know what this means,' he added, slipping the ring over her wedding finger, having first taken off her wedding and engagement rings. He then slid them back on, one by one. 'This means you can never leave me. This binds you to me for eternity. Or at least until one of us kicks the bucket, which is most likely to be me, given the amount I smoke and drink. But then I can haunt you until you join me. I fancy a marble and slate mausoleum with side-by-side coffins. And a huge angel on top. With outspread wings.' He put his head on one side, and grinned. 'What do you think? Perhaps a *little* too ostentatious?'

She reached over to touch his face, and he leant against her fingers. 'It sounds perfectly dreadful,' she said.

'Take note,' he said, sitting back and taking a long drink of the exquisite wine he had chosen. 'I want the whole works when I go. Black horses, great big plumes on their heads, a carriage, the whole shebang. I'm trusting you, you know. No fake wood coffin and a discreet little service. And don't you dare take me back up north. I want to be buried in London. Somewhere smart.'

'But I want to be buried in Yorkshire. In the church, where we were married.'

'Tough,' he said, smiling. 'You're staying with me. I'll have it written into my will.'

* * *

'Mum, you're miles away. What's the matter?'

'Nothing.' Sara brushed away a tear, embarrassed.

'Hey! You're crying. I'm so sorry, it was so thoughtless of me, Emily too . . .'

'It's not that.'

'It's Dad, isn't it? Did he forget?'

'I doubt he forgot,' Sara said. 'Look, darling, it doesn't matter. It's just a day. It's not important.'

'Please don't do that poor little me I'm so unimportant thing,' Lottie said crossly. 'It's bollocks. It *does* matter and tomorrow we're going into Fowey and I am going to buy you a very belated massive present.'

'Do you have any money?'

'No, obviously, you'll have to lend it to me but I promise I will buy you something *great*.'

Sara laughed.

'Did you get a card from anyone?'

'Granny, Catherine, a few friends.'

'I bet Catherine sent you an obscenely huge bunch of flowers.'

'She did.'

'With a note saying, "Chin up, darling, we love you"?'

'Spot on.'

'What happened to the flowers?'

'They died.'

'Dad always used to send you pink roses, didn't he?'

'Mmm.'

'Why was that?'

'A silly private joke, really. He went out to buy me red roses when Emily was born, but he couldn't find any and he ended up at a garage, where he bought me some grotty pink ones which were turning brown and looked like they'd been trodden on by an

133

exceptionally hefty horse. It kind of went on from there.'

'You did really love each other, didn't you?' Lottie sounded wistful.

Sara looked at her, surprised. 'Of course we did. That will never change, Lottie, no matter what happens. What's happened doesn't affect the way we were, and I don't think you should look back and think our time together has been . . .'

'A waste?'

'Not a nice thought, but yes, I suppose so.'

'Are you going to work?'

'If I can find something I enjoy and I'm good at, then of course I will. I can't just sit around.'

'I know you won't.'

'I feel a bit drunk, you know I'm hopeless with wine. I ought to go to bed.'

'Me, too.'

'You go ahead. I'll put Hector out and clear up. Good night, darling.'

Lottie leant forward for a kiss. 'You suit it here,' she said, looking into her mother's eyes.

'Do I?'

'Yes,' said Lottie sleepily. 'You look very peaceful. Younger, too.'

'Catherine said something like that.'

'But only a tiny bit younger,' Lottie said, turning on the narrow stairs, holding her finger and thumb a centimetre apart.

Sara laughed. 'That much? Wow. Goodnight.'

'Night. Love you more.'

Chapter Ten

'This place is going to be heaving in summer,' Lottie said as they wandered from shop to shop, peering in the windows, zigzagging across the narrow main street which ran through the centre of Fowey. They had had to take a little car ferry to get there, which Lottie loved. She loved the fact that the man in the peaked cap who took your ticket charged you ten pence more if he thought you were a tourist. For the first three trips, before Lottie had arrived, Sara had been charged two pounds and twenty pence, but then on the fourth trip the charge had mysteriously fallen to two pounds ten pence.

'That means you're being accepted,' Lottie said. 'You're a local yokel.'

As they floated slowly across the narrow estuary, Lottie wound down the passenger window, resting her elbow on the top of the car door. To her right a huge grey metal ship was moored, a freight liner, with vivid orange stains running down its prow. Beneath the towering keel bobbed several motorboats, anchored to yellow buoys, rising and falling with the tide. The air smelt of salt, and fish, and overhead the gulls wheeled, calling. Small sailing boats chugged up and down the narrow channel, and a sight-seeing passenger boat steamed past the ferry, the cabin crowded with people. A group of teenagers waved at the ferry from the car park on the opposite bank, as they drew near. Lottie waved back.

'This is, without a doubt, my favourite place,' she said, ten minutes later, licking clotted cream from the top of a vanilla cone. 'The other seaside towns round here are a bit "kiss me quick" for my taste.'

'You're becoming a dreadful snob. Look out,' Sara said, as a car inched past them.

At first she had thought that cars were banned from the town, as the roads were barely a car's width, but already a steady stream of vehicles had passed them, meaning that the pedestrians had to press themselves up against the walls. 'I wonder how many people get their feet run over?' Sara said.

'I think you need to get out more,' Lottie said. 'Come on. I want to show you this really wicked shop I discovered when you were getting the ice-creams. I'm sure it's going to have something even you will like.'

The shop in question had a gaily-painted front window, full of the kind of clothes Lottie loved – strappy little tops, baggy shorts, mini skirts designed to hang low on the waist, brightly coloured flip-flops and cheap, colourful jewellery. Clothes for teenagers and twentysomethings to hang out in, surfer summer clothes for the beach.

'This isn't my kind of place,' Sara said, looking in. 'Far too young. It's great for you, though.'

'Nope,' Lottie said. 'This is your missed birthday, not mine. They've got some clothes for the more *mature* lady at the back.' Sara punched her lightly on the arm.

On racks at the back of the shop were, indeed, some more expensive-looking and generally more subtle clothes. The majority were made of linen, in washed greys, pale oranges and blues, Sara's favourite colours.

Hesitantly, she fingered the material of a pair of wide linen trousers. She realized she hadn't bought herself anything at all to wear since she had left Matt. She hadn't cared in the slightest what she looked like, just pulling on whatever was nearest and vaguely clean, usually the same pair of jeans, teamed with a baggy T-shirt or sweatshirt, depending on the weather.

One thing she had noticed recently, however, with a sense of pleasure, was how loose her clothes were becoming. Walking Hector every day on the cliffs, she found she could climb far more easily – reaching the top of the hill, which had left her exhausted and breathless in the first few weeks at the cottage, now barely seemed an effort, and she was rarely out of breath during the entire walk. Nor was she snacking in the way she used to – initially, she had had to force herself to eat, because it seemed so pointless and she had no appetite. Now she was beginning to enjoy her food again – the halibut Lottie had grilled last night had been delicious. But she had lost that rather greedy anticipation of food she used to have when she was living with Matt, when she would wake each morning, and lie in bed for a few minutes planning what they were all going to eat that day. Being at home, pottering around the kitchen so much of the time meant that she seldom passed the fridge without peering in, popping a ball of ham into her mouth, or lifting the lid off the biscuit tin in one of the cupboards, when she sat down to have a coffee. Matt loved good food too, although he never ate puddings, and didn't put on weight because he had such a fast metabolism and went jogging most mornings. But just looking at a carbohydrate seemed to make her fatter, especially in the last ten years, or so. Growing old, she thought, wasn't fair at all – food made you fat, coffee gave you a hot flush and just a few glasses of wine produced a hangover.

* * *

The linen trousers slid easily over her hips. Fastening the zip, she realized they were far too baggy. 'Look at this,' she called to Lottie, having put her head around the changing-room door. Lottie, who was holding a little white top decorated with pink roses against herself, put it back on the rail, reluctantly, and walked over. 'What?' She slid into the changing room and closed the door behind her.

'Too big!' Sara said, with some pride, holding the waistband inches away from her stomach.

'Blimey, Mother,' Lottie said. 'So they are. I'll get a smaller size.'

Sara could not remember having been a smaller size for – what – five years? Ten? More? Sliding the trousers off, she looked at herself, critically. In the unforgiving neon light her thighs were still dimpled with cellulite and there was a pad of fat above each knee, but her thighs were definitely slimmer, and her stomach was flatter. She stood up straighter, pulling in her stomach muscles. Goodness – it was nearly flat. She could never remotely be called skinny, but she looked strong, and healthy. She leaned forward, and examined her face in the mirror. Her skin was lightly tanned and freckled, the slight colour making her wrinkles less obvious. She smiled, and the skin at the sides of her eyes creased into crow's feet, but the skin beneath her eyes was definitely less baggy. She did look better. She ran a hand through her hair. She ought to get it cut, it was falling past her shoulders. Then she thought, I suit it longer. She had always told herself that long hair was for younger women but now she could see that it softened her features. It did need more shape, though – she'd like some layers at the front to frame her face. I'll book an appointment, she thought. I know exactly what I want.

'Try these.' Lottie's disembodied hand appeared around the door. Sara slid the smaller size pale grey trousers over her hips, and could have cheered as she pulled up the zip without difficulty.

'Are you decent?' Lottie asked, through the door.

'Yup.'

Lottie pushed it open, and she stood with Sara, looking at her reflection. They both smiled. The trousers were definitely flattering, if rather too long.

'They'll be OK in heels,' Lottie said. 'You always wear your trousers too short. That's an old-person thing to do. They ought to brush against the ground.'

'But then they fray.'

'Get a life. Who cares? It's better than having them swinging around your ankles like a granny.'

'Who indeed cares?' Sara said, her head on one side. 'I like these. Do they have any in blue? Don't worry, I'll pay.'

'You're paying anyway,' Lottie pointed out, sliding out of the changing room. 'If you get two pairs of trousers,' came the sound of her voice from beyond the door, 'I get that pink and white top.'

'Deal,' Sara called, smiling. 'Are there any shirts which would go with these trousers? Something plain?'

'I'll have a look,' Lottie called back.

'I can't wear that,' Sara said moments later, looking in surprise at the pale blue linen top Lottie was holding up in front of her. It had long sleeves, which was good, but it also had a big ruffle down the front, which was not. 'It'll make me look like a lizard,' she complained.

'It's fashionable,' Lottie said, exasperated, shaking it. 'Just try it on, you old fossil. You don't know what's going to suit you until you try. Honestly, you seem to have lived in the same boring clothes for twenty years. Live a little. Try something new.'

139

'I'll try it on,' Sara said. 'But I won't like it.'

But she did. Instead of making her look ridiculous as she had expected, it actually suited her. It looked – and she had to concentrate hard to get her mind around this concept – it made her look pretty. Both feminine, and pretty.

'Wow,' Lottie said disbelievingly. 'That *does* suit you.'

'I'm going to buy it as well as the two pairs of trousers,' Sara said, faintly dizzy with pleasure. 'How extravagant can you get?'

Handing over her credit card, she found herself smiling. It was such a long time since she had enjoyed shopping for clothes – the last time she had bought anything was the black dress for Matt's fiftieth birthday party, and she had not enjoyed that shopping trip at all, it had been more like a duty than a pleasure. For a moment, she stood stock-still, by the counter, as the shop assistant put her clothes in a carrier bag. That seems a lifetime ago, she thought. I'm not sure I am even the same person. The dress hadn't suited her so much, certainly nothing like these outfits – but Matt had said she looked beautiful. She glanced sideways at herself in the mirror between the rails of clothes, as the assistant pushed her credit card into the chip-and-pin machine.

'Would you think I am beautiful, now, Matt?' she wondered, staring at her reflection. Or did you only say that at the time because you felt so guilty? Had I long since ceased to be beautiful to you? Did you compare me to Karina?

Twenty-five. She had been beautiful, at twenty-five, the year after she had married Matt, the year before she was pregnant with Emily. She would never be so beautiful again.

'Can you put your number in?'

'Sorry, I was miles away.'

What *is* my number, she thought. Her heart started to beat faster, and a sensation of panic and confusion rose in her throat. My number, my number. Come on. I use it nearly every day. Work, brain. She turned, to see Lottie standing next to her.

'What on earth's the matter?'

'I can't remember my pin number,' she said, and for an awful moment, her eyes filled with tears.

'Oh, bloody hell,' Lottie said. 'Move over.' Swiftly, she punched in the four digits.

'It's a good job I know it, isn't it?' She smiled apologetically at the shop assistant, shrugging her shoulders as if to say 'senile', and then turned back to Sara. She stopped as she caught her expression. 'What's up with you?'

'Nothing,' Sara said hurriedly. 'I just need some fresh air. I'll see you outside. It's rather warm in here, isn't it?' She felt the beginnings of a hot flush, her internal thermostat rising, as sweat prickled her upper lip. Clenching her fist, she thought, I must get out of here, or I will faint.

Outside, she stood on the pavement, breathing in the fresh, cool air, feeling her body temperature beginning to drop and her heart rate returning to normal. These hot flushes had been coming for several weeks now. Marvellous. On top of everything else, she had hit the menopause. Not only had she lost her husband, her hormones were in the process of doing a bunk as well.

Opposite her a small line of people were queuing for pasties outside a bakery. She looked briefly to the right, and stepped forward. She would buy Lottie a pasty for her lunch.

'Look out!'

A pair of strong arms grabbed her shoulders from

behind as a car appeared from out of nowhere, travelling far too fast on the narrow, busy street. She was pulled back sharply.

'Bloody idiot,' said the voice, just above her head, as the car rattled past, only inches from her. The voice was deep, masculine, young, with a pleasant West Country inflection.

'Do you mean me, or the driver?' Sara said, spinning round. Behind her stood a young man, about in his late twenties, she guessed. His hands remained on her shoulders, even though she was quite safe on the narrow pavement. He smiled at her, his dark brown eyes gleaming in amusement. He had long wavy dark hair, very tanned skin, and was wearing a faded blue T-shirt over baggy shorts. Around his neck was a gold cross, and twined around his left wrist, which was currently resting on her shoulder, were a tangle of love beads and a copper bracelet. 'Both of you, I guess,' he replied, grinning. 'You OK?'

Sara smiled, embarrassed. 'Just a bit shocked. I'm sorry, I wasn't looking where I was going.'

'Happens to people all the time,' he said, shaking his head. 'It's amazing we don't kill more tourists.'

'I live here,' she said quickly, and then felt rather foolish. 'I mean, I'm not a tourist. I need to get used to it, I've just moved to this area.'

'It's a great place to live,' he said, casually, smiling at her. She felt the most remarkable frisson of – what? Attraction? That was so silly. Flustered, she glanced down at her feet, and then back up at him.

'You take care,' he said, dropping his hands from her shoulders, and stepping backwards, he moved away from her. 'Crossing the road's quite easy, really – you just look left, and then right.'

'The green cross code?'

'What?'

142

'Before your time.' She smiled.

He raised an eyebrow at her, and then turned, strolling away down the street. Feeling rather stunned, Sara watched him go. What a gorgeous, gorgeous man, she thought. Or boy, rather. Then she shook herself. You silly woman, as if he would flirt with you. She must have been imagining it. But how confidently, how easily he had touched her, letting his hands rest on her shoulders, a fraction longer than had been necessary. And how lovely it was to be touched by a man, no matter how briefly. She stood there, watching him walk away, before realizing this could be construed as gawping, and glanced back into the shop, to look for Lottie. When she glanced back down the street, he had gone.

'What's up with you?' Lottie appeared out of the shop, laden with carrier bags. 'You're all red.'

'I'm fine,' Sara said laughing, suddenly filled with an absurd sense of joy. 'The most extraordinary thing just happened. I nearly got run over and this man – boy – saved me.'

'You really aren't fit to be let out on your own, are you?' Lottie said, shaking her head. 'What with feeling faint in shops, forgetting your pin number and then stepping out blithely into the road, regardless of traffic. What was all the weirdness in the shop about, as well?'

'Nothing. I was just upset at forgetting my pin,' Sara admitted. 'It's so silly, you wouldn't understand. I hate that feeling – I try to think of something but it's gone, there's just a blank, and the harder I try to think the more I can't remember. So annoying.'

'Alzheimer's,' Lottie said succinctly. 'Only a matter of time before you're sticking post-it notes to the kettle to remind you what it is.'

'It isn't funny,' Sara said crossly, then started to laugh. 'Oh, maybe it is. I'll have to write my pin number down. What if I was on my own? It would be so embarrassing. I can't go around forgetting things like that. Really, people should have thought about menopausal women when they brought in these blasted pin numbers. At least you can normally remember your own name.'

'Come on,' Lottie said. 'You can buy me some lunch.'

'I was going to buy you a pasty before I nearly got flattened.'

'Gross.' Lottie made a face. 'Glad you didn't. I'd much rather have a prawn salad or something. There's a really nice café I spotted just down the road.'

Sara followed her, carefully keeping to the narrow pavement. Maybe she was becoming senile. Maybe that was why she kept getting the night-time panics and feeling she didn't know who she was. Excellent. Senile *and* menopausal. She was only fifty, for God's sake. What else did she have to look forward to? Unwanted facial hair? Unexpected flatulence? Gout?

'Here it is,' Lottie said, pausing in front of a door which was painted a shocking pink. Nailed to it was a blackboard menu which announced, 'Fresh fish today!' beneath which had been chalked a list of appetizing dishes such as crab claws and king prawns in garlic. The name of the restaurant, 'Pip's', was emblazoned in vivid green lettering across the window. Another blackboard, propped up against the wall on the pavement by the door, said, 'LIVE MUSIC! THURSDAYS.' Lottie pushed open the door.

Inside, Sara was surprised to see that every table was full, and there was a little group of people standing at the bar, at the back of the room. The café was smaller than it looked from outside, the tables crammed closely together, with an assortment of non-matching wooden chairs and benches. On the walls hung posters from old films, and signed photographs of rock bands. A green T-shirt, with the name 'Pip's' across the front was pinned above the bar. Two young waiters, wearing T-shirts with the same logo over baggy shorts with black aprons tied around their waists, scooted about carrying overloaded plates of seafood and salad.

'I don't think there's going to be . . .' Sara said, loudly, above the pounding rock music.

'What?' Lottie said, turning to her.

'There isn't going to be a table,' Sara shouted, just as one of the waiters stopped in front of her, his dark hair tied back in a ponytail.

'For two?' he mouthed.

'Yes. If there is a table,' Sara said, loudly.

'I'm sure I can find you something,' he replied, smiling into her eyes.

Lottie raised her eyebrows at Sara. 'That would be lovely.'

'Sure. This table here's about to leave, aren't you, guys?' A group of teenage girls smiled flirtatiously up at him. 'There you go. Wait just one minute. Can I get you a drink?'

'Two glasses of white wine,' Lottie said, holding her mother firmly under the elbow, propelling her towards the bar.

'At lunchtime?' Sara said faintly.

'It's your birthday,' Lottie replied. 'Kind of.'

'Why not?' Sara experienced the same mildly reckless feeling she'd felt in the clothes shop. Why not, indeed? She found herself smiling. The sun was shining, she'd bought two pairs of trousers and a ridiculous ruffled top *and* she'd recently been rescued from being squashed in the street by an exceptionally

145

handsome man. She felt decidedly happy. Lottie looked at her, closely, as she lifted her glass to her lips. 'What are you grinning about?'

'The man who saved me in the street. He was quite, quite beautiful.'

'Mother!' Lottie was genuinely shocked. 'You can't go about calling young men beautiful, not at your age. How beautiful?' she added, leaning forward.

'Very. Long dark hair, soulful eyes like a spaniel, a wicked smile. Broad shoulders, too.'

'I'm beginning to worry about you, picking up men in the street. Bloody hell,' she said, looking over her mother's shoulder. 'Don't turn round now, but you think *you* saw a gorgeous man.'

'Calamari, scallops or can I tempt you with our fabulous garlic prawns?' he said, a few minutes later, his pencil poised against the pad, his eyes dancing with amusement as he looked down at her, apparently enjoying her confusion.

'Scallops,' Sara said firmly, putting the menu down on the table with a definite air. She was really not going to be made to feel so foolish by an attractive young man. This was ridiculous.

'And for you?' he said, turning to Lottie.

'What?' Lottie said, stunned. 'Oh, um, whatever. The prawn thingy.'

'And some wine?' he asked.

Sara looked at her glass. It was still half full. 'No,' she said. 'Some water. Still, please, not sparkling.'

'Live a little,' he said, grinning. 'What's the harm? Have half a bottle. Or you can order a bottle and then just leave it. We'll owe you one next time.'

'Next time?'

'You live here, right?' he said. 'You'll be back. We've got the best food and at night this place *really* rocks.' From the kitchen came the sound of loud singing, vaguely in tune. He smiled. 'The chef. He's a frustrated pop star.'

'I bet it's great,' Lottie said. 'We'll have to come along, won't we, Mum?'

'Possibly,' Sara said, primly.

'I hope you do,' he said, turning athletically on his heel, and walking away.

'Oh God,' Lottie said, sinking her head into her hands. 'I said I would come to a place full of the most devastating men I have seen in a long time with my *mother*. What will he think? That I have no friends?'

'I did tell you he was lovely.'

'You didn't say he was a waiter, though.'

'How would I know? I only saw him in the street.'

'Bit humble, isn't it, a waiter?'

'Does it matter?'

'He can't be all that bright.'

'Maybe it's a holiday job,' Sara speculated. 'On his gap year. He might be studying nuclear physics or something like that.'

'He looks a bit older than a student. And not, I would say, like a nuclear physicist. Surfer, yes. Boffin, no.'

'Adult gap year. Who cares? It's just nice to be flirted with.'

'He wasn't flirting with *you*,' Lottie said, taking a sip of wine. 'He was obviously flirting with *me*. He's only being nice to you because you are my mother and he wants to make a good impression. But you do look quite reasonable, today, actually.' She stared at Sara, her head on one side. 'Younger. More relaxed. You always seemed so stressed out at home.'

'Did I?' Sara was surprised. 'I always thought I was a very laid-back mother.'

'Hardly. You were always so busy, so many things to do, you never stopped. You had this little worried

147

frown,' she reached forward, touching Sara gently between her eyebrows, 'just here. It's gone.'

'See you soon,' he said, an hour later, holding the door open for them. 'Ciao.'

'Ciao?' Lottie said, as they walked away up the road towards the car park. 'Cheesy. I bet he's like that with all the women. He probably gets a flirt bonus. Women will leave more tips.'

Sara smiled. She felt light-headed from the wine, fuzzy and irresponsible. He had been right. The food was delicious.

'What shall we do at home?' she said, linking her arm through Lottie's.

'I don't know about you,' Lottie said. 'But I'm going to snooze in the garden and improve my tan.'

'I need to take Hector out. I'll just take him up the cliff, and then I shall join you in the garden. What shall we have for dinner?'

'Let's eat out again,' Lottie said, smiling, holding her mother's arm close to her side. 'It's still your birthday. Kind of. Come on. Like the man said, live a little.'

Chapter Eleven

'I brought you some eggs. Extremely free range, as you know.'

'That's really kind of you.' Sara had answered the door to find Helen standing outside, holding a loaded egg box.

'Can I let Nigel out? What do you think? Dare we risk it?'

Sara turned to look at Hector, lurking behind her legs. 'Go on, then. I suppose they have to meet at some point.'

'Brace yourself,' Helen said, moments later, as what did indeed look like a curly mountain bounded down the corridor and into the kitchen. The dog seemed to fill the house, his great hairy face grinning up at Sara, his stump of a tail wagging furiously. Hector took one look at him and dived under the table. The Airedale promptly followed him, and both Helen and Sara lunged forward just in time to save the vase of roses.

'Let's put them out in the garden,' Sara said faintly.

'Good idea.'

'Is he always like this?' Sara asked, as Nigel gambolled about, rushing backwards and forwards, planting two big feet on Helen's chest and licking her face, before returning in frantic pursuit of Hector.

''Fraid so. He's just so full of *lurve*, for everyone. He hasn't tried to mount Hector yet,' Helen observed. 'Good sign. I think they're going to be friends. It'll be nice to have someone to walk with, I get so bored going for walks on my own. I end up talking to myself and then I'm really embarrassed if someone overhears me and I have to pretend to be talking to Nigel. Which is probably worse.'

'Hector, go on,' Sara said, pushing the dog, who was trying to take refuge behind her, away. 'Go play.' Hector looked up at her. 'Save me,' his eyes pleaded. Nigel had found an old piece of rope in the long grass by the wall and was leaping about with it swinging from his mouth. Hector, glancing at Sara to see if this was acceptable behaviour, advanced cautiously towards him and hesitantly took one end. Nigel began growling furiously and, quite forgetting his timidity, Hector braced all four feet and started to tug back. Helen laughed. 'There you go. They're like children. You just have to ignore them and they find their feet. Now. One of the reasons I came over was to bring these.' She let her shoulder bag fall to the ground, and, reaching down, she unzipped it, drawing out a sheaf of A4-sized paper. 'I've done some very rough sketches I thought you might like to see.'

'Let's go back inside,' Sara said. 'I'm sure we can leave them out here, there's never any traffic down the lane even if they get out.'

Carefully, Helen spread the papers out on the circular kitchen table. 'I thought we might knock through the front rooms as you suggested – although we will need some kind of support in the middle, like a pillar or possibly a central fireplace – and extend the kitchen out to the side about so far. What do you think? Ignore all the technical figures, that's just the scale.'

'It looks brilliant,' said Sara, studying the plans with a rising sense of excitement. 'But won't it be hideously expensive? Knocking down the walls and all the building costs?'

'Not if we use my favourite builder and his team. He's not the cheapest, but if he gives you a quote he sticks to it, so you know where you are. His name's Jim – he's getting on a bit now, although he's very fit, and he only takes on the jobs that really interest him. Besides, he's in love with me.' Helen said this in a very matter-of-fact way.

Sara laughed. 'Is he really? That's one way of getting things done.'

'You've got to make use of every weapon, haven't you?' Helen replied, smiling. 'He keeps asking me out, though, and I'm running out of excuses.'

'Have you been out with anyone since your husband died?' Sara asked, and then hesitated, thinking it was a very personal question to put to someone she'd only met twice. God, she was turning into Catherine.

'A couple,' Helen said. 'But really, I'm not so bothered. I had such a good marriage everyone else seems so boring in comparison with Jack. He made me laugh like nobody else, he was great company. I was very lucky, I know, you don't often get to be friends as well, do you? Besides the thought of even contemplating going to bed with someone who isn't Jack . . .' She pulled a face at Sara, who burst out laughing. 'Well, it would be quite a thing at my age to get naked in front of someone who is effectively a stranger. Sorry, that makes me sound as if I go out with men just for sex, which I assure you I don't – it is nice to be taken out, to have male company. But they do want sex, don't they? Even the older ones. They see a woman living on her own, and they think you must be desperate. I just can't be bothered any more. I'd far rather keep tham as friends, and I know this sounds rather mad but I feel that Jack is with me, all the time. I talk to him a lot, when I'm alone, at home. It's one of the reasons why I kept Nigel too, he's like a constant connection to Jack because they were always together. I'm a firm believer that death isn't the end, are you?'

'I'm not sure,' Sara said cautiously. 'The only person who was really close to me who has died is my father, and yes, I suppose, thinking about it, I do feel that he's with me. I ask him a lot of questions in my mind, and he generally gives me a sensible answer. He was a lovely man, my Dad. My Mum has coped brilliantly without him, but she misses him so much.'

'What did he say about your marriage?'

'Before, or after his death?' Sara smiled.

'After.'

Sara glanced at Helen. 'That is a very interesting question. You know, he told me to leave. Matt had an affair, you see. With a very young girl, just twenty-five, who works for him. He's still with her now, apparently. My father told me to get out while I had my dignity intact. My friends – one in particular – thought I should boot Matt out of our home and then take him for every penny. Another said I ought to hear his side of the story, and that really, a lot of married men had affairs on the quiet and it wasn't worth disturbing my lifestyle. Matt was quite well off, you see. But I couldn't do that. If I'd stayed, and fought him for money, he'd still be a big part of my life. And there would be all that anger and bitterness – at least, being here, I'm away from all the repercussions. Now, looking back, I don't feel I am the same person any more, and it's only been a matter of months.'

'Do you miss him?'

Sara smiled. 'Oh, yes. All the time. Like you, we were – at least, I thought we were – great friends.

We talked all the time, discussed everything, and I loved his company. Everything was an occasion, with Matt. He loved to entertain, he couldn't bear to be bored. But now – well, the awful thing is that I don't know if I bored him. Or if he'd stayed with me for years because of the children, or he was worried that I'd take his money – oh, I don't know. So many awful thoughts run through your mind. It's the not knowing, you see – thinking that you knew someone inside out and then discovering that they had this whole other side to them. Apparently his – affair – had only been going on for a year but he must have been receptive, mustn't he – and how do I know this was the first?'

'Did he say it was?'

'You know,' she said, smiling sadly, 'We haven't even had that conversation. I've only talked to him once since I found out. Everything else has come via the girls or friends. I don't trust myself, to be honest, to either see or speak to him. And the crazy thing is that I don't have to – I know what he is thinking. When Emily, my elder daughter, relays his comments I know exactly what's behind them, what effect he wants his words to have on me. In some ways, I do still feel manipulated by him. He's currently trying to make my daughters, well, Emily at least, believe that I'm a menopausal hysterical woman who's gone a bit potty, which is why I've rushed off to Cornwall. I don't think he honestly believes I can stand on my own two feet, and he keeps offering me money. I suppose it assuages his conscience, and I also think he hates the thought that I can be independent from him. I presume he'd like to set me up in a nice house, pay me a monthly sum and then tell himself he's been very generous.'

'And you're not going to make it that easy for him.'

'Exactly. He can fuck off, quite frankly.'

Helen laughed.

'Well, I'm not some kind of pet, am I? I refuse to be patted on the head and made to slip quietly away. I'm here and I'm me, and he has no idea what I'm doing and has no idea exactly where I am living. He hates that. He hates not being in control. I'm unfinished business.'

'You have become mysterious,' Helen nodded.

'Mmm. Not so boring now, am I?'

'I think you're absolutely right. Good for you.'

'I sound very brave, but I'm not awfully brave, really. It's been horrible a lot of the time.'

'How did you find out about the affair? Sorry, I don't mean to pry . . .'

'That's OK. At his fiftieth birthday party. His best friend, who was extremely drunk and angry with Matt because he wouldn't give him money to bail out his business, announced the fact during the speeches.'

'No!' Helen looked at her in amazement.

'In front of all the other guests. It caused quite a stir, as you can imagine,' Sara added, sardonically. 'Not the best night of my life.'

'Were the girls there, too?'

'Yes, that was the really awful thing. I mean, finding out was pretty shocking, obviously, but I do wish it hadn't happened in front of them.'

'What did you do?'

'That night Matt just, well, ran away, and then the next day, I left.'

'Left?'

'I know, it's extraordinary, really. I don't know where I found the courage. But I was so angry with him, I thought I was really not going to sit about waiting for him to choose to come back to me, so I left him. I didn't want to hear him defend himself, or tell me any more lies . . .'

'How *did* you know it was true?'

'His face,' Sara said, simply. 'I just knew. He didn't deny it. He looked absolutely stunned, then livid at being found out, so publicly. Matt was – is – a very proud man, and I think he just couldn't bear the humiliation. That's why he left, that night. And then I found a text message from her which seemed to confirm it. Leaving us like that was unforgivable,' she added. 'He left the three of us alone, to cope. Without one word of denial, or contrition, or apology – he just ran away. It was the action of a coward. That was really why I decided I had to put some space between us. And the longer we were apart, the harder it was to bridge the distance, until the gap became impassable.'

'Do you know her?'

'She's one of his account managers,' Sara said. 'Twenty-five, stunningly beautiful, clever. Bit screwed up though, I think – her father, who's Russian, is phenomenally wealthy and from the few times I met her I got the impression she'd been given an awful lot of material possessions but not a lot of love. She struck me – hmm, yes she did – as being a rather needy, insecure person. They travelled together a lot, on business. I suspect she targeted him – she made it quite obvious she found him attractive, well, there he was, her boss, very good-looking and well preserved for his age, charming, witty, powerful. I guess she just set him within her sights and he could not resist. The silly thing,' she added, 'is that I knew other women on his staff found him attractive but I thought he wasn't the type. That what we had was much too deep and the unspoken trust between us meant he would never be vulnerable. I was a fool,' she shrugged. 'You do live and learn, don't you? And how can I compete with someone like her? I'm fifty. I look OK, but I'm no Joan Collins, I've never been a glamourpuss. I'm a homely, mumsy woman who looks OK in a good light but standing next to Karina I'd look like her mother. Would you like a coffee? Sorry, I am going on. I didn't mean to tell anyone, to be honest, but it seems silly to be so mysterious and besides . . .'

'We're going to be friends.'

Sara smiled at her, gratefully. 'I hope so.'

'I hope so too. I have got to know people round here, but there's no one I've found who could be described as a soul-mate. There's so much I love to do, you know, going to the theatre, and cinema, art galleries, concerts . . . I'm a bit of a culture vulture, really.'

'Me too.'

'I knew that. Isn't it funny? I knew that immediately. I'd love a coffee, by the way. You know,' she looked at Sara thoughtfully. 'Divorce might be the best thing. Get it all settled and over with, then you really can begin your new life.'

'I don't know. You're probably right, but I hate thinking about it. Oh – hello, darling. Did you sleep well?'

Lottie wandered into the kitchen, wearing a vest top and a baggy pair of men's pyjama bottoms. Her hair was a tangled mess, and she rubbed sleep from her eyes. She looked extraordinarily beautiful. She raised a sleepy hand to Helen in greeting. 'Like a log,' she yawned. 'What's all this?' She gestured at the plans laid out on the table. 'Oh, cool, is this for the house?'

'Yes,' Helen said. 'What do you think?'

'I need tea before my brain will work,' Lottie said, plonking herself down on one of the uneven kitchen chairs, looking pleadingly at her mother.

'All right,' Sara said. 'I've put the kettle on anyway.'

Helen looked at her watch. 'Actually, I'm going to have to skip the coffee, I had no idea that was the time. I wonder where those dratted dogs have got to?'

'They're digging holes in the garden,' Lottie said. 'I

saw them from my bedroom window. Great teamwork.'

Helen groaned. 'I am sorry. I'll help you fill them in.'

'Don't worry,' Sara said. 'It's not as if there are many plants to dig up.'

At that moment Hector trotted into the kitchen, his eyes full of guilt. Lottie burst out laughing. 'If you could hold up a sign it would say, 'It wasn't me, it was him.' Hector flopped down at her feet, and she stroked his head. Next there was a loud bang as the kitchen door hit the wall and Nigel crashed into the room, his face split into a great gummy grin.

'You are a delinquent, aren't you?' Lottie said, lifting up her feet as Nigel dived under the table, and then swiftly reversed.

'I'll take him home,' Helen said apologetically as he blundered past her, catching him expertly under the collar. 'Ring me later – I'll give you the name of my lovesick builder.'

'Is everyone around here completely insane?' Lottie asked, once Helen had closed the front door. 'Who is the lovesick builder?'

'It's a long story,' Sara said, gathering up the plans and folding them neatly, before putting them away safely in a drawer. 'You know, I think I am going to have to get a job.'

'Bravo. What brought on that brainwave?'

'There's no way I can fund all this without using Dad's money.'

'Dad texted me last night.'

'Did he?'

'He wanted me to ring him. So I did.'

'And what did he say?'

'The usual, how was I, that kind of stuff. He's going to France next week, and he wants to see me before he goes. We just had a bit of a chat.'

'Oh,' Sara said guardedly, putting toast under the grill and rooting about in the cupboard above the sink for Marmite. 'And?'

'He said we needed to talk about next year. He's going to sort something out so that I don't have to worry about money,' she added hesitantly. 'Is that OK?'

'Is he really? That's generous.'

'He would have paid for uni, anyway, wouldn't he, Mum? He said he'll try and work out a way of making it more tax effective. You know Dad. He's always trying to save as much money from the taxman as he can.' She bit into the toast Sara had put down in front of her. 'What were you saying to Helen about a divorce?'

Sara grimaced. How much had she heard? 'I have to go to London too remember, to see his solicitor.'

'We could go together.'

'I'm not seeing Dad,' Sara said quickly.

'Oh, for goodness sake,' Lottie said, putting down her toast crossly. 'You're like a pair of kids. Dad waited at least ten minutes before he asked about you, really casually, and then he tried to pump me for information.'

'Such as?'

'Like what the cottage was like, what you were doing all day, if anyone had been to see you . . .'

'And what did you say?'

'I said it was very dull,' she said.

'Gee, thanks.'

'I don't mean that. I just mean there's no big drama. That you were getting the house together, and talking about getting a job.'

'And what did he say about that? I bet he thought that was hilarious.'

'He did laugh,' Lottie admitted.

Sara felt irritation rising in her throat. '*Why* did he think it was so funny?'

'He said the world had moved on a long way since

you'd last worked, and that he doubted if you could stick it, nine to five.'

'How rude,' Sara said furiously.

'But it's kind of true, isn't it? How long has it been since you had a proper job? I don't just mean working for Dad, doing bits and pieces at his office?'

'I did rather more than bits and pieces,' she said crossly. 'I wrote most of the sales pitches for quite a few of his early clients, and I supervised launches. The only thing that stopped me getting more involved was because I wanted to be at home when you were both little, I didn't want you brought up by nannies, and nor did Dad. So it wasn't as if I was trying to skive off work – and it was a joint decision.'

'I know, I know, keep your hair on. I'm not criticizing, Mum. I'm just saying that it has been a long time since you had a real job.'

'I know.' The thought had been worrying her. 'I do want to do something I'm really interested in. I would hate to work nine to five in an office, Dad's right. Besides, who would look after Hector?'

'Your life is beginning to revolve around that dog,' Lottie said. 'Why don't you start your own company?'

'What?'

'You know,' Lottie said, flicking through yesterday's newspaper lying on the table. 'A little business. From home. Then you wouldn't have to go anywhere, would you?'

'Doing what?'

'I don't know, use your brain. You must be able to think of something.'

For some reason Sara could not fathom, the name of the wildlife trust flicked through her mind. 'I found this dead dolphin on the beach . . .' she said.

'No!' Lottie said, looking up, horrified. 'You didn't tell me. When?'

159

'A few days after I moved in. It was tagged, and the name of a wildlife trust was on the tag. They're based in Fowey, I've seen the offices. I wonder if they would like any help fund-raising? I'm quite good at that.'

'Sounds a good idea to me,' Lottie said.

'I used to work for a charity after university, before I started working for Dad, and that's what I specialized in, raising corporate sponsorship.'

'I can't imagine you doing a proper job,' Lottie said, her head on one side.

Sara laughed. 'Thanks. I haven't always just been your mother. It would be nice to do something that's actually useful. Maybe because we're living so far out in the country, I'd like to get involved with something which benefits the environment.'

'Since when have you been green? I used to nag you and Dad all the time about recycling and buying organic food.'

'I know. It just seemed like too much of an effort. But here, I don't know. It seems to make more sense.'

'You could do a lot of it from home. We can get broadband, dead easy. I need it too, anyway. I cannot sit in front of that laptop and listen to it making little grunting noises while nothing happens on-screen, for one moment longer. I nearly killed my laptop last night with my bare hands.'

'That's a good idea. I would need broadband.'

'You could . . .' Lottie stared into space, thinking hard. 'You could set up a kind of consultancy which advises people how to get, like, sponsorship and raise money for green projects. I could help you. I can make calls, stuff like that.'

'It's not a bad idea,' Sara said slowly. 'I must get started. I must stop putting things off.'

'Exactly. And you should come with me, to London,

next week. You need to see Dad. You can't hide from him for ever.'

'OK,' Sara said. 'But I'm coming back the same day. I can't leave Hector.'

'You are turning into your mother. Helen would look after him.'

'I don't think I could subject Hector to that.'

'Maybe not.'

Sara realized, with a start, that she had no desire to stay one night away from the cottage. She looked about her, at the peeling walls, the rickety furniture, the old-fashioned sink and ridiculous little stove. This had become home.

Chapter Twelve

Sara was on Lottie's laptop, reading about the local wildlife trust on the Internet, when Lottie burst through the door.

'I've seen him!' she shouted. 'Here! In the village!'

'Who?' Sara asked, looking up, bewildered.

'Him, him. You know, the man, the waiter dude. The yummy one. He was getting into a beat-up old car, with a surfboard on the roof, just next to the Spar. He saw me!' Her eyes shone. 'He saw me and he *waved.*'

'Lottie,' Sara said, smiling at her daughter's excitement. 'Perhaps *you* need to get out more, not me. It can't have been *that* thrilling. He only waved at you.'

'Oh, it was exciting all right,' Lottie said, punching both hands into the air and doing a little dance. 'Yippee! The beautiful man lives in our village! He's going to like me, he really likes me, he's going to marry me . . .' She sang, clicking her fingers and dancing around her mother's chair.

'You big banana.' Sara turned her attention back to the laptop. 'Are you sure he hadn't just been shopping at the Spar?'

'Nope,' Lottie said, leaning her elbows on to her mother's shoulders and looking over her shoulder at the screen. 'I saw him close a door right next to the shop and lock it with a key. He lives here. He actually lives here.' She sighed. 'Now all I need to do is a lot of shopping. You name it. Milk. Newspapers. Bread. Tinfoil. Binbags. Crappy rental DVDs we don't want to watch. You name it, I'm there, shopping away. If only we could see the village from here.'

'We could put a telescope on the roof.'

'Ha, ha. Just wait till I tell Emily. I'm going to ring her now. Who would have thought that life could be so *brillianto* in this backwater? She reckons there are no good-looking men in London and do you know why? Because they're here! They're all here! I love Cornwall.' She leant forward slightly and kissed her mother loudly on the side of the cheek. 'Great hair, by the way. What are you doing?'

'Trying to find out more about the wildlife trust.' Sara gestured at the screen, running her other hand through the troll-like fluffy hair she had just washed but couldn't be bothered to blow-dry. 'It's fascinating. Do you know they log all the sightings off the coast of things like dolphins, seals and sharks? Someone spotted a basking shark last week just a hundred and fifty metres from the shore and it was eighteen feet long! Imagine. Very ugly, though, look at the picture. Dolphins turn up all the time and play with surfers and swimmers. They come into the bays into pods, and apparently they love to romp about with whoever is in the water. Beyond cute – see.' She gestured at a photograph of a dolphin, which appeared to be smiling into the camera. 'The trust *is* a charity – it gets some local authority and European Union funding, but mostly it relies on donations and sponsorships, and it obviously does all kinds of amazing work, running lots of projects with local schools and whatnot. You know, I think I really could help – I reckon they must be desperate for fund-raising ideas.'

'Yo, Mother. This could be big business. Just remember, when you've made your first million that this was all my idea.'

'I'm highly unlikely to make a lot of money,' Sara said. 'They won't want to pay me much at all, I'll probably have to negotiate a small percentage of the money I raise. But it's better than nothing, isn't it? And more important than that, it could be fun.' She leant back against Lottie, who wrapped her arms around her mother's shoulders. 'You know, I feel really enthusiastic about this. It'll be great to have a proper purpose to life, instead of just drifting about doing things for other people. I should have gone back to work, you know, once you were at secondary school. God knows why I didn't stand up to Dad.'

'He wasn't an easy person to stand up to,' Lottie murmured, a shadow passing over her face.

Sara reached up to touch Lottie's hand gently, which was resting by her chin. 'I know, hon, I know.' She sighed. 'I'm never ever going to make as much money as Dad, obviously, but it will be great to actually earn something myself. All I need to do is make enough to keep us and pay for the renovations.'

'Dad's just bought a black Porsche Carrera. Em told me. So now he's got that and the Range Rover. Not very environmentally friendly, is it? How can he drive two cars at once? Emily says the Porsche is the dog's doodahs, but then she's easily impressed.'

'Sad.'

'Mmm. Love you. I'm just going to wash my hair before I nip back down to the village. What do you want from the shop?'

'Nothing.'

'Hey ho. There must be *something* you need.'

'He'll be at work,' Sara pointed out. 'He won't be home for ages. You'd be better driving into

Fowey and marching up and down outside the café.'

Lottie looked at her mother's reflection in the screen, outraged. 'I can't make it look *too* obvious,' she said, unwinding her arms and standing up straight 'It's got to be a casual, accidental meeting. An "Oh, gosh, do you live here too? Fancy that, how amazing."'

'Now you know what time he leaves for work,' Sara suggested, twisting round in her chair to look at Lottie, 'you can happen to be walking into the shop, can't you?'

'Excellent idea. Top thinking.' Lottie wandered away up the narrow stairs, still singing 'He really likes me, he wants to marry me . . .'

Sara smiled, and turned her attention back to the computer. She could offer her fund-raising advice on a consultancy basis to lots of different projects needing sponsorship. Thinking about it, she decided she would concentrate first on conservation and environmental organizations. So many seemed to struggle to get their message across, because even though 'being green' was becoming much more popular and mainstream, the general public – and business – did tend to think this type of organization was run by people with beards, wearing sandals, and Matt had said that the more militant, active groups like Greenpeace made big business rather jumpy. He'd run a couple of publicity campaigns for the larger green charities. But now being environmentally friendly and recycling was becoming so much more of an accepted part of most people's lives, Sara presumed that companies looking to give away sponsorship and donations – usually because of the tax breaks involved – would now look to the green charities.

Living here, she felt a much stronger commitment to the environment. Perhaps because the landscape was so beautiful, the conservation of wildlife and nature seemed a far more pertinent issue. She was definitely beginning to feel more personal responsibility – she realized there was a lot just one individual could do to make a difference.

Two days ago, after she'd walked Hector over the cliffs to Polperro, she had paused in the old cobbled town square to read the noticeboard. It was full of finger-wagging notices about the need to recycle. A local couple called Bob and Pat had put up a note saying they were willing to collect people's old Inkjet cartridges for recycling, because apparently the things will never biodegrade, not in a trillion years, and would probably be the last things left on earth after a nuclear holocaust. The note hadn't said those words exactly, but Sara got the picture. She thought of all the Inkjet cartridges she'd gaily lobbed into the bin over the years, and felt extremely guilty.

Using Google, she surfed around other conservation websites, based on Cornwall. Clicking on to the first one listed, she was met by a banner headline which screamed 'Subscribe NOW To Pesticide News!' across the top of the home page. Possibly tomorrow, she thought, closing that website down. Or maybe the day after that. It depends just how committed I become. Quite possibly not *that* committed, she reluctantly admitted to herself.

At her feet, Hector thumped his tail, indicating that he was bored with all this inactivity and needed some attention. At least he was at her feet – over the past few weeks whenever she'd sat down, he had decided it was time to make a bid to become the largest lapdog on the planet. He would slide a paw on to her knee, and then, looking in the other direction – and quite possibly whistling to himself – he would lever his not inconsiderable bulk on to her knee and perch there like a great hairy bird. Once ensconced, he would peer into her eyes with all the love and devotion he could muster, breathing hot doggy breath into her face from far too close a range for comfort. He was revelling in Sara's undivided attention, and had taken it upon himself to stay as close to her as possible at all times. Hector, my Protector, she smiled to herself. He had always been rather wary of Matt, who said he ought to be treated more like a dog, and less like a furry person. It drove Matt mad when he came home unexpectedly and found Sara talking to him, which she did, she had to admit, quite often. Matt would put on a goofy Hector voice and say, 'I don't know what you're saying, Mummy, because I'm just a *dog* not a real life *human being* and I have a brain the size of a *peanut.*'

'I know,' she said, as Hector's nose emerged from under the table, having slid forward on his stomach. 'You want to go out.' At the sound of her voice, the thumping redoubled and he climbed to his feet, stretching out his front legs and arching his back. Sara pushed back her chair and stood up, stretching too. She looked out of the window. The leaves on the oak tree in the middle of the lawn were beginning to unfurl, like green and pale orange feathery fingers, from the ends of the lichen-covered branches. Spring was becoming summer. To the far side of the cottage lay a small dell which had been filled with bluebells, but these were now dying, wilting into the wild garlic. Each morning as she opened the front door, she was overwhelmed by its feral smell, heightened by the dew.

In the kitchen, she gathered up Hector's lead from the dresser, and called up the stairs to Lottie that she wouldn't be long. She glanced at her watch – it was eleven o'clock.

Time seemed to have taken on a quite different meaning, here at the cottage. In London, every day during the week had a strict timetable – Matt was up at six, ready for his morning jog, and at precisely quarter to seven she'd hear the whir of the power shower. As he washed, Sara got up, reluctantly, and put out his clothes for the day – black trousers, bespoke tailored shirt, usually white, and his favourite black suede Church brogues – he had ten identical pairs. He refused to wear anything but cashmere socks, which were a complete nuisance as she had to hand-wash them, or else they would shrink. Sara rarely dressed before he left, pulling on a comfortable old cream dressing gown and without bothering to brush her hair she would wander into the kitchen to start the tedious business of juicing oranges. Matt insisted on fresh orange juice, and freshly-ground coffee without milk or sugar. He would only eat muesli she made herself, as he said the bought varieties had too much sugar. His one concession to indulgence was to have banana sliced over the top. Sara seldom ate before he left. He tucked his newspaper under one arm as he departed, kissing her on the cheek while simultaneously checking his Blackberry for urgent overnight messages.

Once he had gone Sara would put a butter croissant into the baking oven of the Aga, and gratefully sit down to read the second newspaper. When the girls had still been at school, breakfast time was a whirlwind of lost jumpers, homework and arguments about hair and chipped nail varnish. Once they left school and were off at university or travelling like Lottie had been, Sara savoured the peace of the empty apartment, with time to enjoy her breakfast and plan the day.

Her day, she now realized, had centred almost entirely around Matt and his needs – shopping for the food he liked, taking his clothes to the dry-cleaner, tidying the apartment so it was welcoming and neat when he came home. Goodness, she thought – it wasn't much to show for a life, really, was it? A very tidy home and food in the fridge? What had happened to her goals? At university she had agreed with her friends there was no way she was going to give up her career when she had children, but it had just happened, somehow – she couldn't bear to hand them over to a nanny and Matt had made it clear he wanted her to be at home. Her life had been pleasant, certainly, but why on earth hadn't she been frustrated by so little challenge? Had she lived most of her life, vicariously, through Matt? I lived in his shadow, she thought, sadly. My life was . . . inconsequential.

Looking back it seemed to Sara almost as if she had been sleepwalking. Why hadn't she insisted that she wanted to have her own career, rather than being little more than a housewife? If anyone new asked her what she did, she used to say that she worked for her husband, but actually once the children were born she had done hardly anything, just odd hours here and there when Matt needed her. She wasn't by nature an idle person, and she had not liked being financially dependent, even though Matt never made an issue about the money she spent, as she was naturally far more frugal than he was. If she'd wanted to, in the later years, she could have blown a fortune on designer clothes and pampering herself with beauty treatments and visits to health clubs, but that had held no interest. Besides, she could never quite rid herself of the guilt, the feeling that it wasn't her money as she hadn't earned it.

I was, she thought, as she walked down the lane, swinging Hector's lead, far *too* dependent. She was beginning to realize why Matt might have found it so easy to deceive her – she rarely asked him why he was late, or where he had been. She just accepted it was part of his career, to stay out late, entertaining clients. I put him on a pedestal, she thought, and believed everything he told me. I did not challenge him, in any sense of the word.

Hector trotted from side to side of the lane with his tail held high, and ears pricked. There were so few cars, she didn't need to put him on a lead.

She was also beginning to understand how Matt had controlled her, and moulded her into the person he wanted her to be. How he used his temper, which he knew she hated, as a weapon to make sure he got his own way. Sara loathed shouting, as did Lottie, and would go to any lengths to avoid confrontation. Over the years, she had become adept at sidestepping any issue which might make him angry. Why *didn't* I stand up to him, she wondered. She had always believed that their relationship was based on equality – but she could see now that this was simply not true. Whoever earns the money inevitably held the balance of power in a relationship, she thought. Matt was, effectively, my boss. He felt *superior* to me. Why did I let him tell me what to do? When we married, I was working full-time, I had so many interests outside of the home and a career I really liked. Then one by one I began to give things up – my job, certain friends Matt did not like, interests and hobbies he did not share, until almost all of my attention was focused on him, the children and our home. That isn't healthy, she thought. No wonder he thought my life was – well, less important than his. That somehow he owned me, and he could do what he pleased. Karina is a career girl, she's very good at her job, she presumably has lots of interests – she must be opening up a whole other world to him. Not to mention her youth. She has all the promise of her youth.

Out of the corner of her eye, Sara saw a sudden movement. She turned, just as a huge dark brown bird of prey launched itself into the sky from a post at the side of a five-barred gate by the bend in the lane. She paused to watch over the gate as it swooped down low over a field, and then soared, effortlessly, to the top of a distant oak tree, which swayed violently as it landed. She wasn't very knowledgeable about birds, but she thought it might be a buzzard, or perhaps a kite. She could see the bird had white feathers under its wings, and she was fairly sure that meant it was a buzzard. Sara craned her neck, trying to see it more clearly, but it was hidden by leaves. She looked up at the cloudless sky. All she could hear was the faint rumble of a tractor in the distance, and birds singing. Smiling, she turned away and walked on down the lane.

It was bordered on each side by a high grassy bank, filled with a tangle of ivy, cow parsley, pink geraniums, tiny white dog roses, nettles and layers of sticky bindweed. At the next gate she stopped again, and rested her elbows on the top, breathing in the fresh, wild-garlic-scented air. Before her the fields stretched away, neatly bordered by stone walls and hedges. Amidst the grazing land were fields of oilseed rape, vibrantly yellow, the breeze creating undulating ripples through the crop like waves on the sea. In the distance she could just make out the spire of St Just's, the Norman church in the next village to Lanteglos. Helen had mentioned she went there every Sunday – not because she was an especially committed Christian, she said, but just because it was a good chance to catch up with all the local gossip and feel part of the community. This phrase was accompanied by a slightly self-deprecating smile. She found it, Helen said, an oddly comforting thing to do. The rector, she told Sara, was known locally as the sprintin' vicar because as well as delivering sermons in the three village churches which made up his parish, he also ran marathons.

Sara decided, leaning on the gate, that she would go to church this Sunday. Lottie was unlikely to want to join her – she hadn't been in a church since the end-of-term services at school, and would no doubt accuse her of turning into Granny.

Smiling to herself at the thought, Sara stepped back from the gate and called Hector, who had disappeared around the corner. He came trotting back, his ears pricked at the sound of her voice. 'Home,' she said. As she turned, she was abruptly buzzed by a very large fly. It was a nasty black thing, which hovered in the air like a small alien spaceship, legs dangling, peering intently into her face as if to say, 'Aha. Earthling.' It circled her, slowly. 'Edible,' it appeared to have relayed to its cronies, and they suddenly appeared from nowhere, buzzing around her ears and eyes. She flailed about, shouting, and at that precise moment a very battered white car came round the corner, too fast. Tyres squealing, it slewed to the side, just missing both her and Hector, and came to rest against the far grassy bank. There was a surfboard on the roof.

Panting, Sara stopped waving her arms, aware of how ridiculous she must look, and tugged down her T-shirt, which had ridden up from the waistband of her jeans. Hector jumped towards the car, barking, and she lunged forward to clip the lead on to his collar.

'I'm really sorry,' she said breathlessly, as the driver opened his door. 'It's just so few cars come round here, I really ought to keep him on a lead, I know . . .'

'No worries,' he said, stepping out of the car, and walking round to look down at his front bumper. 'Another dent to add to my impressive collection. Are you OK?' He looked more closely at her and then laughed. 'Oh – it's you.'

Sara smiled. 'I'm sorry, I do seem to be something of a liability at the moment. I'm not normally as away with the fairies as this. I'm Sara, by the way.'

Smiling, he took her outstretched hand. 'Ricky. And this is . . .' He gestured at Hector, who was standing between them, feet firmly planted on the ground, back arched, his face a mask of aggressive masculine protection.

'This is Hector.' She stroked her hand over his neck, feeling the ridged hackles.

'Hector. Cool.'

'Were you . . .'

'I . . .'

'No, you go on.' She smiled. 'Are you heading to the beach? It's just that the road doesn't lead anywhere, we don't normally meet . . .'

'I'm going surfing,' he said, jerking his head at the board. 'It's pretty good in the cove, the tide's about right now. The best beaches are up in the north, but I don't have the time to get there at the moment. Most of my friends surf up there, but I'm happy here, I like to get out on the water alone.'

Sara looked at him, surprised. It was an odd thing to say. 'It must be hard to find time, with work . . .'

'Yeah.' He stood for a moment, one hand on the open car door, looking at her. He seemed quite comfortable with the silence, giving no hint of embarrassment or unease. His long dark hair was caught behind his head in a ponytail, and he was wearing a baggy orange T-shirt over a black wetsuit which had a lime green stripe down the side of each leg. His feet were bare.

173

'Do you live round here?'

'Yes – at the white cottage above the cove. I moved in a few months ago.'

For a moment, he looked shocked. Then he recovered himself. 'I heard someone had bought the place,' he said coolly. There was a curious expression on his face, one she could not fathom, as if he was weighing up whether to say something and deciding against it. 'Normally I surf here a lot, but I've been so busy . . .' His words tailed off.

When she had met him before, she would have described him as a confident happy-go-lucky kind of person. But today there was a thoughtfulness, a sense of melancholy in the curve of his mouth. He shrugged his shoulders. 'You're lucky. It's a great place to live. Amazing views.'

'Oh, yes. I love it. I'm about to start renovating, extending . . .'

'Are you?' His eyes registered a flash of intense interest, but then the expression was gone. 'Well, hey,' he said. 'I'd better get going or I'll lose the tide. No doubt I'll see you around.'

'No doubt. Nice to meet you – Ricky.'

'You too.' He held up his hand in a casual farewell, and then climbed back into the car, slamming the door.

Sara stepped back against the hedge as he drove past, and he raised his hand to her again without looking at her, his face thoughtful, a frown creasing his forehead.

'You'll never guess!' Lottie met her at the door when she walked in ten minutes later.

'I know,' Sara smiled.

'He's here! Right now. In the cove. Come on.' She took Sara's hand and, pulling her mother forwards, they tiptoed across the front garden. Lottie peered over the wall at the stony beach below them. Sara stepped back. 'Don't,' she said, lowering her voice, worried he might be able to hear them. 'This is embarrassing, it looks as if we're spying on him.' Besides, she said to herself, he seemed to want to be alone. As if he had a lot of things to think about. He was, she decided, a far more complex and interesting person than she had first thought. Slightly older, too – possibly in his early thirties. Rather too old for Lottie, she decided.

'Move back!' Sara said, more sharply than she had intended.

'Why? Hey, what's eating you?'

Sara reached out and took hold of Lottie's arm. 'Come inside and I'll tell you.'

Lottie took one last look at the beach. He was tying a rope from his surfboard to his wrist, staring out to sea. He clearly hadn't heard them. Reluctantly, she followed her mother into the cottage.

'So?' she asked, when they were both in the kitchen.

'I spoke to him. Just now, in the lane.'

'And? Tell me everything. Every tiny little word.'

'There's not much to tell. I was daydreaming, and he nearly ran me over.'

'Not again,' Lottie groaned. 'He's going to think you're bonkers, as if you have a death wish or something.'

'He got out of the car to make sure I was OK – well, actually I think he wanted to make sure his car wasn't too bashed up, as he hit the bank. And then we had a bit of a chat.' She shrugged.

'Yes? God, this is like trying to get blood out of a stone.'

'His name's Ricky. He does live in Lanteglos and . . .' She sighed. 'That's about it.'

'Oh, impressive, Mother. Full marks for interviewing skills. Is that really all you gleaned?'

For some reason, Sara felt rather protective of him. She didn't want to reveal anything more – as if, well, as if she wanted to keep most of the details to herself. There had been something haunted, she thought, something decidedly odd in the way he'd reacted when she told him they were living at the cottage. There was something quite mysterious about him.

'He seemed very nice,' she added lamely.

'Nice? Nice? He's fucking gorgeous, that's what he is.'

'Don't swear.'

'Sorry. It's just . . . oh, Mum, I am a bit bored and it would be so cool to talk to someone who has half a brain. Meet some new people. You've got la-la-loon Helen, but I haven't made any friends yet. Couldn't you have invited him here, for a cup of tea or something?'

'He doesn't look very much like the cup of tea type.'

'You know what I mean. Get chatting, in the way that it's OK for old people to do, invite him over. I can't start chatting him up, he'll know that I fancy him. I have to be aloof and mysterious. For a bit, at least.'

'I'm not sure . . .'

'What?'

'I think he's older than we first thought. Maybe thirty, thirty-one.'

'What difference does that make?'

'Oh come on, Lottie, that's way too old for you.'

'I don't want to *marry* him,' she said crossly. 'I just would like to go out at night and have some fun.'

Sara smiled. 'I thought you wanted to marry him, you really liked him . . .' She sang.

Lottie put her hands over her ears. 'Do not, ever, sing. God, you are completely tone deaf. I am severely disappointed in you. This was a golden opportunity.'

Sara turned around and switched on the kettle.

'Are you so very bored?' she said. The thought made her feel rather hurt.

Lottie shrugged. 'A bit, Mum, even you can see there's not a lot for a twenty-year-old to do round here, is there? I mean, it's fun to like plan what to do with the house but I really miss my friends, even vile Emily . . .' She sighed. 'I think I do need to get out more. Would it look too obvious if I went for a walk on the beach?'

'Yes. Leave the poor man alone.'

'I could say I was rock-pooling or looking for shells.'

'You are not,' Sara pointed out, 'ten years old.'

'Walking the dog?'

They both looked at Hector, who at the word 'walk', began to back away.

'You'd need castors to get him out again today,' Sara said, laughing.

'Come on,' Lottie said, 'Let's sit outside. We can move the table away from the wall,' she added hastily. 'Not that I can understand why it's such a big deal. He might be desperate to meet me, have you thought of that? He might be lonely, too.'

Hector followed them out and flopped down, before rolling over to rub his back on the warm grass, his stomach rising and falling with exhaustion, pink tongue lolling out of the corner of his mouth. He grinned up at them from his upside down position, wagging his tail when Lottie reached down to rub his tummy.

Sitting up, she stretched her long slim tanned legs out in front of her. 'If I say it myself, I am looking pretty damn brown. I must paint my toenails,' she added, peering at her feet. 'Can I borrow your red varnish?'

'Of course.'

177

Lottie looked up at the cloudless sky. 'I didn't mean to moan,' she said, turning to smile at her mother. 'I do love it here, you know.'

'I know.' Sara rolled her head around on her neck, hearing a click. 'Gosh, I'm stiff. You're right, though, we do need to meet more people, get on with things. It's been fun just mooching about, but I think now is the time to take positive steps forward. I must ring up the council about the planning permission, and I need to actually do something about getting a job. As do you.'

Lottie looked at her sharply. 'What?'

'You need to get a job and earn some money,' Sara said firmly. 'You've got ages before university and you're not just floating about here all summer doing nothing. You need to pull your weight financially.'

Lottie closed her eyes tragically. 'Dad will give me some money.'

'Lottie!'

Lottie's eyes flew open. 'What's so wrong with that?'

'Everything. You cannot rely on Dad as a meal ticket.'

Lottie raised an eyebrow at her. Sara held up her hand. 'I know. I know. Which is precisely why I feel so strongly about it. I was wrong, Lottie, not to earn my own money. If you live off someone else, it makes you too vulnerable. You always need to be able to stand on your own two feet.'

'Women's lib, coming from my mother.' Lottie laughed, raising her face to the sun.

'I didn't think anyone used that term anymore. But yes, I mean it. Women should not depend on men.'

'Do you feel bitter?' Lottie turned to look curiously at her.

Sara shrugged. 'I did. But I'm not sure I do now. More than anything, I feel, well, excited about the future.'

178

'Weird that Dad buggering off with someone else has made you stand on your own two feet.'

'Thanks. So delicately phrased. It was a savage kind of way to have to change my life, but it's done me good, yes. I was far too complacent.'

'Could you see Dad here?'

Sara laughed. 'Could you?'

'No. No way.'

'This is mine,' Sara said. 'And I like it that way.'

'When did you last speak to Em?'

'A couple of weeks ago.' A look of gloom passed over Sara's face.

'You two have got to make it up,' Lottie pointed out.

'We haven't exactly fallen out,' Sara said slowly. 'It's more unspoken, I suppose . . . she seems to think that moving here was unjustified and I think she's still angry with me for leaving London. And she . . .'

'Sides with Dad,' Lottie finished off for her. 'She's still living at home most of the time with him, you know. I don't know why she bothers to keep that flat. I bet Dad's paying the rent too, she's such a jammy git.'

'They were always close,' Sara said. 'Very similar, in lots of ways.'

'Yup,' Lottie said, watching a gull wheel overhead. 'He always loved her much more than me,' she added, in a calm, factual voice.

'No!' Sara said, shocked, although she knew this was true. 'He loves you both the same.'

'That's bollocks, and you know it, Mum. It doesn't matter. I came to terms with it ages ago. He thinks I'm a wimp. Not brave and feisty like Em. I don't stand up to him like she does. You know, in lots of ways Dad . . . he isn't always right, is he? It was like at home we were always made to think that he was right and we had to listen to him, and you used to defer to him all the time. Well, now I know he isn't perfect. He's a very selfish man.' She shrugged, her mouth turned down at the corner. 'I don't know how to talk to him. I can't think of anything to say. When he rings we're like really hesitant with each other and we can't talk about anything *real*, it's all just platitudes, how are you, what's the weather like, how's work? It is quite freaky. It's like not having a real dad.'

'Maybe you should go and stay with him for a while. Build bridges.'

'But you need me here,' Lottie said.

'No I don't. Not all the time. I mean, I love having you here but you mustn't feel you can't go off . . .'

'I know. I'll plan a holiday, go and see some mates.'

'And get a job. You could work in Fowey, there are lots of cafés and shops which must have holiday work.'

'Nag, nag.' Lottie grinned and reached over to touch Sara's arm. 'But I can't leave you,' she said, peering into her mother's eyes. 'You need me here as spiritual support.'

'Feck off,' Sara said.

'Mother! You swore!'

'Not technically. Anyway,' Sara said, turning her own face to the sun. 'I'm all better now. I think I can just about manage without you for a few days.'

Sara was tidying up the kitchen when Lottie wandered in half an hour later, her arms full of washing. 'I just spoke to Em on her mobile,' she muttered through the clothes, which she then dumped on the floor in front of the washing machine.

'And?'

'I've arranged to see her on Wednesday. She said what about having lunch with Dad too, and I said OK. Is that cool with you? Look, Mum, *why* don't you come? Please? You've got to see Em, it's getting weird.

And maybe Dad too. I would like to see him, actually. We have got to be adult about this,' she added.

Sara laughed, bending down to begin stuffing the clothes into the machine, noting that Matt's old cashmere jumper was in the middle of Lottie's pile of washing. She lifted it out, and put it on top of the machine ready for hand-washing. 'Lots, do be careful. I know this is old and full of holes, but you'll ruin it if it goes on too hot a wash.'

'Never mind that,' Lottie said, impatiently. 'Will you come with me? I think Em really misses you, although she'd never say it.'

Sara straightened up, her face creased with thought. It did worry her a great deal that she hadn't seen Emily since moving to Cornwall, and whenever she rang to ask Emily to come down, there was always a reason why she couldn't come. She seemed so involved in her new job, her life in London with her friends, and with Matt. With Matt and possibly Karina? Now that was an odd thought. She could not imagine Emily taking kindly at all to another woman in her father's life, let alone one practically her age.

'Does she see, um . . .' Sara clicked the machine door shut and began to pour in the washing powder. She noticed that Lottie had previously filled the wrong tray, she'd have to clear it out – how very annoying. Lottie was so careless.

'Karina?' Lottie said. 'Yes. She doesn't like her at all.'

'Dad's girlfriend,' Sara mused. 'What a bizarre concept.'

'What do we call her? Girlfriend? Partner?'

'She's not really old enough to be a partner,' Sara said. 'More like a ward, really.'

Lottie snorted. 'You're not acting at all like you used to, you know. What with swearing and fancying younger men . . .'

'I do not fancy younger men!'

Lottie raised an eyebrow at her. 'Oh, really? So why are you so keen to warn me off the lovely Ricky, then? "He's far too old for you," ' Lottie said, mimicking her mother's voice. Sara picked up a sock which had sneaked away from the washing pile and threw it at her.

'Rubbish. He may be too old for you, but he's far too young for me. Besides, even though I feel much happier I am certainly not ready to begin dating.'

'Thank God for that. I'm not sure I could cope with a mother with a sex life.'

'Lottie!'

'Well, it's true.'

'I promise I am not intending to rush off with anyone. So does Emily see them, together? Come on, I can cope, I'm a grown-up. I won't tell her that you told me.'

'Yes,' said Lottie. 'She does. Which I think must be beyond freaky.'

'And is she − Karina − actually living with Dad? That must be very uncomfortable with Em there most of the time.'

'This is like twenty questions. Do you want to know? Does it help?'

'I'm not sure it helps, but yes, I think I do want to know.'

'Well, she is, on and off. You know Dad's got a buyer for the apartment? He says it's too big for him now.'

So that's probably why he is pushing for divorce, Sara thought. He wants to get our finances settled. How do I feel about our home being sold? She thought hard. Nothing. She felt nothing. This was home now.

'Karina doesn't live there all the time,' Lottie continued. 'I think she's got a place of her own as well.'

'Ah. And how does Emily feel about it?'

'Livid,' Lottie shrugged. 'But there's nothing she can

do. I don't think Karina is all that thrilled with Emily living at home either. I guess Dad's caught in the middle of them, ha, ha. Serves him right. I get the impression that Emily might have met her match with Karina, you know. She's just as tricky as she is. How weird for Dad, to have to try to keep the peace between his girlfriend and his daughter. Anyway, Mum, make a decision. You're going to have to see Dad's solicitor anyway and it'll do you good to go to London. You need to see your friends. How long has it been since you saw Catherine? Em said she met her in Harvey Nicks the other day and she practically pinned her to the wall to get all the latest news about you.'

'This is like having my own personal psychiatrist. Catherine does keep leaving messages on the answerphone but, oh, I just can't be bothered to call her back, I know it's awful but I don't want to talk about how I *feel*. It seems such a long time ago, almost a different life. What I'm worried about is that if I go to London it'll all get stirred up again and I don't want to feel like that . . . it took me such a long time to feel even remotely normal.'

'But you *have* to face things,' Lottie said impatiently. 'Dad is always going to be my Dad, even if I think he's been a pillock. And I think you need to have at least some kind of relationship with him, if only for our sakes.'

'You're getting awfully wise, Lottie. It's a bit worrying. Who is the parent here?'

'It's being the victim of a broken home,' Lottie said dramatically. 'I have been forced to grow old before my time.'

'Enough already,' Sara said. 'All right. I'll come.'

183

Chapter Thirteen

Sara could not rid herself of the feeling, as she sat on the train heading towards London, that she was travelling from Arcadia into Hades. She had risen that morning, very early, to walk Hector before they left, having arranged with Helen that she would come and let him out at lunchtime. She promised him, as she held his big head between her hands and his whole body drooped with the realization that he was being left behind alone, that she would be back *soon*.

She had taken the path leading down to the cove just as the sun was rising, and the air was very still. The rooks were beginning to flap from tree to tree, their glossy black bodies silhouetted against the pale sky. As she had stepped out of the front door she had found a black feather lying in the grass. Turning it over in her hand, she marvelled at the beauty of the colours – rather than being uniformly black, it shone with flashes of iridescent green, turquoise shimmering at the tips. She held it against her cheek as she walked down the path, avoiding the little brown and yellow spiders which scuttled away across the pebbles.

Reaching the point where the path became stone steps, she looked down at the sea. Twenty feet below her, the early morning tide surged against the rocks at the base of the cliff, breaking into a spray of foam as the waves met the land. The sea was very clear today as the wind was relatively low, and just beneath the surface of the water she could see submerged rocks, gleaming ghostly white, like bare bones. Overhead, the gulls languidly rose and fell in the air currents, calling to each other. Sara smiled, thinking of another notice she had seen on the board at Polperro. It was a photo-copied picture of an extremely cross-looking gull with a message below it, 'This is the enemy! Do not feel the gulls – they WILL bite!'

Which was rather unfair, she thought – they were hardly the enemy, more opportunistic creatures who were extremely partial to a sandwich or an ice-cream cone. She'd had to stop herself laughing, a couple of days before, when a particularly large gull had swooped down by the harbour in Polperro and swiped an entire baguette from the hand of a large woman misguidedly wearing shorts. She couldn't laugh out loud because the woman had been genuinely frightened by the great bird swooping down towards her with its wings outstretched, but the raid had been so flawlessly timed and executed it was all Sara could do to stop herself clapping and shouting, 'Bravo!'

She was becoming much fonder of the little town – at first, like Lottie, she'd thought it was rather touristy, with too many pasty and ice-cream stalls and shops selling tat like plastic sandals and key-rings. But the last time she had walked there with Hector, she had taken the time to wander the quieter narrow streets which led up the hill, away from the harbour. There, she had found much more interesting shops selling beautiful paintings by local artists, antiques, pottery and unusual clothes such as brightly-coloured ethnic skirts and flip-flops decorated with shells and beads.

At the time she had wished she had brought more money, so she could have bought a pair for Lottie and for Emily. She had returned, yesterday, and bought them each a pair. She would give Emily hers today – as a token, a small peace offering.

Approaching Polperro on foot via the high, winding mountain path was the best way to fully appreciate the charm of the old town, she thought. Turning the headland, the town lay before you, a picture-postcard jumble of white, pale blue and pink-washed cottages, stacked in higgledy-piggledy rows up the steep sides of the inlet. The moss-covered stone walls of the harbour formed a small lagoon and brightly-painted fishing boats bobbed on the dark green water. When Emily and Lottie were young they had loved a book called *The Mousehole Cat*. The story told of a cat who lived with a fisherman in a Cornish town which looked very much like Polperro. Every night the local people would come out of their cottages to hold up lanterns, guiding the little fishing fleet home into the safety of the harbour walls. She remembered the charm of the illustrations. One night the fisherman's boat had been all but engulfed by a huge grey Storm Cat, which curled its dangerous grey paws around the fisherman's little boat, tossing the boat about on the violent sea and preventing it from reaching the security of the harbour. Eventually the Storm Cat was driven back by the lights of the villagers, who would not leave their posts until the boat was safe. The girls, snuggled down in their pyjamas in bed, demanded she read it again and again, loving the sensation of being scared for the fisherman from the comfort, safety and warmth of their own beds.

Sara leant back against the rough material of the train seat. In front of her lay a glossy magazine, unread, and a particularly nasty chemical-tasting cappuccino, which tasted nothing like real coffee. They had left the cottage just after half past seven, Hector staring forlornly out at them through the kitchen window as Sara backed the Volvo into the lane.

'I wish dogs could read,' Lottie said, looking at his mournful face. 'What will he do all day?'

'Sleep sporadically, turn repeatedly in circles, lick himself and quite possibly chew the leg of one of the kitchen chairs in retaliation at being left,' Sara predicted with a fair degree of accuracy.

She was astonished at how much of a wrench leaving had been and realized, with a start, this was the first time she had travelled more than ten miles from the cottage in months. Maybe Lottie was right – maybe she was in danger of becoming a hermit. She must get a job, if only to force herself back out into the big wide world.

Next to her, Lottie was sitting slumped against the window, fast asleep, exhausted by such an early start, a small trickle of transparent saliva tracing its way down the golden skin of her chin. How brown she was, and then she looked down at her own hands, realizing she was equally tanned. The pleasure faded, however, when she looked at them more closely. Hands did reveal your age in the most brutal fashion, she thought. Whereas Lottie's hands, currently cupped under her chin, were smooth and beautiful, hers were creased with hundreds of tiny criss-crossed lines, the skin pouching over her knuckles when she flexed her wrist. On the third finger of her left hand was a white band – odd that the sun hadn't filled in the gap. Perhaps the skin was too deeply indented.

Her wedding, engagement and eternity rings lay in a little jewelled box on top of the chest of drawers in her bedroom. She had taken them all off, that first night in the service flat, and there they remained, amidst a jumble of earrings. Hidden, but not forgotten. Occasionally she thought about giving them to the girls, or even throwing them, symbolically, into the sea. Then she thought that would be an absurdly over-dramatic gesture, and besides, they were rather beautiful. Both Emily and Lottie, she knew, would not want her to throw the rings away and they did hold, if she was honest, a great deal of sentimental value. Still a part of her, if not worn next to her skin.

This morning she had chosen what to wear with a great deal of care, while consciously trying not to envisage possible scenarios. Even so, she couldn't help herself. How would she feel when she saw Matt? She pictured him turning, seeing her . . . How would he react? Would he look hunted, nervous, guilty? Lottie had said he had behaved quite differently towards her before she had left London, far less confident and take-charge. Sara tried to picture a humble Matt, and failed. She decided he was much more likely to be businesslike and detached, and hoped they would be able to treat each other politely and calmly in front of the girls. But oh, what would he think of her? Would he see a frumpy, plump middle-aged woman and immediately compare her to Karina, counting himself a lucky man? No, she said, firmly, looking at herself in her bedroom mirror as she slipped on a discreet pair of pearl earrings. I am not going to 'go there', as Lottie would say. Who cares? Who cares what he sees? I am comfortable in my own skin and I do not care what he thinks of me. I no longer need his approval to feel good about myself.

Taking a sip of the vile coffee and grimacing, she glanced down at the blue ruffled linen shirt she had bought with Lottie, and her pale grey linen trousers. It was certainly a different look, more relaxed and up-to-date. Gazing at herself in the full-length mirror behind her wardrobe door, she'd been pleased. She did look slimmer and the sun had not only tanned her skin but turned her hair a lighter shade of gold. The grey wisps looked less obvious and she liked the way her longer hairstyle framed her face. No one's going to take me for thirty, she thought, but I could get away with being in my forties. Above all, she thought, I look happy.

Please don't let today threaten that. Don't take away my self-confidence and make me feel insecure. Leave me be, Matt. For what felt like the hundredth time, she wondered why on earth she had agreed to this meeting. I was fine as I was, she thought.

She had also chosen to wear a new pair of shoes, raffia wedge sandals, with a brown and orange flower above her toes. Hmm. She leant back to look at them under the train table. Maybe they were a bit too hippie-looking. They had looked pretty when she had tried them on in the shop in Fowey, but now she wondered if they looked rather – well, girlish. A bit too much as if she was trying to look young and she really did not want to give that impression. She had kept her make-up light, as she always did if she even bothered with make-up at all, just pale pink lipstick, a little eyeliner around her eyes and a quick flick of mascara.

'D'you want anything from the trolley?' A woman wearing a stained overall stopped by her seat, and Sara's head jerked up from the magazine she'd been gazing at without taking in a word.

'No,' she said, 'No thank you.' Should she wake Lottie? She nudged her. 'Darling,' she whispered, 'do you want a drink, or anything?'

Lottie moaned, opening her eyes slowly, extending

189

long, tapered fingers, ending in bitten nails, out in front of her. 'No, thanks,' she said, looking out of the window. 'Are we nearly there? I was like totally asleep.'

'I know,' Sara said. 'There's about two hours to go. No, we're fine, thanks,' she said, to the woman, who clattered her trolley away down the aisle.

Lottie slumped back against her seat. 'God,' she said. 'It is such a long way. Why didn't we drive?'

'Because that would have taken longer and . . .' Sara didn't want to admit that the thought of driving in London frightened her, because that sounded rather pathetic. After all, she had driven around London for nearly thirty years. 'We might not be able to find anywhere to park,' she added a touch lamely. 'I'm terrified of getting clamped, and there's the congestion charge to pay as well. It just seemed much less hassle to come on the train.'

'Where are we meeting Dad?' Lottie asked sleepily.

'A restaurant near the station,' Sara replied. The meeting had been arranged initially between Lottie and Emily, and then Sara and Matt had finalized the details via brief text messages. Sara gave thanks for texting – it meant she hadn't had to speak to him directly on the phone. No matter how terse the conversation, she would have been able to gauge so much from the sound and inflection of his voice, by what he didn't say as much as the information exchanged. He had even managed one, brief, joke – 'Glad 2 c u r texting,' he said, in reference to the fact she'd never mastered the art before.

'And what am I going to do while you go to see the solicitor?' Lottie asked.

They had arranged that after lunch they would go on to see Matt's lawyer. He'd been Sara's lawyer too, not that she had ever needed him, and she supposed now she'd have to get her own family law solicitor as she doubted the sleepy practice she'd used to buy the cottage in Liskeard would welcome taking on a divorce case. *If* it came to that, she told herself.

Having made the difficult decision to agree to meet Matt, Sara thought she'd rather get everything over with in one day.

'You can shop?' Sara suggested.

'Yeah, right, what with? As if I have any money.'

'I can lend you ten pounds.'

'Yay. I'll go completely mad in Topshop with that, won't I? Why do you have to see the solicitor, anyway? Why couldn't you and Dad talk about all that stuff over lunch? You're bound to have rows if you start talking through lawyers.'

'Because I don't want to discuss things like that in front of you and Emily,' Sara said, rather primly. 'It's private.'

'Oh, for God's sake,' Lottie said, looking out of the window, at the countryside flashing past. The sky, which had been a clear duck-egg blue at home, had turned pale grey, the clouds overhead threatening rain.

'What *are* we going to talk about?' she said, turning back to her mother.

'I don't know,' Sara replied, picking up her magazine. 'It was you who insisted we all have lunch together,' she pointed out, flicking over the pages.

'You're not going to make this really weird, are you?' Lottie turned to look at her accusingly.

Sara put the article she had been glancing at down. 'What do you mean?'

'You know. Sit in silence, or start an argument, or bring up . . . you know.' Her brows furrowed at the thought.

'Well, what can we talk about?' Sara asked patiently. 'The weather? The cottage? The flat Dad intends to

191

buy? How much money he wants to give us? Whether he has any plans to marry Karina?' As soon as she said this, she wished she hadn't. She had meant it to sound facetious, but in fact it made her sound bitter. No! That was absolutely not what she intended. She was intending to be mature and gracious and relaxed – and just a teeny bit patronizing towards him. She was, after all, the injured party – the person with moral rectitude on her side. She would be patience on a monument, she thought, perfectly able to deal with whatever transpired.

Lottie sighed. 'Please, Mum.' She lifted a hand and put it over her mother's. 'Just chill. I know this isn't easy for you, but it isn't going to be easy for Em and me either – or Dad.' She looked down at their hands. 'And I don't quite know what to expect, to be honest.' She snorted suddenly. 'What if he asks me to start calling him Matt rather than Dad? Last time I spoke to him on the phone he kept saying "cool" – most off-putting.'

Sara laughed.

'Just don't ask me to call you Sara,' Lottie added, shuddering. 'I don't want you to be my friend. I've got enough friends. I need you to be my mum.'

Sara gently slipped her hand out from under Lottie's and, putting her arm around her thin shoulders, hugged her. Lottie let her head rest against her mother's shoulder. 'I will try to make sure it is perfectly civilized,' Sara said. 'Dreadful cliché, but it is important we all try to be adult about this. Raking up the past and bickering isn't going to make a scrap of difference and will only make the situation much worse. We've all moved on, haven't we?'

'It's been less than eight months,' Lottie reminded her, quietly. 'Since Dad walked out on the night of his birthday.'

Sara looked at her for a long moment. 'I'm sorry,

darling. I didn't mean to sound insensitive. It's just that I've had to really wind myself up for this and I don't want to think too deeply about how I *will* feel, in all honesty. I think we just need to keep things fairly calm and yes, a little superficial. I'm not sure any of us are ready for confrontation.'

'Let's hope so,' Lottie mumbled, sliding her chin down to her chest, pulling the ends of the sleeves of her jumper over her hands. Sara thought how sore her bitten nails looked.

'You must stop doing that,' she said. 'I'll buy you something from the chemist in Fowey.'

'Whatever,' Lottie said.

Sara's heart was beating unnaturally quickly as they stood in the taxi rank outside the railway station, and she had to tell herself to breathe slowly, thankful they had escaped from the crowds on the platform. She had accidentally stumbled and almost fallen to her knees amidst the rush of people heading towards the ticket barrier when she had got off the train. Several trains had arrived at the same time and there were so many commuters talking urgently into their mobile phones, a sheer, suffocating weight of humanity, pushing relentlessly forward. No one stopped to help her – Lottie was a few feet ahead and had not noticed she had tripped.

Standing outside in the street, Sara breathed in the hot, arid smell of traffic. Around her rumbled the constant sound of voices, car horns, brakes squealing, car alarms and in the distance a police siren wailed. Her senses felt so assaulted, she thankfully climbed into a taxi and slammed the door on the cacophony of the city.

As Lottie sat beside her, texting a friend, Sara gazed out of the window. So many people flowed along the

193

pavements they became less distinguishable individuals, more a homogeneous mass without discernable characteristics. The buildings towered over her oppressively, blocking out the sky.

Suddenly overcome by nerves, she plucked apprehensively at the ruffle on the front of her linen shirt. 'Do you think this looks OK? Not too girly?'

Lottie looked up, briefly, from the screen of her phone. 'Will you stop fussing? No, Mother, trust me. You look lovely. You *do* look lovely, actually,' she said, with some surprise, examining her more closely. 'You've really caught the sun. Have I?' She turned her face to Sara, closing her eyes and pursing her lips, sucking in her cheeks in the impression of a model.

'Yes, you know you have. You look lovely.'

'I don't look like I come from Cornwall, do I?'

'Lottie!'

'Well, some of the people who live there do look a little as if they come from the land that time forgot.'

'I didn't hear that.'

'It's nice to be back,' Lottie remarked, gazing out the window. 'It's nice to see *people*. And, wow, look at all the amazing shops. So much to buy.' She turned to Sara and grinned. 'Don't worry, I love Cornwall too. It's just I'd forgotten how – well, *fun*, it is here.'

Sara saw Matt the moment she pushed open the elegant swing doors to the bar of the restaurant. He was sitting with his back to her, facing Emily, who was wearing a smart black suit she hadn't seen before. She stopped dead, and Lottie bumped into her from behind.

There he was. Just from looking at his outline she could instantly conjure up in her mind's eye every contour of his face, the shape of his eyes, the way his hair stood up from his forehead, the planes of his cheek, the lines running down each side of his mouth which deepened and curved when he smiled. She took a deep breath, just as Lottie gave her a little push in the small of her back.

'Go *on*,' she whispered in her ear. 'It's OK. I'm here.'

His broad shoulders, in a dark jacket she didn't recognize, seemed tense. Usually he lolled in a chair but today he was sitting very upright, a small gap between his body and the back of his chair. She had to stop herself calling out his name, but just at that moment he turned, as if he knew instinctively she had come. They stared at each other, a lifetime together held in that one concentrated moment.

'Dad!' Lottie broke the spell, running past Sara to throw her arms around Matt's neck. She saw him reach up to put his arms around her, his eyes suddenly clenched shut, the lines of his face etched with love as he held his youngest daughter.

Sara moved forward, awkwardly, to stand a few feet away from them.

'Hello, Matt,' she said. Lottie's eyes were shining, like a child unwrapping a present. You do love him, Sara thought. Of course you do. Oh Matt. Oh, Matt. He lifted his face to look at her over Lottie's shoulder. His eyes were full of tears, his mouth twisted into the ghost of a smile. My husband. My beloved husband. You could not be more familiar to me. What have we done? Our family is here, the four of us together. How can we have initiated these splits, these sharp angles which wound us all? How can we call ourselves adults? I'm sorry, his eyes spoke. I am so very sorry.

For several moments they stared at each other, as Lottie looked from her father to her mother. Sara found she was smiling, as was Matt, and in that one instant their eyes said I love you, oh I love you, how could I have thought it would be different? I know you better than anyone else in the world. What *have* we done?

'Dad?' Emily's voice cut through the moment. His gaze jerked away from Sara's, and the connection was lost. He coughed, twisting back in his chair away from her, leaving Sara standing behind him, embarrassed. Lottie stood up from bending over her father and pulled out a chair.

'Sit here, Mum,' she said, her expression scared, watchful. Don't cry, her eyes pleaded with Sara. Please. Not now.

Mutely, Sara moved forward and looked over at Emily, who was imperiously holding out an empty wine glass towards her father. Emily's gaze flicked up at her. 'Hi,' she said. 'How was the journey?'

'Long,' Lottie cut in, swiftly. 'It took ages, didn't it, Mum?' The words rattled out of her. 'We were going to drive but Mum thought it would take even longer and she was worried about finding a parking space, and now you have the congestion charge it was just . . .'

'Enough already,' Emily said, holding up a manicured hand. 'I don't need a blow by blow account, OK?'

'How are you?' Sara said to Emily.

'I'm fine,' Emily said, in a brittle fashion. 'How are you?'

'I'm really . . . well, I'm fine too. It's lovely to see you. You look very . . . smart.'

'Thanks. I'm normally a bit more scruffy for work but I thought I'd make an effort because Dad was bringing us somewhere so nice.' She looked over at Lottie critically. 'Glad you didn't bother to dress up, Lots. God, you're not still wearing that old jumper, are you?'

'It used to be mine,' Matt said recognizing it with

196

surprise. 'Mum bought it for me, in Scotland . . .' His voice tailed off as Sara looked at him.

'I remember.' She smiled. 'That was ages ago, I'm amazed it hasn't fallen to bits.'

He returned her smile. 'You look great. That's a new shirt. And new trousers.'

'Mmm. I treated myself.'

'You've lost weight.'

'Have I?'

'Yes. It suits you. I like your hair like that.'

Out of the corner of her eye, she saw his hand move, as if he was going to reach over and brush a hair away from her cheek. Her eyes met his, and they both froze. Don't touch me! her eyes warned – don't, please don't, I could not bear that. For a second they stared at each other, appalled. They no longer had the freedom to touch.

'Would you like a drink, madam?'

She turned to find a waiter hovering by her chair. She looked at Matt and Emily's glasses. 'Yes,' she said. 'I'd like a glass of white wine, please.'

'House wine, or we have a list of different wines by the glass. Perhaps if I bring you a . . .'

'House white will be fine,' Sara told him.

'You don't normally drink at lunchtime,' Matt remarked, surprised.

'Now I do,' Sara said. 'Things have changed.'

Lottie, who'd been holding out her wrist to show Emily a new bracelet, glanced over at her, warningly.

'They have,' Matt said, frowning, and looking down at the menu. 'They certainly have.'

Well, of course they have, you bloody man, Sara screamed inside. You changed them! Here we are, the four of us, having lunch, and it could be lovely, and normal, and instead we are about to talk about divorce and our two children feel as if they have to walk on

197

eggshells and nothing will ever be the same again because you took that selfish step, that eminently selfish step of thinking you had to have something that you wanted – not needed – and in that one, thoughtless, greedy action you broke our lives. Don't make me feel bad about any of this. Don't you dare, don't you dare make me feel as if this awkward, tense, surreal situation is any of my fault. I am not going to have that. Her hackles were raised, and the immense, warming sense of love she had felt when they first saw each other was receding, to be replaced by all the feelings she had spent so long suppressing – anger, bitterness, helplessness . . .

'What would you like?' Matt handed her the menu. The words swam before her eyes.

I'd like this year never to have happened, she thought. That is what I would like. But I would like the woman I am now to be the woman who was married to you then, because if that was the case you might have thought twice before deceiving me.

'I'll have the scallops,' she said, and suddenly had an intense longing to be out of this smart, formal atmosphere and sitting in Pip's.

'As a main course? No starter? You can have one, if you like.'

Well, thank you, Sara thought. How generous. 'I don't need to be told what to eat,' she said, coolly. 'I'm not really hungry.'

She looked up, and saw Lottie's mouth was twitching.

Emily glanced over anxiously at her sister, and her sharp expression softened. 'You OK, Lots?' she murmured.

Lottie sniffled, and reached down into her bag for a tissue. Matt shifted in his chair, uneasily.

'So tell me about the house,' he said brightly.

'It's great,' Lottie said, looking up. 'We love it, don't we, Mum?'

Emily's expression changed. 'I'm glad you've both settled in so well,' she said sarcastically.

'That wasn't what Lottie meant,' Sara said.

'Whatever.'

'I'd love you to come and stay,' Sara said. 'Maybe at a weekend, or when you have a holiday?'

Emily glanced over at her father. 'I'm really busy,' she said.

Matt looked from his elder daughter to Sara. 'I don't mind . . .' he said, then stopped abruptly.

'You don't need your father's permission,' Sara said.

'Perhaps I just don't really want to come,' Emily replied, staring at her mother.

'Oh.' Sara nodded, her heart beating faster. There was a deathly silence around the table. 'Well, that's brutally honest, if nothing else. It's up to you, of course. You're an adult now.'

'Please can we not have a row?' asked Lottie faintly.

Matt smiled at her. 'No one is rowing, Lots.' He raised his hand in the air, to signal a waiter to come and take their order. 'We had better order,' he said, glancing at his watch. 'We've to see my solicitor at three, and then I've a meeting I couldn't rearrange, he's flying in from the States.'

'I need to get back too,' Sara said.

'Oh?' Matt replied, raising his eyebrows.

'Hector,' Lottie explained. 'Mum hates leaving him for too long.'

'Oh yes,' Matt said. 'Hector. How is he?'

'Still a Labrador,' Sara said. Lottie snorted.

'I mean, does he like living in Cornwall?'

'Seems to,' Sara said. 'We all do, the three of us. It's very healthy. We go for lots of long walks.'

'How jolly,' Emily muttered.

'I am sure,' Sara said, keeping her voice level, 'that if you came you would enjoy it. Try to meet me half way, Em.' Their eyes locked, and in that instant Sara saw how lost and lonely her eldest daughter was actually feeling, behind the bravado.

'I miss you,' Sara said simply.

Emily's face seemed to crumple. 'I miss you too,' she said, quietly.

'Let's go and eat,' Matt said.

'I hear you're moving,' Sara remarked, as the waiter brought their main course.

'That's right. I'm glad Emily's keeping you up to speed.'

'Why shouldn't I know?' Sara asked. 'Is it a secret?'

Matt laughed nervously. 'Of course not.' He put his glass firmly down on the table, as if determined to wrest control of the direction this conversation was taking.

'It's not far from home. Smaller, but then I don't need the space.'

'Don't you?' Sara said. 'Why?'

'Because Emily's got her own flat and I can't imagine Lottie will stay with me very often when she's at university – although you're very welcome, Lottie, obviously – and, besides . . .'

'You're going to live there alone?' Sara hadn't meant to say anything like this, but the words just tumbled out of her. Both Lottie and Emily stared at her, appalled. Matt hurriedly reached forward and took a long sip of his wine.

'Yes,' he said. He and Emily glanced at each other, and then Emily looked away.

Sara had almost finished eating her scallops – which proved to be delicious – when Matt said they must talk about money.

'We've got to start making some practical decisions about the future. Given that . . .' He looked down at his empty plate, as if searching for inspiration. 'Given that Mum has the, um, Cornwall, and the contracts are close to being exchanged on my new home – flat – I want you all to be secure,' he added. His mouth turned down at the corners, and, for the first time during the meal, Sara felt a tug at the very edge of her heart.

'Maybe I have been . . .' he could not meet Sara's gaze, and he looked over her shoulder out of the window. He took a deep breath. 'Maybe things have . . . I don't want any of you to feel that I am not supporting you. I have a responsibility to you all,' he continued, looking around the table, 'and that will never change, whatever happens. As you know,' he said to Lottie and Emily, 'you both have trusts . . .'

'I didn't know I had a trust,' Lottie said quickly. 'Did you, Em?' Emily shook her head.

'Well, you have,' Matt said. 'It just didn't seem, there was no need to go into it before. Anyway, I can release some money to buy you a flat when you feel ready, Emily, and for you, Lottie, if you want a place of your own in your second year at university, so you don't have to waste money on rent. It'll get you started on the property ladder. I'm going to set up a monthly allowance for you both, for clothes and holidays, things like that. Now, Sara . . .' He turned to her, in a businesslike fashion.

'I don't need your money, Matt,' Sara said, putting down her fork and looking at him coolly. Matt glanced at her, irritated.

'I know you didn't want to take money initially but principles are one thing – the reality is that . . .' He was beginning to sound pompous.

Sara held up the palm of her hand, as if to stop him. 'I appreciate what you are trying to do for the girls –

but I really don't want them to think they can just click their fingers and you'll send round a wad of cash. It doesn't give them much of an incentive to work, does it, if you are going to supply them with an allowance indefinitely? Don't you think this has more to do with obviating your guilt than a desire to provide?'

Matt stiffened in his chair. 'I don't think that is fair at all. I am their father. Frankly, I can do what I want. I don't need your permission to give money to my children.'

Sara took a deep breath. I am not going to lose my temper, she thought. 'Isn't it fair? I think it is, actually. They are my daughters too, and I have a say in this. I happen to think it's good for them to have to work for their own money. I don't mind you giving them the deposit for a flat, but I draw the line at a monthly allowance.'

'It's up to Dad,' Emily said quickly.

'Oh, is it? I suppose you would be keen to agree, though, wouldn't you?'

'Oh shut up!' Emily shouted. The people on the next table looked over at them in amazement. 'What has it got to do with you? I am so sick of your holier than thou attitude, that we can all manage on a shoestring. Well, I don't want to manage on a shoestring. I don't want to live in a horrible falling-down shitty little cottage in the arse end of nowhere just so you can prove a point and make Dad feel really bad! I'm not surprised he left!' Her shoulders heaved. She threw down her napkin and ran out of the restaurant.

'I'm sorry,' Matt said, and put his hand over Sara's. 'I'm sure she didn't mean it.'

Sara snatched her hand away. 'Don't touch me,' she said sharply. Lottie pushed her chair away from the table, glanced despairingly between her parents, and rushed after her sister.

'Ah,' Matt said, watching Lottie's departing back. 'That went well, didn't it? Well done, Sara.'

Sara sank her head into her hands, groaning. 'That was not my fault! What did you expect, Matt? That we'd meet up and it would all be happy families and you'd give us money and pat us on the head and we'd go away contented as clams? This isn't about money! It's about the fact that the children love us, both together, and it's breaking them in two to see us like this. Emily wasn't furious about money, she was furious about the fact that we are living hundreds of miles apart and that she has to see you with . . .'

There was a long pause. 'I wondered when you would bring that up,' Matt said

Sara looked up at him. She felt mentally and physically exhausted, and suddenly had an intense longing to be at home. 'I don't necessarily mean . . .' she said, wearily. 'Honestly, Matt. Of course it has hurt me, you'll never know how much, but I think I'm finally over it now and if she makes you happy then . . . fine. Get on with it. Do whatever you want to do. But be sensitive to the children's needs. They don't just need money, Matt, they need your time. They don't want anything to change – we – you – took away their security, their home, the parents they took for granted.'

Matt bristled. 'I see Emily a great deal. It's your fault that Lottie won't see me – I've asked her time and time again to stay. Actually, I was trying to sort everything out. You may not think money is important, Sara, but then you've never had to live in the real world.'

Sara stared at him horrified. 'It's my fault I didn't work? It's my fault I dropped my career to have your children? Oh, thanks, Matt. Thanks very much. I am so glad to think that over twenty years of my life were apparently a waste of time. I wasn't living in the real

203

world, was I, I was a spoilt little housewife? So now I know.'

'That wasn't what I meant,' he said. 'Honestly, Sara, you have become very argumentative and difficult.'

Sara laughed. 'You mean I don't agree with you? No, Matt, I don't agree with you and if I don't like what you are saying I will bloody well say so.'

'Sara! You never swear.'

'Oh, yes, I do, Matt. I do now.' She sighed. 'Look. This isn't getting us anywhere. Neither of us is completely blameless and I'm not going to start recriminating. What's the point? What's done is done. Here we are. Apart. Possibly even about to divorce. Maybe you're right. Maybe my attitude is upsetting the girls. Emily has a problem with me, she always has had. You were her favourite and now we've split the family right down the middle, haven't we? Well done us. Full marks for excellent parenting. At least we waited until they were old enough to cope. No. Scrub that. They are never old enough to cope. You know, Matt, it is better we don't meet. It's always going to end in chaos because there is just too much – just too much history, feelings, emotions for us ever to be calm and normal with each other because the situation is so very far from normal. You live your life, Matt, and I'll live mine. Let's keep communication down to the bare minimum.'

Matt put down his napkin and gazed out of the window, before turning to look at Sara.

'Are you happy?' He looked long and hard into her eyes.

'Don't do this,' she said. 'That isn't fair. I haven't asked you if you are happy.'

'You asked me about – Karina.'

'I know. Maybe I shouldn't have. I'm sorry. That is your private life. Look, let's just keep things nice and polite, shall we? Let's not try and be honest.'

'I miss you,' he said.

Sara sat back in her chair and stared at him. 'Oh. What do you expect me to say? Thank you?'

'Don't be silly. Do you miss me?'

'Oh, no, I am *not* doing this. Do you want to know the truth, Matt? That you ripped out my heart when that bastard Richard stood up and said what he did and brought my world crashing down around my ears? The safe, cosy, cushy little life that you obviously despised and bored you, because otherwise you wouldn't have . . .'

He reached over to grasp her hand, so hard she winced. 'It's not as simple as that,' he hissed. 'You have no idea the . . .'

'What? *What* do I have no idea about? Aside from the obvious deception?'

He looked away and the pulse beat beneath his eye. Under his tan, Sara thought how strained and exhausted he looked. 'Are you OK?' she asked.

He turned back to look at her. 'No,' he said. 'I'm not. Not at all.'

'I have to go,' Emily stood by the table, staring at her parents defiantly. Sara saw how red her eyes looked.

'Darling . . .'

'I have to go back to work. I'll call you, Mum,' she said. Suddenly the hostile set of her shoulders seemed to relax. She bent down to kiss her mother's cheek. 'Look. I'm sorry I went off on one. It's just all so . . . I will try to come down and see you, honestly. As soon as I can. Say bye to Lottie for me, will you?'

'Didn't she come into the loo?'

Emily looked surprised. 'No, I haven't seen her.'

'Tell her to come back, if she's outside,' Sara said. 'Please.'

205

'I will. I'll call you later, Dad. Can I come over tonight?'

He nodded. 'Of course.'

Emily walked away. Suddenly, Sara remembered the shoes. 'Emily!' she called. Her daughter stopped in the doorway. 'What?'

Sara lifted the bag. 'I brought you something.'

Emily walked back to the table. Reaching into the plastic bag her mother was holding out, she pulled out the pretty flip-flops. Without saying a word, she turned them over in her hands, examining the small pink and white shells sewn on to the narrow leather bands. 'They're beautiful,' she said slowly. 'Thanks, Mum.'

'That's OK. I'm sorry they're not very . . .'

Emily shook her head, tears starting in her eyes. 'I love them,' she murmured. Then she turned and walked out of the restaurant.

On the doorsteps of the solicitors, Matt reached up to touch her face, in the way he had when he was saying goodbye. For a heartbeat, she rested her cheek against the warmth of his fingers. And then they had looked at each other without animosity. Don't go, his eyes told her. Please, don't leave me.

You are lost without me, Sara thought. The idea gave her no pleasure. This was a dreadful, chaotic, emotionally draining mess and showed every sign of going on being so for months, years to come. They had found Lottie leaning against a tree in a small park opposite the restaurant, sobbing as if her heart would break. Sara had folded her into her arms, while Matt stood embarrassed and uneasy beside them. 'Shall I leave you?' he asked, but then Lottie had reached out with one arm, without looking up from her mother's embrace, to take Matt's hand and she pulled him,

206

physically pulled him towards her, so Sara had to stand crushed between her daughter and her husband, almost unable to bear the feeling of the warmth of his body, his arms awkwardly looped around the two of them. As soon as he could, he stepped back, and Lottie looked up at him, as if the scales of innocence were falling from her eyes. She held up a hand. 'I'll see you then,' she said coolly. He took a step towards Lottie, but she moved away. 'I'm sorry,' she said, looking down at the hard baked earth by the base of the tree. 'I guess that was rather embarrassing for all of us, wasn't it? I'll try to be more adult in future.'

'Don't,' Matt said, his voice breaking. 'Please.'

'Come on, Mum. Hand me the dough.' Lottie held out her hand, refusing to look at Matt, and Sara reached into her bag.

'Let me . . .' Matt said.

'No,' Lottie said quickly. 'I don't want your money. A tenner is fine. I'll see you at the station, Mum, at five. OK?'

Stuffing the money into the back pocket of her jeans, she walked away from them, hunching her shoulders. Matt and Sara stood together, watching their daughter leave. She looked up at Matt. His expression was incomprehensible.

'Goodbye,' Sara said on the steps of the solicitors, and leant forward to brush her lips against his cheek, his hand still on her face. He smelt as he always did, of aftershave and cigarettes. She took a deep breath, and then stepped back from him.

'Was it . . .?' He gestured upwards, towards the office of his solicitor.

'I don't want it, Matt,' Sara said. 'Put the money in trust for the girls if you want, give it to a cats' home. I don't care.'

'I'm not going to let you starve.'

Sara laughed. 'Stop being so condescending! We're not starving, Matt, honestly. I've still got some of Aunty Lucy's money left and I'm going to get a job.'

Matt raised an eyebrow.

'Don't *do* that. Please. Just let me be. Have some faith in me. I'm perfectly capable of standing on my own two feet, you know. You don't have to support me, or keep me like a kind of pet you no longer want but feel you have to look after.'

He laughed. 'That isn't how I feel about you at all.' He stared at her. 'You're an extraordinary woman, Sara,' he said.

'I know,' she said. 'And that's something I am only just discovering. I have a lot to thank you for, really, although I can't say I felt like that immediately.' She smiled ruefully.

'Can I call you?'

'Why?'

'I don't know. To chat about the girls, I suppose, just to keep in touch . . .' His voice tailed off.

'I'm not sure there is much point, Matt. The girls can call us.'

'I'd just like to think I could pick up the phone and talk to you.'

'You want everything, don't you, Matt? I'm sorry, but it's true.' She shook her head in disbelief. 'You want me at the end of a phone, like some kind of security blanket, and you want the excitement of life with her. It won't wash, Matt. You can't have everything.'

'I'm beginning to realize that,' he said. Then he turned, and walked away.

Sara stood for a moment, watching the easy way he moved. A woman he passed turned to stare at him. Still a head-turner, aren't you, she thought. She closed her eyes wearily. I can't let myself think this. I can't imagine falling back in love with him; have I ever stopped? Honestly, honestly, Sara, have you ever stopped loving him? No, she thought. I haven't. Not even through the anger and the hurt.

At home, once Lottie had fallen exhausted into bed, Sara poured herself a glass of wine. Quietly opening the front door, she stepped out into the twilight of the garden. Hector had been beside himself with joy when he had heard her key in the door, and even brought them the tartan blanket from his basket, which he'd never done before, dragging it down the hall behind him like Marley's chains. He now sat at her feet, looking up at her, as she stared ahead unseeingly. The fir trees rustled as the rooks settled down for the night, and overhead the bats flew, their tiny black shapes darting and swooping in the still, warm night air. Now I know, she thought. Now I know. You are a silly, deluded woman. Let go. Let go.

After Matt had left, she turned round and went back into the solicitor's office, as she needed the loo. She had seen a toilet by reception on the first floor, and thought it wasn't too much of a cheek. She planned to walk back to the station – it was a fair distance, but she had a little time to kill and the weather, although not as hot and sunny as it had been in Cornwall, was warm. She thought she might do some shopping, if she had time, but most of all she wanted to think. To think about the effect Matt still had on her, the way she had felt when he touched her face . . . She put her hand up to feel her cheek where his fingers had lain. The girls were so devastated – was there a chance, any chance, that she might forgive him? He seemed so lost, so desperate to keep in contact. Lost in thought, she climbed the stairs. Halfway up was a window, which looked out on to the street. Idly, she glanced out.

About two hundred yards away a black Porsche was waiting by the kerb on double-yellow lines, the engine running and smoke billowing from the exhaust. Whoever was driving seemed to be revving the engine, and even through the window she could hear the roar of the powerful engine. Her attention caught, she saw a figure which looked very like Matt approaching the car. Looking more closely, her face almost touched the glass. It was Matt – she could see his white shirt, dark jacket slung over his shoulder, the way he ran his hand impatiently through his hair. Hardly able to breathe, she saw the driver's door open. He would have thought she had long gone, she had told him she was getting a taxi back to the station straight away.

Karina stepped out, wearing a beautiful pale blue halter-neck dress, her long dark hair flowing over her tanned shoulders. In the gentle breeze, the silk of her mini-dress clung to her slim thighs. Her mouth was opening and closing angrily, as if arguing, and she was gesticulating as she walked around the front of the car. And then – and then. Matt had put his hands behind her head, underneath her hair, and pulled her towards him. As if to silence her, he bent his head and kissed her so passionately a couple walking down the street towards them stopped to stare. Sara felt as if she might faint. She saw Karina's arms slide up around Matt, her body mould to his, and together they exuded such a white-hot sexuality it was almost indecent. Sara closed her eyes, letting her hand trail down the cold glass.

Chapter Fourteen

Sara had intended to spend the day chasing up the builder, whose name and number Helen had written on an envelope and left on her kitchen table when she had come to walk Hector, while she was in London. She must get on with it, because otherwise the summer would be over and she'd be dealing with builders tramping through the house in the autumn and possibly even winter, bringing in trails of mud and unable to mix concrete in the rain. She had decided she wanted the exterior of the house painted too, once the work was complete, and that had to be done during the dry weather. She had thought long and hard about this, and decided that the cottage should be painted pink. Not a vibrant pink, but the gentle, washed pink she had seen on many other Cornish cottages. In the sunlight, it would appear mellow, and in the winter, when the skies turned dark and the sea became a surly steel grey, the house would look warm and welcoming.

She had decided to keep the open fireplaces in all the rooms, and planned to put a log burner at the end of the kitchen – she loved the idea of having a real fire in the kitchen, with possibly an armchair on either side, so she could sit and read with a glass of red wine, snug and warm on a cold winter's evening as outside the wind howled around the house.

Time was getting on and she needed to make plans. But, today, she could not motivate herself to do anything, paralysed as she felt by the emotions of the day before. Whenever she thought of it, an icy hand clutched her heart. Despite the wine, she'd been unable to sleep and had tossed and turned in bed, far too hot, replaying the kiss over and over in her mind. Had he ever kissed *her* like that? Presumably yes, in the beginning of their relationship when they were both much younger, but certainly not latterly. Their love-making had been gentle, familiar and reassuring, rather than white hot and passionate. No wonder, she had thought, angrily, turning over again, no wonder Karina holds such a fascination for him. Perhaps he was just being *kind* to me, she thought. He just wants to make sure that he is doing his duty by me so he can enjoy his new life with Karina without the ties of guilt. How very deluded I must have been to have even begun to imagine he still wanted me, in any sense. Who am I, next to her? He called me an extraordinary woman. Well, clearly not extraordinary enough. If he does have any feelings of love towards me, they are simply those of habit. That is all. As the mother of his children. Not as a woman, a sexual woman. Will anyone ever love me like that again? she thought. Will I ever be desired?

She had managed to drift off just before Hector's cold nose was pressed against her cheek. His face split into a welcoming morning grin. Sara groaned.

'At least you don't find me repulsive,' she muttered. Hector thumped his tail and peered winningly at her, as if the idea was absurd.

'But that's because I feed you,' she added, crossly,

levering herself out of bed and stumping off towards the bathroom on stiff knees.

Now she lay on the wooden lounger in the front garden, a book open but discarded on her chest, trailing a hand idly along the top of the still dew-damp grass. Behind her closed eyelids, the sun burnt a vivid orange. Overhead the rooks cawed raucously, their calls slicing like a chainsaw through the gentle musical birdsong of the garden. A fly landed on her face. She heard the buzzing noise and then she felt its feet tickling her skin, irritatingly. She tried to wave it away, but it kept circling and landing again. Crossly, she opened her eyes, looking up at the sky. Am I never to have peace, she asked herself, slapping at the last place the fly had landed on her face. A faint buzzing told her she had missed. She sighed. Stop it, she told herself. Stop torturing yourself.

So what if you are a fat old woman with an arse like a rhino? You have poetry in your soul. What had Ricky said to her, smiling at her with those wicked dark eyes? Live a little. Come *on*. She must not brood. Matt was gone, he wasn't coming back and she was never, ever going to be able to wear a halter-dress like Karina's and have thighs like that. I must cultivate my hidden depths, she thought, so people – men – will look past my cellulite. I look good for my age and I must not compare myself to a young floozy with thighs like a gazelle. She laughed out loud. That was better. Karina was probably very dull, beneath that stunning exterior. She was obviously hard work too, which pleased Sara. I hope she gives him hell, she thought. She sighed again.

What shall I do today? I know, she decided. I will buy something. She looked up at the sky once more. The beautiful colour made her think of Cornish blue and white pottery. I will treat myself to an extravagant amount of Cornish pottery in Fowey.

She had pulled her chiffon summer skirt up above her knees to tan her legs, and now she looked down at her thighs critically. They were slimmer, but there was still a long way to go. She stretched one foot out in front of her, and a bulge by her toe caught her attention. The side of her foot was swollen and pink. It must be her new walking boots. Lord, she was getting a bunion. Oh, wonderful, she thought. A bunion. She stared at her foot, flexing the ankle crossly. She'd always had nice feet, and now this one was misshapen. She sat up, letting the book fall into her lap, looking around her.

The lounger was surrounded by almost foot-high long grass, the spindly stems topped with white and grey feathery leaves, interspersed with fat dandelion clocks and a sea of daisies. She must buy a mower. There was no earthly reason why she couldn't mow, it wasn't an exclusively masculine activity.

'Are you going to do nothing *all* morning?' Lottie flopped down beside her. 'Yuck, this grass is still wet.' She was wearing a wide-brimmed sun hat, the tight white top with daisies she had bought in Fowey and tiny denim shorts, and was clutching a large sketchbook in her arms. 'I must get my portfolio together,' she said, plucking at one of the long stems of grass and putting it into her mouth, hugging her knees. 'I'll have to go and collect a load of stuff from Dad's, most of my artwork is still at the flat. I better grab it before Dad moves. In fact I need to get all of my things. Can we drive into London? I won't be able to carry it all on the train.'

'No,' Sara replied, closing her eyes. 'I can't face that at the moment.'

'Well, could Dad bring it here?'

Sara's eyes flew open. 'Definitely not,' she said firmly.

'What did you think of him?' Lottie gazed at her thoughtfully.

'Who?'

'The Pope. *Dad*. Who do you think I mean?'

'He seemed pretty much himself,' Sara said cautiously. This was the last thing she wanted to discuss. 'A bit tired, maybe, but he's probably working too hard. His hair's rather long, though. I honestly think he's started blow-drying it.' She deliberately kept her tone light.

Lottie laughed, relieved they could make a joke out of the gruesome lunch. 'I think you may be right. He's trying to look a bit too cool. I mean, Dad's always looked good but longer hair on older men is not a great idea.' She paused, chewing on the end of the grass. 'I don't think he seemed himself, actually. I thought he was kind of jittery, on edge.'

'It was quite a strange situation, you must admit.'

'It was more than that. I can't put my finger on it, but he was just . . . different.'

'We haven't seen him for a while,' Sara pointed out.

'He kept staring at you, as if he couldn't believe how much you had changed.'

'Did he?' Sara said. 'I don't think . . .'

'He did. Whenever you weren't looking he kept taking these quick glances at you – I caught him once, and he actually went red. I've never seen Dad blush before. I think . . .' She sat back on her heels. 'I think he might still be in love with you.'

Sara twisted sideways on the lounger to look down at Lottie, the book falling from her lap in the sudden movement. 'Oh no, darling, he isn't. He really isn't.' My love, she thought. How much you want to believe it.

'How do you know?' Lottie's face was hurt.

'I just do. Can we leave it? I don't think there's any point dissecting the day. We met, we had a conversation, of sorts, the ice is broken and now we can all move on.'

Lottie looked away. 'I didn't mean that you were like going to get back together. I'm not a child. I don't think Dad's going to come to his senses, get rid of the tart and we can all be one big happy family again.' She plucked angrily at the grass. 'I just meant that he obviously still has feelings for you.'

'You can't rub out twenty-odd years,' Sara said, sorry she had been so sharp. 'I know what you mean, darling, don't be upset. Of course I still have feelings for him. But I know he isn't in love with me. He's in a new relationship, it's obviously not just a fling, and hard as it is, we have to respect that.'

'Respect her? Are you bonkers?'

'Not respect,' Sara said. 'But accept that she isn't going to go away and she is a part of Dad's life. I am sure he loves her. Perhaps not in the same way that he loves you – us – but he does.'

'She looks like a twig,' Lottie said. 'I can remember what she looks like. Skinny, witchy and cross.'

Sara laughed. 'You can talk. She's no slimmer than you.'

'She has a beaky nose.'

'She's very beautiful,' Sara said.

'Nice clothes, I'll give her that,' Lottie said grudgingly.

'I'll make some tea,' Sara said, standing up. 'Do you want to come into Fowey? I feel the need to buy something reckless and extravagant.'

'In that case,' Lottie said smiling. 'I'm just the girl to join you.'

'And stretch . . .' If I stretch any more, Sara thought, something is going to snap. This is not normal. My arms are not supposed to reach forward like this while one foot is bent under my thigh and the other is stretched away behind me, and I cannot walk my fingers forward any further because I am about to either break in two, collapse sideways, or fart, and I don't know which would be worse.

'Now, sit up, gently,' said the irritatingly calm voice of the Pilates instructor. She was a rather dumpy woman, which pleased Sara, because she had thought she would be a jealousy-incurring ultra-slim goddess and all supple and bendy like a pipe cleaner.

In fact she was a sturdy little thing with fatter upper arms than Sara's. The voice of Sting flowed caressingly out of the CD player, and Sara glanced sideways at Helen, who looked as if she was trying not to laugh. 'I did warn you,' she hissed. 'I said it was harder than it looked.'

Having reassembled her outstretched legs, Sara was now sitting, cross-legged, on a spongy blue yoga mat on the wooden floor of the village hall. Natalie, the Pilates instructor, had spent the first ten minutes of the class moaning about the fact that the sound system wasn't working *yet again* and fiddling about with her headset, which shrieked and yowled, forcing the class to cover their ears. Sara recognized several women – she had either bumped into them in the village shop, or met them out walking with Hector. There were a couple of definitely oversized women in straining leggings, and one game old girl who must have been well over seventy, but who was as trim and wiry as a little bird. Helen had told her she had been doing Pilates for a year now, and it had made such a difference to her flexibility as well as toning her muscles. 'It won't make you slim,' she warned, 'but it will make you feel stronger.' Sara didn't know if this was a direct criticism of her weight, but didn't really care. She was never going to be skinny, but it would be good to try to reduce some of the cellulite at the tops of her thighs, get rid of the spare tyre around her middle and that dratted floppy skin under her upper arms. She had no intention of becoming obsessed with the way she looked, like Catherine, but she did think it would boost her confidence to be able to wear jeans and summer skirts without having a roll of flab hanging over the top of the waistband. She would have more energy, too. *Mens sana in corpora sano*, she thought. A new mantra for the new me.

'Now, slowly, stand up,' said Natalie, her lips pursed in concentration. 'You are becoming a tree. Lift your leg and place the sole of your foot against your thigh, if you can reach so high, knee for those of you new to the class,' she added, looking patronisingly at Sara, 'and now reach up, up, into the sky, lift your gaze towards the sun.' Immediately, Sara started to wobble, and her tree became a shrub and then she fell over. Helen snorted with laughter, but then she could, couldn't she, because she was being a beautiful, tall tree without a wobble in sight.

'Now take your woo-chi ball . . .'

'What's a woo-chi ball?' Sara whispered.

'Shhh,' hissed Helen. 'Concentrate.'

Sara tried to copy the others, placing her hands either side of the metaphysical ball, and moving it about in front of her. She kept getting behind the others, waving her non-existent woo-chi ball above her head when they were swooping it down to the earth. This is like trying to rub your head and pat your stomach at the same time, she thought crossly.

'Sun Salutations next,' said Natalie, and obediently, everyone but Sara turned towards the middle of the room and raised their arms, outstretched, above their heads, before suddenly swooping down in a swan dive to rest their palms flat against the floor. Sara bent over, but there was no way her hands could reach so low down. The most she could do was wave them vaguely about at calf-height. She looked over at Helen, feeling absurdly envious. This is childish, she thought. No wonder Helen looked so trim, if she was doing this kind of palaver twice a week. Sara made a concerted effort to touch her fingertips against the floor, but her stomach seemed to get in the way and the back of her thighs shrieked in agony. She was worried she was going to get cramp, and then she realized that the rest of them were no longer bent over like paperclips, but were making an upside-down 'V' shape on their mats, palms flat, balancing on their tiptoes, bottoms in the air.

'Down Dog,' Natalie intoned. 'And then – slowly – forwards into the plank . . .' Now this really did hurt, Sara thought, trying to hold up her entire body weight on her outstretched arms. 'Sink into the crocodile,' floated Natalie's voice. Slowly, Sara levered herself down to try to hover just above the ground as the other women were doing with their elbows bent close to their bodies like grasshoppers, but she couldn't support herself, and flopped on to her front. She wondered if there was a Pilates position called Beached Whale, because she could do this, no problem.

In seconds, Natalie was beside her, her voice full of sympathetic concern. 'You mustn't do too much on your first lesson,' she said quietly, but not quietly enough for the rest of the class not to be able to over-hear. 'When you're rather *out of shape*, it *will* take time. Just take it slowly – I promise,' she lowered her voice, 'it *will* come. You can't force it. The body will give when *it* wants to give.' Sara gritted her teeth. Out of shape, eh? What did she think she was, then? Shaped like a weeble?

The class ended with a long stretch lying flat out on the mat, eyes closed. 'Let the body and mind relax,' droned Natalie. 'Fill your mind with happy thoughts, and just drift away . . . you are lying on a bed of flowers . . . the sun is high . . . every muscle in your body is floating . . . let your karma relax . . .' Sara opened one eye and saw Helen had her eyes open too. Helen raised her eyes to heaven, and Sara had to stop herself giggling.

'What did you think?' Helen asked, as they emerged, blinking, into the sunshine.

'God, she'd drive me round the bend if I had to listen to that more than twice a week,' Sara said. 'Let your body float away . . . you are lying on a bed of hot air listening to a load of shite from an overweight midget . . .'

'Shush,' Helen said, snorting and nudging her. 'She's just behind you.'

They both turned and smiled at Natalie. 'Thank you so much,' Sara said, hastily straightening her face. 'Goodbye. It was, what can I say? *Truly* enlightening.'

Natalie regarded them beadily, before turning to stow her sports bag into the boot of a blue sports car, and departing in a swirl of gravel.

'Do you think she heard?' Sara asked, worried. She really didn't want to be unkind.

'I'm not sure. Do you fancy a coffee?' Helen said. 'I can't face going back home to work, it's far too sunny. I've got loads of stuff to do but what I really want to do is flop about. Come on. Have you ever been to Holly Murphy's?'

'No,' Sara said. 'What is it?'

'A café in Fowey. The coffee's great and they do the most amazing paninis.'

'Doesn't that rather negate the effect of the Pilates?' Sara said, primly.

'Absolutely not,' Helen said firmly. 'The point about exercising properly is that you can then eat whatever you want, within reason. I never diet.'

Sara looked at her slim, strong figure. 'You're lucky,' she said, glumly. 'I think it must be genetic. I only have to look at a baguette to put on weight.'

'Didn't you exercise before?'

'I should have done, I suppose, but there never seemed to be the time, and, besides, Matt never complained I was putting on weight.'

'But exercise is about feeling happy too,' Helen pointed out, climbing into her car. 'It makes you feel more positive and optimistic.'

'True. I could do with that. Things are still – a bit, well, tricky, sometimes.'

'How did the meeting with Matt go?'

Sara turned away from her, pulling the passenger door shut.

'It was fine,' she said slowly. 'Well, no, it wasn't, it was pretty grim really and both the girls ended up getting upset. There were all these subconscious emotions seething around, most of which went right over Matt's head. Men aren't very good at noticing things, are they? And nothing was his fault, as usual, despite the fact that he was the one who brought all this about by rushing off with a toddler.'

Helen barked with laughter. 'What happened?'

Sara paused, thinking. 'Well, it was so hard seeing Emily. She resents me deeply for leaving and I'm not sure she can ever forgive me for that. But then she's very unhappy seeing Matt with his new girlfriend. You know – it is such a mess. She's twenty-three but she's still a child at heart, trying to be very grown-up and understanding about the whole thing, whereas I think she's actually far more screwed up about the break-up than Lottie. It sounds awful but I think Emily *would* be better living with me – I bet Matt never talks to her about the situation and I think she needs to talk. I know she and Lottie chat a lot on the phone, but I worry I'm losing touch with her . . .'

'And Matt?'

Sara turned her head away from Helen to glance out of the window. Then she looked back at her friend

221

and shrugged. 'I'm not even sure I can begin to explain.'

'You don't have to, if you don't want to.'

'I know.' She smiled. 'Well, we started off OK and then it got very prickly, and he really got my goat by telling me I never had to live in the real world.'

'Ouch.'

'Precisely. Hardly justification for buggering off, is it? And it was all so confusing – one minute he was telling me off and being bossy about money, the next he was stroking my face telling me how much he missed me and how dreadful he felt.'

'Oh dear.'

'Mmm.'

'And how did you feel about that?'

Sara sighed. 'Manipulated, mostly, as if he wanted me . . . as if he wanted me to be still in love with him.'

'Bastard.'

'There is that. And the awful thing is that even though we had a couple of stormings off and then we found Lottie really upset outside the restaurant, which was very traumatic – there was a teeny bit of me which was thinking, "maybe", and "what if . . ."'

'So what happened?'

'Oh, it was marvellous. I was skipping about thinking maybe he does love me and I'm not so repulsive after all and he'd said how great I was looking and then . . .' She stopped.

'What?'

'I saw him snogging the teenager out the window. He thought I'd gone. Honestly, Helen, it was pretty off-putting, he was eating her face off in the street.'

Helen laughed so hard she bent over the steering wheel. 'What a prick!' she howled.

'I know. Grim, isn't it? Like I'm so trendy and cool I kiss my girlfriend in public. Look at me with this beautiful young woman.'

'I can't wait to meet this guy.'

'That will not be for some time yet,' Sara said levelly. 'I am currently at the stage of wanting to punch his lights out. How dare he give me all the "you-look-so-great-I-have-made-such-a-mistake" and then whip off five minutes later and stick his tongue down her throat?'

'I'm so glad you are seeing this without rose-tinted glasses.'

'Oh-ho, yes. I see right through that man. How did I ever trust him?'

'Because you loved him?'

'Sadly, you are quite right. But I don't anymore.'

'Definitely?'

'Definitely.'

'Chin up,' Helen said, negotiating the Land Rover onto the ferry. 'She'll probably want babies.'

'He's had the snip,' Sara said.

'It can always be reversed. Can you imagine dealing with babies now?'

'God, no. Grandchildren, yes, but you can hand them back.'

'Exactly. Let's hope he has to start all over again with howling infants, shall we?'

They grinned at each other.

The conversation had not started well. Sara had been in the middle of mopping the floor, and snatched up the phone, irritated at having been interrupted when she had finally got around to a job she had been putting off for days.

'Yes?' she said, ungraciously.

'Chill, Mother,' Emily said. 'It's me.'

'I'm sorry, darling, I was just in the middle of something.'

'I'll call back if you're *so* busy.'

223

'No!' Sara said, quickly. 'It was nothing, only boring housework. How are you?'

'Fine,' Emily said guardedly.

'It was lovely to see you.'

'Yeah. Ish. Not a howling success, was it?'

'We had to all meet up some time, I suppose. How's work?'

'OK.'

'Just OK?'

'No, I like it. It's just – different – to how I imagined.'

'Different in what way?'

'They expect me to know stuff without telling me how to do it, and some of it is really technical.'

'Well, it is radio,' Sara said reasonably.

'I thought there'd be more real journalism and less fiddling about with tape recorders.'

'It's all digital now, isn't it?'

'Yes. And that's really hard, we edit our stuff on screen and it took me ages to get the hang of it.'

'But didn't you do that at university?'

'Yeah, but we used a different form of software. I have to work so quickly, too, the deadlines for turning copy round are really tight.'

'But is it fun?'

'Bits of it are fun, I suppose,' she said dispiritedly.

There was a long pause. 'How's the flat?'

'Dad's new one?'

'No, yours.'

'Oh, that. It's OK. I can't wait to move out. Dad said he'd help me find somewhere to buy.'

'But how will you pay the mortgage?'

'I'll manage,' Emily said testily. 'Dad said he'd pay anyway, didn't he?'

When are you going to grow up and stand on your own two feet? Sara thought, but said nothing. It was a novelty for Emily to actually ring her. Normally Sara had to be the one who phoned and then Emily was always in a hurry to dash off.

'What's the weather like in Cornwall?'

'Sunny. We had a thunderstorm yesterday, but it's cleared up now. What's it like in London?'

'Boiling. I can't wait until Mauritius and I can lie on the beach and sunbathe, rather than have to work in all this heat.'

'Mauritius?'

'Didn't I tell you? Dad's taking me on holiday in August.'

'Just the two of you?'

There was a long pause. Then Emily said quietly, 'No. Unfortunately.'

'Ah.'

'She's such a . . .'

Sara cut her off. 'Darling, I don't know if it is any of my business, really. I don't particularly want to discuss your father's relationship.'

'You don't know what she's doing to Dad!' Emily's voice rose suddenly.

Sara stared at the phone. 'What on earth do you mean?' she asked.

'Nothing. I can't. I don't . . .' Her voice tailed off, and Sara realized she was crying.

'Darling, what on earth is the matter? What's going on? What's *wrong* with Dad?'

'I can't tell you.'

'Why?'

'I'm not absolutely sure if . . . It's very hard to know definitely . . .'

'What? Please, Emily, tell me.'

'I shouldn't have said anything.'

'This isn't fair. You can't get me all worried and then not tell me what it is, exactly, which is worrying you so much about him.'

'Everything's changed, Mum, you've no idea. Dad's quite different. Without you he's . . .'

'He's bound to be different,' Sara said, as calmly as she could. 'I don't think that is such a cause for concern.'

'You're so bloody naïve, Mum,' Emily said unexpectedly. 'You really have no idea, do you?'

'And how do you expect me to know, if you won't tell me?'

'I'm scared,' Emily said.

'Why? What about?'

'No,' she said. 'It isn't worth it. Forget I said anything. There's nothing you can do, anyway.'

'You're probably right, not that I have the faintest clue what you're talking about. Come and stay, darling, and then we can have a proper chat, face to face. It isn't the same on the phone. Besides, I want to show you the cottage. You'll love it here, it's really relaxing. We can walk, and sunbathe, go shopping, eat out – there are lots of lovely places to eat.'

'Maybe. I hardly get any holiday, though, and I'm using two weeks to go with Dad.'

'You could come at the weekend.'

'It's such a long way.'

'It isn't so far. Only four hours or so. You could be here by ten, if you left work at six on Friday night.'

'Hmm.'

'That doesn't sound very positive.'

'I will try. I do miss you.'

'I miss you too. Are you sure Dad isn't ill? He looked very tired.'

'No,' Emily said definitely. 'He isn't ill.'

Chapter Fifteen

Sara gazed up at the church roof, as around her the congregation sang a ragged but enthusiastic rendition of 'All things bright and beautiful'. She hadn't heard the hymn since primary school, kneeling on an itchy sampler cushion, her hands clasped in a facsimile of piety as her lips moved noiselessly, while she was actually planning where to go on her bike with her friends.

Back then, the air within the Yorkshire village church had seemed stale and oppressive, but here the atmosphere was bright and airy. The morning sun poured in through the huge stained glass windows, a colourful rainbow of light dappling the heads of the congregation.

The church had a magnificent roof, with arched wooden timbers. Why were church roofs so high? Sara wondered idly. To encourage you to feel the majesty of God? Were your thoughts bound to soar with seemingly infinite space above you?

Every seat in the pews was taken – when she was handed her hymn book by John who ran the village shop, who was also apparently a churchwarden, Sara spotted practically everyone she knew from the village. Helen was right – it was oddly comforting, she thought, to be part of a community drawn together like this. There were lots of children in the congregation too, dressed in their Sunday best, and Sara thought how sad it was that in most parts of Britain religion was no longer a uniting force of the community.

The conversation with Emily was plaguing her, and here, in the peace of the church with half an ear to the sermon and prayers, she had time to think. Something was evidently worrying Emily deeply about Matt. It wasn't just that she disliked Karina – that was obvious and she was bound to feel jealous. What she had said – or not said, rather implied – was that Matt was hiding something, that he had changed in a way Emily did not like – or feared, even. Emily's worries corresponded with her own – when they had met he had been contradictory and nervy. And even though she had joked with Helen about the street-kissing incident, it really was not in character. Matt was quite a private person, and disliked public displays of affection. Perhaps it was simply his lifestyle with Karina which was pushing him close to the edge – she probably encouraged him to burn the candle at both ends and would have all the energy of youth, able to stay up late without feeling completely exhausted the next day. Matt may look young for his years, but he'd still feel the effects of repeated late nights, Sara thought. Karina presumably wanted them to go out clubbing, out drinking with friends. Emily was possibly just very worried about how tired and irritable his social life was making him feel.

That must be it, she decided, looking at her hymn book. I'm tired of worrying about him anyway, she thought. This shouldn't be a sad day – yesterday they had heard through the post that Bristol was prepared to offer Lottie a place.

* * *

'I'll take you to Pip's,' Sara said, as they had a celebratory cup of tea. 'Treat ourselves.'

'Brilliant.'

'Can I ask Helen?'

'No,' Lottie said. 'This is a family celebration.' She hesitated, smiling. 'Well, all the family we can muster for now.'

'You'd better ring Granny.'

'Do I have to?'

'Yes, go on, she'll be thrilled. It's about time we gave her some good news.'

'Have you told her about your plans for a job?'

'There's nothing to tell, yet, is there? Anyway, I want to make sure it's going to happen before I start telling anyone, I don't want to look foolish. You should ring Dad too.'

'Mmm.'

'And French Granny.' This was the family term for Matt's mother, a tiny, bird-like woman who smoked constantly and still lived in the council house in which Matt had grown up in Manchester. He had tried to persuade her to move down south, but she said all her friends lived in the area and there was no point. She was a very nervy woman and Sara realized she did not have the confidence to make such a dramatic life change. She absolutely doted on Matt, her only child, and after his father had left – which was a relief to both of them, he was the hard-drinking feckless kind of Irishman – she poured all of her hopes into her clever, good-looking son. Sara and she had never seen eye-to-eye and the girls didn't enjoy visiting her, mainly because her house stank unbearably of smoke. Sara felt guilty the girls were much closer to her own mother, but then she found visiting Matt's mother a trial too. His parents had met when his mother was

229

working in a hotel in Manchester as a chambermaid, having come over from France when her parents died unexpectedly, and he was a porter. An illustrious upbringing Matt would say, with a smile. But the combination of cultures had given him his dark good looks plus a determination to succeed so he never had to experience life in that way again.

Lottie had hugged her mother. 'I'm so pleased! I have a place! Let's go up to Bristol soon and have a good look around. Maybe Dad will buy me a flat.'

'Please, Lottie,' Sara said. 'Don't go there.'

'I'll have to make a whole load of new friends,' Lottie said, her face suddenly worried. 'And I don't want to leave you on your own.'

Sara smiled. 'You won't be leaving me, silly. It's hardly any distance from here, no more than two hours or so. I can easily pop up to see you, or you can come home at the weekends. Anyway, the cottage is going to be like a building site soon, you'll be well out of it. I may well come and live with you, if things get too uncomfortable here.'

'No way,' Lottie said, firmly. 'I'm not having an ancient mother cramping my style.'

The thought of this conversation made Sara smile, as she mouthed the words to the hymn 'Jerusalem'. Helen was singing very loudly, if tunelessly, beside her. Sara had felt a warm sensation of pleasure when she'd walked into the church and seen Helen, who motioned she was saving a seat for her. Like being back at school, Sara thought.

On the way out of church, she joined the queue to shake hands with the sprintin' vicar.

'Call me Bob,' he said, when it was her turn. 'So

pleased you've found us. You've moved into Tremain Cottage, haven't you?'

'That's right,' she said. 'I'm Sara Atkinson. I'm sorry I haven't been before, I'm still settling in.'

He waved his hand carelessly. 'That really doesn't matter. We're just pleased you came. If there's anything I can do to help, I know nearly everyone around here,' he added. 'If you need anything, do call. I'm not just useful for spiritual guidance, you know. I'm an expert in local plumbers as well.'

Sara laughed. 'That's very kind of you. I'm about to start renovating the house, Helen's helping me,' she added, turning to look at her friend.

'Ah, Helen,' he smiled. 'Now she does know how to get things done. Gets us all organized. I'm not going to put any pressure on you whatsoever because I know you must be so busy, but we do have a few little groups here you might enjoy. A reading group, on a Tuesday, and we're always looking for help with the church flowers. Have you met Pam yet? She's the chairman of our Women's Institute. Or should I say chairwoman? I do get confused. She can come across as a little . . . intimidating, but her heart is definitely in the right place and they do some tremendous good works.'

That's it, Sara thought. I have become my mother. She smiled. 'I'm not sure if I'm Women's Institute material,' she said. 'And I'm rather useless at arranging flowers. But I will try, if you like.' Amazed, she realized that the thought pleased her. She liked the thought of decorating the church, working inside the calm, cool walls during the week, when it would be quiet.

'Marvellous,' he said, smiling. 'I'll tell Pam. She'll pop round, if that's all right, not an imposition?' He looked at her questioningly. 'I don't want to rope you in, but if you'd *like* to get involved . . .'

'I would,' she said firmly. 'I didn't go to church, before I came here. Not often, anyway. I'm afraid I am something of a lapsed Christian.'

'That doesn't matter,' he said airily. 'We all have our reasons for being here. God means many different things to different people, doesn't He?'

'Church, blimey,' Lottie said, sitting at the table in the garden, munching toast. Sara was browsing through the Sunday papers she'd picked up on the way home, as the village shop was open until twelve on a Sunday. There really were too many supplements, she thought, opening a glossy magazine. At least five brightly coloured leaflets fell out on to her knee. 'I do wish they wouldn't put in all this rubbish,' she said crossly.

'You're turning into a grumpy old woman,' Lottie said, drinking a mug of tea. 'Did they get you on the flower rota, then?'

Sara smiled. 'I rather think they might have done,' she admitted.

'That's it,' Lottie said. 'Tweed skirts, sensible flat shoes, hairy chin and big knickers. Old age has set in. What's the vicar like?'

'Rather nice,' Sara said. 'Young, a beard, two small children. He runs marathons, looks terribly fit. Not a fogey by any means, the sermon was all about Iraq – quite political, really. I don't think he's out of touch. It was very soothing, actually.'

'Soothing!' Lottie laughed, from behind the newspaper she'd picked up. 'What with Pilates and God, you'll end up completely catatonic.'

'Hardly,' Sara said.

'By the way, when are you going to get around to doing something with that toy box by the fridge? I nearly fell over it this morning.'

'Oh,' Sara said. 'I meant to clean it up, it's rather

232

beautiful, isn't it? It just needs sanding and re-waxing. The wood is lovely. Although it's not ours, is it? I wonder who it did belong to.'

'The old man who used to live here?'

'I suppose so. But apparently he died without leaving any family, so maybe it does belong to us, now. There was nothing else of any value in the attic, just that load of old documents in cardboard boxes. I really ought to have a bonfire, start clearing the rubbish.'

'Have you ever actually made a bonfire?' Lottie asked, putting down the newspaper and looking at her mother with some concern.

'No. Fires were always Dad's domain. But it can't be so hard, can it? I've got a can of petrol in the shed – we should just collect all the rubbish together and then pile it up outside the gate – not in the garden, there isn't room, and it's a bit too near the house.'

'I have a bad feeling about this,' Lottie said. 'You plus petrol strikes me as a dangerous combination.'

Heaving everything down from the attic was a marathon job which took Sara and Lottie well into the afternoon. At first they kept getting sidetracked by reading old newspapers, but then realized how long it was going to take at that rate, and started piling everything regardless into black binbags. Most of the documents Sara found were old insurance policies and bank statements, dating back up to fifty years, so she decided it wouldn't do any harm to get rid of them. Once they had cleared the entire attic, Sara sat back on her heels, pleased with their industry, as Lottie tied the last knot in the final binbag full of paper.

Above her, the bats swung gently in the breeze – she had opened the tiny skylight in the roof to try to get rid of some of the dust. It really was quite a big area –

maybe Helen was right, and they could put a little staircase up from the landing, and make this into one big bedroom or studio, even have a little shower room at the end. But what about the bats? She regarded them balefully. Blasted protected species. She was sure Lottie, who would probably end up having the attic room, could not co-exist with bats. Their droppings stank, as her hands testified.

Lottie stood under the hatch, as Sara heaved down the binbags.

'How many more?' she complained. 'I want to go to the beach. I fancy a swim.' She looked up at her mother. 'Do you want to come?'

'I'll come to the beach, but I'm not going in. It may be officially summer, but that water will still be freezing. I'd need a wetsuit to get me in.'

'Coward. Go on, Mother. Live a little.'

'Hmm. Maybe.'

'Whose idea *was* this?' Sara was standing up to her knees in the chilly water, as it surged and eddied around her increasingly numb feet. Fortunately there was no one else on the beach – she doubted she would have got this far if there had been anyone watching. She had managed to unearth a swimming costume. It was not flattering, bagging around the stomach and lacking in support at the top.

'Come on!' Lottie called to her. She was wearing a tiny pale yellow bikini, which showed off her tan, and she'd put her hair up into a bun. She was already standing up to her waist, holding her arms outstretched at either side of her. 'It's not that bad, Mum, really. You get used to it.'

Sara looked up at the cliff. The rock face, eroded into a series of ledges and crags by the tide, was covered in yellow gorse towards its summit, and its steep sides cast long shadows over the water, blocking out the warmth of the sun. Pebbles and rocks were sharp under her feet, and she winced as she edged forward, then recoiled as her toes touched a slimy clump of seaweed. The water around her was very clear, a pale, translucent blue, but beyond Lottie the colour darkened to steel grey towards the misty line of the horizon. The image of the basking shark flashed through Sara's mind. Harmless, she said firmly to herself. No teeth. It just sucked in plankton, gummed it about a bit and then spat it out. No danger to humans whatsoever, as were the porpoises, dolphins and grey seals. The most they might do was accidentally bump into you. You were more in danger from jelly fish. Then another thought flashed through her mind. A great white shark had been spotted off the coast of Cornwall last month. Surely it wouldn't come in so close to the coast? She peered out to sea, imagining a sleek grey fin scything through the water, heading towards them with deadly intent . . . She let out a little squeak.

'What on earth is the matter?' Lottie called. Then, seeing her mother was still upright, she held her breath and dived under the surface of the water. The next thing Sara saw was a pair of neat white heels as Lottie disappeared.

'Lottie!' she cried, suddenly overcome by a quite irrational hysteria. Moments later Lottie reappeared, shaking her head, laughing, some twenty feet away from Sara.

'It's amazing!' she said. 'So clear! I kept my eyes open and there were these little tiny grey fish, a great shoal of them! Honestly, once you're under you don't feel the cold. You get acclimatized.'

'Numb,' Sara corrected.

'Oh, come on!' Lottie said impatiently. 'What harm can it do? Swim, Mother.'

At that moment, from behind Lottie, a rising crescent of water appeared. Sara stared at the wave horrified, quite unable to move. Until now, the tide had been little more than a swell, barely a foot high, just lifting the sea further up her legs in a gentle, pushing motion. But this was a definite breaker. As she watched, the water began to define itself into an overhanging curve, before erupting into a thin snow-like crust of spray. 'Lottie!' she called, pointing. 'Look out!' Lottie turned, just as the wave hit her, and she screamed as it lifted her clean off her feet. Then she disappeared. Sara felt rooted to the spot – she turned to try to get back to the shoreline but the previous much smaller wave was pulling her back. She was, inexorably, being drawn into the path of the wave. She felt herself being lifted up, tugged backwards, and then the water broke over her. The wave was huge, at least eight feet high, and for an instant her world turned upside down as she spun, helplessly, the salt water rushing up her nose, choking, trying to keep her mouth closed, feeling her thighs, her knees, crashing against the stony bottom of the sea, and then it passed, leaving her floundering on the surface, her chest heaving, her eyes, nose and throat full of water and sand. She turned, rubbing her eyes.

Lottie was treading water some thirty feet away. 'Are you OK?' she called. 'That came out of nowhere!'

'It certainly did,' Sara shouted back. She was OK, nothing was broken, she'd survived. It was only a wave. Why had she been so fearful, when there was nothing to fear? 'Wait there,' she called. 'I'm coming.' With an awkward, jerky breaststroke, holding her head high out of the water, she made her way over to her daughter.

Lottie was right, once you were fully submerged, the shock of the icy water became almost warm against your body. She'd never liked swimming out of her depth, but now, treading water next to Lottie, she realized there must be at least twenty feet of sea beneath her. But she did not feel afraid. Tumbling in the chaos of water, seaweed, sand and stones, she had realized that as long as she remained calm the sea would not hurt her. There was nothing to fear.

Chapter Sixteen

'Pleased to meet you, Sara,' he said, lifting a banana skin off the chair and dropping it into an overflowing waste-paper basket. 'I'm Nick, by the way, and this is Tom.' Tom waved a greeting without looking up from his computer. The office, Sara noted, was extremely untidy, with piles of papers and photocopied pictures teetering on each of the desks, amidst a litter of empty coffee cups. Sara had to suppress the urge to have a good tidy-up. But they probably had far more important things to do than worry about mess.

'Your letter came at just the right time,' Nick said, lifting up a pile of documents which had lain beneath the blackening skin of the banana, so Sara could sit down. A girl with long dark hair and a pencil in her mouth wandered by. Ignoring Sara, she leant over the desk towards Nick. '*The Echo* called about a quote, you know, the shark thing. What shall I say?'

'Tell them Jaws is definitely not coming to town,' he said sharply. He turned to Sara apologetically. 'Sorry, but we get one sighting of a great white two miles out to sea and suddenly it's Amityville Horror around here. No one has ever been attacked by a great white off the coast of Cornwall, but if this story goes any further we'll have all manner of idiots driving their motorboats up and down the coastline, ladling fish guts into the water, which attracts all kinds of predators into the shallow water and affects the whole ecology of the coast. Honestly. It plays havoc with the marine life and last time we had a scare like this about thirty harmless sharks, like reefers and hammerheads, were unnecessarily baited, caught and killed.'

'That's awful,' Sara said. 'But surely people know the difference?'

Nick raised an eyebrow at her. 'Sadly not,' he said. He was a rather good-looking man, Sara thought, then checked herself – goodness, she must stop looking at men who were young enough to be her son and noticing how nice-looking they were. He had long, light brown hair, tucked behind his ears, and small rimless oval glasses.

'Don't you have a press officer?' Sara said.

'Nope,' he said, picking up and scanning the letter she had sent him about helping the organization to fund-raise and find corporate sponsors. 'Can't afford it. We're working on a shoestring here. Look, I love the idea of you helping us to bring in more cash, but we wouldn't be able to pay you much at all. Could you work on commission? You know, the more you bring in, the more you get paid?'

'That's what I expected you to say,' Sara smiled. 'That would be fine. Do you have a good relationship with the local papers?' she went on. 'It's just I think we might need to raise your profile first, and let people know what a valuable job you are doing, before we start contacting sponsors. Do many people around here know what you actually do?'

'Not many,' he admitted. 'We tend to keep our heads down and just get on with the work in hand. To be honest, the whole media thing is a bit of a distraction, a nuisance. We're too busy to chat to journalists,' he said. 'And they always sensationalize everything; it's really hard to get the facts across. All they want to hear is that we have a giant man-eating shark in our midst which will make a great headline for them and sell papers. I mean, we try to do our bit by getting out into the local community and we go into schools fairly frequently.' He thought for a moment. 'We've got the website too, but we don't publicize that much.' He sighed. 'There's probably a lot more we *could* be doing if we had the time.'

'I could do that, too,' Sara said.

'What?'

'I could handle your press as well as fund-raise,' she said. 'I used to work in a marketing company, I dealt with journalists all the time, and I know how to write a press release.' She smiled. 'It would be fun.'

Nick was looking at her appraisingly. 'I'm sorry, I don't mean to sound rude, but why would you want to work for us? I mean, you're . . .'

'Rather mature?' Sara said smiling. 'I know. I haven't worked for a while, but I've recently separated from my husband, moved down here and I need to work. That's all.'

'We *could* only pay a pittance and it's very chaotic. We should have someone running the office too, but we can't afford a full-time secretary.'

'I could sort your office out, if you like. I'm quite good at organizing. Most of all, I'd like to do something where I feel I am doing something worthwhile. I've become quite interested in conservation, although I don't know much about it. Now, how do you send out press releases?'

'I put it off until the very last minute and then I just bash something out,' Nick admitted.

'If you want, I could interview you, write the press release, and then you could check what I've written,'

Sara said. 'A kind of practical test. No cost,' she added, hastily. He grinned at her. 'You're on,' he said. 'Fire away.'

'OK,' Sara said, banging the front door behind her and striding purposefully into the kitchen, where Lottie was reading the newspaper still wearing her pyjama bottoms and a hoodie sweatshirt, Hector snoring at her feet. 'While you were slumbering in bed your mother has got herself a *job*.'

'No!' Lottie looked up from the paper. 'How on earth did you swing that?'

'Cheek, mostly,' Sara said. 'The chap from the trust – Nick, the one you heard me phoning yesterday to check he'd received my letter – said he'd see me this morning. I managed to talk him into taking me on, not just fund-raising, but writing press releases. They are not,' she added, smiling, 'going to pay me much at all, but at least it is gainful employment of a kind. It was nice to be in an office again, actually, although they were all so *young*. Only a bit older than you. And it was such a mess, I itched to clear up. How they find anything I don't know. They only want me a few days a week initially, but it's a start. I can work for other companies, too. It is *so* exciting!'

'What do you know about writing press releases?' Lottie asked suspiciously.

'Quite a lot, actually, I used to do it for Dad all the time. It was funny how quickly it came back, interviewing Nick and then writing up the press release. He was really pleased with the result,' she added happily, 'and he said I could go in tomorrow and look through their list of sponsors and think of new people and companies to approach.' She continued, her eyes shining, 'They emailed it over to the newspaper right away! It might be in the newspaper tomorrow!'

241

'They'll change it all,' Lottie said grinning. 'You know they will. I can't believe how excited you are.'

'The thing is,' Sara said, 'it's a start. I did it, all on my own, through sheer cheek, and the thing came off. Gosh, maybe I can make a go of this after all.'

'We're only talking about one tiny charity,' Lottie pointed out.

'I know, but there are plenty more out there, aren't there? And I can do a lot of the work from home, on your laptop, so I don't have to leave Hector on his own.' At his name, Hector thumped his tail against the floor under the table. 'This really feels like a new start.'

'But what will *I* do?' Lottie asked pitifully. 'I thought I was going to help you.'

'You can help me.'

'Only if it's raining, actually,' Lottie said grinning. 'I've decided I must teach myself how to surf.'

'I wonder why that might be?'

'A girl needs many weapons in her armoury,' Lottie said mysteriously.

Chapter Seventeen

Sara swung her colourful striped cloth handbag as she walked towards the trust offices in Fowey. That morning, she had looked at herself sternly in the mirror and said, 'Right, this is it, Sara Louise Atkinson. You have no one to depend upon but yourself, and you need to look businesslike and smart now you are back in the world of work. Which means make-up and nice clothes. You have to start making an effort.'

Although she had to admit that Nick and his fellow staff were unlikely to notice if she walked in wearing a binbag. But when she did get out and about to meet potential sponsors, she'd need to look the part.

She had decided that she was going to have her hair cut in a more fashionable style, and she was also going to buy some more clothes. All the walking and the twice-weekly Pilates sessions were definitely having an impact, and she might even have dropped another dress size.

Last night she had felt so fired up about the prospect of work she could not sleep, but this sleeplessness was so very different from the dreadful first nights at the cottage, when she had struggled to stop herself wallowing in nameless fears. She was wakeful now because she had so many purposeful ideas buzzing around her head. This morning she had woken feeling both energized and enthusiastic. She would have to be far more proactive: she could organize events and launch campaigns. After all, she had been running a home and family for years – now she could put all those organizational skills to good use.

In the middle of the night she had remembered about the discarded fishing lines. The death of the dolphin was unlikely to have been a one-off incident. Perhaps she could help the trust launch a campaign to stop fishermen dumping discarded nets and lines off their boats. She had read recently on the Internet that over a million sea creatures died each year through the debris of nets and lines in the oceans. Now that really would make her feel as if she was doing some good. Above all, she thought, as she lay staring at the ceiling, it is lovely to feel that I am needed, that I have a purpose to the day.

Just by the trust's offices she stopped to buy a copy of the local newspaper. As she walked into the shop, the headline splashed on a billboard by the door caught her eye. 'NO PANIC OVER GREAT WHITES!' it read. Almost unable to believe what she was seeing, she rushed into the shop, bought the paper and hastily scanned the front page. They had repeated her press release, literally word for word. Nick would be thrilled. She had a spring in her step as she reached the offices and a huge smile on her face. Pushing open the door, she was greeted with hoots of appreciation and Nick put down the apple he was eating, walked round his desk, and hugged her. 'I think we really do need you, Mrs Atkinson,' he said.

At lunchtime she offered to go out and buy everyone a sandwich. Nick looked at her gratefully. 'We often don't have any lunch,' he said. 'We just seem to forget.'

'Well, you must eat,' Sara said briskly, straightening a pile of papers as she walked past his desk. 'What does everyone want?'

Armed with a long list, she headed for the sandwich bar next to Pip's restaurant. She couldn't stop herself peering into the window. It was dark, and seemed empty. She turned to walk on. Just as she was doing so, the door opened.

'Hi,' he said.

'Oh, hi,' she said, casually. 'I'm just going to buy some sandwiches.'

'I see,' he said gravely.

'Sorry, that sounded rather mad. I've just started work, well, part time really, helping out, at the trust.' She waved her hand up the street. 'I said I'd get lunch.'

'The wildlife trust?'

'That's right. I used to do some fund-raising professionally and I thought that rather than sitting about at home surrounded by builders and getting in their way, I would see if they needed some help, and they do, so here I am.' She finished off her sentence breathlessly. She paused. Why was she talking gibberish?

'Good for you. They do a great job.'

They stared at each other in silence for a moment before Sara said hurriedly, 'Did you have a good surf? The other day, in our cove?'

'*Your* cove?' He smiled and Sara realized she had forgotten just how very attractive he was. 'I thought the sea was free. Not bad. It's still so cold though. The waves aren't really up to much on this stretch of coastline but I only get one day a week off, and I'm so knackered after all the late nights I need to kip. So I have to make do with whatever is available nearby.' He smiled again and Sara thought how perfectly white and even his teeth were. 'Are you in a rush?' he asked suddenly.

'No,' she said, startled by the question. 'I'll have to get back reasonably soon, but I'm free for a few minutes, if that's what you mean.'

'Cool. Would you like a coffee?' he asked. 'I'll treat you.'

'OK,' she said. 'Why not?' She was glad she'd made an effort with her appearance this morning, if only for her self-confidence.

'May as well have one here,' he said. 'We're not open for lunch today. I'm just setting the tables up for tonight.'

'I thought you were treating me?' Sara teased.

'OK. I owe you one,' he said. 'Next time.'

Sara perched on a bar stool as he walked behind the bar and switched on the big coffee machine. As he turned away from her, she found herself studying the back of his head, thinking how thick his hair was, as black as a raven, curling down to the top of his shoulders in gleaming waves.

'How do you want it?' he asked, turning to her, and Sara realized he must have caught her staring at him, and blushed. She suddenly had the urge to giggle. Tonight she was going to her first Women's Institute meeting at the village hall, and here she was, apparently being chatted up by a beautiful young man who appeared, for whatever insane reason, to be genuinely interested in her. Life was full of surprises.

'White,' she said smiling.

'What's so funny?' he asked, a puzzled look on his face.

'Nothing,' she said. 'Just a silly thought.'

'So how are you enjoying living here?' He put a white porcelain cup as large as a small bowl in front of her, sprinkling chocolate powder on to the top of the coffee from a steel pot on the bar. She took a sip, before wiping the froth from her top lip.

'I really love it. We both do. Lottie – you've met my daughter, haven't you? – says it feels as if we have lived here for years. But it's going to be chaos for the next few months,' she added.

'Oh, yes, I remember. You're having some building work done, aren't you?'

'That's right. It'll be murder. At least working here in town will make life a little more peaceful.'

'It's not *so* peaceful here,' he said, raising an eyebrow. He leant towards her, his elbows on the bar. Sara breathed in his warm masculine smell, with a hint of aftershave and salt water. His hair was still slightly damp – perhaps he had been swimming or surfing this morning. Discomfited by his proximity, she sat back in her chair and crossed her legs. She took a sip of coffee. Her heart was beating rather faster than usual. 'Why isn't it peaceful?' she asked in a high voice, and then coughed.

'It's like a party here every night, we don't shut until at least two.'

'But that's at night. I'll be working during the day.'

'Nothing to stop you joining in,' he smiled. 'Most of the locals end up down here on a Thursday night, when we have live music. It's a riot. You must come. Bring your daughter.'

Aha, Sara thought. So that's why you're being so nice to me. She smiled to herself. Delusions, again. She must stop forgetting that he would look at her and see a woman almost as old as his mother.

'It would be fun,' she admitted. 'Lottie would love it. I do worry she's getting bored, she misses all her friends in London. We meant to come a few weeks ago but we just didn't get round to it. We were celebrating – Lottie has a place at Bristol University in September.'

'Good for her.'

Was Sara imagining it, or did that odd melancholy

247

look she had seen before flit across his face? He turned away from her, using a J-cloth to wipe the nozzle which had just frothed the milk.

'So you came from London?' he remarked casually, turning to wipe the top of the bar.

'Yes.'

'Big change.'

'For the better.' Why had she said that?

'Good.' There was a long pause. Now he's wondering why he invited me for coffee, Sara thought. What could we ever have in common? Then she noticed he was smiling at her encouragingly. 'Look, come this Thursday. Everyone ends up dancing. Even the staff have been known to join in.' He shrugged. 'You'll have to promise to save me a dance, though.'

'I haven't danced in years,' Sara said laughing. 'I'm not sure I still know how to. You kind of grow out of dancing, you know.'

'Well, you shouldn't,' he said, leaning towards her again. This time Sara did not move away.

'I think,' she said, 'you may be quite right.' For a heartbeat, they looked steadily at each other.

The door banged behind them. Sara jumped, and turned to see the waiter with the ponytail standing behind them.

'This is Jake,' Ricky said. 'Jake, meet Sara.'

'Hey,' Jake held up his hand in greeting.

'How's the hangover?'

'Killing,' Jake replied, walking round the bar. 'Get me some black coffee, will you, man? I'm still drunk, I didn't get to bed until five. How did you get home? You couldn't have driven.'

'I didn't,' Ricky said. 'I ran. Quick dip in the sea, then came in here. I'm shafted, mate. Still on cloud nine.' Jack laughed. Sara felt as if a spell had been broken. How could she have thought they might be friends? He was of a different generation. Lottie's generation, of wild parties and staying up all night. She was slippers and a glass of wine by the fire before a nice early bed with a good book. She smiled to herself. 'I must be going,' she said. 'Thanks so much for the coffee.' She slid off the bar stool.

'No worries. Do come on Thursday. It'll be cool,' he said.

'Bye,' Sara said, as casually as she could manage. 'See you. Nice to meet you, Jake,' she added. He smiled at her and held up his cup of black coffee in farewell.

'Ciao,' Ricky said, bending down to run the tap under the bar to rinse out some glasses from the previous night.

'I saw you,' Helen whispered. 'Disappearing into a doorway with a gorgeous young man.' They were sitting in the back row of the village hall, while a woman called Gloria ran through a not very brief account of a recent holiday hill-walking in the Alps, accompanied by many slides of the Alpine flowers she had encountered along the way. Sara giggled. 'Have you got spies everywhere?' she whispered back.

'You didn't notice me, you were so wrapped up in your toy boy,' Helen murmured. 'I was in the delicatessen. I called hello, but you didn't hear me. Or blatantly ignored me, which is far more likely.'

'I'm sorry, I was miles away.'

'I bet you were.'

'He was only chatting me up to find out about *Lottie*,' Sara said, out of the corner of her mouth. 'Sadly.' A woman sitting in the row in front turned to glare at them. Gloria had reached Italy.

'At least she didn't need an elephant, not with those thighs,' Helen muttered.

Sara snorted. 'Shush. You'll get me thrown out, and this is my very first meeting.'

Helen ignored her, leaning forward and turning her head towards Sara to muffle her words. 'Come on, tell me all about it. Honestly, your heads were so close across the bar they were practically touching.'

'You were spying on me!'

'I just happened to walk past the window and couldn't help glancing in,' she said nonchalantly. 'So, go on, what did you talk about?'

'I was telling him about the plans for the cottage.'

'Is that all?'

'Well, what did you expect us to discuss?'

'I don't know. Something much more riveting than that. We're starved for gossip around here.'

'Do you know him?'

'Only to wave "hello" to,' Helen said. 'He moved into the village about a year ago, I think, setting many a young heart a-flutter, not to mention a few old ones. I don't know much about him – he seems very friendly, but I don't think he likes to volunteer too much information about himself. I've no idea where he comes from, or why he's here. He'll probably move on soon, after another season. A lot of young people come here for a few seasons and then just drift away.'

The woman in front turned round furiously. 'Will you be *quiet*!' she hissed. She had a very tight, curly perm, and the cross, beady expression of a bird whose mate had snatched the worm.

'Sorry,' Sara whispered back, and tried to compose her face into an expression of sincere interest. Gloria clicked a hand-held device to bring up yet another close-up of a very small flower. 'And this is a really pretty pink one,' she said. Helen put her hands around her throat as if to throttle herself, as Sara bit the inside of her lip.

Standing in the queue for a cup of tea what felt like days later, Sara murmured, 'Tea? Nothing more stimulating?'

'Nope. Tea and digestives, that's it. Hello, Martha, how are you? No? Your hip's still bad? I know, the NHS waiting lists are a scandal. You poor thing.'

'This is making me feel rather old,' Sara said, as they took their tea in faded green cups and saucers with a biscuit each balanced on the rim, to sit at a rickety table. 'I thought the WI had become much younger in outlook. More racy nude calendars than jam and Jerusalem.'

'*We're* the young ones here,' Helen said. 'Which is quite nice, really. I keep getting called a girl, which is very refreshing. The young mums in the village can't get out because there aren't enough babysitters to go round, and even if they could get one, they're hardly likely to come to the WI, are they? They'd rather go to the pub.'

'I hear you've moved into Tremain Cottage.' A woman who must have been well into her eighties put a tiny, gnarled hand firmly on Sara's arm. She was bent almost double, with her neck stretched out like a tortoise from a severely curved spine.

'That's right,' Sara said. Even sitting down, her head was almost level with the woman's. 'In Lanteglos,' she added, loudly and clearly.

'I know.' The woman twisted her head to look at her, the skin stretched tight like parchment over the bones of her face, her eyes black and bright as a little bird. 'That house is haunted, you know,' she said.

'Is it?' Sara said, surprised.

'Come on now, Beryl,' Helen said. 'Don't go frightening Sara, she's only just moved in. You'll scare her away. I've never heard anything about that.'

'I've been there for nearly seven months now and I can't say I've seen or heard anything unusual,' Sara said smiling.

'She killed herself, you know. Threw herself off the cliff.'

Sara looked at her in horror. 'Who did?'

'Same age as my grand-daughter,' Beryl continued, shaking her head. 'Sixteen. Such a beautiful girl, too. It was a tragedy. It all but killed him, you know, what with his wife having gone as well. He never recovered. Hardly ever left the house after that.'

She peered into Sara's face. 'There *were* rumours of a child, but we never saw it. She'd gone away for a while, you know, and then she came back. That's when it happened.'

'How awful,' Sara said, genuinely shocked. 'Was that – Mick's – daughter?'

'That's right,' she said, nodding. 'Charlotte.'

Sara locked the car and walked round the house to her front door. There she paused, looking up at the dark sky. The poor, poor man. No wonder he had lived almost as a hermit, if something so awful had happened to him. To have had a child die in such a tragic manner – and so young. The thought was unimaginable. *Why* had she killed herself? And then he was left with no one, his wife having died. The baby was probably just a rumour – he would have looked after it, surely, if he'd managed to raise a daughter on his own? Sara was not scared by the talk of ghosts – she had known, as she entered the cottage on that very first cold, windy day back in January, that there were no ghosts here. There was sadness, yes, and loneliness, but no spirits.

She pushed open the front door. Lottie's TV was on

in her bedroom, so she was still awake. Hector appeared, dragging his blanket. This had become something of a habit.

Moving into the kitchen, she poured herself a glass of wine. Sliding off her shoes, she rested her feet on Hector's comforting warm back, and stared out of the window. One of the tall firs was silhouetted on the left hand side of the frame, the dark contours like a child's drawing of a Christmas tree. Beyond its outline, the sun was sinking in shades of pale gold and ochre, the soft light broken by a line of dark cloud, like faint smoky grey brush strokes against the sky.

Chapter Eighteen

He lay with his back to her, the duvet hunched up over his broad shoulders. As she opened her eyes, he turned over, and she smiled at the way his face had lost all its tension after a good night's sleep. They lay very still for a moment, staring at each other. Slowly, he raised his hand, to brush her tangled hair from her face, and she felt the warmth of his fingertips against her cheek.

'You were hot again last night,' he said.

'Was I?'

'Yes,' he smiled. 'It was like lying next to a very sticky stick of rock.'

She laughed. 'I'm sorry. It'll pass.'

'Just one of those things, I guess. You ought to get it checked out, though.'

'I know. I did. The doctor says he'll put me on some kind of herbal supplement I know I will forget to take.'

He laughed, and rolled over on to his back, staring at the ceiling. The hairs on his chest were beginning to turn silvery, she noticed. She lifted herself up on one elbow. If she lay back and closed her eyes, she knew she would go back to sleep, and she must get up. From down the corridor came the sound of a shower being turned on – one of the girls was awake.

'She's up early,' Sara said dreamily, as she reached up to wipe away a tiny piece of sleep from the corner of her eyes. She swung her feet off the bed, feeling them sink into the soft rug which lay over the polished floorboards. She pulled down her nightie, which had ridden up in the night, as she'd tossed and turned, too hot, even though the window was wide open. Outside the open window the city was waking, with blaring car horns, shouts, dogs barking and the steady rumble of traffic. Conscious that he was looking at her, she pulled down the hem further, noticing, looking back, how the sheets had concertinaed into a series of fine pleats beneath her body. She ought to take the supplements, it was just she knew they would make very little difference. Age happened, just another phase, to be endured. Reaching up to take down the cream-coloured dressing gown which hung on the back of the bedroom door, she turned to ask Matt what he wanted to wear that day. But the bed was empty. She noticed the curtains were flapping against the wide open window, and her hand flew to her mouth. Surely not. Oh God, surely not. He wasn't well, there was some-thing wrong, but please God he would not do that. Not jump. Not jump from the cliff . . .

She woke, sweating, to the sound of knocking on the front door. For a moment, she felt quite lost – where on earth was she? She had to get Matt's clothes ready – oh, my God, what had he done, he'd . . . ? She took a deep breath as she looked around her, taking in the familiar details of her bedroom, as the world slowly righted itself. She was here. This was home. Matt was in London. Quite safe, as far as she knew, and that sound was the builder knocking on the door. Her eyes flew to her clock. Lord, how had she slept in until nine? She could hear Hector whining downstairs as she had, for once, slept with her bedroom door closed. She was getting rather fed up with being woken by a staring dog.

'Coming,' she called, loudly and pointlessly, because there was no way he would be able to hear. Lottie's bedroom was nearer, but it would take a bomb to wake her up, nor would she regard letting a builder in as part of her daughterly duties. Sleeping in until midday, yes. Leaving toast crumbs and an empty Marmite pot on the kitchen table every morning, yes. Sleeping with her TV still on and discarding a trail of clothes from the bathroom along the upstairs corridor, also, yes. Sara muttered to herself. Now she had secured a job, it really was time that Lottie found gainful employment as well. She was doing nothing at the moment, apart from sleeping, sunbathing and the odd bit of painting. When pressed on the issue, she said she was conserving her energy for the hurly-burly of life as a student, which made Sara humph even more.

Hurriedly, she pulled on her dressing gown and pushed her feet into slippers. But the dream still lurked in her subconscious, disturbingly, as if she were living between two worlds. She could feel the warmth of Matt's body against her skin, breathe in his smell, notice the way his mouth turned up at one corner when he smiled . . . She hesitated on the stairs, one hand on the rail, breathing deeply to slow her racing pulse. It's just a silly dream, she told herself firmly. Just a dream. He would never do anything so foolish, and anyway, he is not my responsibility. All is well.

Hector was waiting for her at the bottom of the stairs impatiently, tail thrashing, glancing backwards and forwards from her to the front door. He barked, twice – his deep, manly bark designed to repel all intruders.

'Hang on,' she called loudly. 'I'm coming. I am

sorry.' She tied the belt around her dressing gown more tightly in a knot and then slid back the bolt on the door, before opening it. Hector shot past her and positioned himself squarely in the doorway. He barked again fiercely. The man, wearing paint-stained blue overalls, seemed quite unperturbed and reached out to pat him on the head. Hector stared up at him, bemused. The stranger was supposed to be *terrified*. This was his very best bark. He'd been saving this particular deep-throated vociferous version for moments of real crisis.

'You're a handsome fella, aren't you? That's all right, ma'am, don't worry, I'm used to dogs. I am a bit early, I hope I didn't disturb you.'

Hector swiftly realized this was going to be friend, not foe, and did a remarkable about-turn. From scary guard dog he was instantly transformed into tail-wagging grinning-faced friendly Mr Labrador, weaving backwards and forwards against the man's legs, pushing his head ingratiatingly into his outstretched hand.

Sara smiled at the man, who held out his hand. 'Jim,' he said. 'Pleased to meet you.'

Sara shook it, taking care not to stretch out her arm too far in case it loosened her dressing-gown belt. Poor man, he hardly knew where to look. She quickly put up a hand to stop the robe falling open to reveal her cleavage. He was tall, well over six feet, and had a pleasant, open face. His thick hair was greying, and although he must have been well over sixty, he looked strong and fit.

'I overslept,' Sara explained, rather obviously. She stepped back. 'Come in, come in. I'll put the kettle on for some tea. I am normally up by now, honestly.'

'Don't mind me,' he said, taking care not to look at the top of her dressing gown. 'Tea would be grand.' He reached down to begin unlacing his heavy brown workman's boots.

'You don't have to take those off,' Sara said.

'I will, if you don't mind,' he said. He had a deep voice with a broad Cornish accent, very attractive, and Sara suddenly thought how nice it would be to have people in the house, a man around. There were so many other jobs which needed doing too.

As he walked in she moved forward to close the door, glancing out into the garden. It was a lovely morning. The leaves on the oak tree near to the front door were trembling in the light breeze, each, according to its size, appearing to move to a different rhythm. The newest leaves were the delicate pale pink of a baby's skin. Sara was finding it fascinating to see the garden gradually revealing its summer secrets – the top of the low stone wall at the front was now dotted with tiny pink and white geraniums.

When she had first seen the cottage in winter the garden had looked so bare – the trees, apart from the tall firs, swayed in the wind like grey skeletons and the flower beds were empty, brambles and bindweed the only visible plants. But ever since February little green shoots had been appearing. First came snowdrops, by March daffodils and crocus were blossoming, and now that summer was here the roses she had planted by the wall had produced the most stunning yellow, orange and pink flowers. Next year, she promised herself, the cottage garden would be in full bloom and she aimed to research and plant old-fashioned varieties such as phlox and hebe.

In the kitchen, she poured Jim a cup of tea, which he then sipped slowly. She began to sidle out of the door. 'I'll just . . .'

'Ay, you get on. I'll have a bit of a look round down

here and remind myself what's what before the boys arrive.'

Boys? Sara thought, climbing the stairs. Maybe he had a team of young lads.

The plan was to start with the really messy stage – the demolition of the internal walls between the two front rooms, taking away the corridor which ran down to the kitchen from the front door. Sara had had two site visits from the planning officer, and she and Helen had gone over the plans repeatedly, spreading the drawings out on the kitchen table and mulling them over with a glass of wine. In her mind, Sara had established exactly what shade she wanted to paint the walls, and thoroughly enjoyed wandering around mentally placing items of furniture and pictures. Having lived with the depressing, old-fashioned and shabby décor for so long, she was desperate to transform the cottage into a warm and welcoming haven.

She and Lottie had agreed on a cream-coloured range for the kitchen, as it would create much needed warmth in the winter as well as heating the water. Helen said she might want to put in an electric cooker as well, especially if she planned to cook for a number of people. Which, in turn, made Sara think of Christmas. Jim had told Helen that hopefully the building work should be finished by then, five months hence. It would be tight, he had told her on the phone, but they would try their very best.

As she climbed the stairs, Sara found she was actually looking forward to the festive season this year. Certainly, it could not be worse than last. What a long way I have come, she thought. She hoped Emily would come to stay this Christmas. Lottie would be home from university, and she could even invite her mother down, if she could bear the thought of her two boisterous dogs. The image of Matt flashed through her mind. No, she thought. Not yet. Maybe next year. If he could leave Karina, that is. If, in fact, he was still with her by then. She sighed. She ought to invite Catherine and Milo too – the girls would enjoy his company. Her mind ran on ahead. She could invite Helen for lunch if she didn't have her family staying or wasn't going up to see her son Daniel in the Midlands. Her daughter was in Australia, and wasn't planning to be back until Easter, having found a job and a boyfriend out there. Sara had a sudden, pleasing mental image of everyone sitting down to a meal at her new dining table, under the glass atrium in the extended kitchen. She began to look forward and sketch out menus.

If, that is, Emily would come. It was now a month since they had met up in London, and they had only spoken twice since the conversation about Matt which had so worried Sara. In two weeks Emily was due to fly out to Mauritius with him and Karina – she didn't think this was a particularly good idea, but there was nothing she could do about it. If she interfered, Matt would be furious.

'God,' Lottie said at lunchtime, looking at the four elderly men sitting on the stone wall outside, eating their sandwiches with a steady dedication. 'It's like being invaded by dinosaurs.'

'Shush,' said Sara giggling. These were Jim and his 'boys' – they were even older than he was. She and Lottie were looking out of one of the front windows, having inspected the quite extraordinary amount of necessary damage wreaked by just one morning's work. Of course she knew it would like a bombsite, but Sara hadn't quite been prepared for the clouds of dust and the sheer amount of rubble created. A fine grey silt seemed to have settled over everything, even upstairs. I'm going to have to block any thought of tidying up until all this is over, she told herself firmly. Otherwise, I will go rather potty. Going out was the answer. Just close the door and leave it all behind until they had finished – then she could face the marathon task of cleaning up.

She'd asked Nick if she might work from home for a few days this week, to supervise the builders, but she now decided this was a mistake. The chaos of the office with its overflowing bins and stained coffee cups suddenly seemed a haven of order and tranquillity.

Another problem she had encountered was that the cottage was so small there was nowhere for things to be stored, so the cream sofa and chair were currently sitting on a spare roll of carpet in the front garden, covered by a sheet. It was hardly ideal, and Sara was terrified of a summer shower. She realized she would probably have to find a storage company, because she couldn't leave her furniture outside indefinitely.

Jim told her that all his 'lads' were officially retired, but liked to take on the odd job now and then. Sara guessed they were probably bored sick of retirement, especially if life consisted of pottering about the garden and being bossed by their wives. As she gazed at them, one of the men reached down to put a screwed-up ball of cling film back in the Tupperware box at his feet. It was like watching a film in slow motion. Mesmerized, Sara watched him carefully peel back all four corners of the lid, place the cling film inside, stare thoughtfully at the contents for at least five seconds, and then click each corner back with absolute precision. Then he sat up, put his hand back on his knee and stared ahead of him into space. Moments later, his eyelids began to droop as he rocked gently backwards and forwards in the warm summer sun. Sara smiled to herself. How on earth had they managed to knock the walls down so quickly? They must be very good at conserving their energy.

Lottie nudged her. 'When did you say they said they were going to be finished? Christmas? More like *next* Christmas,' she said.

'Oh ye of little faith,' Sara said. 'You know what effect they are having, though? They're making me feel positively young.'

'It must be something in the air here,' Lottie said, gazing at the row of sleeping builders. 'Gradually, the pace of life slows all your bodily functions right down to zero and then you just – stop. They may even be zombies. It's a good sign they are eating.'

'One thing's for sure. I'm going back to work. All this mess is going to drive me mad and once they get started it's impossible to hear yourself think, let alone make phone calls,' Sara complained.

Jim briefly opened his eyes and reached up into his mouth to very slowly dig out what might have been a piece of trapped ham from between his teeth, with the edge of his fingernail. Sara watched him with appalled fascination. 'I can't see him and Helen together,' she remarked.

'What?'

'He's a widower. Apparently he fancies Helen. Keeps asking her out. Actually, I think he seems an absolute sweetheart but perhaps not the most dynamic of men.'

'Poor her. It would be like being kissed by a fossil.'

Sara laughed. 'I'm going into Fowey. Do you want to mooch about while I do some work? Or perhaps you could call in a few places and enquire about the possibility of a summer job. Honestly, the summer is going to be *over* before you earn any money.'

'I'm an *artist*,' Lottie said dramatically. 'I don't do menial labour.'

'My arse.'

'Mother!'

'Well, you've lazed about long enough. If you get a job you really like then they might take you back during your university holidays so you can earn some extra money. I'm not funding a party lifestyle at uni, you know.'

'Da . . .' Lottie caught the look on her mother's face and stopped. 'OK, OK, I'll try to get a job. I'll just spend my last days of freedom washing pans, if that makes you feel better, you mean person.'

'a) You are unlikely to be washing pans and b) this is not your last summer of freedom. You've got three years of university ahead of you, and trust me, it's not exactly hard labour. That comes when you get out into the real world of work. Most jobs only allow you five weeks' holiday a year.'

'Five weeks a *year*!' shrieked Lottie. 'That's inhuman!'

As they drove towards Fowey Lottie said, casually, looking out of the window away from Sara, 'Actually, do you mind if I go on holiday? I had a call from Katie. She's going inter-railing around Europe. I wouldn't be gone long, no more than three or four weeks.'

Kate was the friend with whom Lottie had travelled to Thailand.

Sara glanced over at her. 'Of course I don't mind, as long as you can earn enough to pay for it.' Lottie groaned. 'Well, I'm not simply handing over money for you to drift around Europe. If you want to go you must pay for it, and don't you dare ask Dad.'

'Slave driver.'

'Hardly.'

263

'You know, I might go and see Catherine when you're away,' Sara said. The thought had just occurred to her. 'I ought to catch up with old friends, I can't hide down here for ever.'

'Good idea.' Lottie nodded approvingly. 'You know Em's going away with Dad?'

'Yes, she told me.'

'What do you think? Sounds like hell to me,' Lottie said, sliding a CD into the player, adjusting the volume so they could talk. 'I mean, the hotel will be fantastic, you know what Dad's like about luxury, but oh, being with him and Karina would be murder.'

'Does Emily talk about her much?'

'A bit, not a lot. They don't like each other at all, obviously. And I bet Karina's not that thrilled, either – imagine going on holiday with your new bloke and his *daughter*.'

'It is a bit odd,' Sara admitted.

'I think Dad feels really guilty about Emily. He'd probably feel guilty about me too if I was still living in London, but I'm not as in his face as Em. I'd love to have been a fly on the wall when he told Karina their fabulous luxury holiday was going to include Emily.'

Sara laughed. 'It's up to him, though, isn't it? He'll be paying.'

'Maybe I'll ask Em if she'd rather come with me and Katie.'

'That's a good idea. Although Dad's going to have paid for the room and the flights by now, isn't he?' Sara was worried that Emily's relationship with her father was becoming a little *too* close. It was as if Emily felt she had to *guard* Matt, had practically taken on her, Sara's, wifely duties of looking after him. Perhaps that's why she was being so dramatic about his health. Emily needed to spend more time with people her own age, Sara thought. Live a normal life.

* * *

'How long have I got?' Lottie asked, leaning on the ticket machine in the car park in Fowey. They'd had to wait for a parking space – the streets of the little town, since the beginning of July, had been transformed into a sea of tourists and all the shops and cafés were doing a roaring trade. Sara felt absurdly resentful of the cheerful holidaymakers in their shorts, sunhats and flip-flops, browsing around the shops, taking up space choosing things they didn't really need, simply fancied. Don't you know some of us have to actually work here? she thought, crossly, as she queued for the ticket machine.

Sara pushed the pound coins into the slot and then pressed the green button for her ticket. She turned back towards the car. 'About two hours,' she answered Lottie. 'That should be enough, so many people seem to be away it's almost impossible to get anyone to commit themselves to anything at the moment. You could have brought your own car, Lots.'

'No petrol,' she admitted cheerfully. 'Two hours is cool. I'll see you back here. Don't work too hard.' She span on her heel and disappeared into the crowds. Grr, Sara thought, trying to walk the half mile from the car park into town above a dawdling pace.

Chapter Nineteen

'Are you sure you don't mind me just dropping by like this?'

Ricky was standing by the wall at the front of the cottage, shading his eyes from the sun, as Sara bent over the border, trying, with a great deal of effort, to pull up the roots of the elder and bindweed which invaded the flower beds. She knew this was not her best side – Lottie said that when she bent over it was like a total eclipse of the sun. From behind them came the muffled thump of falling masonry.

'Not at all,' she said hastily straightening up, pushing a lock of hair behind one ear, her hands in thick green gardening gloves, smearing soil on her forehead in the process. 'It's nice to see you.'

He smiled, and, reaching down to place a hand on the wall, he vaulted athletically over the top. 'It's great to get some peace. At work we are just *crazy*, they're queuing for tables down the street. What the hell are they doing in there?' He turned to look in the direction of the noise, the hair by his forehead darkened with sweat. He had been out for a jog, he had told her, and was desperate for an excuse to stop.

Pulling out one of the garden chairs he sat down, easing off an old pair of white and blue trainers, flexing his rather grubby bare feet in the sun. He had a curious ability, Sara thought, to make himself at home wherever he was, like a cat. Sitting at her table, he seemed as relaxed as if this were his home.

'Man, my feet hurt,' he said, rubbing the sole of his left foot. Amidst the tangle of love beads and copper bracelets on his wrist he had added several leather shoe-laces. 'I'm shit at jogging. I've got such a stitch, I really must get fit.'

'Doesn't surfing keep you fit?' Sara asked. She felt very self-conscious as she was wearing a pair of shorts and they did not hide much. But really, what did it matter? He was only being friendly, and he'd probably called in on the off chance of meeting Lottie. Her thighs, she told herself, were not an issue. She slid the gloves off and laid them on the wall.

'Surfing? Not really. You need a lot of strength, but it uses energy in short bursts, not real stamina.'

'It must be lovely to be able to surf, it looks so graceful when you're standing on the board. I wish I could have a go, but I'm sure I am way too old to learn now.' She laughed.

'Rubbish. I'll teach you. I'm lucky. I learnt as a kid, and it's like riding a bike, you never forget.'

'Have you lived here all your life?' she asked, and then remembered that Helen had told her he'd only moved into the village about a year ago. 'I mean, have you always lived by the sea?' She paused, also remembering that Helen had said he didn't like to volunteer much information about himself. She sounded, she feared, like a nosy old woman. 'Did your parents teach you when you were young?'

His easy smile disappeared as he looked up at her. 'No,' he said shortly. 'I'm adopted.'

She stared at him. What a curious thing to say. 'You learnt on holiday, then . . .' Her voice died away, embarrassed, as she pulled up a chair to sit down, pulling her shorts as far over her thighs as they would go.

'Yeah. We used to come to Cornwall when I was young. I was an only child, and I used to wander off on my own, bought a board one day and taught myself. My parents were kind of old, I can't imagine my dad surfing.'

'That must have been difficult,' she said thoughtfully.

'What?' His eyes searched her face.

'Having much older parents. As well as being an only child.'

He looked at her gratefully. 'Yeah. It was. I used to look at these families on the beach . . .' He shrugged. 'There were these kids jumping about in the sea with their dads and mine was sitting in a deckchair with a rug over his knees.' He shook his head. 'I used to lie. I used to say they were my grandparents.'

'Did you ever . . .' Sara stopped suddenly, aware it was a very personal question to ask someone she had really only just met.

'Go on.' He was looking at her curiously.

'Try and trace your real parents?'

He looked away from her, out to sea, and when he turned back Sara was astonished to see his eyes had filled with tears.

'I'm sorry,' she said. 'I really shouldn't have asked you, it was thoughtless . . .'

He reached up and ran the back of his hand over his eyes. Then he grimaced, his eyes full of a distant memory. 'That's OK. Really, man, it is. I did, but . . .' His voice tailed off and he twisted in his chair to look back at the cottage. 'So tell me, what are you doing to this poor little house? It sounds as if it's being knocked down.'

'I am slightly worried the whole thing *might* fall down,' Sara admitted. 'But the builders seem to know what they are doing. I'm knocking the two front rooms into one. The views are so lovely the plan is to make the windows much bigger so you get the best views, and also put a big fireplace at one end.'

'That's a very good idea, those rooms are way too small,' he said. 'Last time . . .'

Sara glanced at him swiftly. 'Last time?'

He looked away from her, his face flushed underneath his tan. 'When it was on the market I came and had a look,' he said casually. 'But there was no way I could afford it.'

Sara smiled. 'I see. No wonder you seem to know so much.'

'Yeah,' he said. 'That's it.' He looked out over the sea again, then tilted his head back, staring up at the aquamarine sky. Sara thought how sharp his jawline was and how beautifully long his neck, before it met the grubby white T-shirt. She examined him more closely. Oh dear, she thought, he really could do with some tender loving care. His T-shirt was filthy and full of holes, and his shorts, she had noticed before he sat down, were torn. His feet, one of which was resting on the wall, had very long dusty toenails. She had the sudden urge to run him a bath, and smiled to herself. She was turning into an old mother hen. She pulled her shorts even further down her thighs, and saw him glance over at the sudden movement.

'I like your hair,' he said suddenly. 'It suits you.'

Sara put her hand up, touching it, surprised he had noticed. 'I went to the hairdresser's in Fowey. They're really good. It's a younger style, but I do think it suits me.' She smiled. 'Not that I care so much, at my age.'

'What age?' he said. 'You're what, late thirties? That's not old.'

Sara looked at him steadily. No one would mistake her for being in her late thirties. Not even in the dark. 'Thanks,' she said. 'Although I don't believe that's how old you think I am for one moment.' Do you always flatter, Sara found herself thinking, as a way of keeping people at arm's length?

'So how old are you, then?' he asked, leaning forward, his eyes holding hers.

'What a personal question,' she replied smiling.

'You asked me one,' he replied. 'Fair do's.'

'OK. I'm fifty,' she said.

'No!' He seemed genuinely surprised.

'How old are you?'

'I might not tell you,' he said, teasingly, twisting one of the shoe-laces of his discarded trainers around his finger. 'Guess.'

'This is a bit silly,' Sara said, grinning to take the sting out of her words. 'OK. Twenty-nine. Thirty.'

'Not far off. I'm thirty-one,' he said. 'And still a waiter. Impressive, huh?'

'It's not a bad job. I mean, the lifestyle down here is wonderful, isn't it, you can surf and it sounds as if there are a lot of parties . . .'

'Oh, there's no shortage of women and parties,' he said.

Sara felt a sudden pang in the pit of her stomach.

'I just don't know what to do next,' he continued, his smile fading.

'How did you come to live here?' Sara asked curiously. 'Where are your parents from?'

'Somerset. Not so far away. I don't see them, though . . . we . . . well, they think I'm kind of drifting about. Wasting my life. I guess I never turned into the son they wanted.' He shrugged his shoulders.

'Did you go to university?'

'Yeah. Didn't last though, I kind of got into the drug

thing and then I just dropped out and went off travelling. I only meant to travel for a year but then I found work and one year turned into three or four. I lived in Canada for a while – I met a girl there. But she wanted to settle down, have babies, all that shit. I realized I didn't love her so I moved on.'

'What did you study at university?'

'Architecture.'

'How interesting. Couldn't you go back to it?'

'I guess I could. I just . . .' Sara noticed a movement under the table, and realized it was his knee moving rapidly up and down. He lifted his hand to put his fingernail into his mouth, and she saw how bitten they were, the skin around them raw. 'It was easier to pick up jobs here and there. I couldn't face going back to university, couldn't afford it, anyway. I came to Cornwall because . . . I guess I was looking for someone.'

'And did you find them?'

He drew his dark eyebrows together. 'No,' he said. 'I was too late.'

'They'd gone?' Sara asked, her heart touched by the pain on his face.

'Oh yeah,' he said. 'They'd gone. Long gone. But it was so beautiful I stayed. I like the job. It's easy, the people are fun, there's a good *craic*. I don't have to think too hard and I can surf.' He lifted his head and stared at her. 'What about you? What brought you here?'

Sara bit her lip. 'It's rather . . .'

He leant towards her. 'What?'

She sighed. Why not tell him? 'My husband left me,' she said simply. 'He was having an affair with a much younger woman and I found out and then . . .'

'You kicked him out?'

'Not exactly. You could say I ran away. I ran here,

271

miles away from home. We lived in London . . .'

'I remember you saying.'

'I suppose I wanted to put as much of a distance as I could between him and the pain. No, not pain, really. Anger. Humiliation. You know, everyone whispering and saying, "Poor Sara," and it drove me mad. I wanted to be somewhere new. Be someone new, I suppose.'

'That's brave of you. To start a new life . . .'

'At my age?' Sara smiled.

He smiled back at her. 'Touché. Had you been married a long time?'

'Twenty-six years.'

'Wow.'

'I know. I have two daughters, my eldest, Emily, still lives in London. She's twenty-three – Lottie is nearly twenty.'

'How did they take the split?'

'It's been hard,' Sara said. 'But we're coming through it now. I love living here, it's so peaceful . . . well, usually,' she added, laughing.

'Kind of spiritual?'

She looked at him, surprised. 'Yes,' she said. 'It is.'

'The sea gets in your blood,' he said, looking over at the headland, which cast a long dark shadow over the water. A fly landed on his hand, and instead of brushing it away, he watched it march across his skin, and then jump off on to the table, where it paused to wash its face with spindly front legs. He smiled. 'I don't normally talk this much,' he said. 'You're a good listener.'

Sara laughed. 'Thank you.' They sat in silence for a few moments, and she was surprised how easy she felt in his company. He had a scar, she noticed, running across one black eyebrow, a thin white line, like an arrow.

'Do you mind if I call in again?'

'Why would I?' She smiled.

'You're pretty cool, Sara,' he said. 'I'm glad you live here.'

He lifted his foot off the wall, and, standing up, he leant forward with his right hand. Gently, he rubbed his fingers over the skin of her forehead. 'You've got a mark,' he said. 'Just here.'

Chapter Twenty

'I hate her,' the angry voice proclaimed. 'I want to chop her up into little pieces and feed her to the fishes.'

'Who?' Sara asked, although she already knew.

'*Karina*,' Emily said. 'You've no idea, Mum, what she's like. She resents absolutely every tiny thing about me – Dad said I could have whichever bedroom I wanted in the new flat and I was free to stay over any time, but now she says I can't because she needs my bedroom to keep all her bloody clothes and shoes in. She has millions, and she's moved all the stuff I left with Dad out, just plonked it in a cupboard, not even folding anything. She doesn't think about anyone else, *ever*. It's just me, me, me.'

'Not even Dad?' Sara couldn't resist saying.

'Oh, she's all over *Dad*,' Emily spat out the words. 'It's sickening. I hate seeing her with him. She's always pawing him, holding his hand, smoothing his hair, picking bits of fluff off his jacket. It's all look, I own this person, he's mine, not yours. Like we're in competition or something. She's so childish. And Dad just takes it. Well, he used to, but I think he's starting to get fed up with her as well. She's so self-centred, she spends hours and hours gazing at herself in the mirror and she's always in the bathroom. The apartment is like totally covered in her stuff, not just clothes and shoes but beauty products and magazines. You know how tidy Dad likes everything, really anal? Well, he's always picking things up after her. Can you imagine that? And she never cooks, when I go over we always have to eat out and Dad says he's going to run out of money at this rate. And he's bought her a car, a black Porsche like his. It's enough to make you vomit.'

Sara had to stop herself laughing at her daughter's sulky voice. She felt for Emily, she really did, but there was a hint of come-uppance. 'Do they have matching number plates? His and hers? How charming.'

'It wouldn't surprise me. And Dad looks really knackered, Mum. She wants to go out every night and stay up late and she's always complaining that Dad isn't enough fun, although she seems perfectly happy spending his money. They're forever going to expensive restaurants.'

'She does work for him,' Sara pointed out.

'*Supposedly*,' Emily said, her voice full of venom. 'She seems to spend most of her time shopping or having her bloody nails done. I'm not going to Mauritius. I told Dad last night. I can't face it, it would be just so ghastly watching her drooling over him and there'd be no escape. Plus the fact that the last thing she wants is me tagging along, she's made that clear. Actually, that's about the only reason to go, just to piss her off. But I still couldn't bear it. Lottie said I could go round Europe with her but that'll be so studenty, staying in youth hostels and stuff, gross. And now it's too late to arrange anything with my friends. Work is driving me round the bend. I'm doing ten-hour days and I earn a pittance. Honestly, nothing is going right at the moment.'

'It's your first job,' Sara pointed out. 'You can't

expect to earn a fortune, and journalism always means working long hours.'

'I know, I know, don't nag. Dad and I had a big row last night.' Her voice dropped. 'I said I was sick of seeing him running round after her and that she was the most selfish person I've ever met.'

'I bet that went down well.'

'Not very. Dad said it was none of my business, which is really rich, isn't it? I mean I'm his daughter, I'm perfectly entitled to my opinion. But he won't listen to me. I just hope he gets more and more irritated by her. And she's so . . .'

'What?'

'Oh, nothing.'

There was a long pause. 'Come on, Emily, spit it out. She's so what?'

'Such a baby,' Emily said quickly. Sara realized that wasn't what she had been about to say at all.

'Emily, is there anything you're . . .'

'It drives me mad. She's such a princess. I was working on a late shift yesterday so I nipped round first thing in the morning to see Dad before work. He took ages to answer the door – I still haven't got my own key – and – well. She expected me to make her coffee, like I was her slave or something.'

'Doesn't Dad mind her being so lazy? We all used to run around after him.'

'He's put up with it so far, it's so weird, although she seems to realize she can't push him too far. When he gets cross with her she has this way of looking up at him from under her eyelashes, as if to say, poor little me, and you just know she's got him wrapped round her little finger. It's like she has some kind of hold over him.'

Which she clearly does, Sara thought, sexually, but she could hardly say this to Emily.

'So work's not going well?'

'No it isn't. It's so bloody boring having to *be* there all the time.'

'But that's what having a job is like,' Sara said patiently.

'Fat lot you know,' Emily said rudely. 'You never even worked full time.'

'I did, actually, before you were born. I do know what it's like.'

'Yeah, but you didn't face the prospect of years and years of this, endless crappy pay and hardly any holidays. Honestly, I'm going to find a rich man and marry him. Roll on the money from Dad'd trust, I say.'

'But having a career is important,' Sara said. 'Trust me, I wish I'd spent more time establishing my career before I had you two. I'm glad I could be at home with you when you were little but I should have returned to work, even if it was only part time. It's so hard getting back into the workplace after such a long time at home.'

'Do you really wish you hadn't given up work?' Emily's voice was surprised.

'Yes, I do. I think it's important you have something for yourself so you aren't beholden to someone else. Stick at it, Emily. You can't rely on Dad for ever, you know. You're a grown-up, you have your own life. I thought Dad said he was going to buy you a flat.'

'Hmm, that's gone suspiciously quiet and I bet Karina has something to do with it, she doesn't want Dad to spend money on anyone but her. I wish you and Lots weren't so far away,' she added suddenly.

But it's been your choice not to come and see us, Sara thought impatiently, but didn't say anything. You sided with Dad and you haven't once asked me how I am feeling.

'I think I'm going to go off travelling,' Emily said sulkily. 'Take a year off.'

'What would that solve?' Sara asked.

'It would be fun.'

'Undoubtedly, but you're already had a gap year before university and you'd have to come back eventually and start all over again at the bottom, when everyone you left behind had been working their way up in your absence. Besides, when you go away for a long time, it is really hard to settle when you get back. Especially if you haven't established a career properly.'

'How do you know?'

'A friend told me,' she said.

'Which friend?' Emily asked suspiciously.

'A new friend,' Sara said.

'What's it like down there?' Her voice was curious.

'Noisy and dusty,' Sara said. 'I've got the builders in. You should have come before I started the renovations. You'd hate it at the moment, we're camping in a cloud of dust and everything we eat seems to be covered in a layer of grit. I'm sure Lottie's going to Europe to get away from all the mess.'

'It's good about Bristol, isn't it?'

'Yes, we were thrilled,' Sara said. It suddenly struck her that saying 'we' was ludicrous. It was as if their family had been split in half. 'Do come soon, never mind the mess,' she said. 'We miss you so much.'

There was a pause at the end of the phone. 'I really miss you, too,' Emily said in a very small voice. 'I hate this. You have no idea . . .'

'We can't change the situation, darling. You just have to make the best of it. It's one of those things.'

Emily laughed. 'That's a very Granny thing to say. I'm sick of being a grown-up,' she said. 'It sucks.'

'Don't make any rash decisions,' Sara said. 'Look, Lottie and I are going to look at Bristol next week, before she goes on holiday, just to have a wander around and maybe look at halls, that kind of thing. Could you take a day off and meet us?'

'That would be cool.' She hesitated. 'There is something I think I need to talk to you about.'

'What?' Sara asked, alarmed.

'I can't talk about it on the phone. It's kind of – complicated. I'm not sure. I'd really love to see you both – could we make it Wednesday?'

'That would be lovely. Are you sure you can't tell me now?'

'No.'

Chapter Twenty-one

'I wish I could live here,' Lottie said, looking up at the beautiful, honey-coloured Georgian terraced houses set around a square, with a leafy communal garden in the centre.

'I bet you do,' Sara said, consulting the directions the rental agency in the students' union had given them. 'But the halls we are looking for are not, unsurprisingly, in this area. We go to the end of this street,' she turned the little photocopied map upside down, 'turn left and keep walking for about a mile. But these houses are gorgeous, aren't they?'

'Fabulous,' Lottie said dreamily, running her hand over the black railings. 'I wonder if Dad would buy me a house here? Bugger halls. It would be like living in a Jane Austen novel.'

'I doubt even Dad would run to a four-storey Georgian terrace in Clifton,' Sara said sharply. 'Anyway, there's no point buying anywhere too soon, you need to be into halls to make friends. That was part of the problem last time, wasn't it, you isolated yourself.'

'It was mostly from being somewhere really crap and depressing in the first place,' Lottie said, swinging on the railings. 'This is totally different. I can tell I am going to be happy here.'

'Come on,' Sara said. 'We've only got an hour before we're due to meet Emily.'

Lottie saw Emily first, as they ducked their heads under a low beam at the entrance to the restaurant. She was standing at the bar, and, as Lottie called her name, she put the mobile phone she'd been checking for messages back into her handbag and turned towards them.

Sara's first thought was that she had lost weight – too much. Emily was wearing a white and blue flowery halter-neck dress, and it was hanging off her. She had always been plumper than Lottie, although never fat. Now Sara could see her clearly defined collarbones, like little chicken wings poking through her skin, and her arms were like matchsticks. She looked very tired too – as Sara moved nearer to her she could see the dark shadows under Emily's eyes. Although their hair was a different colour, she and Lottie now looked much more similar. But beside Lottie's healthy tan and shining hair, Emily seemed pallid, fragile. It was only two months since Sara had seen her daughter, but the change in her appearance was remarkable. Sara felt a stab of guilt. Should she have insisted that Emily take time off work to come and stay in Cornwall? Or should she have come to London to see her? It was awkward as she had nowhere to stay, but she could have slept on the floor at Emily's rented flat. What did comfort matter? I have been blinded by my hurt at your support of your father, Sara thought. Which is neither mature, nor the way a mother should feel. You come first, not me.

'I love you,' she murmured, pressing her lips against Emily's cheek, breathing in her perfume, the fragility of her skin. 'I've missed you so much.' Her heart felt so full she could barely swallow.

'I love you too,' Emily said, biting her lip. Sara looked into her shadowed eyes. With a trembling hand, she wiped the tip of a red-nailed finger underneath her eye, tears smudging the line of mascara. Sara leant forward and gently rubbed the mark away.

Emily rested in her mother's arms, her body curiously lifeless, as if completely exhausted. Then she pulled away, blinking, and forced a smile which did not reach her eyes. 'God, you two are *so* brown,' she said. 'You must spend every day sunbathing. It's all right for some. Look at me. Not a hint of colour. *I* have to spend all week inside, slaving away. Honestly, Lots, I can't wait for you to start work. It's *dreadful.*' At the end of the sentence her voice cracked, and she glanced away from them. Lottie looked at her mother in alarm, raising her eyebrows.

'We have been lucky with the weather this summer,' Sara admitted, keeping her tone light. She reached down to take hold of Emily's hand, squeezing it hard. 'I can even work in the garden if I want to, I just take the laptop and a mobile outside. We're walking a lot, too – Hector loves it, we can go for miles on the cliffs. He didn't at first, but he's so fit now you wouldn't recognize him. He looks years younger.'

Emily's bottom lip trembled. 'I miss Hector,' she said. Rather than taking away her hand, she held on tight to her mother, and Sara thought, I must never let you go. Never again. I *love* you, her hand clenched around Emily's repeated. Love you, love you. Do not doubt it.

Lottie looked sceptically at her sister. 'Really? You used to say he was a useless waste of space and so smelly he must have his own eco system.'

'I didn't mean it. I miss him now. I miss . . . lots of things,' she added, looking into Sara's eyes. She took a deep breath, slid her hand out of her mother's and rested it on the bar. Sara noticed it was shaking. 'How's your new job, Mum? Is it fun?'

'Not fun, exactly,' Sara replied. 'Most of the time it's like banging your head against a brick wall, trying to get money out of companies and convince them it will do their image good to sponsor the trust. I had planned to approach other charities but I'm so busy I haven't time at the moment.'

Emily's smile was brittle. 'Really? Can we have a drink? I haven't ordered one yet. I was waiting for you and you're *late*.'

'Mum's gone all ecologically friendly,' Lottie said grinning. 'We have to, like, recycle everything and she threw away some of my make-up last week because she thought it might have been tested on animals.'

'We must tread lightly on the planet,' Sara said. 'It's my new mantra. Of course we can have a drink. What do you want? Wine?'

'Mm. Just a glass though, I have to drive home . . . back to London.'

Lottie raised her eyebrows at Emily. 'See? Mantra? We have a New Age mother.'

'You *do* look different,' Emily said, looking her mother up and down. 'You've lost weight.' She seemed to be regaining her poise, but Sara could not rid herself of the urge to snatch up her daughter, bundle her into the car and take her home where she could run her a bath, put a hot water bottle into her bed and feed her hot Ribena, as she'd always done when she was ill or off colour as a child. I need to take care of you, she thought. No one is looking after you. Perhaps, she thought, you only stop being a child when you have one of your own.

'A little,' Sara nodded. 'Although not enough.'

'And bought some new clothes, I see.'

'Lottie helped me.'

A flash of jealousy crossed Emily's face. 'They suit you,' she said generously.

'A compliment?' Sara smiled.

'Don't get carried away. I don't mean you look ten years younger or anything, but you do look – good. Three glasses of dry white wine, please. Thanks. Dad . . .'

'Yes?'

'Nothing. I've found us a table, by the way, on the terrace. I thought we'd sit outside, it's so lovely and sunny.' They each reached forward to take a glass, and Emily led them out of the bar.

As they followed her, Lottie whispered in her mother's ear. 'There's something up with Em. She's being *polite*. And why is she so thin? She's never been thin. I'm the thin one.'

'Mum's fallen in love with a young bloke,' Lottie remarked casually, as their starters arrived. Emily looked at her mother in horror. The waitress, who was serving them at the time, smiled down at Sara as if to say, 'Good for you, honey.'

'No! Please tell me you haven't found a toy boy. That would be *gross*.'

Sara smiled. 'I have *not* got myself "a young bloke", thank you, Lottie. There's just a . . . a young man, in the village, who calls round occasionally and we chat.'

'He's dreamy,' Lottie said, spearing a prawn. 'You'd love him, Em. He's got long dark hair and great big eyes like a spaniel, just your type. Fit, too, he's an amazing surfer.'

'How did you meet him?' Emily asked.

'We bumped into him. Literally.' Sara said. 'He stopped me from being run over in the street. He works in a café in Fowey, the pretty town where the trust is based. You'll love it, Emily it's very "you".

Then we found out he lives in our village. Anyway, Lottie's exaggerating. We hardly know him.'

'What a weird thought. You being friends with someone our age.'

'He's older than you, actually. Anyway, why?' Sara asked. 'Surely age is purely relative.'

Emily raised her eyebrows. 'No it isn't. How old is he, anyway?'

'Thirty-one,' Sara said.

'I didn't know that!' Lottie was indignant. 'You never told me you'd asked him his age.'

'You never asked me. Besides, I don't have to tell you everything, you know. I do have a private life,' she smiled.

'No you don't,' Lottie said. 'You're our mother. Actually, Em, there is a big difference in the old mother.' She turned to look at Sara. 'You're more relaxed about things, generally, aren't you, Mum?'

Sara smiled back at her. 'I think I've needed to be, don't you?'

'Don't you miss London?' Emily asked curiously. 'Home?'

At the word 'home', Lottie cast a surprised glance at her sister. 'Cornwall is home now,' she said.

A shadow passed over Emily's face. 'No, it isn't,' she said. 'It's not *my* home.'

'Not yet,' Sara said quickly, as Emily chewed her lip, her eyes bright. 'Come as soon as you can. You must be able to get time off work and Dad won't mind.'

'What's Dad got to do with it?'

'Nothing, I just thought that you might not . . . might not want to hurt his feelings.'

'Don't be bloody silly, Mum, why would he mind me?'

'He wouldn't, of course he wouldn't. I'm just being silly.'

'He doesn't care anyway,' Emily said suddenly. 'All he cares about is *her*.' She slammed her fork down. 'No one thinks about me.' She sobbed, pushing back her chair. 'I'm going to the loo.'

Lottie sat back in her chair, watching her sister's rapidly disappearing back. She waited until she was out of earshot before she spoke. 'What on earth is the matter with her? She's gone completely bonkers. She told me she never wanted to come to Cornwall,' she said.

'You shouldn't tell me things you've been told in confidence, Lottie. Be a little more sensitive. This must be really hard for Emily, she feels we . . .'

'Well, she's making it sound as if we abandoned her! She *chose* to stay in London – I know she had to for work but she didn't have to carry on living with Dad, not to mention letting him pay for everything. He's bought her loads of new clothes. My theory,' Lottie said, tapping the table with her finger, 'is that Karina's fed up with having her hanging around Dad's new flat and is forcing her out. That's why she's being so nice to us.'

'That's really unfair, Lottie. I think she feels very alone.'

'Hmm,' Lottie said darkly. 'You don't know what she's been saying about you . . .'

'And nor do I want to. Be quiet, she's coming back.'

'Were you talking about me?' Emily asked, staring between the two of them. She rubbed a hand over her forehead with trembling fingers. Her eyes were pink.

Lottie looked up, her face a picture of innocence. 'The world does not revolve entirely around you, Emily.' She took a sip of wine. 'This is yum. Can we have some more?' She looked pleadingly at Sara. 'Please, Mummy.'

'Sit down, darling. Everything is fine. We were talking about you, but I just said I was worried you seemed so thin. But it suits you,' she added hastily. 'I don't want another whole bottle,' she continued. 'Lottie, darling, could you go to the bar and get us three more glasses of white wine? Tell the barman to put it on the bill.'

'You want me out of the way, don't you?' Lottie said crossly. 'What do you need to say that I can't hear? It isn't fair.'

'Just *go*,' Sara said. Lottie trailed away reluctantly, making a face at her mother over her shoulder.

'So,' Emily said trying to sound bright, once Lottie was out of earshot. 'Tell me about the cottage. Have you brought any photos with you?'

'No,' Sara said. 'I haven't. Darling . . .' She reached forward and put her hand over Emily's, noticing that below the smooth varnished nails, her cuticles were bitten. 'Please tell me. What is the matter? I know you inside out. Please, please do not think that I had any intention of leaving you behind in London. I wish, more than ever, that I had insisted you come with me but you had your new job ... I wasn't thinking clearly. I have been at fault, and I have not been a good mother over the past six months. I haven't put you first, but oh, darling, don't ever think that I haven't thought about you every day. I would love you to come to Cornwall. It's so quiet and beautiful – the house is a bit of a tip at the moment but it's going to be wonderful and you'll be able to really relax there. I want you to have your own bedroom, put your own things in it and you can come whenever you want, even if you just want a day out of London. It's your home too, darling, as much as mine and Lottie's.'

'It isn't really that, Mum. I know you love me, stupid.'

'So what is it? Is it something to do with Dad?'

'No.' Emily dropped her head and Sara had to lean forwards to hear her. 'Yes,' she said, almost inaudibly. Sara gently put her hand under her daughter's chin, tilting her head. She saw that she was crying.

'Oh, my love. We've put so much pressure on you. What on earth is it?' she asked. 'Please, darling, tell me . . .'

'It's OK.' Emily brushed away her tears. 'Oh, it's everything, really. Not being able to see you, you and Lots being so far away, having to cope with my new job and seeing Dad with that . . . that bitch. It's horrible, Mum, it's all wrong, as if life has gone completely insane. And there's something else as well, something big . . . I shouldn't tell you, though, I promised . . .'

'Is it to do with Dad? Is he ill?'

Emily took a deep breath. 'Look, Mum. I really don't know if I should say this or not, it may even be none of my business, or yours, but . . .'

'Here you go.' Lottie cheerfully plonked the glasses of wine on to the table.

'What?' she asked, looking from her sister to her mother with bewilderment. 'What's up with you two? You look as if someone had just died. God, there was such a queue at the bar.'

'Emily was just – do you mind saying whatever it is in front of Lottie?'

'What on earth is going on?'

'There's no reason why Lottie shouldn't hear this,' Emily said quickly. 'If I tell you, I may as well tell Lots.' She looked up at the ceiling, screwing up her face as if trying to find the courage. 'This is so hard. Dad . . . Dad has a . . . a problem.'

'Well, we know that,' Lottie said. 'Her name is Karina.'

'Don't joke, Lots. It is so not funny. There's no easy way to say this.' She took a gulp of wine.

'For God's sake, Em, spit it out,' Lottie said.

'Dad's taking drugs.'

'WHAT!' Sara's hand jerked forward in a spasm, knocking her wine glass over. The contents spilled out over the table like a river, into Lottie's lap, who jumped backwards squealing.

'Ssh,' Emily said furiously.

'What kind of . . . drugs?' Whatever Sara had been expecting, it was not this.

'Coke, mostly. Karina's an absolute cokehead, she takes it nearly every night. Most of her friends do too, and they're the ones Dad's been socializing with.'

For an instant, the idea seemed so ludicrous to Sara she thought she might laugh.

'Dad? Taking cocaine? At his age?'

'Lots of people do, Mum,' Emily said. Sara remembered Catherine. They did, didn't they?

'But he's always hated drugs. He said only losers took them . . .' Sara shook her head, unbelievingly. 'I'm sorry, but I find this so very hard to comprehend. How could he be so stupid?'

'He's been taking it for ages, you know. He told me one night, when he was quite drunk.'

'Ages?'

'Years.'

'While we – while Dad and I were together?'

'I think so, Mum. I'm sorry.'

Sara sat back in her chair. So many things began to make sense – the shaking, the nervous tic beneath his eye, the jittery behaviour, the irrational decisions he had made over the past two years, culminating in his affair with Karina. What could have sparked it off? The sale of the company, she suddenly thought. It could well date from around then. She had known he was very stressed because the pressure seemed endless, but she thought he had it under control through natural methods, by running, by the hours he spent in the gym. He had an addictive personality – all that manic energy was poured at the beginning of their marriage into keeping the business afloat, and then making it such a huge success. He was a man who never did anything by halves, and she could see that if he tried something like cocaine, something which instantly took away the fears and worries flooding his hyperactive mind, making him feel super-confident and on top of the world, he would find it irresistibly attractive. And yet, she had thought *she* was the one who knew how to keep him calm and happy. By making his home and family as loving, safe and secure as possible, taking away as much pressure as she could from him. She had a sudden, crushing realization. Not all of this had been his fault. He was not acting rationally. *Had* he stopped loving her? How much of an influence had coke been on his affair with Karina?

'He and Karina share the same dealer,' Emily said, mirroring Sara's thoughts. 'I think it all started from that.'

Sara looked at her unbelievingly. The entire conversation felt totally surreal, everything she had regarded as their previous normal middle-class life was being blown to smithereens. Poor, poor Matt. What a tragedy, what an awful tragedy that he'd fallen into such a state, and she had been so unsuspecting. You're right, she thought. I didn't live in the real world. I lived in a little happy bubble while you were out there on the edge.

'I'm really, really worried about him,' Emily said, her voice cutting through Sara's thoughts. 'He's started having panic attacks, he says he can't breathe. I said he ought to see his doctor or even go into rehab. He passed out one night, it was awful. I was staying with him and I found him on the floor in the kitchen.

But Karina's like, he'll be fine, just leave him. Thank God he came round, I was about to call an ambulance but he was frantic that I didn't tell anyone.'

'Why didn't you tell *me*?' Sara said.

'I nearly did, several times, but he begged me not to – he made me promise,' Emily grimaced at the memory. 'He tried to reassure me, saying it wasn't a big deal, he was just exhausted and he had it under control. And because he's my dad and he's always been the one in charge, I believed him. Now he's so worried about the new people who own the company finding out – he's got to stay in his job for another two years, hasn't he, to get the full pay out? And Karina's spending so much money – this holiday to Mauritius is costing a fortune, which is why he was so livid with me for pulling out. She insists on flying first class.'

'But surely he's far too intelligent to put himself in such a vulnerable position?' Sara said, almost to herself.

'He's changed so much,' Emily said. 'He's lost without you, Mum. I know he brought all this on himself, but he's really paying now. I think he's having a kind of breakdown. I guess it all started to fall apart the night Richard told us about Karina.'

'But it seems as if all this – the drugs and Karina – had been going on a long time before that night,' Sara said.

'But Richard brought it all to a head, didn't he? Maybe before Dad was only doing a bit here and there, because he was with you, but once you'd gone there was no one to stop him, was there? There was no one to put on the brakes.'

'This can't be my fault,' Sara said.

'I know, Mum,' Emily said. 'I didn't mean that. I just mean that since you left he's out of control, and Karina is the very worst person for him to be with. She's never going to stop him taking it because she's so hooked on the stuff herself.'

Lottie gave a sob, and Sara reached over to put her arms around her. 'It's *horrible*,' she moaned into her mother's shoulder. 'Like a nightmare. What can we do?'

'I don't know,' Sara said slowly. 'It'll be very hard to interfere. Dad's a grown-up, after all. It's his life.'

'It's not *interfering*,' Emily said. 'Mum, face the facts. Dad could *die*. He could have a heart attack or something.'

Tears were running down Lottie's face. Sara tightened her arms around her, rocking her gently. What could she do? What should she do? She took a deep breath. 'I need to see him,' she said decisively.

Chapter Twenty-two

There was a tiny break in the clouds, a small sliver of ocean blue amidst the pale grey masses billowing overhead. The grassy banks at the side of the lane were slick with water, rain dripping methodically off the ivy, brambles, wild geraniums and ferns. For so long it had been dry, the pastureland yellowing, arid and parched, but now the heavy thunderclouds hung low in the sky and the rain had come.

Perhaps it will clear up this afternoon, Sara thought, driving the Volvo slowly along the lane leading away from the cottage, peering up at the sky as her windscreen wipers beat a rhythmic crescent-shaped pattern through the raindrops. But even as she watched, the curtains of cloud drifted together, swallowing the sliver of blue sky, the tiny promise of sun.

It was odd, she thought, how much the weather affected one's mood – as she had looked out of the bedroom window this morning, and watched the rain dripping off the tarpaulins the builders had left draped over the trestle table outside, soaking the pile of sand to the colour of dark red clay, she had felt her spirits fall, and she moved listlessly around the house, unable to tidy up, to focus on any one thing.

It was such a frustrating time of year, she thought –

work was so slow, all the big corporations she was approaching for sponsorship didn't want to make decisions now, with directors away on holiday and the skeleton staff unwilling to commit themselves. Nick was backpacking around New Zealand, so there was no one to report to anyway.

She had gone to the office yesterday, but felt as if it was quite pointless. She was planning a big campaign about the danger of discarded fishing lines for September, and she could make some calls about that, but, oh, not today. Not while the rain beat down and the worry about Matt hung so heavy on her shoulders. He was in Mauritius now, lying on a beach with Karina. Doing God knows what. What could she do? What *could* she do?

It was his life but what if, as Emily had speculated, something dreadful happened and he became seriously ill? How would she feel if she hadn't intervened? Lottie had even said she didn't want to go off to Europe with all this worry. But Sara pointed out that Dad was away himself, and there was nothing they could do until he came back. She had gone, but kept ringing up to see if there was any news.

How impossible it is, Sara thought, watching the windscreen wipers beat backwards and forwards, to have so little influence in his life. To be unable to intervene and say, 'You must let me help you.' Because, she thought, it is no longer my place. But she was still tied to him because of the girls, and those ties would be broken only by death. I must do something, she decided. I have to. I owe it to them. I cannot bear the thought of losing you to something so wasteful, so pointless. After all you have done with your life, Matt, all the success you have achieved, to allow yourself to become hooked on something so destructive. Even though you make me so angry, you have caused me so much hurt, at least I know you are alive somewhere in the world. She had thought it would be easier for her to bear the separation if Matt had died. Now, that thought was rendered ridiculous.

All these thoughts ran through her mind as she drove towards the ferry at Bodinnick in the rain. She wanted to look at some material for curtains for the new living room, in Fowey. She should have driven round the headland, really, because the two pounds ten pence for the ferry added up when you were making the journey all the time, but today she could not be bothered. The worry was making her feel ill, and she was desperate for distraction. Much of the frustration lay in the fact that there was nothing she could do until Matt came home. She could ring him in Mauritius, she supposed, but how could she have this conversation over the phone?

As she rounded the sharp bend just before the village she met a big estate car, being driven too fast. She stopped dead, and with squealing tyres, he braked too, bringing his car to a halt just inches from Sara's bumper. Groaning, she twisted in her car seat to look behind her, beginning the tortuous process of reversing as she knew she was nearest to the next passing place. Reversing around a bend was awkward at the best of times, but with the rain falling so hard, she could barely see through the rear window. She had become quite expert at this, however, and manoeuvred the long car into the wider space, pulling as close as she could into the grassy bank at the side. Opposite her, the red earth was lined with tyre tracks, and rivulets of water ran down either side of the lane.

She sighed. The garden needed the rain, but this would mean the front of the house, with the sand and the dusty remains from plastering the walls, would become even more of a boggy mess. John was being as tidy as he could, but inevitably there was stray dust, which blended into a nasty grey slush by the front door. This week Jim and his team had begun digging out the footings for the extension, the area marked out with wooden crosses, string tied between them. The new dimensions for the study, laundry and kitchen stood at forty-five by twenty feet, but it didn't look very spacious, marked out on the ground. Jim said that was always the case, and that once the walls started going up she would get more of a real idea of the size.

Upstairs the extension would provide an extra bedroom and bathroom – they had given up on the idea of extending into the loft, so Lottie would not get her studio, but at least Emily and Lottie would have a bedroom each. Sara was very worried about how much the whole thing was going to cost, but it would be such bliss to have three bedrooms and two bathrooms.

She loved her work – at least, she would, once everything got going again after the summer – but even she had to admit it was paying hardly anything at all. Now that Matt had sold their flat, what he deemed 'her share' was sitting in a high interest account. She was so determined not to touch it, but she might have to – she could not bear the thought of being overdrawn. That money, she had formerly decided, would be for Emily and Lottie, but she did not want them to know it was theirs – they had to have some kind of work ethic. Lottie still hadn't found a job, and was unlikely to now that she was off in Europe for nearly a month.

Neither of the new bedrooms would be very big – but there was nothing they could do about that. Emily, used to Matt's spacious flat, would think it was tiny, when she came to stay.

The driver raised his hand in thanks to Sara, as he squeezed his car past hers, just an inch between their wing mirrors. The rain was so heavy now she had to put her windscreen wipers on double time, and, arriving at the ferry queue she found that she was the only car waiting.

A song was playing on the radio that she and Matt had loved. She wondered what kind of music he was listening to now. Karina's choice of music? How odd it must be, she thought, to have nothing culturally in common. To have no births, no deaths, no shared experiences between you.

A small stream of cars turned the sharp left-hand bend and drove towards her, signalling the arrival of the ferry. Moments later, she drove slowly down the jetty, hearing the familiar clunk, clunk, as her wheels passed over the iron ramp onto the deck. Tim, who took the fares, was today swathed from head to foot in yellow oilskins, and he smiled when he saw Sara's car. She pressed the button and her window slid down a fraction, and he said, through the gap, 'Morning, Sara. Bloody awful, isn't it?'

'I know. I hope it clears up.'

'No young lady with you today?' He peered hopefully into the car. Sara smiled. He must have been nearly forty, but he blushed a deep red whenever he saw Lottie. Sara teased her that if she failed to find a boyfriend in Europe or at university, there was always Tim.

'Sorry,' she said. 'Not today.'

'Where is she? On holiday?

'That's right. In Italy at the moment. At least, she was when we last spoke. She's travelling around, inter-railing.'

'You tell her I was asking about her. She brightens my day, that one does.'

'I will,' Sara said smiling. He was such a sweetheart.

She handed the coins over through the top of the window, and he gave her a little yellow ticket before dropping the money into the leather satchel he wore around his neck. Waves buffeted the ferry and he was standing with his legs far apart, balancing against the swell. Anchored to their buoys, the small sailing boats in the estuary rocked violently from side to side, and, once the ferry had set off, it took twice as long to sail across, the winch having to fight the powerful tide as they drifted towards the sea.

Sara realized that there would be days in the coming months when the ferry might not run at all. Life would be quite different, she thought, in the winter. When she had moved in the early spring, the villages were just beginning to wake as if after a long winter sleep. Awnings were being unfurled, window frames painted, paths brushed – there was a general air of everyone gearing up for the influx of holidaymakers with their pounds jangling in their pockets. When the tourists left, Fowey would feel like a ghost town once more. A sudden thought occurred to her. Would Ricky leave, once the work slowed down and the stream of visitors to Pip's became a trickle? Perhaps he might move on this year. She smiled to herself. Why would that matter? It was just, she thought, she'd become so used to him. His visits to the cottage had become a regular occurrence – he jogged past nearly every day and would stop for a glass of water. Sometimes Lottie was there, before she left on holiday, and the two of them had developed an easy, joking relationship. There did not seem to be any sign of romance – Lottie had admitted to her mother she found him a bit too old. He also regularly appeared in the trust's offices – he and Nick were friends and Ricky would perch on the end of a desk, teasing her, bantering with Nick, until she shooed him out, saying he was getting in the way and they had work to do, even if he didn't. It was ridiculous, she thought, how much she looked forward to seeing him.

The ferry hit the concrete jetty with a resounding bang, and Sara switched the engine back on. She'd been looking forward to choosing material for the curtains, and had spent many a happy half-hour browsing through sample books, trying to imagine what the room would look like once it was finished.

Indicating, she turned into the car park, waiting as an old woman negotiated her way out of a space, her husband sitting glumly in the passenger seat, staring miserably out at the rain. At least Matt and I never had the time to run out of things to say, she thought.

Chapter Twenty-three

'I'm usually in *bed* by this time, never mind going out,' Helen said, as they pushed open the door to Pip's. The noise inside was deafening, and the heat hit them like a tidal wave. All the tables appeared to be full and there was a crowd of people ten deep at the bar. Ricky, Jake and the two other waiters had to manoeuvre themselves with immense difficulty through the packed tables, plates held high over their heads. When Ricky saw Sara standing by the door all he could do was raise his eyebrows in greeting. Having served his table he fought his way over to them, taking Sara under the elbow.

'I've saved you a table in the far corner,' he said in a muted bellow. 'Christ, this place is insane tonight. I've had to beat people off with sticks to keep this for you,' he added. 'See how much I care?' Sara smiled.

As they reached the table, he deftly slid their chairs back for them. 'Now, what can I get you to drink?' he asked. His hair, slick with sweat, was tucked behind his ears, and his face was dripping with perspiration. It must be boiling in the kitchen.

'I don't know,' Sara said, turning to look at Helen. 'What do you fancy?'

'I can make you a cocktail,' Ricky suggested, leaning

forward and tapping the drinks menu lying on the table between them. 'We do a brilliant house cocktail. Two of those and you'll be first on the dance floor.'

'Dancing?' Helen asked faintly.

'Didn't I tell you there's a live band?' Sara shouted. 'I thought you knew. That's why I booked the table for so late. I'm normally in bed by now too!'

'I'm not sure I can last that long,' Helen replied grinning. 'Aren't we a bit old for a live band? It's going to be very loud.'

'Live a little,' Sara said, studying the menu. Ricky grinned. 'I've had a frustrating week at work, the weather is awful and tonight I think I may drink too much. Just warning you.'

'Yey,' Ricky said, smiling at her. 'I, personally, am looking forward to that a lot. Sara finally lets her hair down.'

The band was indeed deafening. Having warmed up with various squeaks and yowls, they launched into their first number only ten feet from their table. Sara had forgotten the effect of live rock music. It was years and years since she'd been to a concert. Now she suddenly remembered the way that the bass beat through you, quickening your pulse, making your heart race. Making you feel as if anything might happen.

Ricky and Jake had moved the vacated tables in the centre of the room away, creating a small clear space.

Sara peered at herself in the small mirror above the hand basin in the toilet, after they had hurriedly finished their meal. What do you think you are doing? she asked herself sternly. You have drunk very nearly a bottle of white wine and it is quite possible you will drink more. You will regret this, you know you will. No matter how worried you are about Matt, you cannot use that concern as an excuse to blot everything out. Plus the fact you know how bad your hangovers are these days, they seem to last for ever. And you are too old to be out of control, especially in the light of what is happening to Matt. What would the girls think? But she and Helen had decided they were going to have to get a taxi home anyway as they were both over the limit. She stared at herself for a long minute. It won't do any harm, she told herself. I think you deserve one night to be just a little irresponsible. After all you have been through. Tears started in her eyes. Oh stop it, she said. It's only the wine. Put on some more lipstick, get out there and smile. In the morning you can be sensible responsible Sara again. She drew a little more liner around her eyes. I do look OK, she thought, noting how deep her tan was, how her eyes sparkled. Even her face seemed slimmer, somehow, less lined, although that could have been the deliberately low light in the toilet.

'Oops. Ow.' She tipped forward, and hit her hip bone against the basin. She grabbed a tap to steady herself. Goodness, she thought. I haven't been so drunk for years. Water. I need to drink *a lot* of water.

As she emerged from the loo, people had begun to dance, the wooden floor of the restaurant vibrating under her feet. As she fought her way over to stand next to Helen, she saw Jake appear in front of her, holding out his hand. Smiling, Helen took it, and he pulled her into the sea of bodies. Heavens, Sara thought. I hope she isn't going to do anything she might regret.

'I said you had to dance with me.' His lips were very close to her ear.

'I told you,' she said, turning, their bodies touching. 'I haven't danced for years.'

'You don't forget,' he said. 'It's like riding a bike.'

'I was never a very good dancer anyway. Far too inhibited. The girls say my dancing makes them want to hide under a table.'

'Shut up,' he said, taking her hand. 'Live a little.' He stared at her. 'You look great tonight. Really amazing.' His hand was warm in hers. She looked down at them, noticing how his fingers twined in and out of hers, like a child.

'OK. Although I warn you – you may say I am too beautiful, tonight. But the illusion will be lost once I start dancing.'

'I'll risk it,' he said smiling. 'If you will.'

Chapter Twenty-four

'God, it's hot.' Catherine was lying on a sun lounger on her roof terrace, fanning herself with a weary hand. 'Why am I still in London? Everyone I know is in the South of France or somewhere glamorous. I'm going to book a holiday tomorrow. Only I haven't got anyone to bloody well go with. Why won't you come with me?' She turned angrily to Sara, who was lying next to her with eyes closed.

'You know I can't,' she said. It felt far hotter in London than at home, probably because there wasn't the sea breeze. 'I've got work.'

'Oh work, schmerk,' Catherine said. 'It's not a proper job, is it? It doesn't matter if you're there or not. Please, darling, come on. I'll pay. We can go to St Tropez, or Marbella, anywhere you fancy.'

Sara suddenly realized she had absolutely no desire to go on holiday. Living in Cornwall was like being on holiday every day. Besides . . .

'What are you grinning at?' Catherine pushed up her sunglasses to look at her.

'Nothing,' Sara said. 'Really, nothing.'

'Matt's back from Mauritius, you know.'

Sara's eyes flew open. 'Is he? I thought he was coming back at the end of the week.'

'Apparently they had to come home early,' Catherine said. 'No idea why. You know, I think that relationship is in injury time. Melissa saw them out two weeks ago and she said . . .'

Sara held up her hand. 'Please, Catherine, I do not want to know. The only link I have with Matt now is the children, and his relationship with Karina is of no interest to me.' Only, she knew, that wasn't strictly true. She had to speak to him, and now he was back in London, she could. Oh, bugger and blast. The shadows returned, returning at a time when she had this tiny chink of happiness inside her, this possibility of something, well, something quite extraordinary. If. Well, there were far too many if's. The only way she could see forward was not to think what anyone might say. Especially the girls. Oh, especially the girls. She closed her eyes again.

'Are you planning to see Matt?'

'I didn't know he was back.'

'Now you know he is.'

'Mmm.'

'Mmm? Is that yes, mmm?'

'Mmm.'

'You're annoying me, Sara Atkinson. Talk properly.'

Sara sat up and looked at Catherine. 'I might see him. I haven't made up my mind. There is something we have to discuss.'

'What?' Catherine was all ears.

'Nothing.'

Catherine glared at her. 'Do you want to go shopping this afternoon?'

'No.'

'Out for lunch?'

'Not really.'

'Can I just say that you are being really rather dull? I am trying to entertain you and give you a taste of

305

life, and all you seem to want to do is sit in the sun.'

'I just want to relax,' Sara said. 'My house is such a tip it's bliss to be somewhere tidy, and I had a bit of a heavy night a few nights ago. I'm still recovering.'

'With a man?' Catherine was agog.

'No,' Sara said. 'Not with "a man". With a friend.'

'Have you met anyone, you sly fox? God, how could you have kept this from me? Me, your oldest friend?' she added dramatically.

Sara smiled. 'Meet someone in Cornwall? Hardly.'

'You'll have to start looking for a man eventually,' Catherine said. 'You can't moulder away down there like an elderly spinster.'

'Trust me,' Sara said. 'I'm not mouldering away.'

'You *have* met someone.' Catherine's eyes were wide. 'Remember how long I've known you. Just like all your life. Don't hide this from me. Tell me, tell me all.'

'There's nothing to tell,' Sara said firmly.

The slap, slap of Catherine's flip-flops woke her from a brief doze. Catherine set a tray holding a bottle of white wine and two glasses between them, before gathering up her chiffon sarong to sit down. Shifting about to get comfortable, she lay back and moved her sunglasses from resting in her hair to cover her eyes.

'*I* saw Matt and Karina in Knightsbridge together,' she said conversationally. 'Last month. He was buying her some jewellery. He went bright red when he saw me,' she added. Sara opened her eyes and lifted herself up on one elbow. Catherine lay back, her face turned up to the sun. 'He looked all right from a distance, but when I got closer I thought he looked a bit peaky. I don't think she's good for him at all. Pretty, yes, I'll grant you, but she has a very predatory look about her. Couldn't be more different from you.'

'Thanks. I'll take that as a compliment. Did you chat?'

'I tried to, but she was shooting me evil looks and tugging at his arm. He looked very harassed. Nowhere near as sleek as normal. You know . . .' She turned her face to Sara. 'I think he is missing you. He didn't look cared-for at all.'

'I don't think so,' Sara said. 'I doubt he ever thinks of me.'

'Well he should,' Catherine said, raising her sunglasses to look more closely at Sara. 'You look really good, you know. Are you sure you haven't had anything done? Come on. You can tell me. What is it? Botox? Caci? Liposuction? Don't forget I am the expert.'

'It's just clean living and lots of fresh air,' Sara said smiling.

'I think there is a man.' Catherine was like a dog with a bone.

'I'd tell you, I promise, if anyone remotely interesting strayed across my path. Look, do you mind if I see someone this afternoon?' As she said it, her heart was sinking, but she thought, I must. I have to. For them.

Catherine sighed. 'Oh, just leave me, I don't care. It's not as if I haven't seen you for ages or planned lots of lovely things to do. Who?'

Sara thought hastily. She could not tell Catherine she was going to try to see Matt, because she would get the third degree when she came back. She hunted about mentally for a plausible alternative.

'Rachael,' she said.

'God. No! Not really? Oh, well, go ahead if you want to be bored to death. See if I care that you'd rather spend time with her than me. She's so menopausal, she positively thrums. Shall I book somewhere for dinner? Come on, darling, let's have *some* fun.'

'OK,' Sara said. 'I'll be back by seven.'

* * *

Her heart beat impossibly quickly as she dialled Matt's Blackberry number. She was standing in a doorway a couple of streets away from his office. He'll be fine, she told herself, Emily might have been exaggerating, he can't be so foolish . . . A sudden mental image of Ricky flashed through her mind. The way his eyes had closed as he bent his head to kiss her as they stood by the harbour, the lights of Fowey reflected in the water, the feel of his lips on hers, the way her stomach had seemed to disappear as his lips parted hers and she'd had to move away from him, putting her hand over his mouth as he protested, 'Why? Why not? I want you so much, Sara. What harm can it do?'

Matt should have been at work as it was three in the afternoon, but for some reason he didn't seem to be answering. She had nearly given up when she heard him say, abruptly, 'Yes? Matt de Lall?'

'Matt, it's me. Sara.'

'Sara! Good God! How are you?'

'I'm fine. How are you?'

'OK. A bit stressed, busy, you know. Where are you?'

'In London.'

There was a stunned pause. 'Why?'

'I'm staying with Catherine. Just for a night.'

'Oh.'

'Can I see you?'

'Is it something to do with the girls?' His voice was suddenly wary.

'Kind of. I can't explain on the phone.'

'OK.' He paused. 'Can you meet me in the Starbucks by the office? How far are you away?'

'Ten minutes,' she said.

'Fine. I'll see you there.' His voice changed as he said crossly, away from the phone, 'It doesn't have to go off now. Just *wait*. OK. I'll see you there,' he said to Sara.

Sara watched him walk towards her in the café. His olive skin was tanned a deep mahogany and he was wearing a beautifully-cut dove-grey silk suit, with a pale pink shirt. Contrary to both Emily and Catherine's reports, he seemed perfectly fit and healthy.

Sara had bought him a black coffee, and he took a sip as he slid into the seat opposite her. For several moments they sat, looking at each other, in silence.

'I . . .'

'You . . .'

Sara laughed. 'You first.'

'You look well. Great, really – really, well, I don't know. Even better than before. Life there must be suiting you.'

'You look good, too.'

'Thanks. I had a good . . .'

'In Mauritius.'

'Yes. And you?'

'What?'

'Have you been away?'

'I don't really need to. It's like being on holiday all the time.'

'I suppose it is. How's the house?'

'In a state of chaos. I'm renovating.'

'I'd love to . . .'

'What?'

'Nothing. Never mind.'

'How's work?'

'The usual. Stressful. It's fucking murder effectively working for someone else. I hate it. Tossers. Still, I have to tell myself that soon it won't be my problem.'

'And the new apartment?'

'Not the same.'

She looked at him, surprised.

He smiled, but it did not reach his eyes. 'It's fine. Somewhere to live. I'm thinking . . .'

'Yes?'

'I don't know. I might buy somewhere abroad. In the sun.'

'France?'

'No,' he said. 'Not France. Maybe Barbados. Anyway, how are you? We couldn't really talk before. Have you met people? Made friends?' He smiled and Sara was irritated that there was a trace of condescension in his voice.

She looked at him defiantly. 'I have. Quite a few, actually.'

'That's good. I'm glad you're not lonely. Although, of course, there's Lottie . . .'

'Honestly, everything's fine. I am OK, happy. Look, Matt, there's something . . . the reason why I wanted to see you.'

'Oh?' He looked guarded. 'What's up? Have you a problem? Is it money? I told, you, Sara . . .'

'It isn't me,' she said. 'It's you.'

'What? What on earth can it be to do with me?' He sat back, smiling.

'I don't quite know how to say this.' The café, which had been full of chatter, suddenly seemed very quiet and Sara looked about her nervously. She lowered her voice. 'It's just . . . I was told something very worrying . . .'

'What on earth can this be?'

'Look, this is really hard. The only way I can deal with it is to just come right out and say it. Look, Matt, I heard from someone that you're taking . . .'

Matt cut in sharply. 'Why on earth are you looking so serious? What the hell are you trying to say?'

She took a deep breath. 'I heard you were taking cocaine.'

'WHAT?' He seemed almost to explode, rocking back in his chair. She knew immediately from the expression on his face that it was true.

'Who the hell told you that?' He was genuinely stunned. 'And, to be honest, even if it were true, what has it got to do with you? Putting it politely, you're not my mother, Sara. You don't have the right to tell me how to live my life.'

'Does it matter who told me?'

'It was Emily,' he said.

'No it wasn't,' Sara said quickly. 'Anyway, that's not important.'

'I fail to see,' he said, breathing slowly as if he was trying to keep his temper. 'What this has to do with you or why you feel it is your responsibility to even mention anything so . . . ridiculous.'

'Don't you think that I *should* know? Especially when it affects my children?'

'*How* does it affect your children?'

'Well, Emily was living with you for a while. She might have seen you . . .'

'Do you honestly think I would let my daughter see me taking cocaine? Look, Sara,' he said, leaning forward. 'I'm a big boy now, honestly. Hands up, I might have taken it once or twice. But it's hardly ever – just the odd line with friends, it's no big deal.'

Oh, Matt, Sara thought, you are lying. You are lying again, and I don't want to be here, now, with you, listening to this. I don't want this responsibility, but who else is there to tell you that what you are doing is crazy?

'I can't believe this,' he said, running his hand through his hair. 'Do you really think I would be so stupid as to let it get out of control?'

Sara noticed his confidence seemed to be ebbing away as his hand was shaking. 'I would hate to think

311

so, Matt. But I don't know how well I do know you, now.'

'I promise you, Sara, it's fine. It's nothing. I don't have to justify myself to you, anyway. Christ.'

'How long have you been taking it? When you were still with me? Something else I didn't know?'

He stiffened in his seat, stared at her, and then looked away. 'Only occasionally,' he said dismissively, the nervous tic beating under his eye. 'When I was away on business. Sometimes late at night, when you were asleep. Hard as it is for you to get your head around this, I am always under a lot of stress, especially when the sale of the company was going through. It was fucking murder, they wanted blood. It helped, Sara. You wouldn't understand.'

Don't dismiss me, Sara thought. You think we lived on different levels, don't you?

'You're a fool, Matt,' she said. 'I can't believe you would do something so reckless. In your position. At your age.'

He glanced impatiently at his watch. 'I have to get back to work. Was this the only reason you wanted to meet me? To tell me off? To make me promise not to do anything naughty?'

Sara felt her temper rising. 'Oh, for God's sake, don't be so childish. Matt! This isn't "naughty". This could kill you. Try to think of someone other than yourself! The girls are worried sick.' The moment the words were out of her mouth, she regretted them.

'The girls? So it was Emily who told you.' His face seemed to close down on itself. 'I see. Thank you.'

'Don't you dare mention this to her! She loves you, Matt. Lottie loves you. Don't you care what they think? Is your life ... now ... more important than that?'

'And you? What about you? Do you care?'

She stared at him. Oh, you bloody man, she thought. 'Yes,' she said. 'I do.'

'I thought you'd written me off.'

'I cannot write off twenty-six years, twenty-seven, since we met,' she said wearily. 'No matter how hard I try.'

'Sara –', he reached out urgently across the table to try to grab her hand. Sara pulled it quickly away and bent down to pick up her handbag.

'Don't do this,' she said, sitting up. 'Please. It will affect you, Matt, no matter how much you think you have it under control. Think of the girls. They need you. What kind of example are you giving them? What kind of a father are you being?'

At these words Matt seemed to suddenly slump in his seat. Then he looked up at her, his eyes full of tears.

Reacting instinctively, she reached out to put her hand over his. He bent down, until his face was almost touching her fingers and she could feel his tears wet against her skin.

'Ssh, darling,' she said, as if to a child. 'It's OK.'

For a moment he let his cheek rest against her hand. Then he sat up and stared at her.

'I'm sorry,' was all he said.

Chapter Twenty-five

She had to walk quickly to keep up with him, and by the time they reached the cliff above the bay, she was breathing hard. She wished she hadn't put a jumper over her swimming costume instead of a T-shirt, as she was beginning to sweat. But the sky had looked grey when they set off, as if it might rain. The weather had been changeable like this all week, since Sara had returned from London.

At the top of the path, they paused together for a minute, looking down at the sea. The beach below was deserted – few people walked this far along the headland, because there was another bay much nearer to the car park, and the path down to this beach was very steep. But Sara loved this cove, the rocks forming a perfect half-circle, sheltered from the sea breezes. A yacht sailed past, far below them, its white sail curving in the wind.

'Can you sail?' she asked idly, admiring the way it glided so smoothly through the water, perfectly silhouetted against the pale grey horizon. He put his arm around her, and she leant her head against his shoulder.

'I crewed on a boat in Australia, but I didn't really

know what I was doing, I just blagged it. Probably pulled all the wrong ropes.'

She laughed. 'I've never learnt to sail. There is so much I haven't done.'

'It's never too late. Why don't we take off, Mrs Atkinson? Let's travel round the world. I'll teach you to surf and sail, and you can teach me . . .'

'What can I teach you?' She smiled, looking up at him.

'I can think of lots of things, if only you would let me.'

'Stop it.'

'I love you.'

'No, you don't.'

'Yes, I do.'

'How can you, you foolish boy?'

'Because you're beautiful.' He moved around to stand directly in front of her, shielding her from the wind, drawing her close to him. Reaching down, he tucked a stray lock of hair behind her ear. Sara allowed herself to lean into him, resting her face against his chest for a moment. He felt so warm, so safe. Glancing up, she watched the wind lift his hair, mesmerized by the way it moved. This is like living within a dream, she thought. A dream in which I allow myself to fall in love with a beautiful young man, a dream in which he does not leave and I will be left alone once more. I *can* control . . . this, whatever it is, she thought. These two weeks are nothing more than a window in my life, as if I have stepped outside of reality, and when Lottie returns my life will go back to normal, and no one will ever know that I let this man hold me and, yes, kiss me, once. He can tell me he loves me and that if I do not let him make love to me he will go mad, because I know he means it now, but tomorrow he would change his mind and I would mean nothing.

'What are you thinking?'

'I'm thinking,' she said carefully, 'that this is like living in a dream.'

'Why?'

'Because it cannot be real.'

'Don't say that.' He held her, close and warm, as the breeze blew around their bodies and the moment was held in time.

He lay with his head in her lap, as she read her novel, holding it high above his face. His eyes were closed. Around them lay the remains of the picnic, the crusty end of a baguette, a slice of blue cheese half-eaten in its cling-film wrapper, several slices of tomato lying on top of a crumpled white paper bag. There was less than an inch of wine left in the bottle, which stood a few feet away from them in a narrow stream running down to the sea. Hector lay, panting and covered in sand, close to them, his eyes on the remains of the baguette.

Before their picnic they had swum. The sea was still freezing, despite the weeks of hot sun on the sea. Plunging underwater, Sara let her eyes drift to the grey, stony bottom and watched the dark patches of sea-weed waving in the current, as if in the wind. Beneath her a fish seemed to hang, glimmering pale green in the murky light, its body undulating, trembling fins outstretched.

Afterwards they flung themselves down onto towels and dozed, before Sara woke crusted with salt and chilly.

Now she sat reading, as he slept. The world felt far away and for a second she looked up from her book, savouring the moment of perfect peace. She realized the sun, barely visible through the cloud, was much lower in the sky and the light was beginning to fade.

She put her book down, and Hector lifted his head, enquiringly. Sara moved her legs restlessly, and Ricky's eyes opened.

'Sorry,' she said, looking down at him. 'I've got pins and needles. And it's getting late.'

'Sure,' he said sleepily, lifting his head. Slowly, he turned on to his side and rested on one elbow. 'God, man, I was fast asleep. What time is it?'

'After six, I would guess. I'm not sure.'

She reached forward, and began to massage her legs. 'We ought to go,' she added.

'Why?'

'Aren't you working tonight?'

'Nope,' he said, running a hand lazily through his still-damp hair. 'Can I stay with you?' He rolled over on to his stomach. 'I promise not to try . . . anything.' He grinned up at her.

'Don't worry,' she said dryly. 'I feel I can just about resist you.'

'Such a hard woman.' He flopped over on to his back. 'I wish I could stay here for ever.'

'Why can't you?'

'Because I need to do something with my life.' He turned his head to look at her. 'I'm thirty-one. I can't stay a waiter for ever.'

'Why don't you go back to architecture? I know you'd be fantastic.'

'I don't have the confidence.'

'Don't be silly.'

He reached out beside him, letting a trail of damp sand trickle through his fingers.

'I'm not sure I do. I've been a failure so long I don't think I know how to be a success. I'm happy with drifting, because that way no one has any expectations of me and I can't let anyone down.'

'Like your parents?'

317

'Yeah. Like them.' He stared up at the sky. 'Marry me,' he said.

'What?' Sara stared at him, astonished.

'You heard me.' He put his hands behind his head. 'Marry me. I could work then, if I had you beside me, telling me sensible things.'

'You're crazy,' Sara laughed. 'Come on. We must go home or we'll be trapped by the tide. It's coming in.'

Half a mile from the cottage, he stopped in front of her, looking down at the little house below them. The sky was a deep, unearthly pink, the sinking sun casting long surreal shadows. He put down the rucksack, and turned to her. 'There's something I haven't told you,' he said. 'And now is the right time.'

'What?' she said. 'Don't be so mysterious. You're worrying me.'

'The reason I came here,' he said, slowly. 'The reason I stayed . . .'

'Yes?'

'Charlotte was my mother.'

Chapter Twenty-six

She sat watching him as he slept, safe in Lottie's bed. His eyelashes flickered as he dreamt, the dark curling hair creating feathery shadows on his cheeks. If you were my child I could never leave you, Sara thought.

'That one word,' he had said as they sat together in the garden late into the night, as the sky turned a dark midnight blue, shot through with the vivid colours of the sunset. 'Dad. But there was this really weird kind of comfort in it, you know,' he said, gazing into his wine glass. 'Because I really wanted to believe that if she'd been alive, she would have come to find me. I knew they could never have been my parents, even before they told me I was adopted. All my life I had this thing inside me, this restless thing, telling me I had to leave and look for someone. When I was a kid, I used to stare out of the window at night, fantasizing about sneaking out into the dark, opening the front door and just running, running down the road towards ... I had no idea what. I just knew that I wasn't loved, not really loved. I saw my friends with their mothers and it just killed me. My mother never hugged me, barely touched me. She used to look at me as if she was kind of *scared* of me. Of course they were a lot older, I don't know why they even wanted a child.

Maybe it was to save their marriage – they didn't seem to like each other's company, so I failed at that, too. And then when I found out I was adopted, everything fell into place. These people were strangers, there was nothing connecting us beyond a sense of duty. Out there was my real mother, and all I had to do was find her. My life became a kind of quest. Crazy, huh? I used to look for her all the time, in the street, in restaurants, anywhere there were people, crowds. I followed a woman once, who had dark hair like mine. I stalked her for hours. I was only nine. But once I got close enough, I could see she did not look like me. You wouldn't know . . .'

He sighed, draining his glass. 'It's like you're half a person, half of you is a total mystery. You invent so many kinds of things, you fantasize that your mum is the most perfect woman in the world, and if only you could find her, she'd put her arms around you and you would be safe and happy for ever. Not an outsider anymore but part of a family.' He shrugged, looking at Sara, his face a mask of sadness. 'And then when I did find her, she was dead. She'd been dead all my life. All the time I'd spent looking for her, there was nothing to find. Just bones in the ground.' He shut his eyes tight. 'And I killed her.'

'Don't be ridiculous,' Sara said quickly, reaching out to put her hand over his. 'How could it have been your fault? You must not think that.' If anything, she thought to herself, it was the agony of having to give you up which killed her. But she did not say anything.

'If she hadn't got pregnant with me, she would never have killed herself, would she? It's the violence of her death which has haunted me since I found out the truth. I dream that I'm falling. They say that if you ever hit the ground in your dreams you will die in real life, but I do, Sara, I hit the rocks and my body breaks, and the pain is real. When I first came here, I used to stand on the cliff, just beneath the cottage, and imagine. I tried to picture myself letting go, falling forward into the air. There was such an extraordinary kind of beauty to that feeling, as if it was what I *should* do. I tried to put myself into her mind, to imagine how she felt, giving up her child and feeling she had nothing left. But she did. She had me. She had that baby lying in his cot and none of this needed to have happened. Ever since I have lived here I wake hearing her screaming as she fell, screaming for me.'

He paused, and Sara tightened her grip on his hand. 'Maybe it's weird that I stayed here, but it's as if this is the only home I've ever had. The nearest I have to a family, a home, is to be close to the place where my mother died.'

'Is that why you say you love me?'

'What?'

'Because I could be her?'

He laughed. 'That's kind of crazy,' he said.

'I don't mean I could be your mother, obviously, I just mean . . . I just mean that I maybe represent a kind of security to you.'

'So marry me.'

She smiled at him. 'Now that really would be weird,' she said.

He smiled back at her. 'I cannot tell you how much peace unloading all of this has brought me,' he said. There were tears in his eyes. 'I know this sounds insane, but I feel as if I have come home.'

Chapter Twenty-seven

'Six across, a type of sleeping sickness, ten letters, begins with an "n".'

'Narcolepsy,' Sara said instantly. 'How did we do yesterday? What was six down, in the end?'

'Fornication,' he said grinning.

'Rubbish,' she said, standing up and snatching the newspaper from him.

'Fabrication.' She looked at the crossword answers, smiling. 'You are so immature at times, you know that?'

'At least I'm not over half a century old,' he said, throwing a peach stone expertly into the bin. 'What shall we do this afternoon?'

'Aren't you working?'

'Nah. I took the afternoon off. We're not busy at all. I told Jake he may as well shut up shop until the week-end, there's hardly anyone around.'

'I know,' Sara said. 'It's like a ghost town.'

'I like it. Gives me time to study. And at least with it being so fucking – sorry, *absolutely* – freezing, I don't look out of the window all the time and long to get out on the water.'

Sara, who had peered at him reprovingly over the top of her tortoiseshell half-moon glasses, began to tidy up the coffee cups and lunch plates which lay on the table.

He leant back on his chair, rocking it on to two legs.

'Don't do that,' she said automatically. 'You'll break it.'

He let the chair crash back to the floor before picking up the local newspaper, flicking through to the classified advertisements.

'I'm going to have to get another job to pay my college fees,' he said.

'I told you,' Sara said, without looking up. 'I said I'd lend you the money.'

'But I don't *want* to borrow it,' Ricky pointed out reasonably. 'This is going to be all my own work. God, there's nothing around at the moment.' Putting the paper down angrily, he drummed his fingers on the kitchen table, staring dispiritedly out of the rain-soaked window. 'So what shall we do?'

'I ought to work,' Sara said. 'I've got reams of calls to make.'

'Sod that. Let's take Hector to Polruan sands. The wind's up, the surf will be magnificent. Come on, there's a cave I want to show you.'

'OK,' she said, reluctantly. 'By the way, I had a letter from the solicitor's.'

'Oh, yes?'

'They need your birth certificate.'

'Whatever for?'

'Something about the deeds, I didn't read it properly.'

'You deal with it, I hate paperwork. Although, you know, I still think you're rushing into this. There is no reason to be so generous.'

'This is your home as much as mine,' she said.

Hector ran towards the sea, barking, but stopped dead

when he saw the height of the waves. They towered above him, the water a deep, vibrant green, before they rolled over into a crystal shower, the noise roaring in his ears. He turned tail and fled. Ricky tucked his arm through Sara's as they picked their way through the streams of water in the rippling sand. 'I could watch the sea for ever,' Sara said, standing still, looking out over the water.

'I told you it gets into your blood,' he said. 'Anyway, you can.'

She turned to him, smiling. 'Why?'

'Because you won't leave. Not now. This is your home.' He pressed her arm against his side. She reached up to smooth away the hair which was blowing across his face, like a mother would a child.

'Come on,' she said, her words caught and hurled away by the wind. 'You may not feel the cold, but I certainly do. I want to sit by the fire and read my book.'

Chapter Twenty-eight

'Why do I always choose the ones which go sideways?'

'Let me have a go.'

Sara stood obediently to one side and he took the handle, shoving violently. The trolley immediately skewed off to the left, knocking into the legs of a woman standing with her back to them, who had been gazing thoughtfully at a row of cereal packets. She turned around crossly, and Sara realized it was Gloria from the Women's Institute. Gloria of the alpine flowers.

'I am *so* sorry,' she said. 'He doesn't get out much.' Ricky snorted with laughter and wrenched the trolley backwards to try a different track.

'Ham?' Sara paused by the chilled meat counter, having decided it was safer if she steered. The trolley was piled high with food, and Sara thought, not for the first time, how much feeding Ricky was costing her. Compared to the girls he seemed to eat continually, even whole loaves at a time.

Ricky had kept his rented flat by the Spar shop – Sara pointed out he must surely want the privacy – but he often stayed over at the cottage, sleeping in the bedroom allocated to Emily. It was, Sara thought, like having an overgrown child in the house, full of jokes, clumsiness and a shocking inability to tidy up after himself. She found his company highly entertaining and he seemed to derive, what seemed to Sara, a real sense of comfort from being with her in his mother's former home. An odd relationship, but one which suited them both. Helen said they were the talk of the village, but Sara could not find it in her heart to care. She knew the truth, and that was all that mattered.

'Do you want honey roast or plain ham?' Sara asked, a joking edge to her voice. 'I know it's a tricky decision. Shall I choose for you?'

Ricky was standing with his hands in the pockets of his leather jacket, looking away from her, whistling. 'Sorry,' he said. 'I wasn't listening. Supermarkets make me lose the will to live. Do you mind if I get some fresh air? Whatever. You choose, you know I'll eat anything.'

'No, go ahead,' Sara said wearily. 'Just leave me to do the weekly shop all on my own.'

'Thanks,' he replied cheerfully, and wandered off in the direction of the door. Sara watched him go affectionately. Even though she did most of his washing, there was still much of the gypsy about him – today he was wearing a favourite pair of frayed baggy jeans, a T-shirt which frankly should have been thrown away and his very battered old leather jacket.

As Sara stood in the queue for the check-out, she saw him sitting with his feet up on the red metal chairs behind the tills, reading the notices on the pin board. Looking up, he realized she was watching him, and flicked a finger at the board behind his head. 'Salsa dancing classes? Polruan village hall?' he mimed at her, and put both thumbs up enquiringly. She shook her head. He glanced behind him again.

'Yoga for the over fifties?' he mouthed. 'That's one for you. I could wait outside.' She laughed and made a face at him. He grinned.

'Would you like any help with your packing?'

'No, thank you. I can manage.'

'Do you have a club card?'

'No, thank you.' She peered at the badge. 'Cheryl.' The girl on the till looked at her gratefully and smiled.

'It's turned ever so chilly, hasn't it?'

'It certainly has.' Sara rubbed the plastic carrier bags between finger and thumb to open them, and began to pack away the shopping. After a while she turned to Ricky. 'Come and help, you great lazy lump.'

'Oh *God*,' he moaned as he stood beside her, to Cheryl. 'She's so bossy, aren't you, my lover?' He said the last two words, jokingly, in a broad Cornish accent.

At the check-out till next to them Sara saw Gloria's head snap up, as if she had been electrocuted.

'Don't *do* that,' she said, as they pushed the trolley together towards the car, Ricky making it zigzag irritatingly into the path of an oncoming car.

'Do what?' he asked, his face a mask of innocence.

'You know perfectly well,' Sara said.

'She loved it,' he said. 'It'll be all round the WI like wildfire.'

'I know,' Sara said. 'It isn't you who has to cope with all the staring and whispering.'

'I would imagine it would enhance your image, Mrs Atkinson. Anyway, who cares? Fuck 'em. Village busy-bodies with nothing better to talk about.'

'What do you bring me, you dreadful boy?'

He put down the shopping bag he was loading into the boot of Sara's car, and turned to look at her. For a few moments they stared at each other, and then he wrapped his arms around her, his eyes dancing wickedly.

'Fun,' he said, tightening his arms and lifting her off her feet. 'Without me, your life would be so predictable.'

Chapter Twenty-nine

She stood by the new patio doors which led out on to what would, eventually, become the sun terrace at the side of the house. If the sun ever shone again, Sara thought, looking up at the leaden sky through the glass ceiling in the kitchen roof. There was such a beauty to the landscape, however, she thought, as she drove down the lane to work, looking out over frosted fields framed by the bare skeletons of the trees. Above her, dark grey clouds drifted slowly across the sky. The atrium had been an inspired idea, if she said it herself, creating so much natural light. To her right there was now a wide, picture window, looking out over the front garden, the lawn neatly mown under a covering of frost, the rose bushes pruned and waiting for the spring.

Now the building work was finally finished it was such a pleasure to come home. To push open the door at the back of the house and walk over the newly-laid oak floor down the corridor, into the extended living room, never failed to please her. To Sara the room seemed vast although it was only twenty feet or so long. Used to being cramped in the two small front rooms, this felt an oasis of space. The arched windows, as she had hoped, let in so much light and the views over the bay were breathtaking. She had kept the colours muted – the walls were a thick cream colour, the carpet a natural beige weave and the skirting boards painted a pale dove grey. Framing the windows were long cream heavily-lined curtains which trailed on the floor, and the large sofa and chairs no longer dwarfed the room. At the far end, an open fire flickered in the wide grate, an arched wooden beam above it. It looked, as she had intended, as if it had always been there.

Sara loved to sit by the fire at night, listening to the wind whistling down the chimney, the wisteria tapping on the windows. The cottage felt a warm, safe haven, high above the stormy sea.

'Come in!' She slid open the patio door a fraction, wincing as the freezing wind blew into the warm kitchen. 'You don't have to finish it all today.'

'In a second.' He looked up at her, grinning, and dug the spade hard into the earth, leaning on it as he wiped a hand across his mouth, leaving a trail of earth. He seemed determined to get the foundations for the pergola dug before Christmas, although Sara had pointed out the ground would be much softer in February and there was no rush. Now, with the temperature way below freezing, the ground was rock hard. But once he got the bit between his teeth, it was pointless to try to stop him. Besides, he said, it was a great antidote to the pressure of studying and looming exams.

Emily walked into the kitchen, twisting hair still wet from the shower. 'You look cold,' she said solicitously, and rested her fingers, briefly, against Ricky's cheek, as he leant against the wall, sliding off his wellingtons.

'*Muddy*,' Sara said. 'Put them outside. I don't think it's going to rain.'

'It's your slave-driver mother,' Ricky said. 'She's got me working in all weathers.'

'I did not say you had to dig today.' Sara smiled. 'You chose to do it. I told you that you should wait.'

'Nag, nag. OK, I'm the lunatic. Actually, I'm not cold at all, I'm boiling from all that work.' He pulled down the sleeves of his muddy navy-blue woollen sweater before lifting it over his head, revealing a white T-shirt carefully ironed by Sara and several inches of tanned, flat stomach. He had a hole in the cuff of his jumper, Sara noted. She'd rescue that from the wash and darn it. More jumpers might be an idea for Christmas. Her own tan seemed to have long since disappeared. It would return, she thought, in the spring, when the warm weather came.

'When's Lottie coming home?' Emily asked, picking up the post which lay on the kitchen table. 'Here's one for you,' she said, handing Sara a cream-coloured envelope. 'You must have missed it.'

'Friday, I think,' Sara said, turning it over in her hand. The writing on the envelope seemed familiar.

Tapping it against her palm, she walked out of the kitchen, down the corridor and into the living room. The fire burnt low in the hearth, and she carefully placed two more logs on to the dying flames, which flared up immediately, throwing shadows against the far wall. It was lovely having Emily here – she was taking two weeks off over Christmas. Early days, she thought to herself, smiling. Early days.

She sank into the armchair, slipping off her shoes and tucking her feet underneath her. Hector, who had followed her, circled, sighed, and then lay down on the grey rug in front of the fire, his head on his paws, watching her lovingly. She reached out with one

331

foot to rub the fur on his back, and he closed his eyes.

She scanned the page, turned it over, the lines between her eyebrows deepening. And then she smiled before dropping the letter into the fire, watching it curl, blacken and twist to its death in the flames.

'Be careful!' Lottie said, jumping away from her in mock horror, as Sara eased the champagne cork out of the bottle, having first twisted it a little. She'd never been very good at this, and she half-closed her eyes as the cork began to slide up the neck of the bottle, before it exploded towards the ceiling. 'Quick, a glass,' she shouted and Lottie hurriedly held a narrow champagne flute under the foam, which was pouring down over Sara's fingers.

'Vintage,' Emily noted from where she was sitting at the table. 'Where have you been hiding that, Mother?'

'I bought a case yesterday,' she said. 'Why not? I've had a small pay rise.'

'Cheers,' Helen said, raising her glass. 'Happy *nearly* Christmas, everyone.'

'Cheers,' Ricky said. 'Although I have to say I hate this stuff.'

'Don't spoil the moment,' Emily said, smiling, and their eyes met.

There was the sound of a car in the lane, the roar of a powerful engine. Surprised, Ricky put down his glass and walked over to look out of the kitchen window, into the dusk.

'Who the hell do you know with a Porsche?' he said, peering out, as the sensor outside light flicked on. 'Wow. Look at that. It's gorgeous.'

'Mum!' Lottie looked at Sara, amazed. 'It can't be *Dad*, can it?'

Sara shrugged. 'He wrote to me and said he might

come down, depending on work. But you know what Dad's like. I didn't want to raise your hopes until I knew definitely, but then he didn't write again, or call. I presumed he had changed his mind.'

'But why, Mum? Why would he come down here, now?' Emily's face was baffled. 'I mean he knows your address because he asked for it ages ago, but surely not . . . what about . . . ?'

Sara took a sip of champagne. 'As I said, I have no idea. Please can we not make this into a drama. Not my first Christmas here. Calm down, all of you.'

Easier said than done, she thought to herself, however, as her heart thumped to an unfamiliar beat.

'What did he say, Mum, in the letter?' Emily asked impatiently. 'Why didn't he tell me? I saw him last week. Do you know he's planning to give up the business sooner? He said, and his exact words were, "sod the money".' She smiled.

'Sounds like Dad,' Lottie nodded. 'But what about Karina?'

'I don't know,' Emily said, 'I really don't know. He was very vague on that subject. Like he didn't want to talk about her at all.'

There was the sound of loud knocking on the door.

'Go and let the poor man in, someone,' Sara said. 'He'll be freezing.'

Ricky was standing with his back to her, his hands in his pockets, staring out into the night. Lottie ran away down the corridor, and they heard the sound of the door opening.

'Are you OK?' Sara asked him quietly.

He turned, his face a conflicting mask of emotions. 'I don't know,' he said. 'It's so odd to think I will finally meet him.'

'Do you want to go? Not that I think you should. This is your home.'

He smiled. 'I know. You tell me often enough, even though I now have to sleep on the sofa.'

'It's Emily's room,' she said automatically.

'I know.' He smoothed his hand down Sara's cheek. 'It's OK.'

For a moment, they stood looking at each other. He shook his head.

'What?'

'Nothing. You know best, Sara. You always know best.'

'Don't patronize me.'

'Mum! It *is* Dad!' Lottie, her eyes shining, ran into the kitchen. 'Hey, what's up with you two?'

'Nothing,' Ricky said again.

'Offer him a drink, will you?' Sara said. 'It's such a long way to drive, he must be exhausted.'

'Sara.'

She stood quite still for a moment, one hand on the twisted metal handle of the Aga's hot plate. Then she deliberately moved the pan full of potatoes and boiling water on to the simmering plate, before she turned.

He was standing by the door, in a long dark overcoat, a black scarf around his neck.

'Do take your coat off. Did the girls get you a drink?' she asked.

'Yes. Thanks.' He raised the glass, showing her, before putting it down on to the kitchen table.

'So how are you?'

He smiled. 'I'm fine. Much . . . much better.'

'I see.'

He nodded, biting his lip.

'Good. That's really good.' She took a deep breath. 'The girls are delighted to see you.'

'I know. It's fantastic to see them. Are you sure you

don't mind me . . .'

'No.'

'This is . . .' He looked around him, at the warm, welcoming kitchen, the books on the shelf above the Aga, the colourful local paintings she had bought, primarily of the sea.

'What?'

'Wonderful. Not what I expected.'

'Oh?'

'You look . . . well, so at home.' He began to undo his coat, without taking his eyes off her. Sara reached forward to hang it over the back of a kitchen chair, next to Ricky's jumper. She couldn't help smiling at the contrast of the luxuriously sleek cashmere next to Ricky's bobbly wool.

'Did the girls introduce you to Helen and Ricky? They're staying for dinner.'

'Yes. She's a friend and he's a friend of Lottie's? I couldn't quite work out how he fits in.' He looked at her warily.

'Not exactly.' Sara smiled to herself.

'Ah.' His eyes were puzzled and Sara could see a hint of anger brewing behind the carefully arranged politeness of his expression.

'He's a friend of mine,' she explained. 'It's rather a long complicated story. I'll tell you later.'

Matt stared at her. 'I see,' he said frowning.

'I'm not entirely sure you do,' she replied, smiling brightly back at him.

'Dad brought loads and loads of presents!' Lottie burst through the door. 'And he brought this huge bunch of flowers, for you, Mum. I put all the presents under the tree, Dad, is that OK?' He nodded. Sara reached for the scissors, and began snipping the ends of the gigantic bunch of pale pink roses.

* * *

335

The empty plates lay on the kitchen table. Emily said they all had to play charades now and had herded them into the living room, Ricky complaining loudly that he hated charades. Sara said she would clear up first, she didn't mind doing it on her own.

She didn't hear him walk into the kitchen. A CD was playing, and she hummed to herself as she moved about the kitchen. She was bending over to stack the dishwasher, when she felt his hand rest against her back.

'Stop that for a minute,' Matt said. 'Please.'

'I want to get this finished.'

'You can do it later.'

'What if there is no later?'

'There's always a later,' he said. 'There has to be.'

'Really?' she said. 'No matter how long you have to wait?'

'I love this song.'

'I know.'

'Dance with me, Sara.'

'When I'm ready,' she said, closing the dishwasher, with a click.

THE END